Where Wild Rivers Meet

Where Wild Rivers Meet
A Story for Seasoned Lovers

A Novel by Tom W. Boyd and B. Skye Boyd

Golden Word Books
Santa Fe, NM

Photo of the authors by Michael Griffith.

Library of Congress Control Number 2020932829

Published by Golden Word Books, Santa Fe, New Mexico.

ISBN 978-1-948749-57-2

To Kathy and Terrell, the couple whose love story ended too soon
To W.A. and Alice, the couple whose love story should never have been

Contents

The Subject Tonight Is Love

The subject tonight is Love
And for tomorrow night as well.
As a matter of fact
I know of no better topic
For us to discuss
Until we all
Die!

—Hafiz

An Ending That Is a Beginning

THE QUIET IS EERIE AND IRRITATING AT THE SAME TIME. "STU-dents don't come into these stacks much anymore. That's what Google is for!" Donie mutters to himself, surveying the cramped basement room with disdain. "What am I doing in this place so late on a Friday night?" The campus is virtually empty. Most of his friends have completed their exams and scattered for winter break, waving goodbye to him as they pulled out of the parking lot. While he is quite skilled on his laptop, Donie intends to carry a book or two home with him, just for the pure satisfaction of reading the actual pages for a portion of his research. Given who his mother is, Donie has never lost his affection for the feel and texture of books, as have many of his classmates with their attachments to their electronic devices.

Finally, Donie locates the section he needs. Rummaging disinterestedly through the books rigidly lined on the shelf directly in front of him, he grumbles again, "What am I doing here?" Glancing down at his phone to check for useful titles, the frustrated student finds nothing that speaks to his needs. He shrugs his shoulders and leans back against one of the shelves. As he begins to despair, he spies a title at eye level, on a shelf directly in front of him, *A Personal and Philosophical Reflection on Love and Loss.* Having never heard of the book, he notices that the author is a philosopher. "This will do as a start!" he exclaims.

As fate would have it, in the second year of his studies at the university, Donie took an introductory philosophy course that included sessions on the topic of love. *Why in the world would philosophers study love?* This question puzzled him at the time. He determined to focus on this elusive topic for his senior thesis, and then promptly put the entire project out of his mind until a couple of years later when, on a lonely night in December, he finds himself wandering through the campus library for lack of a more creative effort on his part.

After a week of final exams, Donie set his psyche for escape—back to his beloved New Mexico, where he will see his mother, enjoy sleeping in his own bed and go skiing! Excitement overrides his earlier frustration as he grabs a burger and shake from a fast food restaurant close by his co-op apartment. Before long, his clothes, both clean and dirty, are scrambled together in wads and stuffed into a wilted brown duffle bag, left over from his summer camp days. Donie showers, then collapses onto his bunk bed for much-needed sleep before the daylong tedious drive northwest to Santa Fe.

*   *   *

"Hey Mom! You home?"

"Yes, hon, come on back to the kitchen. I'm doing some holiday baking—your favorites!" Rorie hugs her son and giggles as he groans from her routine ritual of reaching up to brush her slender fingers through his thick brown hair. "Welcome home! I've set the logs for you to light a fire. There's chicken pasta soup in the crockpot. Take your luggage up to your room and then let's get this evening going! Rorie is smiling, her excitement easily evident. Mother and son wander into the living room to stare at the Christmas tree casting sparkles onto the walls. The smell of pine fills the air. Kneeling to start their evening fire, Donie chatters easily about his exams and the drive home. The carefully laid wood ignites and color bursts into the fireplace.

Standing, Donie grins in delight as he puts his arm around his mother before reaching down to tussle with their overly friendly dog, Shama, a four-year-old golden retriever that resembles their formerly beloved dog Flame. Both mother and son had sobbed when Flame died of a cancer in her neck. It had taken a few years before Rorie could replace her dog, but finally she had broken down and fallen in love with a new puppy offered to her by a colleague at work.

Shama jumps at Donie, recognizing him, nudging his knees for a massage behind the ears. "Home again," Donie sighs. "I do like university life, but I really prefer being here in Santa Fe. Thanks for the welcome, Mom! You always know how to make a guy feel good!"

Heading off to his room to drop his duffle and backpack, Donie savors the smells and sights of his home. He and his mother have been the only residents in this condominium apartment since he was a small child. She never married and had not really explained in so many words why he was fatherless. For some reason unknown to him, the topic had seldom been brought up. Strangely, Donie was not curious to know about his missing parent, assuming his mother would tell him if and when she wanted him to know. Rorie did not seem to have a need to tell him the story. He had rarely felt the absence of a father; Rorie had seen to this. They are a pair bonded by time and an easy rapport with each other. Both are content with their arrangement.

When all the holiday folderol passes, Donie announces that he wants to drive up to Taos and meet a buddy of his to share some skiing and snowboarding. Rorie knows better than to interfere, so she sends him off with her usual, "Have a good time. Let me know when you get there, will you? Where are you staying this time?"

"I'm bunking with Jake wherever he's hanging—I think with a cousin. Not to worry, Mom. We'll be fine," he waves off her concerns.

"College kids!" she says out loud, "Though it does sound fun the way they do things these days. Wish I had been that confident at his age," Rorie sighs to herself as she begins to straighten the living room from Donie's usual clutter.

Donie throws his ski gear into his well-used pick-up truck and heads out, traveling up Highway 285 toward Taos. The partially read philosophy book on love has been stuffed into his bag. Snooping around online, Donie has learned that, although Dr. Clayton E. Jacobs had spent his academic career in Kansas, *The author currently resides in Taos, where he continues to write books.* Clay's online biography makes it convenient for Donie to be able to locate the author, or so he assumes.

Donie has not told his mother that he has plans to seek out the writer of the book on *love and loss*, not because he is hiding this fact from her, but because this is not the first thing on his mind. First things first— *skiing!*

After a couple of idyllic days of boarding and skiing in the Taos Ski Valley, Donie and Jake, his best buddy from high school, decide to skip the slopes for a day because overnight the weather has turned sharply cold and miserable. The slopes will be icy today and Donie wants none of that. Though he loves to ski, a traumatic accident when he was ten had taught him not to take foolish risks. Better to stay in town on this blustery Thursday and try to locate "the professor." Using his phone, he quickly finds the address of Dr. Clayton Jacobs. Donie decides not to call, afraid the author will refuse to meet with him. *Better go chase him down and make this personal,* Donie slyly calculates.

Taos is not so large that the college-aged sleuth is concerned he will find it difficult to track down the professor—not at all. However, he does not account for the fact that Dr. Jacobs lives outside of town on the high desert. Thus, he drives around quite a while before discovering the house sitting primly in the middle of a field of sage in full view of the Sangre de Cristo Mountains. The snow-covered peaks are hidden, now covered with heavy dark clouds swirling around them, warning of an impending wintry blast.

Pulling his truck into the nondescript gravel driveway, Donie parks and turns off the engine. Secretly hoping the sounds of the six-cylinder engine will bring the owner to the front door, he sits in the truck for a moment. But no such luck. "All right, I better get this over with," he mutters to himself, now half embarrassed at his strategy to show up without an appointment. Opening the screen, he knocks on the thick wooden front door, returns the screen to its closed position and waits. Donie hears rustling inside, and a dog begins to bark. But no one comes. He tries again, knocking louder this time as the dog starts to whine. Finally, footsteps.

The inner door swings open, and a friendly face gazes at him. "Sorry about that. I was in the back of the house." Donie, noticing wisps of white foam lingering around the man's neck and ears, realizes he has been shaving.

"Umm, I'm sorry. Should I sit in my truck 'til you're through?"

"No. Come on in and wait—who are you?" The professor, used to students dropping by from his days of teaching, has forgotten to follow protocol and check to see who is standing on his porch. A cold wind wafts through the door. To keep from losing the heat emanating from his wood-burning stove, Clay pulls the door closed behind him; they both stand on the porch.

"Hello, Sir, my name is Donie. I'm a student at the University of Texas, and I'm up here in Taos for a couple a days of skiing. I want to talk to you about your book." Suddenly, Donie realizes how foolish this must sound to the author, so he tries again, pulling his jacket closer to his body.

"Sorry. I guess that didn't make much sense. I'm working on my senior thesis paper, and I want to use your book on *love and loss* as one of my resources. So I thought . . . umm . . . maybe you would let me interview you." He stops here to allow his proposal to sink in. The wind is biting his neck and face at this point. As Clay pauses a moment to ingest this information, Donie drops his eyes, regretting his plan.

With a shove, Clay swings the screen door wide open and chuckles, "Sure! That actually sounds like something way better than what I'm working on at the moment. Come on in outta the cold. I'll put on a pot of coffee for us. That sound okay?" Clay grins again, now very curious about the young man standing in his house, shivering, and shuffling snow off his boots. Something about this kid seems "familiar," but he cannot put his finger on it. *Maybe he was one of my former students,* he muses. *There were so many of them. Names are gone. But that can't be right, he's a bit too young to be one of mine. Hmmm . . . I guess I'll soon know.*

"Now tell me your name again?" Clay asked, cocking his left ear toward the visitor.

Donie responds a bit too eagerly, "Donie, Sir. . .it's an Irish name. My grandfather is Irish."

"Is that so?" Clay, amused at the young man's uneasiness, gently teases him. To relieve Donie's discomfort, Clay continues in a more formal tone. "Okay, Donie. Give me just a minute to clean up my face and put on my shoes, and I'll get that coffee brewing." Clay disappears, leaving Donie to figure his way about in the cozy room, decorated with eclectic furniture not of any particular style or fashion.

The dog lingers close to the stranger, sniffing and pawing at him. Absentmindedly, Donie pats the animal's head as he is used to doing with his own pet. *Funny how much Dr. Jacobs' dog resembles Flame. I sure miss that dog.* Allowing his eyes to wander around the space, he shucks his jacket, hanging it on a rack by the front door. Crossing the tile floor where woven black and red woolen rugs have been cast here and there, Donie reaches out for the wood stove to warm his hands. He spots a carved walking stick leaning in the corner. *I wonder if Dr. Jacobs is a hiker?* Just as he is about to walk over to pick up the stick, Clay enters the room. Donie jumps, as if caught doing something wrong.

Clay spies instantly what has caught Donie's attention and says, "Feel free to take a look at it. That one's special. I'd be happy to tell you the story behind it over our coffee. It's almost ready." Donie hesitates, so Clay grabs the stick and shoves it at him. "Here. Give it a look!" Returning to the kitchen to prepare their coffee, Clay calls out, "You a sugar or a cream man?"

"Just a bit of milk, please. That's all."

As Clay reappears, one cup in each hand, he sets the steaming coffee down and ignites the conversation, "So what do ya think of my stick?"

Moving to the sofa to grab his cup and sit down, Donie stammers, "Well, I . . . I guess I wondered if you are a hiker, though that stick seems a bit fancy to actually take hiking. Looks valuable." Taking a sip of the coffee, the impromptu visitor glances at Clay over the rim of his cup, wondering if the question is a bit too personal this early in their conversation.

"You're right there. I paid a pretty penny for that hiking stick, but it wasn't mine for years. I bought it for my dad after I took my first hike down into Wild Rivers gorge." Clay grows quiet and distant, momentarily forgetting his guest. The dog lifts himself off the rug in front of the wood stove and ambles over to Clay, as if in sympathy. Clay's hands find their way into the thick fur around the animal's neck.

To break the awkward silence, Donie asks, "What's his name?"

"Flame."

Donie gasps, but then gives a half-hearted laugh. "I had a dog named Flame when I was a kid. She looked a lot like yours. Guess they're relatives." Clearing his throat, he squirms on the sofa, looking for a way to extract himself from the conversation.

Clay looks up startled, then softens and queries, "You ready to talk about my book? I have an appointment in a couple of hours, so we better get onto this. Tell me what you're after in your project. What's it about precisely? What do you hope to accomplish by talking with me? Why do love and loss interest you at your age?" Clay slips into his professor mode easily and quickly with the young man, waiting for him to respond.

The two men, one older, one younger, but with matching blue eyes, talk easily about the contents of the book, the meanings and interpretations that might be applied to the thesis project. More than an hour zips past before either of them notices. "Hey, Donie, I need to get ready for my appointment and go into town. How long are you planning to be in Taos? Do you want to get together again to finish our work?" Clay eagerly suggests they continue their dialogue. In the past, the professor enjoyed his time with the college crowd, seldom growing tired of their inquisitive minds and open hearts. He volunteers his time to Donie, hoping the bright young man will accept his invitation.

Donie's eyes light up. "Sure, Dr. Jacobs, thanks for the offer. I'm skiing one more day with my buddy, but I'll be coming back through Taos on Saturday morning. Could I buy you a late breakfast, so we can finish our talk?"

"That's a deal!" Ushering Donie to the door, Clay takes the ski jacket off the rack and hands it to him.

"Thanks again, Dr. Jacobs. Thanks again." Patting Flame on the head, Donie bows his shoulders into the cold wind and lopes back to his truck, his head full of ideas and questions. *I made some progress today. Meeting the author is just so cool!*

After Clay finishes with his appointment in town, he returns home, all the while pondering the encounter with Donie. Although his book on love and loss has long since been published, Clay realizes that the morning meeting with the student has awakened his interest in the topic again, this time seen through the eyes of the younger generation. Clay's book had included reflections on the varieties of coupling that fill the human experience. But he had failed to acknowledge that within the experience of romantic love there is also a range of depths. As the two worked together, Clay became aware that Donie is inexperienced in the field of love. His queries were unformed and simple. Yet, Clay could tell the young man sought clarity about this complicated subject of so much human pursuit. *He has a natural curiosity about topics like love. My kinda student.* Clay grins to himself as he remembers Donie's eagerness to understand.

Filling a glass with cool water, Clay strolls over to his favorite chair, worn, with creases in the leather seat, and calls Flame to sit by his feet. Then, after a long drink, he rests the glass on his knee. His mind immediately becomes saturated with memories, some prodding him with red-hot emotional pokers. *My time with Mellie was deeply profound—earth-shaking really. We were devoted to each other in a way that was inexplicable to others. Yet, in the middle of that relationship, when I could not imagine such a connection with any other human being at any level, I met and loved Rorie. How was that possible? Because not only does love shift through levels of developmental stages, from youth to old age, intimate love also contains a range of depths to it. Some love is markedly deeper than other love. I was fortunate to love two women with a depth that bound my soul to both of them. I lost both, and this has shaped my life since. I'm not sure I can explain this to Donie when we meet again. Wonder if I should even try?*

*   *   *

Saturday morning dawns with ponderous skies and frigid temperatures. Starkly white mountain peaks poke through the gray clouds, issuing a warning of things to come. Springing out of bed, Donie begins his exit routine. He loads the truck with his gear, tells Jake goodbye with a guy hug and a fist bump, then heads out for the road back into Taos. He had called Dr. Jacobs the night before and set up their meeting: 9 a.m. at Michael's Kitchen.

"Hey, Dr. Jacobs. Glad you could meet me!" The two men shake hands, and Clay responds by saying, "I think you should call me Clay at this point, don't you?" A grin is sprawled across his face.

"I know some professors who are comfortable with that, but it feels odd to me, knowing that you were a professor at one time. But I will try . . . Clay." Donie nods.

Over hot coffee, scrambled eggs, crispy bacon and tasty pastries, the student and the teacher keep their heads close as they discuss *love and loss* for the next two hours. The conversation is intense, lacking in levity or nonsense. Clay's words about the complexities and complications of their shared topic are some of the most enlightening Donie has heard on the subject.

Feeling overwhelmed and ready to conclude the conversation, Donie comments, "I see here in your dedication that you mention someone named 'Rorie.' My mother's name is Rorie. Isn't that a hoot? That we both know someone with that name? She was named after her Irish grandfather, though I never met him. Never met my father either. Long story." Donie drops his eyes and signals with his left hand that he wants no questions about this situation.

Clay's face turns ashen, then scarlet. "Where did you say you were from? How old are you?"

"Santa Fe. I've lived there since I was a kid. I'm twenty-one. Why?"

"Oh, just curious." Clay feels as though he is suffocating.

A silence grows between them. Donie stands to take his leave. "Well, uh . . . thanks again, Dr. Jac—Clay. I guess I need ta get back on the road. There's a storm blowin' in soon, and I don't wanna get caught in it. I cannot tell you how much I appreciate your help with my project. Could I contact you during the semester if I need more help? He asks awkwardly, worried his request will be perceived as an imposition.

"Of course, Donie. Of course. You have my number. Feel free to use it. Take care. I hope you will let me have a copy of your paper when you finish it—just email the document to me if you wish. And good luck." A strange look crosses Clay's face. Wishing he could hug this kid, Clay grabs Donie's hand instead for a hearty shake, clapping him on the shoulder as they part.

Arriving home, Donie dashes through the front door right into Rorie's arms, as he did when he was a child. Rorie surrounds her son with a huge hug, as if he has been away for a year. "I just love having you home for the holidays, Donie! It won't be long before you'll strike out into your own life, and I won't see you as often." Her eyes grow misty.

"Mom . . ." he drags out the word so that it is several syllables long. "You make it sound like I'll never come home again. That's not gonna happen." The two settle into chairs around the dining table with beers in hand and Donie regales Rorie with his skiing escapades. He withholds recounting the meetings with Clay for a later time, since his mother seems tired from her work. With a flash of loving aggravation, he urges, "Now what are our plans for the rest of the day? I'm really ready to be home! Could we just order in pizza and watch a movie tonight?"

"Sounds great. I'm tired too. Long morning of reading manuscripts, even though I'm not supposed to have to work on Saturdays," Rorie says with a sigh. "Anyway, I'm going to shower. Then let's get into our sweats. Order the pizza, will you? Get what you want . . . and you pick the film this time. Set a fire for us, and we will just hang here this evening. Okay?"

He nods as she leaves the room. Donie's mind is still absorbed by the discussion with Clay. Wandering over to his mother's enclosed bookcase, he opens one of the glass doors and riffles through her books. He never paid much attention to his mother's book collection before. With her career in publishing, books stacked in piles around their home are a familiar scene. Now that he is a college student, her collection takes on more interest. Looking for nothing in particular, Donie skims the titles. Suddenly, his eyes lock onto one book with a red binding and familiar words on the cover: *Where Wild Rivers Meet,* by Clayton E. Jacobs, Ph.D.

Donie had no idea his mother owned this book. Taking it down off the shelf, he stands frozen, staring at the cover for several moments. In the background he hears his mother's shower come on. As he opens the cover to read the familiar title page, a paper drops out and floats to the floor. As he picks up the sheet of paper, Donie notices it is a letter. Without even thinking that it might be private, he opens it.

Dear Clay . . .

Naked

"FLAME! COME ON, LET'S EXPLORE. IF WE DON'T FIND THAT spring before dark, we won't have water." Rorie picked up her daypack and slung it over her shoulder. When she reached for her hiking pole, she watched Flame whirl around her in anticipation. "Look at this trail," Rorie chattered, "shoe prints everywhere . . . not a good sign, but at least most of them don't look fresh." Petting her pedigreed retriever's head, she confessed, "I would like some solitude, wouldn't you, girl?"

Pausing to survey the trail ahead, she consoled herself and the dog, "At least we haven't seen anyone. Not yet." Rorie had lived alone with her dog long enough that she frequently carried on sustained conversations with the creature. On occasion she worried about herself. Talking to a dog like this was only a notch above mumbling to herself in public. Not that she was lonely. Just the opposite—she felt crowded.

Rorie moved up the trail, her long legs allowing long strides. Her thick, auburn-tinged hair, tied back for a hike, was a close match in color to her pet's fleece. Flame charged ahead and then back, circling Rorie to make sure she followed. The animal's frenzy comforted Rorie, and she entered a rare tranquility as the trail climbed through a mass of volcanic rock and up to the higher plateau. She could see the river below, imperceptibly etching an ever-deeper gorge in its southward plunge.

The main trail rambled another half-mile before Rorie began to hear, dimly at first, then steadily louder, a rush of water concealed among an imposing assembly of swaying pine trees towering over the pathway. A stream appeared beneath the needles of the trees. The crystalline water gurgled and leapt from rock to rock, seeking channels between them and finding a moment's rest in a pebbled pool before dashing on with purpose toward a larger encounter with the Rio Grande. Flame had already found the miniature reservoir, lapping in it as she waded upstream.

Sitting on a moist stone near the shimmering rush of water, Rorie drew from her pack her recently purchased purifying system. She had even practiced the process in her home in Dallas, but this was her first time to purify water for drinking in the wild. As she engaged the process, her mind wandered. *I want adventure. I want this! Everything in my world seems so arranged and predictable.* Contemplating what adventure might mean for her, she defended herself. *What, after all, is adventure but taking some risks by doing what I've never done before. I'm staying alone in this canyon for four days. That's an adventure!* She harrumphed to herself.

Rorie remembered from the map of the gorge trail that there was yet another site for camping farther to the north. It had a name: Big Arsenic. She did not know how far away the springs were, but the urge to explore lured her. Fretting briefly about possibly returning to her camp in the dark, she whispered into Flame's ear, "Let's explore!" The dog wagged her tail with excitement as Rorie hid her water container behind a jagged stump and found the trail again.

By the time Rorie spied the next camp shed, the sun hung ever closer to the rim of the west mesa, and the shadow of the pending sunset advanced steadily toward her from across the river. Hesitating for a moment, indecisive, she stepped forward and resumed her trek.

Flame bounded back from her own trailblazing, but this time she fretted and uttered low muted whines. Rorie imagined her companion had stirred some wild creature and wanted permission to pursue. She stroked the dog and spoke reassuring words. Flame did not rush forward, but stayed so close to her that Rorie almost stumbled over her.

Entering this latest outcropping of trees, mostly ponderosa bordered with pinion and cottonwood nearer the gushing water, Flame crept low on her haunches. At first Rorie did not notice but only listened for the source of the sound, which she soon spotted rushing beneath a crude bridge on the trail. Flame was on her belly, whining insistently and staring toward the precipice where the water plunged.

When Rorie came up beside Flame to calm her, she saw movement down below and slightly to the other side of the tumbling waterfall. At first, she thought it must be some sizable animal, and she experienced a flash of panic when she remembered that brown bear and mountain lion inhabited the region. Then she spotted the movement again. Whatever it was, it has a pale, almost creamy color. Curious. Presently she heard a muffled sound humming above the water's roar, and she crouched almost as close to the ground as Flame. The "animal" was a person!

After feeling so alone and secure on the trail, Rorie suddenly felt invaded. Or was *she* the invader? Rising cautiously and moving slightly to her left, she could see through the foliage—a man. He had on no shirt and seemed to be pushing something. She peered at him until she saw that he was rolling a large flat, only modestly wheel-like rock, up an incline. She pondered, *Sisyphus, perhaps?* She muffled her laughter. When he stood upright, she saw that he was naked. A naked man in her bedroom was one thing, but an utter stranger in this wilderness, boldly unclad and alone, was another matter. Should she be afraid or thrilled? Rorie immediately moved to leave the area, then looked around, lest she be seen spying on another human being.

Moments later the man stood balanced on the rock he had moved into place, a small bucket in one hand and a soap bar in the other. Rorie stood stock-still and, hardly blinking, gazing at the stranger. She was drawn to this man's body glistening in the last light of the day's sun. She sensed something visceral within her gut, something so elemental that it canceled all of her conventions and invited, no— compelled her—to stare.

What she witnessed was a figure with arms and face bronze, and all the rest a pale-tinted flesh. He was neither old nor young but fell in the nondescript middle range of life-—somewhere in his 40s. Without fanfare the man poured the pail of water over his head and soaped himself vigorously, innocently, as one does when alone. Rorie could not imagine his bathing so openly. Didn't he realize that other people used the trail and that he could easily be seen? Still she watched, an instant convert to voyeurism. Holding onto Flame's collar, she whispered into the dog's raised ears, "Stay. Stay."

When the man turned facing her, Rorie looked away momentarily for fear he might see her. Then she peered back at him as if under hypnosis and into his face, deeply tanned to his hat-line. He had an agreeable, almost playful appearance, but she also barely detected what appeared to be care lines, especially around his eyes. She scanned his body top to bottom, back to front, the way women inspect each other upon first meeting. She thought about her recent commitment to adventure and awareness came to her again that she had never before seen a naked man outside, let alone in the wilderness.

Stepping off the rock and moving to splash in a pool beneath the cliff, he vanished from Rorie's sight. He would soon finish his bath and might well come up the trail. This possibility prompted her to a serious effort at retreat, but when she heard him start singing, she halted. As Rorie listened to the muffled melody, the sun dropped into the distant mountains, and soft shadows insisted that she leave. What inspired her more urgently was the renewed speculation that he might be with someone else who could see her. *Spies do not like to be spied upon,* she reminded herself and crept away, urging Flame to silence.

Rorie did not realize how far she had walked. The trail back to her campsite seemed so much longer. She grimaced while dismissing the possibility that she could be lost. *Even a klutz could hardly become lost in this gorge,* she chided herself. If she kept on the trail, she would come to her campsite. For a few moments she relaxed for the first time since her vision—or was it an epiphany?—of the naked man.

Twilight overtook Rorie. She berated herself for not putting her flashlight in her daypack. "Novice!" she whined. Flame's companionship became her saving consolation. The day faded into stillness. The only sound around her was the scuff of her boots against the dirt and rocks as she walked. She stopped at the stump, gathered her water and moved quickly on down the trail. A tinge of fear crept up her spine as she increased her pace. *Nothing is so intimidating at the edge of dark as a canyon that appears to reach into eternity, slowly filling the crevices with shadows.*

Finally back at her camp, she tended to a much-needed meal for herself and Flame. The evening chill caused her to shiver and reach for her jacket. *No fire tonight. I'm too tired after a day like this!* Supper completed, she put away her gear, crawled into her tent with Flame, turned off her lantern and nestled down deep into her sleeping bag. She had planned to read a while, but the memory of the man, the guileless naked man, continued to weave through her mind. Her persistent thoughts fixated on the face of this human in the gorge, bathing alone and unencumbered by shame or embarrassment. None of his actions were hurried. He was thoroughly enjoying the water, the bathing, even his own music.

Wriggling in her sleeping cocoon, Rorie felt herself growing drowsy. Flame had already gone limp and was sleeping close by her. *Why did I keep watching him? What made me do that?* As if identifying with the man, her final thought invaded before sleep overtook her. *He knows about adventure too.*

Interlude

Tacking into a side-wind across the Kansas prairie and through the plains of eastern Colorado, Clay guided his antique BMW motorcycle close to five hundred miles, stopping only for gas and snacks. Once the escape-bound traveler came through the first high range onto the mountain plain and veered south, he began to search for a place to camp. Twilight insisted that he follow a sign to Crestone that promised campsites. Clay found a heavily wooded campground with a couple of vacant sites to the back. He did not mind that tonight—too tired to care. He pitched his tent, wolfed down unexceptional food and fell into his tent to sleep, almost in one gesture. He had spent the entire day in free-fall and had felt a purifying emptiness. His body tingled with the day's cycle vibrations, nudging him into a dreamless sleep.

Morning came late but with a start. Sparkling dewdrops covered his tent. His body stiff from the previous day's ride, he wrangled into his boots and jacket for warmth. Before anything else, even breakfast, he wanted to make a call. Retrieving his cell phone, he tried but could not get a signal. Only after a quarter-mile walk out onto the highway did he finally locate an invisible path toward home. Clay had promised Cassandra he would call every morning that he could. The phone gave a dim ring.

"Good morning, Cassie. How's your mother?"

"She's fine, Dad. Well, you know what I mean . . . where are you?"

"I made it to Crestone, Colorado. I'm at a campground in the mountains. I'm worried this call may drop."

Cassandra interrupted, "Good grief, you drove all that way in one day? Why did you do that? What's the rush?"

Halting a bit with his reply, Clay answered, "I just wanted to reach this mountain range before dark, if I could. I suppose I was just trying to get away from . . . you know . . . ." his voice trailed off. Then he realized how this might sound, "Not from your mother, but from illness and the fatigue of it all."

"Dad, it's all right. It was important for you to go. You are so worn out with everything, you're beginning to look old! Let it go for a while—mother will be fine. I'll take good care of her!"

"When you've hung on this long, letting go is not easy, hon. But I did seem to be able to break the spell for a while yesterday and just drift. The phone is cutting out—you still there?"

"I can barely hear you, Dad. Everything is fine here. Mom is glad you decided to go. She rested well last night, and today she's peaceful. Stop your worrying and enjoy your adventure. Like she said, 'Go on.' We love you."

"I'm working on it. Your voice is fading. I'll call again tomorrow. Love you! Bye!" The phone went dead. He dropped it into his pocket with relief that he could continue this journey into his own healing and restoration.

A tiny fire of twigs and the few branches he could scavenge eased the morning chill. This, along with the oatmeal, pan fried toast and coffee gave him a boost into the day. *Why doesn't food taste this good when cooked in the kitchen back home? There's something to breakfast and camping, I must say. Mellie was right: I desperately needed this trip.*

He sat down at a wooden picnic table provided by the forest service, took out his journal and stared at it. He had promised himself to keep notes on the trip, not only about what he was doing but about whatever thoughts he might have, especially for the book. He wondered whether it would ever finally be written, given the pace of teaching and Mellie's suffering. At least he could read some of it to her when he returned.

Opening the notebook, he read his last brief entry and pulled a pen from the pocket of his tan camper's vest:

Monday, August 20, he had scrawled in the log the previous day. The report was brief, because he had had a mind-blank day, and did not want to fill the page with a dull recitation of his long drive. He ended the log with:

It was a good day. I needed to drive fast and west. I needed to be some-where else—here in these mountains.

Then his thoughts turned to Mellie:

How do you stand it? If I have so much difficulty even watching you go through it all, how can you possibly endure this awful disease? When Justin said that it was a great test, I wanted to slug him. Who needs a test like this? You surely do not need it, even if I do. Three years! The doctor said that your decline would be steady, and he gave you a terminal report. What do they know? All they have is what has happened to others. You are not "other people!" This is maddening to me, and here I am run-ning away like a wimpy child who can't take it.

Catching himself falling back into the very morbidity that im-pelled him to take this trip, Clay ceased writing and looked at the splendor of green against blue as the tips of the trees pierced the sky. A chipmunk skittered around his feet, searching for breakfast crumbs. The sun had begun lapping up the dew from his tent. He picked up his pen and continued to write:

Whether it is a test or not, I will turn this into something more than the stark, dreadful ordeal you suffer. The least I can do is to make some-thing of it on your behalf. Writing seems such a pitiful response. Yet, it is the only thing I can think to do, except to scream. But then, who would hear this? And if they did, what would they do about it? For a generally optimistic man, I am coming to the edge of "Yes" and filling up with "No."

Clay paused again, struck by how grim his attitudes and reflec-tions had become in the last year. Then he remembered and wrote one last sentence:

If Mellie would only stop telling me, in that plodding indirect way she uses to say anything, that I must go on with my life, I might be able to keep a steady presence for her. But that "go on" leaves me feeling as aban-doned by her as she would be by me, if I were to "go on."

He closed the notebook, aware that he would never read today's entry to Mellie.

With hardly a backward glance at his campsite, he began loading and strapping his "traps," as he liked to call them, to the cycle. Clay resumed his ride. He found his route to the south, and by noon he was in New Mexico, headed for Taos on a road he had never before taken. Indulging the wind, the brilliant sun and the elegant scenery whipping past him, he rode as light as any "easy rider" ever had. In this frame of mind, Clay was oblivious to those ponderous jottings of the morning.

A sign appeared five miles north of the Hispanic village of Questa. It read, Wild Rivers Recreation Area and, under it, 2 Miles. Clay did not recall ever hearing of such a place. By the time he reached the turn-off, he had decided to take a look.

He turned onto a paved road and wound through the drowsy village of Cerro. Imitation adobe houses in earth tones, cement gray, and shades of pink mingled among mobile homes, all interspersed with dated cars rusting in yards, abandoned mounds of unsightly metal. The hamlet splayed across the plain in no discernible order. It had no specific center of gravity, except for the adobe Catholic church on Clay's right. He slowed as he passed. He wanted to take in the spectacle of this quaint settlement in northern New Mexico. Across the road from the church spread the cemetery, cluttered with white crosses to which paper flowers and streamers clung and danced in the breeze. A fiesta of grief.

When the road turned south, Clay saw the ridge breaking the plain to his right. He stopped at the first turnout, named Sheep's Crossing, and read the tourist information on a tall brown board. The Rio Grande Gorge. He walked down a stony trail that took him to an overlook and stared into the great rift in the earth.

Intrigued and inspired, Clay rushed back to the cycle and continued driving across the open plain, the gorge unfolding its serrated edges to his right. When he came to a sign that read Big Arsenic Springs, he again stared over the cliff edge into the depths of the canyon. Then he saw a trailhead marker pointing down to the river. Without hesitation, Clay pledged himself to camp in those depths by the river that night.

At the Big Arsenic campsite, Clay loaded his pack, locked his motorcycle and started toward the trailhead. There was only one well-worn pickup camper in the area, parked under a juniper to stay cool. *Maybe those folks are down there too.* The air was hotter than he expected, but he assumed it would be cooler in the gorge closer to the water. The trail snaked steeply down the cliffside, causing him to slip and slide from time to time. When he reached the canyon floor, the calves of his legs ached. Obeying a marker that pointed him to the right, Clay paused to stare at the rugged scenery while wiping his forehead with a bandana. *This is stunning! A spectacular reward for that tricky hike into this place.* After a brief trek and another descent, he spied a sign marking the Big Arsenic Springs, where close by he found a metal shed and began to set camp.

By the time he finished driving the last tent stake into the ground, it was late afternoon but still warm in the August sun. He had not bathed for two days, and the call of the water dropping from a bluff toward the river animated him to explore. He found an ideal grotto beneath the spilling flow, hidden away from anyone who might venture along the trail. Rushing back to his campsite to retrieve his toilet kit, Clay strode to the water's edge. He stripped naked. He wanted to bathe while solar heat still inhabited the nook. His spontaneous humming celebrated the occasion. He noted to himself that it had been a long time indeed since he'd felt like humming or singing.

Rolling a stone away from the water's edge and further into the sun, he stood undressed upon it. He recalled how, stripping outdoors and running naked through Nebraska woods and fields of high grass when he was a child had always exhilarated him. After laboriously rolling a somewhat round stone with a flat surface into place, the naked man stood in the beams of sunlight from above the west ridge, delighting in their warmth before splashing a small bucket of water over his head. The water was frigid. Unexpectedly, he shouted at the abrupt coldness. Trembling, he lathered himself vigorously, turning around so that the sun could warm him from every direction.

When Clay plunged for a rinse into the pool beneath the waterfall, the frosty torrent forced him into a loud aria of verbal nonsense. This was his device for not rushing out without rinsing away the soap. He sang as loud as his voice allowed, but the sounds were instantly swallowed by the roar of the fall and the vastness surrounding him. He dripped his way from the tiny lagoon and sat on his rock briefly before dressing to take pleasure in the prickling vitality of his body after this rite of purification.

He dressed with deliberate movements, then began to wander up the path. For an instant he sensed the presence of someone, but he looked around and saw no one nor any movement. He dismissed the notion and made his way to his campsite. As if an afterthought, Clay began to wonder how he would possibly call home in the morning from this hole in the earth.

Escape

WHEN RORIE PASSED WIL'S OFFICE DOOR ON MONDAY, SHE stepped in and interrupted his discussion with an assistant. "Got your invitation," she confided. "What's going on?"

"What do you mean?" he asked, genuinely puzzled and a little offended.

"The formality of a note!" she popped back at him with a demanding stare.

Wil dismissed the assistant and came around the desk, leaning back against it with his arms crossed. "I'm trying to let you know that you are special." He spoke positively, but his face belied another, hidden emotion. He had wanted to add "to me" to his sentence, but dared not.

A minute red flag hoisted itself in the back of her mind, but Rorie tried to ignore it. *Special. This word usually meant this guy was up to something. I do hope he's not going to ask again.*

Twice before, Wil had asked to move in with her. Rorie owned her home and delighted in fussing over it. This house, the first one with her sole ownership, gave her a sense of independence, of belonging to herself. She liked this feeling. When Wil had first hinted at sharing her most cherished refuge, she instantly recoiled with the thought of being invaded. The second time he was more direct. He knew he could not ask her to part with her own home and move into his apartment, but he wanted their relationship to be more defined. Rorie made excuses at first and finally said she was simply not ready for a live-in mate. One of the assurances that made her relation to Wil so comfortable was the knowledge that, on any given occasion, he would eventually leave and go to his own place.

"It's always nice to know you're special," Rorie lamely responded to Wil's overture. "I'll look forward to Friday." With a look that signaled the conversation was over, she spun around on her heel and left his office. Then feeling a bit guilty, she turned back and added, "Of course, I always look forward to Fridays and our time together."

Rorie dressed for an elegant evening, but she was quite unprepared for what it became. Wil, attired in his best suit (*He does know how to dress well when he wants to!*) picked her up at her front door. This itself was unique. They almost always met at some rendezvous.

Driving into the heart of the city, they chattered about the week and their work. Wil was most comfortable in the subject matter of his work. Pulling into the underground parking cavern of the Reunion Tower Complex, the couple exited the car looking quite the part as young, sophisticated Dallas urbanites.

Rorie spoke with trepidation, because they had never been to this club together. "Well, this will be a first, won't it?"

"You betcha! Don't you think it's time we dined on the top of the city?" Wil puffed a bit with pride at the plan he had contrived.

"Impressive," she answered nervously, not actually as impressed as Wil thought she would be.

"It's for the occasion." His eyes glistening with hope.

"Of what?"

"Of impressing a special woman." That word again! Her breath caught in her throat.

The maître d' politely interrupted their banter. Wil gave his name and, placing his hand possessively on Rorie's back, guided her to their table. They were seated on a raised dais overlooking the city. The restaurant, rotating a full circle every hour, was in the round, with floor-to-ceiling slanted windows allowing them a panorama of the metropolitan sprawl below. The twilight skies gave way to moving lights, some blinking in and out of view, others holding vigil for humanity through the night. *I will have to admit this is lovely,* Rorie thought, struggling to give Wil a fair chance at his plan.

They were eating a light dessert when a bustle of activity turned their attention toward the corner of the room. Three men emerged, dressed in tuxedos bearing stringed instruments. They made their way across the room toward Rorie and Wil. He was smiling, but seemed a bit agitated as they approached. Upon reaching the table, the three positioned themselves to play. Soft strains of Rorie and Wil's favorite song sprang from the strings, *The Music of the Night*. Rorie smiled broadly but found herself simultaneously suspicious, then perplexed.

When the music ended, the three men stepped back as if on cue but did not leave. Wil reached across the table, taking Rorie's hand, swallowed and said, "We have been together almost three years, and we have found so much in common. I believe we are meant to be together." *Heavens!* Rorie's mind spun. *He's going to propose right here in front of everyone. What am I supposed to do now?*

"I want to ask you, as honestly and openly as I know how, to be my wife," Wil continued. He drew from his jacket pocket the inevitable diminutive velvet box. Maroon, she later recalled. He opened it to reveal a glittering diamond set daintily upon a gold band, announcing an imposing count of carats.

Rorie began to cry in what appeared to be an obligatory manner, but her tears, unbeknownst to Wil, were expressions of rage. To be exposed in this public setting in this way left her with no avenue of escape. *Did he plan it this way to keep me from saying no? That's not fair!* They had discussed marriage on random occasions but always in the abstract, only for a very distant future. For her, the conversations never marked any serious anticipation of actually marrying Wil, at least not in any future she could conjure. Her rage increased with the comprehension that Wil planned the whole event in this way precisely so that she could not refuse. Her suspicions were correct!

In a stupor of confusion, Rorie allowed Wil to place the ring on her finger. The various patrons around them erupted into applause and the musicians played again, this time, *Endless Love,* a song Rorie had mentioned once to Wil that she enjoyed. As far as Wil and his band of strangers knew, Rorie's tears were a voiceless affirmation of his proposal, and for the moment she played the part in a fit of befuddled humiliation.

Later, as they left the venue, descending into the thicker evening air, Rorie's mind shuffled through a file of possible responses to what she perceived as a disaster for her. Yet, she cared enough for Wil that she could not find the means of confronting him that would not also dismantle his best intentions. She elected to remain silent, clinging tightly to his arm until they reached his black sedan, then from the car to the opera, and back again. She did not even notice the tragedy of love and loss in the opera. It was, as she would have guessed, the great love story, *La Bohème*. Clenching the playbill in her hands, Rorie spent the evening trying to smile while internally she was screaming, telling herself that Wil meant to do everything perfectly and that she should be elated, even grateful. But she held neither of these emotions. She felt a dizzying mixture of sensations that were mostly exposed, raw and trapped.

All she could muster on the way home was one stalling gesture. "Wil, I am not ready to marry yet." The commitment represented by marriage always threw her into a riot of memories revolving around her parents' horrendous divorce, and then her mother's untimely death following soon after. Rorie was ten. The wounds and scars actively lingered in her mind and heart. The phantom of commitment loomed larger than she could comprehend and left her with a vacuous dread.

Wil responded by patting her arm, "I know that. We are in no hurry. There's plenty of time to make our plans. Just relax. Things will be fine, Rorie." Wil spoke confidently, all the while holding the assumption that she would soon change her mind and begin to make wedding plans, at least within the year.

"Would you mind a great deal," Rorie requested, "if we don't stay together tonight? I know this sounds peculiar. We just became engaged. But I do need some time to consider all of this." Avoiding his face, she stared out the window over her shoulder at a park where she wished she could go walk with Flame and just be alone with her jagged thoughts. "I'm exhausted from the week, and tonight, well . . ." her voice trailed to a near sob.

"Rorie, honey, I do understand." Of course, he did not understand at all, but he always tried to be understanding with this complicated woman. Wil continued, "I'll call you tomorrow, and we can talk." Rorie nodded, helpless to speak.

Wil walked her to the door. "You are okay, aren't you?" he solicited. She nodded again. "I'm excited about our future, but there is no rush. Please hear me on this." His dark eyes pled his case as his head tilted toward her. They kissed and parted, Wil practically skipping back to his car.

Rorie held her breath so she would not cry until she was safely inside her home. Flame jumped up to greet her as she entered her sanctuary. She leaned down and hugged the dog as if this was the only friend she had in the world, burying her face in the dog's thick pelt.

That night, Rorie's home became an inner sanctum for her outrage. If there was anything she despised, it was being deliberately cornered, not being given a way to be her true self. Even if he proposed out of "love"—*that damn word*—this did not redeem the fact that he gave her no warning, no option, no time to consider!

At times she calmed herself with the assurance that Wil believed he had her best interests in mind, but she also doubted this. *He has his own best interests in mind. I'm just part of his game plan for fitting into the mold.* Back and forth she swung between her fury and her compassion, creating an emotional pendulum throughout the night. She did not even turn back her covers but flung herself on the bed, then hopped up again, ranging through the house in her pajamas and slippers. Opening the refrigerator door, then closing it, turning the television on and off, pacing the living room floor, Rorie ranted and raged until she wore herself thin. Her agitation gave her mind a focus: *What am I going to do now?* She anticipated the movement of time, wishing morning into existence so she could call Sara. She craved attention from someone who would truly listen and give her guidance.

By eight in the morning, Rorie and Sara were downing lattes at the nearby gourmet coffee shop. Her closest friend and mentor, Sara Fogelman, had been seasoned by a twenty-five-year marriage and three teen-aged sons. The eldest, Joshua, was in his first year of college, with all the trauma of adjusting to roommates and class schedules.

Sara listened to Rorie with deep sensitivity, waiting for the distressed young woman to quiet. When her friend finished her recitation and commentary, Sara responded by laying her hand over Rorie's, "Well, you are not married to the man, ya know. You have made no fatal blunder here. All that has been done can be undone, if need be." She paused to allow her words to puncture Rorie's distress. "Rorie, I suspect that you don't like surprises, and you feel out of control."

"Right! I don't like that for sure," Rorie exploded. "You know what bothers me most?"

"What?"

"It's not that I don't care for Wil. Why would I have spent most of my spare time with him for the past three years if I did not care for him? What drives me crazy is that I allowed my feelings for him to keep me from being honest last night. I hate that! Sometimes I think love is just another name for deception," she mourned.

"Shhh," Sara whispered. "We don't want that idea to become public right here in Dallas, do we? This could destroy a lot of lives." Sara chuckled as she spoke. The two women offered each other wry grins.

Becoming sober, Sara looked directly at Rorie, "You know what's really going on here, don't you?"

Peering over her coffee cup, Rorie complained, "What? That's why I called you. I need advice, and I need it in a hurry."

Speaking firmly and looking Rorie squarely in the eyes, Sara spoke with authority, "You are afraid, Rorie. Your thoughts and actions come from fear. You fear being trapped. Just slow down. Give this idea of marriage to Wil time to simmer. Figure out a timeline you can live with and stick to it. You're in panic mode and this will not help you think very clearly."

Rorie ducked her head. She knew Sara was right. Tears filled her eyes. "You're right. I cannot tolerate the idea of being trapped into a marriage I'm not ready for. But I don't need to mistreat poor Wil. This isn't his fault. He's done nothing wrong. He's just a man 'in love,' as they say. Thank you for meeting with me this morning, friend. What would I do without you?"

The two women hugged and parted with waves and promises to meet again soon. Rorie needed to return home, shower, formulate a plan and follow through. Resolve focused her mind. When she entered the side door into the kitchen, the message machine reported that she had missed two calls, both from Wil while she was meeting with Sara. *Yoga first, shower next, and then I will return his call. He can wait on me for a change.* Her mood was not kind at the moment, even though she was not ordinarily a cruel person. Feeling cornered was not bringing out the best of her character.

"Where were you?" His very question only underscored her worst anxiety about the prospect of wedlock. *When you marry, at least one other person besides your father can always ask that question!*

"I had breakfast with Sara," she answered defensively.

She could hear Wil's sigh of relief. "Good. Say, could we have some time together today?"

"How about later in the afternoon? I have some errands to run, and my garden is desperate for attention." Rorie loved working in her yard, running her fingers through the dirt.

"Fine." Wil agreed. "What if I come by about seven? We can go to the trails and jog for a while. Bring Flame if you want."

"Great!" Rorie felt the need to be outside, moving her body. Stress always tied her in knots and running with Flame was a good release for her.

After being up all night battling her feelings, she felt the bed call to her. She collapsed into a dreamless heap on the comforter, waking sluggishly just before noon. *So much for my resolve to do yoga and garden.* She sat up on the bed, feeling a surge of energy rush through her body. *A plan! I must have some time away from work, away from Wil, away from here.* She looked down at her left hand and the sparkling ring on her finger, wondering whether she should remove it at least for the time being. She could say she feared losing it. This would be true but not the reason she wanted to remove it. The ring was simply far too loud a statement about her future given how she felt at the moment.

The afternoon passed all too quickly. Wil would pick her up any minute and the confrontation ahead would loom over their plans. He arrived right on time. After their run around the lake, they paused to sit on a black metal bench and drink from their water bottles.

Taking a deep breath, Rorie broached her concerns, "Wil, I need to say something." She rushed into the next sentence before he could interrupt her. "Although we have from time to time discussed marriage as a possibility, I must admit that I was profoundly surprised—no, shocked—by what happened last night."

Wil immediately began to apologize. "I didn't mean to. . . ."

Holding up her hand, "I'm not accusing you of doing anything wrong, Wil. You are wonderful. Thoughtful. Devoted. I could not ask for more. I am not talking about you or the proposal at this point. I just want you to hear my response to it all. Could you do this for me?"

"Sure." Wil nodded assent, sitting forward on the bench.

"What I'm telling you is that the proposal caught me off guard. No, by surprise. I am thirty-two years old, and I have never faced a direct proposal of marriage before. I was in only one lengthy relationship in my college years. I haven't spent much time thinking about "settling down" into marriage. I do not take your proposal lightly, but you surely know this about me."

"I do know this about you, Rorie. I don't want to frighten you. But I am also ready to take this relationship to the next stage." Wil spoke firmly.

"I know that—at least now I do. But at the moment, I'm talking about me, not you. When I am surprised by something, I usually stall for time, and that is what I plan to do. I need time."

"How much?" Wil spoke with a thinly veiled panic in his voice.

"Let me finish. I don't mean a decade. I am talking about some time now, in the near future, to sort through my own feelings about how I want to live my life and what it will mean for you to be part of it with me." She nervously pulled on her ponytail, shifting one leg beneath her.

"Well, I've been part of your life for—"

"Yes, you have." *He can never set aside his marketing voice even for an intimate conversation.*

Rorie stalled her internal dialogue and returned to the conversation. "But if—when—we marry, it is supposed to be for the rest of our lives, which I do hope will mean a very long time for both of us."

"Right. Of course!" he concurred.

"Now," she began revealing her plan, "I have some time coming to me at work—"

"Yes," Wil interrupted again. "I know. I have some too. But I thought we might use this for a—"

"Wil, you keep interrupting me to make a pitch for the marriage and to tell me *your* plan. But I need you to hear *my* plan!" Rorie deliberately placed emphases in her reply, becoming exasperated with the conversation.

Biting his lower lip, Wil dipped his head to listen harder to her words, "Of course," he replied contritely.

"All right. Here goes," she sighed. "I am going away for a few days, probably a week. Don't ask me where. I don't know yet. But I insist on being alone. I want solitude—quiet—something that almost never happens in my life." Wil sat quietly, holding his reply.

They paused, waiting for the tension to pass, to glance at Flame chasing a duck back into the pond. Cyclists rode by, and a woman pushing a perky baby in a stroller came down the path toward them. The scene seemed surreal in the middle of their talk, each feeling desperate for the other to understand. In a more comforting tone, Rorie continued, "I promise you that, when I return, I will be prepared to state clearly whether, when and even where we might plan our future together."

"I do not like 'whether,'" Wil admitted.

"But it has to be included. This will be the biggest decision in my adult life, and it cuts across several that I thought I had already made. I want to be clear and sure, and you really don't want to deal with me unless I am clear and sure," she added with a touch of humor, patting his hand.

"Okay, Rorie. I will respect your wishes because I want to. That's how much I love you." This is the first time she heard the word "love" in any of their discussions. *Isn't that odd? Neither of us has used that word since the proposal. It's almost as if we are negotiating a business deal rather than a marriage.*

They stood, hugged each other and called for Flame. The almost-but-not-quite-engaged couple hardly saw each other for the next few days, except for brief encounters in the office. Rorie spent time becoming clear about what she longed to do in terms of her "get-away." For years, she realized, a suppressed passion had nagged her, especially since she had entered the busy world of corporate and urban life. Her fantasy had to do with nature, with being out of doors. Memories of camping with her father on some of his less exotic anthropological expeditions filled her mind and birthed her ideas. Rorie's subterranean image of encountering the wilderness rose steadily closer to the surface of her consciousness. She envisioned hiking and camping alone, a solitary woman surrounded by nature. She had never mentioned this hidden desire to anyone, not even Wil or Sara.

Soon Rorie found herself in camping stores with no particular scheme in mind. Mostly she milled around among the array of gear and bags of freeze-dried food, finding pleasure in reading the labels, handling unfamiliar items and musing at how clever the camping industry had become since she was a child. One Saturday she woke determined to purchase what she needed. *Today's the day!*

Her shopping frenzy netted her a pack, tent, sleeping pad—all the gear she needed for shelter. In addition, she purchased a lantern, packer's cook stove, fuel cans, dish set complete with cup and eating utensils, water purifier, first-aid kit, and a lightweight dish for Flame. Rorie spent the most time selecting her hiking boots and socks, poring over the selections with obsessive attention.

Just as she was ready to complete her purchase, she spotted the hats and realized she would need head cover in the sun. *Hmmm, hadn't realized I am headed for sun, but I guess the decision is made.* Privately, she giggled at herself as she recognized how this trip was unfolding inside her mind. Grabbing a gray-green hiking hat off the hook, she slammed it on her head, the tag hanging off the back onto her long hair, and turned toward the checkout counters. When she drove out of the camp store parking lot, the back of her four-by-four bulged with her bounty.

Three weeks from the day Wil proposed to her, Rorie loaded her car, preparing to escape. She had spoken to him the night before but asked him not to see her off. For Rorie, this was her very own experience. Solo. As a final gesture, she removed the engagement ring with care and tucked it back into its tiny box, then placed it in her dresser drawer. "There! That's a better home for you right now," she whispered to herself, clicking the drawer tightly shut.

The exhilaration, along with a touch of terror, came in waves as she drove away, Flame sitting upright on the back seat behind her. Heading west, Rorie noted that, to her best memory, she had never taken a personal trip on her own to a place where she would know no one, nor have a support system. She had studied abroad in Italy but had traveled with other students and professors. Even her move to Dallas allowed her to arrive with an already-established support team of colleagues. This time she was totally alone, except for Flame.

Up at daybreak, unheard of for Rorie, she and Flame piled into her Jeep Cherokee and began their journey north and west, until the vast open terrain began to show signs of ancient turbulence. The modest remains of volcanic fissures then thousand years past surrounded her. The land swelled into rippled earth, covered with clumped vegetation. Beyond Cimarron, New Mexico, the first hints of the heights made her gasp. They came upon her stealthily, then boldly. The climb became steady. Her heart began to beat with excitement. Her ears popped. Rorie took one final hairpin turn to the left and climbed precipitously to a pass. On the other side lay a motionless silver-gray mountain lake below, guarded by the sleepy village of Eagle Nest. Final stop for the day: Red River. She had a reservation in this village trapped between two mountains. From there, she had no idea where she was headed. She fell into her bed that night feeling bold and brave, Flame already asleep on the floor beside her.

The following morning dawned bright and crisp, the mountain air gloriously cool after the Dallas heat. Rorie asked a woman at the front desk of the quaint inn about the best place to camp. The woman's round, friendly face lit up. With a twinkle in her blue-gray eyes, she spoke of a camp area out on the high plains north of Taos, her "favorite place that nobody knows." She glowed as she shared her secret with Rorie.

Turning north out of Questa, Rorie danced inwardly with exuberance. She remembered reading about New Mexico, that it is not so much a geographical location as a spiritual dimension. This was proving true. She located the sign for Taos and drove twelve miles in the opposite direction, falling under the spell of this sparse, somewhat desolate landscape. The recreation area was marked by official campsites and posted directives pointing down toward the river. After stopping at the Ranger Station for hiking maps and general directions, she drove until she reached the far point. The sign read, La Junta, and an arrow directed her to the right.

Rorie parked and walked through a scattering of empty camp shelters to the point. Her mouth dropped at the vista she found there. More than a mile below she could see the confluence of two rivers. To her left tumbled the Red River, which she had followed down the mountain from Red River. To her right flowed the Rio Grande, until the two bodies splashed together in the distance below her. *Wild Rivers* . . . She turned the words over in her mind, savoring them like fine chocolates. *Wild Rivers. This will do.* "Here, Flame. Let's do this!" Her dog leapt at the excitement in Rorie's voice.

The trailhead into La Junta allowed her a panoramic view of the point below as she began her quest. The horizon stretched endlessly before her, the depths beckoning her to come below. Especially pleased to be hiking down into the canyon with her load, Rorie endured a slight anxiety at the thought of hauling it and herself back up out of the gorge. *Well, at least all the food should be eaten by then, and the pack will be lighter,* she assured herself.

Reaching the base of her descent, Rorie walked down to the point of the confluence, took off her pack and her boots and splashed in the shallow water on the Red River side. Cold. Flame had already bounded into the water, head buried as she lapped a drink. The nearby campsites disappointed Rorie, however, and she surmised that more people might show up here. *I really want to be alone. Not going to risk it.* Consulting her map, she decided to hike north to another site.

After a half-mile, Rorie found a camp shed that looked sufficiently private and shaded. She immediately began to set up camp, tossing her gear helter-skelter on the pine-needle-covered ground. She vaguely remembered a childhood instance of trying to help her father pitch a tent by a lake, but mostly he thought she was in the way and brushed her off. Because the splendid blue of the sky began disappearing behind a mixmaster of clouds rising over the high cliffs to the west, Rorie hurried to raise her tent. She struggled to locate adequate ground for driving her stakes. *Tree roots everywhere. I need a mallet!* She grumbled under her breath. She had practiced pitching the tent in her backyard in Dallas, where the dirt was soft. This ground was a different matter! Locating hand-sized rocks nearby, she pounded the stakes into the dirt. Within an hour, her home away from home nestled under the trees ready for habitation. Flame was animated, sniffing every tree, chipmunk hole and pinecone to be found.

Let the adventure begin! Rorie sighed, contented for the first time in weeks.

Encounter

BY SEVEN IN THE MORNING, CLAY SAT CROSS-LEGGED IN THE tent with a new journal open on his lap. Fresh ideas for the book, emerging from his alpha state, stirred him to thought. Dawn lightened into day. After jotting a few notes, he felt restless, ready for the opening of the day to lay claim to his psyche. Clay could not remain closeted in his cocoon with so much expanse luring him out of the nylon shelter. Shivering in the morning chill, he donned his jacket, unzipped the tent and entered the luminous spectacle offered by glowing, mauve-streaked skies and the jumble of rocks and towering trees in front of him.

Walking to a high point down trail, he tried to raise a signal on his phone. Only silence. He would have to walk up to the rim to make the call, and even then, he might be only able to locate a meager connection.

After surveying his food options, Clay selected dried fruit, a beef stick and a granola bar, stuffed them into his pockets, grabbed a water bottle and headed up the winding trail toward the mesa top. The mile-long ascent allowed him to pant, sweat and feel his body marshaled into a vigor to match the energy of his surroundings. *Hiking really feels good. So glad to be doing this again!*

Even so, he wondered why he had promised to call every day. Although the climb enthused him, the self-conjured impression that he *had* to call *because he had promised* left him with some resentment. *Is this what it means to be a father and a husband? To make and keep promises?*

Clay continued his reverie, realizing that this idea of promise would be important to the writing project he planned to focus on during the fall semester when he began his year-long sabbatical.

What is the role of promises in our daily lives? And why do we make promises when we know from the outset that at any moment we might have to break the vow, or we might even desire to intentionally dishonor our pledge? Promises expose a need we have for connection, from one person to another. They create a future between us, like my promise to Mellie that I would take this trip in order to help both of us. We form vows with good intentions, for the most part, but then as we require ourselves to keep them, they often turn into a burden. Sometimes resentment creeps in, like my pledge that I would call Cassandra and Mellie every day while I am away. They didn't ask me to do this. I simply promised that I would call— probably to assuage my own sense of guilt for leaving. Now, why did I make such an agreement? For their sake or mine? To hold me accountable to them? Is any oath made without an agenda? Can we be conscious enough to make a promise that is reciprocal rather than controlling? Is an unconditional vow possible when death looms ahead for all of us? Death becomes the condition the moment we say, "till death do us part."

The morning breeze that had been so welcome earlier in his climb began to fade, as the usual high noon stillness set in, causing his breath to be labored. *Not a cloud in the sky—yet.* The ascent took him two hours with a steady stride, as he climbed close to the volcanic face of the mesa. Up top, Clay moved around, searching for an avenue for his voice. Once connected, he confessed to Cassandra that he would probably not call again for several days. After their usual goodbyes, and "I love yous" sped across the miles, he closed the phone, turned it off and put it back in his pocket, letting go.

Then a sudden thought struck him: *What if Mellie takes a turn for the worse?* Agonizing about this possibility, the despondent husband felt the heavy weight of promises made. *Yes. I suppose vows made should be kept. Why have our promises become so difficult and binding for my love and me? When might vows be broken intentionally and with integrity? I must deal with this question.*

Since his academic project had led Clay to think about such matters, he found himself lost in reverie about the role of duty and responsibility between spouses, lovers, friends and family. *Am I my brother's—actually, my wife's—keeper? If so, what am I doing here? Is this the proper way to take care of her? Go off and leave her?* Recognizing that this was his guilt taunting him, he shook his head, as if to clear the thoughts lodged there. Then his mind moved on and continued the internal debate. *Yes, I am Mellie's keeper. But the reason I am in this gorge is to rest so that I am able to do a better job of it. So if this is the case, what is my responsibility to her? Am I to sacrifice my life for hers? Is this what duty of love means?*

Clay halted in his tracks beside a fallen log, plunked down and stared at the sheer wall of craggy stone looming before him. *Why did I use the word sacrifice? Was that a Freudian slip? Do I feel like taking care of Mellie is a sacrifice?* These thoughts startled Clay's usually patient and loving self. But the question was authentic and, he realized, must be faced. *Yes, love includes sacrifice. And what we sacrifice are our self-preferences. Because we made vows to each other, Mellie and I agreed to be responsible to and for each other. We promised to be dutiful in our care, faithful in our love and actions. This is the constant test of love.* A deep sigh filled his chest. *We just never imagined our test would be so demanding and constant—and permanent!*

A huge raven arching in a glide over him filled Clay's ears with its caustic screech. As he stared into the sky at the black smear of movement, a thought struck him like a bolt. *Yes, in the end it all comes back to the most common of answers, love. How could it be anything else? If I do not have that urgent feeling of human connection, of the most intense yearning toward others, duty and responsibility begin to sound vacuous. But great day in the morning, I do not know how to take adequate account of the gravity of love itself.*

As he began moving again, his thoughts of Mellie became even more focused and intense. *Yes, I must confess that love is both the puzzle and the answer. Love seems to have the power within the human experience to complicate our lives while at the same time pulling us into that vortex of chaotic emotions, as if we cannot help ourselves. Love is an indefinable magnet that we cannot seem to live without. And those who try are damned before they even begin.* Tramping on down into the canyon, Clay remained caught in his interior muddle on this stubborn issue. His boots left tracks where there was dirt, just as Mellie was stamped across his heart. *Like my tracks, she will disappear. I am not ready for that tie to be broken.*

His angst was affirmed when, next to the trail beneath his feet, he caught sight of a striped desert lizard frozen on a sponge-like piece of tuff. Above it a tiny, vulnerable pale-green butterfly pumped its wings. Abruptly, with a gesture demonstrating that the tongue is quicker than the eye, the lizard flicked the unsuspecting prey into its mouth and crouched, munching. *Sudden death.*

Tears spurted out of Clay's eyes as he absorbed this swift reprise of his and Mellie's story. The lone pilgrim stood helpless while grief overtook his entire body. His shoulders shook as he sobbed, release finally finding its way into his soul. Once the storm inside him passed, Clay pulled out his bandana, wiped his eyes and face, and stared into the distance as far as he could see. The horizon drew him in, restoring him with its fantastical glimpse into eternity.

Along the trail back to camp, Clay found a dead limb and began to fashion a hiking stick. Cutting and carving with lazy, unhurried gestures, he fell under the spell of the land. Late summer beetles marching along the trail, ubiquitous flies nibbling on his bare legs and arms every chance they had, wild blossoms, especially the fiery paint brushes, attracted his gaze. The sun kept him company, by way of his shadow, through the pile and tumble of basalt stones and boulders separating meadows of sage, cedar and pinion. He was on the verge of true rest, despite the suppressed stirrings trailing him from Kansas.

This idyllic spectacle dissolved with the appearance at some distance of an animal. At first Clay could not make it out. He thought it might be a deer or even a mountain lion. He became a safari hunter crouching behind a scrub pinion, stalking the creature with his eyes. His heart pounded loud enough for him to hear. He longed to see a substantial beast of the wild, to admire its pose and prance as it claimed the place for its habitat. Shortly, the recognition that it was a dog disappointed him. A reddish-orange retriever. *And where dogs appear, humans must be near,* he reminded himself with a twinge of displeasure. The dog advanced on the trail toward him with no sign of suspicion or threat. Clay called to the animal and the dog came to him with a cordial strut, head high, familiar and friendly with humans.

Rorie emerged from her tent that morning with self-congratulating enthusiasm at having slept in the wilderness alone for the first time in her life. Her first thought sealed her determination to move her camp closer to water at Little Arsenic Springs. But the water was an excuse. She knew that the naked man camped only a bit over a mile farther, and despite all of her wishes to be alone, she felt an amorphous assurance in knowing he was down in this gorge with her—for safety reasons, at least. She only wished never to actually run into him again, clothed or not.

To Flame's disappointment, Rorie did not immediately strike out for the trail once their morning meal was consumed. She instead puttered with her gear and the tent. Eventually the tent collapsed with the removal of the poles and stakes. Stuffing the tent into its bag, Rorie hoisted the bulging pack onto her back and began hiking toward the springs. Flame shifted from brooding to ecstatic canine frolic.

From walking the trail the previous day, Rorie remembered a camp shed near the springs and made for it in the hope that no one else had settled there. Sweat poured down her face as she tramped in the late morning heat toward yet another home. She was not enamored with the flies or the clicking sound grasshoppers made when she stirred them from their own dining. Although the passage was less than a mile, she was ready to cheer when she reached the vacant site. Within an hour, Rorie laid claim to the spot as her own, like a bird making a nest, while Flame did the same in the fashion peculiar to her kind, circling about until she found a preferred place to lie on the soft pine needles piled under a huge tree.

Strolling toward the river, Rorie found a massive flat rock and sat for some time musing on the tranquil dazzle of her setting. The sun made her drowsy. Only the plunge and stir of the Rio Grande broke her thoughts. For the first time since her arrival in the gorge, she turned to face directly the reason she came to this wild place. The reason loomed large, and she wanted to reduce it to a more manageable size. *Why marriage at all? Why him? Why now? Will I ever truly want to marry?*

These questions tumbled over and over in her mind, like the glistening rocks in the river below tumbled their way within the river's flow. Wil's proposal had thrust Rorie into a space she was not interested in considering. Yet, the idea of marriage persistently nagged at her. *Why not choose marriage? Why am I so hostile to this idea? Wil is fine, as a human being. He's stable, kind, thoughtful. So what's my problem?* Even without asking herself these questions, she knew the answer. She had not grown up with a positive image of marriage, and the very idea of being married created such a deep fear in her that she could hardly breathe when confronted with the thought of it. The identity crisis this situation caused in Rorie played heavily on her mind, prompting anger as well as bewilderment.

Her contemplation ended with the intrusive recollection of the naked man. *He must be up there. Am I too close?* Then she thought about the puzzling blend of infatuation and aversion that the experience of spying on him had produced in her. She wanted to sneak back up to Big Arsenic Springs, and at the same time she wanted to head back to La Junta. Her ambivalence created confusion in her mind. *Enough of this!*

An indistinct but clearly human voice in the distance and Flame's bark interrupted Rorie's ruminations. Flame had wandered off about half an hour earlier, and Rorie had not noticed she was missing. She stood, climbed up the rise behind her tent and walked in the direction of the sounds. Noticing a shadow that came up behind her, she looked up to see the head of a ponderous bank of stone-gray clouds rising over the rim to the west. They ranged from ominous dark at the base to white fluff massing above in the stark blue of the sky. A light wind stirred the shrubbery around her and brushed through her hair.

Turning her attention back to the noises and her concern for Flame, Rorie at first saw nothing. Then, boldly, *he* appeared— the naked man—this time in clothes, thank goodness. She moved toward them, but much more toward Flame. Had her dog come to her, Rorie might have rushed back to the river. Too late. The man was already waving a greeting. *Oh dear, what do I do now? I cannot deal with this man. I have seen him undressed.* She collected herself by the reassurance that he surely did not *know* he was *known* and walked up the trail toward him.

The awkward shuffle of first meeting a stranger was complicated by what Rorie knew and Clay did not. He came toward her, open-faced and grinning. She only glanced in his general direction and then looked away, pretending to be concerned about her dog. She wanted to apologize but could not imagine how. Clay spoke first.

"Your dog?"

"Yeah. Come here, Flame." She touched the dog's head. "She never meets a stranger."

"My kinda dog."

When people meet each other for a purpose or in a familiar set-ting, they generally understand from habit the rules for negotiating the meeting. But neither Clay nor Rorie knew the protocols for this random encounter in the wilderness. Both felt clumsy. Rorie tended toward introversion and was about to dismiss herself and walk away, when Clay asked, "How long have you been down here?"

"Since yesterday."

"Me too. How long you planning to stay?"

"Oh, three or four days. I haven't decided." She paused, then looked around and added, "I could probably live here forever, but. . . ."

Nervous, Clay interrupted to say too much too fast. He noticed but could not stop himself. "I know what you mean. When I found this place, I couldn't believe I'd never heard of it. And then I drove through and found it almost deserted. I still can't imagine why, but I like it that way." Then chuckling, "Present company excepted." He turned his eyes away, gently blushing.

Rorie glanced up and smiled at his acknowledgement. Then she actually observed his face, much as she had the day before, only much closer now. She was struck by how different he appeared up close and in clothes. More self-possessed, more prepared for the world, less exposed. *Clothes.* She became lost inside herself. *Clothes are armor as much as anything else.* Then she pursued her woman's quick dissection of him. Out-of-style sunglasses hid part of his face, but she could see that he had a relaxed, weathered countenance, sturdy yet refined. Guessing that he was in his mid-forties, Rorie noticed the gray socks sticking out of his scuffed, dusty leather hiking boots. *He's been hiking already today,* she surmised. Above the socks his legs were pale, just as she remembered from her voyeurism. She noticed a wedding ring on his left hand, a plain gold band. *This will provide the distance I need and keep me in check. Thank goodness!* She announced this internal message to her heart that was beating a pace too quickly.

Clay, much less intimately observant, was aware that Rorie was tall. A word shot through his mind, *lithe.* She wore stylish, recently purchased hiking clothes. Blond-streaked-sharpening-into-auburn hair framed her face, with a bit of fresh sunburn across her nose. Her eyes were bright green in color, surrounded by golden lashes. But what stood out most about her face was the defensive tightness tucked around her lips. Only gradually did this canyon visitor let down her guard as the two strangers chattered innocuously with each other.

Wondering whether to pursue the conversation further, Clay turned to peer upward. The sky had abruptly become shades darker. Wind danced through the taller timber, working its way down to the meadow of shrubs and stunted cedars. Occasional glances reported to him the steady weather changes. He considered leaving for his camp before the worst struck. But at that instant a chilling gale swirled up-canyon. Simultaneously a stunning blast of thunder echoed through the gorge, announcing the pending storm. Rorie leapt; Flame swung around her feet.

"I can tell something is about to happen," she exclaimed, moving to take her leave.

Clay, turning toward the trail, shouted above the roar of the wind, "I'd better hurry, or I'll be caught in this." But as he looked back over his shoulder in the direction of his campsite, he witnessed an off-white shroud extending from clouds to earth, so common to big sky summer storms. It marched across the river and down through the gorge as if coming to capture them. Then the first dust-settling globules of rain, those heavy grand drops that mark the beginning of a New Mexico downpour, already surrounded them.

They both endured a momentary paralysis before Rorie spoke. "You'll never make it all the way back to Big Arsenic without getting soaked. Let's head down to my shed for cover." With a burst of energy, she started running.

How did she know I'm camped up there? Clay stood frozen for a moment. Before he could form the question out loud, the rain increased to a deluge, and without further negotiation they charged toward the camp shed. To his astonished chagrin, Clay stumbled over a stone hiding behind a shrub of sage and fell headlong downhill. Rorie rushed back to help him, her wet hair swinging in her face, but he immediately sprang up and sheepishly ducked into the shelter.

Once under the metal awning, they both laughed at their modest crisis. Flame ran in behind them and shook herself all over them. They laughed again, and Clay sputtered, "Why do dogs always want to dry themselves off as close to you as they can?"

"It's their way of being friendly," Rorie quipped. As she spoke, she also saw Clay's mud-spattered clothes spackled with bits of grass and weed, and they both laughed even harder. Rorie dashed over to her tent and reached in for a hand towel. It took a moment to locate, and by the time she returned, she was wet to the skin. Again, soft chuckles as she wiped away the excess mud from Clay's shirt. She grew more serious when she saw his skinned knee and asked about it, but until she mentioned the wound, Clay was unaware that he was bleeding. He put out his hand for the towel, held it out in the rain and then wiped off the laceration.

"Does that hurt?" Rorie questioned him with concern showing on her face. Her query made her forehead wrinkle and creases appear around her mouth.

"It stings a bit, but it's only scraped skin." Clay observed Rorie's concentration on his wound as he wiped away the blood, their faces a bit too close together. *It's been a while since someone took care of me,* he noted to himself.

As they lifted their heads, they smiled awkwardly at each other, this time with a touch of shared unease at knowing they were trapped together in the cramped space for as long as the storm lasted. Clay stuck out his hand and volunteered, "Well, since we are going to be huddled here for a while, we might as well get acquainted. I'm Clay." His blue eyes sparkled with the levity of the moment.

Nodding, she said, "Rorie." When he appeared surprised at her name, she added warily, "after my grandfather."

They perched on the wooden picnic table like marooned castaways, a comfortable silence growing between them. Flame, curled in one corner of the shed, yawned loudly and her breath came in slow drags as she settled into a nap. The beat of the rain on the metal roof made it nearly impossible to converse. The wind shifted, forcing them to pull the table further back into the shed. They resumed their perch, watching the heavens open up and dump sheets of rain on the roof. Each in their own way felt safe, even cozy, in this makeshift haven. Little embarrassments slipped into oblivion.

The rain abated for a brief time. They discussed whether the storm had passed, though the skies did not look compliant. Clay noticed Rorie shivering and was about to ask whether she had something she could put on when a clatter of pellets struck the roof. "Hail!" Clay studied her tent outside the shed. The flap was open. "If those become large enough, they could damage your tent. We should drag it in here, now!" His voice was urgent.

Without hesitation, Rorie bolted toward her lodging and began pulling up stakes. Clay followed just as the hail began to pound the earth. They stuffed the tent into the shelter, throwing themselves in after it. "Whew!" Rorie exclaimed. "That was close."

Digging around inside the folds of the crumpled tent, Rorie searched for her fleece-lined windbreaker. *Ah! Success.* She slipped the black jacket on over her thin wet hiking shirt and zipped it up for warmth. Next came a foray into her backpack to find a foil emergency blanket, the only other covering she had. She handed this to Clay. Remembering her first aid kit, she retrieved a Band-Aid, which she applied to his knee before climbing back onto the table to sit beside him and watch the marvel taking place outside their metal cave. The hail fell like white marbles, striking the earth and the shed, bouncing and piling within minutes into a summer snow.

As quickly as the clouds came, they rumbled away eastward toward the Sangre de Cristo Mountains. At the first hint of sun, the world around them sparkled with the sheen of a fresh bath, and the aroma of residual moisture thrilled their senses. Nature's drumbeat temporarily stopped, and a serene hush reigned, punctuated only by lingering drops falling on the shed from an immense ponderosa close by. The soundless sight of the momentary sheet of ice that covered the canyon floor engaged their attention, and the pair joined the stillness engulfing them. Flame roused and came to stand by Rorie at the edge of the table, peering out, wondering when she would be able to go beyond the bounds of the shed to relieve herself.

"Wow! Would you look at that?" Rorie muttered.

"Winter in the middle of summer," Clay agreed. Then recalling his own camp, he spoke with worry, "Wonder how my tent made out? It was under a big tree, but this was a heavy storm." Before Rorie could reply, he recalled the question he had wanted to ask her earlier.

"Say, how did you know I'm camped at Big Arsenic?"

Rorie's face turned crimson at his inquiry, but she soon recovered with a question of her own. "Isn't that the next camping area up trail?"

"Yes, it is," he answered without paying much attention to her discomfort. She felt relieved and clever at having skirted the little secret she increasingly cherished. She wanted to tell him, so they could both laugh about it, but she was not confident enough to know if he would find her spying on him so funny.

"I just assumed, I guess, that you were there, I mean." She stuttered as she looked away, afraid he could see the truth in her eyes.

The sun spilled forcefully back into the gorge and began doing its work. The bullets of hail melted within minutes. Faint streaks of a rainbow appeared against the sky. Ambivalent between leaving and continuing their conversation, they glanced up to witness the colors before turning their attention to the wet tent and its contents. As they were straightening the tent, Rorie's book fell out. Clay's eyes caught sight of it and he asked her, "What're you reading?"

"Oh, just something a friend recommended," she dodged the question, hoping he would go no further.

No luck. "May I take a look?"

"Sure," she replied, reluctantly handing Clay the book.

He read, *The Path to Love*. "That's a tough path, and I wager it does not lie in this canyon," raising his eyebrows in question at her.

Smiling and nodding, Rorie looked into his eyes, "Probably not." After a pause, "I actually haven't started reading it. I was about to, but I heard Flame's bark. And then there were the two of you."

"Ah, saved by an intruder, huh?"

"From what?"

"Having to take *the path*," he chuckled at her.

"Oh well, it doesn't hurt to read the map, even if I don't take the trip," she quipped back.

Rorie's insightful remark triggered Clay's interest. Here was a person who had a thought or two. He liked that. *Mellie was that way, at least before.* . . . He said, "Yep, you're probably right about that. I spend more time thinking about that subject than about anything else these days." He waited for his thoughts to clear and then moved on, "Well, almost anything." And she caught the wistfulness in his voice.

Rorie was taken aback by a man confessing out loud to a virtual stranger that he thought about love all the time. She had earlier noticed his wedding band, so she assumed the reference was to his wife.

"What sort of thinking about love are you doing?"

"Well, for instance, do you love your dog? What's his name?"

"*Her* name."

Clay looked under the table at the animal who had nestled there, and said penitently, "Sorry 'bout that." Rorie liked that.

"Her name is Flame."

"Perfect! She looked like a camper's fire walking up the trail to meet me."

Rorie refusing the joust, headed around to sit on the table again. Responding to the heart of Clay's inquiry, she asked, "Now, what was your question?"

"Oh, the question. Yes. Do you love Flame?" At the sound of the name the dog roused and looked at Rorie from her snug cradle of sand. Clay slid onto the edge of the table to be able to look at Rorie when they spoke.

"Do I love my dog? Certainly—" Clay was on the verge of interrupting her again, but Rorie held up her hand and continued, "—but only as much as Flame is capable of being loved," thinking instantly of Wil and his irritating aloofness.

Rorie's qualification stunned Clay. He had asked her his question trying to locate the reasonable boundary for appropriately using the word *love* but had never before entertained this idea. *Is it true?* His thoughts spun through fresh synapses, *that we can only love to the extent that the beloved can receive our love . . . or return it?* Clay agreed, "If this is how you see it, then you can probably love Flame to some degree, but can you love your car or your house? They have no way of "responding" the way a dog or another human might."

Rorie, perplexed at how this conversation could be transpiring here in this outback country between the two of them, explained, "I have not actually thought about it, you know, all that much. But it does seem to me that love requires some degree of response. I like my car, enjoy it—in fact, it's a great car!" She paused for effect, "But to say that I *love* my car stretches the word too far for me."

"So then love has to involve a 'two-way deal,'" Clay concluded.

"Sure," said Rorie, "but the deal is almost never absolutely equal. What if you loved someone, and they wanted to return the love, but for whatever reason they couldn't? Or, what if they just don't love you in return?" Rorie is now thinking intensely about Wil. *Is what I feel for Wil love? I'm not sure, since I don't want to marry him.* Frustrated with her line of thinking, Rorie shrugged and turned her attention back to Clay, who seemed adrift in his own thoughts at the moment. The silence between them was natural, easy, at least for the moment.

Clay's mind raced to Mellie's bed, where she would inevitably die. He knew how desperately she must long to return his constant gestures of affection, but. . . . For a few seconds, Clay became so melancholy that tears formed in his eyes. He caught himself: *This is insane. I cannot begin to blubber here in front of this total stranger. Am I nuts?* Rorie noticed the flicker of his eyes but did not ask what the tears meant. Composing himself, Clay nodded, "That is, uh, it would be extremely difficult, I imagine."

Rorie insisted, "I don't believe love has to be absolutely equal. Is that even possible? Most of the time I think it probably isn't. For instance, I guess you could say that I love my employees, the people who work for me." Clucking with amusement, "Well, most of them, most of the time. But the relationships are unequal in so many ways. And what about the love between parents and children? That's certainly not equal, at least for a few years, if ever."

Clay puzzled a moment and then observed, "This sounds too much like love is out of balance most of the time. You can have more or less of it, depending on the type of relationship it is. And then there must be a receiver of love. Did I get that right?"

Rorie, feeling cornered, held up her hand again as if stopping traffic. "Hold it! This line of discussion has already gone way past what my mind is ready to absorb at the moment. How did we get into such a deep conversation, anyway?"

"The book!" Clay turned a huge grin to her, pointing at Rorie's book. "That's how."

"Why are you so interested in the topic anyway?"

"It's part of my work."

Dear me, she thought, *don't let this guy be a shrink. I cannot stand the thought of being analyzed right now. This is my trip, and I do not need anyone poking around in my psyche. That's my job.* She asked with trepidation, "What *is* your work?"

"I'm a teacher, of sorts."

"Of what sort? What kind of teacher?" Panic was beginning to rise in Rorie's mind.

"I teach at Kansas State University, in the philosophy department."

"You're a philosopher? I should have known." She responded to him suspiciously. "What kind of philosophy do you teach?" she asked, remembering the one course she had taken in collage and thoroughly disliked.

"The kind that likes to study topics like 'love,'" he replied to her with a grin at her obvious disdain for his academic discipline. "I'm currently writing a book on the topic."

"You mean a philosophy book on love?" Rorie, being relatively ignorant of philosophy, was incredulous.

"Right." The look on her face tickled him. "By the way, why did you bring that particular book on this trip?" he asked pointing again at the book in her lap. Seeing the look on her face, he knew he had gone too far with his questioning.

Pulling her bandana out of her pocket, Rorie absentmindedly wiped her forehead. "The reasons are too complicated to go into right now." Her voiced faded into a mutter, and she fumbled about for some way of offering a comment that would end the conversation. *That's too close for comfort. I am not willing to share my story with a man I've seen naked in the wilderness. Nope!*

She shook her head defiantly, though he saw no reason for her behavior. Their brief encounter, their conversation was closing the gap between the two of them, forcing a kind of intimacy on them that made Rorie increasingly uncomfortable.

Sensing her restlessness, Clay scooted off the table and stretched. His movements gave her permission to pull away and create a safer distance between them. Clay handed her the foil blanket and ventured into another tone, "That was a delightful way to escape the rain and hail. Thank you!" She smiled and stepped out of the shed, leading him toward the trail as a signal that she was done with their encounter.

As they stood at the trail's edge, Clay said, "I can still smell the rain." He sniffed the air, like a beast seeking some aroma to guide him back to his home. Nodding, Rorie looked in the direction toward Big Arsenic and confessed, "These sights and smells do create feelings I'm not used to having."

"Enough said." Clay was lighthearted as he turned to retreat up the trail. "Perhaps I'll see you before one of us leaves."

"How long did you say you plan to stay?" The question unexpectedly popped out of Rorie's mouth.

"Not sure. Probably two or three days."

Waving at him, Rorie shouted, "Have the vacation you need." As an afterthought, she added, "I hope your tent is okay!" She could not help but quip with a grin, "And I hope it loves you as much as you love it."

Clay, having already headed up trail, waved over his shoulder. He bent to pick up the stick he had abandoned when they ran for cover. Rorie noticed as he walked away that he favored his left leg slightly.

Turning back to face the mess in front of her, Rorie started staking her tent again, this time inside the shed for double shelter against the weather. Her mind wandered. *What an odd guy. But one thing is for sure, he is not boring.* In Rorie's world that was no small compliment.

It had been an eon since Clay could even remember a conversation so satisfying. The walk back to his camp allowed him time to recount and savor it. A quality day. A day of healing for himself. Back in his camp area, Clay had to stake his tent again because the weight of the hail had all but made it fold over. Removing the rainfly, he hung it over a bush to dry in the sun. The wind had scattered some of his gear about, so he spent some time picking up his things while fussing at himself for such "greenhorn" camping patterns. *I know better than this.*

The rest of the day passed in the glow of a red and gold sunset cascading down into the gorge. He felt his shoulders and neck release some of the stress he had felt after he called Cassandra earlier in the day.

The night embraced him. He slept long and deep.

Ordeal

AT DINNER, DURING THEIR CASUAL REVIEW OF THE DAY, MELLIE told Clay, "This morning, Dana and I played tennis for a couple of hours. Strangest thing happened. Three different times, my racket flew out of my hand. I didn't actually lose my grip. It was like the racket had a life of its own. One time, it landed on the other side of the net." She cackled at herself. "I couldn't get the ball over, so I tried the racket."

Clay laughed with her, then became a bit more serious, "Better hang on tighter next time."

Neither of them gave the tale too much attention after their conversation. Both were too involved in their respective routines. Mellie edited a small journal for the history department at the university. Clay spent most of his days organizing to begin writing a manuscript in his field of study. Through all the details and distractions, they wove a marriage with relaxed rhythms and few crises. From the beginning, when they first met in college at the University of Nebraska, Mellie and Clay knew they were a match. Aside from the predictable tensions in adjusting to each other's patterns and idiosyncrasies, they had endured only predictable marital conflicts—hanging up clothes, choice of wines, whose turn to cook.

Friends, especially Dana, remarked more than once, "You two are the most boring couple I know. Nothing ever happens at your place but sweetness and light." Mellie usually joked back that she did look forward to a mid-life crisis just for something interesting to happen.

Mellie, always healthy and never an alarmist, began noticing minor difficulties, such as in turning the key in the ignition to her car or dropping things around the house. When the incidents increased and began breaking her concentration, she finally announced to Clay that she had set up a doctor's appointment. The family practitioner found only minor signs of loss in her reflexes but suggested she see a specialist in Topeka. They made the trip together.

The specialist worked with Mellie far longer than either she or Clay had planned. Soon Clay became aware that the examination was taking a long time, and he lost his concentration on the article he was reading. He began to pace about in the waiting room.

A nurse called him into the doctor's private office, where Mellie and the physician soon entered the room, without smiles. With little emotion in his voice the doctor said, "I've found nothing definitive, but there is some loss in neurological function, especially in Mrs. Jacobs' right arm."

"What does that mean?" Clay cut in before the doctor could explain further.

"I'm not sure. The nervous system is a labyrinth, and this can require considerable testing to interpret, and—"

"We'll do whatever testing is necessary," Clay urged, almost getting out of his chair.

"No need for alarm yet, Mr. Jacobs," the doctor spoke impatiently. "But I do recommend further diagnostic testing. We can do it here, but I really suggest you go to Kansas City. Facilities there are more sophisticated, and they can offer a better diagnosis. More thorough."

As usual, Mellie kept the level head and subdued Clay's anxiety. The doctor assured them his office would arrange for the necessary tests and concluded by passing the worried couple off to his nurse. Clay and Mellie left the medical complex, arm in arm, quiet but determined, as in the past, when she had twice miscarried. They would weather this storm together. This had been their pattern over the years and nothing would change this.

The medical tests in Kansas City were scheduled for the end of the semester during final exams for Clay, which created more stress for him. However, he was determined that nothing would be allowed to interfere with their intention to find a verdict. When Mellie's ordeal ground to an end, it turned out to be only the beginning. A week later they returned for results. A team of three doctors, two men and a woman, took them into a consulting room. As they motioned for everyone to sit, Clay's mind raced through the possible diagnoses, but none of them came close to the conclusion.

"Mrs. Jacobs, from the evidence of your test results we find that you are suffering from amyotrophic lateral sclerosis," said a tall, thin woman with cropped gray hair. "ALS is the more common usage."

"What is that?" Mellie whispered, with a hoarse voice.

"It's commonly known as Lou Gehrig's Disease," the younger male doctor blurted out, "which is an unfortunate way to identify the disease—" He ended abruptly when the female doctor glared at him.

Neither Mellie nor Clay said anything. They knew the news was bad, but they could not begin to put their minds around the implications of what the doctors were saying to them. While the white-coated physicians droned on about the condition and how the two of them might cope, a primal question formed in Mellie's mind. She broke into the trio's presentation, "Is this condition terminal?"

Silence filled the room. Finally, the female doctor responded with an antiseptic answer, "Yes, it usually is, but lifespan can and does vary widely."

Clay squirmed in his chair. The promise of grueling years ahead for both of them began to take hold in his mind. Shock surged through his body. Posing his own question, Clay asked, "Are you absolutely sure of your diagnosis?" All three shook their heads in the affirmative. They did, however, encourage Mellie and Clay to seek further consultation if they felt the need.

Turning to leave, Mellie walked out the door. The youngest doctor volunteered, "If there is anything—"

Somewhere between Kansas City and Manhattan, Mellie observed quite casually, "I felt so sorry for those doctors. You could tell they did not know what to say, except the facts. Not one of them wanted to be in that room, and for that matter, neither did I," she said wryly, making a sound, guttural, somewhere between a laugh and a cry.

Here sits this remarkable woman, Clay thought in amazement, *with a death sentence hanging over her, and all she can talk about is how dif-*

ficult it must have been for the doctors to tell her. Why doesn't she scream or throw a tantrum? Managing only barely to control himself, Clay responded to Mellie's observation with modest commiseration. "Medical schools don't necessarily teach compassion these days. It's all about science and facts." His voice bordered on anger as he spoke.

When Cassandra came over from her apartment to hear the report, she knew without asking by the look on her parents' faces that the news was ominous. Clay nervously started to explain to their only child, but Mellie interrupted him. She insisted on being the bearer of the news, as if she were working to take control of the diagnosis by speaking it out loud. Cassandra broke down before Mellie could finish her explanation of what lay ahead for all of them and moved immediately into her mother's arms. They clung to each other for a long time, but Mellie never for a moment shed tears.

Clay struggled, *how can I go nuts when she is so together?*

Later Mellie told him, "When they explained what I have, it was as though I awoke for the first time ever. I could suddenly see and understand things . . . about my life. You know . . . how it is playing itself out. The story was horrifying and glorious all at once. I saw the arc of my life, and I've been totally awake and more alive since we left the medical center than I ever have been before. Why is that, I wonder?"

Clay had no response to her question. He simply took her in his arms and held her tightly, not yet knowing that at some point he would no longer be able to tightly embrace his mate.

In the weeks following her diagnosis, Mellie said little, so little that Clay wondered if they should go to a counselor. Clay wanted to understand Mellie's silence. This was so unlike her. When he finally approached her about talking with him, she agreed, "Yes, we do need to talk. I apologize for being so distracted, but. . . ."

"No! You do not need to apologize. I just don't want to be walled out," Clay confessed. "This is happening to both of us, don't forget."

"I know. I'll be ready soon. I promise," she said contritely.

Clay and Mellie pursued all of their options, including more medical examinations, but the verdict remained constant. Mellie became thinner than she was, it seemed to Clay. Over the summer months that passed in a blur, her lively gait became a trudge. By the anniversary of the diagnosis, she began to use a wheelchair more frequently. Her ascent and descent of stairs halted. Mellie, as was her way, joked about everything, especially the chair, her "new wheels" or "my carriage." Her condition showed no signs of arrest. Though the effects of the disease were slow, they were steadily stealing her ability to remain mobile.

After the third year of watching her become more debilitated, a sense of heaviness settled into Clay's shoulders and his heart. At Mellie's request, they found a counselor to visit her weekly. Clay did not know why, but after a few weeks the counselor surprised him at his office. "Mellie wants to sit down with you and Cassandra to discuss her funeral." Clay caught the message and was stirred into resistance.

"Why do we need to do that now?" She's not in any danger of dying at the moment." Clay was indignant.

"Well, she says with her voice failing, she wants to have the discussion before she can no longer speak."

Clay breathed deeply and faced a reality he had begun to notice months before. *Mellie is losing her voice. I need to face the fact that her sound will soon disappear.* "Yes, of course. I understand. When do you want to do this?" Clay dreaded the encounter but knew at some level in his gut that this day had been coming for quite a while.

On Tuesday the following week, Cassandra was free to come over, and the four of them sat at the round pedestal table with Mellie in her chrome chair. She chose that spot where so many light and laughing moments had transpired, to tell her family how she wanted her death handled. Because her speech came with increasing labor, she asked her counselor, Daniel, to explain.

"Mellie insists on cremation, and a memorial service, out of doors if possible, with no somber words or music. She has divided the service into three parts. One part for all her friends who will be gathered. One part for reflecting on who she is. And the final message for the two of you from her." He waited to see if Clay and Cassandra were absorbing his words. When they said nothing, he continued.

"Here's how she would like the service to unfold. Mellie wants someone to sing *Morning Has Broken* to open the service." At that point Mellie began to cry, which only aggravated her condition, and Clay, himself in tears, insisted that they cease the process. Mellie sputtered out rasping sounds in rebellion, "Go on!" She made it clear that they must proceed. Throughout the half-hour ordeal, tears continued to flow down Mellie's lined face, frequently laced with sobs that shook her thin shoulders. No one could persuade her to stop crying. It was her time of agony with her family, and she wanted no evasions.

The counselor took a deep breath, and said, "Mellie has chosen a reading. I'll give you the title, so you can find it. She says it's in a book of her favorite poems." Clay nodded, knowing exactly what poem Mellie wanted. Daniel moved on. "Her friend Dana is to do the eulogy. You can choose anyone else to speak for the family as you wish." Then the counselor rushed on before Clay or Cassandra could reply. "Clay, for you and Cassandra, Mellie wants the final song to be sung as a message to you both from her. She has chosen *We've Only Just Begun.*"

At this point, Cassandra set up a wail that could be heard throughout the house. Clay hugged her close, as she sobbed into his shoulder. This song was Clay and Mellie's "love song," used in their wedding ceremony years before. Once Cassandra was born, they included her in their circle and the poignant music had become their family ballad, usually sung while doing dishes together.

Daniel completed his role by stating, "The service will conclude with *Ode to Joy* and a benediction." By now he and everyone else at the table were so choked with emotions, spoken and unspoken, that only silence and sobbing remained. He stood, hugged Mellie, embraced Clay and Cassandra, then departed. The catharsis ended with Clay watching his wife's last shudders from crying. He loved her more than ever before. Her bold, doe-soft brown eyes called to him, and he kissed her fully on the mouth. *This woman will live inside me forever.*

Mellie declined rapidly in the ensuing months, becoming more and more limited in her ability to speak or remain in control of her movements. The precise shape her debilitation would take was unpredictable. Clay studied the condition, learning more than he wished to know. *Only the outcome,* he growled to himself on the edge of bitterness, *is definite. Why couldn't she have been one of the ones who kept their voice and mobility? This is going too quickly!*

The most difficult loss was Mellie's speech. With her alert mind and wit, she and the family needed her voice. They rigged a computer so that she could manipulate it with one finger, but even that capacity eventually declined. From her hospital bed placed in the sunroom downstairs, she helplessly watched her family buzz around her all day. Finally, her communication reduced to a batting of her eyes in response to questions, one bat for "yes" and two for "no." An alphabet board and her yes-no responses allowed her minimal expression.

The progression of Mellie's condition took what seemed like a lifetime. It was obvious she would not live much longer. The atmosphere in the home grew more and more somber.

After over three years of the grinding routine and the horror of watching the one person whose life claimed him more than any other, struggling to stay alive, Clay's weariness reached a depth untouchable even by himself. He could find no way to serve his wife that led to any heartening result. Helplessness, hers and his, evolved into frustration, and frustration threatened to lead to his own paralysis. He resisted this tumble into his basest emotions, but he was tired. Not just tired, but weary to his core.

In the fall term, a classics professor approached Clay to teach a course with her for a special program. She wanted to deal with the great love poems of history and to call the course, "Love in the Western World." Reading in the vast resources on love, Clay found himself reflecting on his own love of his persistent but dying mate. He continued to long for her to make some advance against her mortal enemy. Frustration occasionally brought him to rage, but never in her presence.

At times, in the darkest of his brooding, he longed for her death. Not for himself, but to set her free. He even fancied his own death, so he could accompany her into the nether world beyond. Then he would chide himself to the point of laceration, only to have the notion push its way back into consciousness when he was most fatigued and could not battle his negative thoughts. One night, Mellie insisted they watch a movie rerun on television. It was a story about a terminal patient who insisted on his right to simply die. Afterward, Mellie blinked out the message that she admired the young man but that she was not ready to go that far. After that exchange, Clay never again wished for her demise. He saw her strength and courage, modeling his own desires after hers. *What an astounding human being she is! I have so much to learn from her yet!*

Mellie's endurance and his intense engagement with the subject of love led Clay to believe he could somehow help Mellie, in some indirect way, through his writing project. One night, after waking to check on his wife, the idea came into focus. He would write on "love and loss" and use this great personal calamity as the testing ground to understand the relation between human love and the reality of separation and loss, particularly loss through death.

After Mellie had her evening meal each day, Clay usually read to her. Once he discovered the heart of his project, he wanted to discuss his work with her. Mellie sensed in his voice that here at last he had found some way to wrestle with the demons her sickness produced for both of them. She urged him with her eyes to talk more about it. She saw in this enthusiasm more of the Clay she had known and loved before, and she probed him with questions now batted out on an alphabet board.

In Mellie's fourth year of illness, on Clay's forty-fifth birthday, she enlisted Cassandra in a plot to have Clay take a trip by himself, to spend some time working on his book and relaxing, really finding rest. At first, Clay adamantly vetoed the idea. After all, he insisted, he had time to write at his office during the summer. By early August, however, Cassandra had undermined her father's resolve by assuring him of her own ability to cover the bases at home. She also reminded him daily of how tired he appeared and how he could best prepare for his upcoming sabbatical and writing project by first resting and finding a change of scenery.

One evening, Mellie motioned with her eyes toward an accent table in the room. Clay looked toward it but at first saw nothing. She insisted, and he walked over. A note which she had composed, with Cassandra's help, lay on the table. Picking up the paper, he read it slowly. *Clay, we both know this condition is terminal. We just don't know when. You cannot wait forever. You must go on with your life. That will make me happier than anything else you can do. Go on with your own life. I need this in order to let go myself.* Her husband read the note again, walked back to her bedside, and tenderly embraced her withered body.

"I cannot imagine going on without you, Mellie. There's no such thing." Clay's eyes filled with tears and his body sagged under the weight of her request.

Standing in the kitchen later that evening, he spoke to Cassandra of Mellie's plan. His daughter answered firmly, "Mother means for you to find your own way without allowing her illness to define your life. She's accepting her ending, Dad. To give her peace, we have to accept it too. All of it." Her voice cracked with the weight of her words.

Clay spoke with aggravation. "That sounds like she's already gone. She is here! She *does* define everything that I am and do. How can I do anything without Mellie in my plans? She's the center of my world." Turning his back on Cassandra, he reached for a glass so he could pour himself some wine. "Would I prefer her to be well? Sure! But she's not! So I accept what I have of her and it's enough." His face was defiant.

"Sometimes, Dad, I think you don't understand Mother at all."

"What are you saying?" Clay's voice had risen to a pitch loud enough that Mellie could probably hear him.

"She knows you are utterly loyal to her, but the person she used to be, the Mellie you fell in love with, no longer exists. What good is life to Mom, if she drags you down with her?"

"She's not. . . ."

"Yes, she is. And she can see it. That's how she feels, anyway. Here's what she wants you to do. This idea will make her happy and give her a sense of release. She wants you to return to New Mexico, where the two of you spent such wonderful times together, hiking and camping. She wants you to make a trip for the two of you and then come back and tell her everything, so you can both move on. Just do this so she doesn't have to watch you fade away too." Cassandra's eyes were pleading with her father.

Clay answered in astonishment, "Did she actually blink through all of that?"

"Yes, she did, indeed." Cassandra laughed for the first time in months. "She cracked me up when she got through the message. She was so proud of herself."

Clay knew Mellie well enough to know she had won this battle, in her own style. There was no way to argue her out of the idea. Within two weeks, Clay announced his plan to drive to New Mexico. Mellie smiled broadly as he shared his plans with her.

He thought, *this plan is certainly a weird one. I'm going on a quest for release, for Mellie . . . and for myself. For the "us" we used to be.* He assured her that he would visit some of their favorite haunts and convey her greetings to each of them. Working hard to release his guilt about leaving Mellie, Clay turned his attention to packing his gear and mapping his trip.

Fascination

A FTER A SECOND NIGHT OF SLEEPING AN INCH FROM MOTHER Earth, Rorie awoke with anticipation, crawled out into the crisp air and stretched toward the sun. Flame stretched beside her, in dog fashion, paws extended before her. Rorie congratulated herself, *an entire day to myself to do whatever I please!* Then she immediately recalled that, in addition to her respite from civilization and its rushed routine, she did come with one self-imposed assignment: Wil and the proposal.

After a hearty camper's breakfast, cleanup and campsite reconnoiter, Rorie took to the river's edge with a bag of fruit and nut mix for munching, her book, and a poncho. Spreading the military-green plastic poncho on the sand as a ground cloth, she sat down to listen and look at the passing river. Its music soothed her. The sun fired its golden streaks of warmth into the canyon, landing on her hair and turning it to gold. Her relaxation was complete at this point.

Opening her book without zeal, she began reading sporadically. After a few sentences her thoughts turned to Wil. Reading about love drove her mind toward the task that she carried around her shoulders like a lead weight. *The exchange I had yesterday with Clay prompts my intention to consider the marriage proposal to Wil as a burden rather than a love story. Why didn't I realize that what I am wrestling with is whether I truly love Wil or not? I have been debating the marriage question, not the love question. This is an important distinction and not one I am prepared to sort through at the moment. Who is this guy Clay to stir up my thoughts so that now I am more confused than ever about Wil's proposal?* She sighed deeply and closed the book momentarily, holding her finger inside the pages while her thoughts raced.

Then quickly, as if dodging the more difficult inner work, her thoughts shifted to the image of Clay and their unlikely conversation from the day before. Every time she began reading she presently became lost in unsolicited fantasies about Clay, and foreboding thoughts about Wil. Her mind merged them into one person at one point. Called back to the present moment by the cry of a raven overhead, she chided herself for her loss of concentration, only to fall prey to more recurring unsought daydreams. Finally, she surrendered, laid the book aside, lay back on the ground covering and gave vent to her imagination.

Time passed without her awareness. Sitting bolt upright, Rorie realized she had fallen asleep and wondered what time it was. She wondered what Clay was doing. She fancied that she could simply hike in that direction and see what he was up to for the day. *But why?* She asked herself. *I came down here to be by myself, not to hang out with some guy I met in the wilderness.* She could not seem to abandon the idea of seeing Clay, and she found herself devising a plan while feeling a bit like a stalker—again! "Come on, Flame, let's go. It's time to walk!" she said dismissing her own self-manipulation.

Clay's own morning included reminiscences of the day before, though not as persistent. Stewing over not calling home to check on Mellie and Cassandra, he forced himself to take a brisk hike across a field of boulders where he had to attend each and every step, in order to dismiss that nagging sense of neglect. The effort energized him and took his mind away from all other considerations.

When Clay reached a high protrusion of basalt laced with cracks which caused some of the rocks to resemble weathered faces, he perched on the highest point and looked south. *Perhaps I can see her camp shed from up here.* His mind betrayed him. Moving around and scanning intently, he could not make out her location, only the general vicinity. Too many trees and boulder masses. In a surge, he relived the day before, especially his stumble and the animated conversation with Rorie. A chuckle erupted under his breath.

Retreating down the rockslide, Clay decided to make some notes for the book and perhaps write in his journal. The day was clear, without a single cloud over the rim, and he could hear the river running below him, steady and reliable. On reaching his tent, he picked up his daypack, threw it over his shoulder, and found his way down a steep, partly overgrown path to the river's edge. Lounging on a sun-claimed rock partially buried in the sand, he put himself into a trance by staring at a red harvester ant working hard to move a grain of food. Shaking himself loose again, Clay wrote in his journal about the woman who loved her dog, but only to the extent that the dog could be loved. He made marginal notes about that idea and what use he might make of it in his manuscript.

Standing to give his legs relief, he walked closer to the water's edge and tossed a stone at one of the huge-moss covered boulders rising out of the water. The pitching flow gobbled up his effort. *I need to relax. This is why I came.* He shook his shoulders, hoping the tension would fall away. Returning to his personal stone stool, he noticed that the sun had warmed it. He moved his pack into the shade of a ponderosa pine and sat down lotus style facing the river. He began to breathe deeply, slowly, deliberately.

When Rorie first saw Clay from the trail, he appeared to be fishing, but she could see no rod or line. She stood watching him for several minutes, but he did not move. Holding Flame's collar so that the dog would not run to the sitting man, she wondered whether she should approach him or continue her hike up-trail. Perhaps she could see him later. Before she could take either course, she recognized that he was actually in a meditation posture. What surprised her most was the realization that this instance of seeing Clay focused on his interior self was considerably more intimate than seeing him naked.

Rorie moved away, glancing back and forth between Clay and the path ahead. She held onto Flame, whispering to her. Once she was back on the higher trail, she let the dog go and began to strike toward the more remote reaches of the canyon. She walked for over an hour. Her eyes feasted on the landscape from side to side and ahead of her. *What stunning views! This canyon has been here for eons, changing and staying the same. And I never knew until now.*

Finally, Rorie was tired enough to stop in a small grove of aspen, which seemed out of place at this juncture of the canyon. Her green eyes stared through the trees at the river winding its way to its destination. She heard a golden eagle cry overhead. Pausing to lean on one of the larger aspens and enjoy its shade, Rorie found her mind wandering again to the problem with the marriage proposal. *I am beginning to realize my issue may be whether I am capable of loving Wil at all. I'm not convinced I know how to "fall in love" with anyone. The sound of that phrase actually frightens me. Maybe I'm the problem, and not Wil.* Flinching at this self-revelation, Rorie startled out of her reverie and pushed away from the tree, ready to move again. Flame, who had been lying beside her feet, roused and stood, ready to join her. "Flame! Time to walk some more."

Heading back toward her campsite, Rorie noticed in herself an increased anticipation of seeing Clay again. As she passed by, Clay looked up and squinted into the sun at the sound of footsteps. He saw Rorie picking her way down a sharp incline in the trail. Flame came bounding toward him, and they greeted one another before he called out to Rorie, waving as he had the day before.

"How did you slip past me on this trail without my noticing?" he asked.

"When I came by, you were busy down by the river."

"Yes, I went down there and wound up meditating. But you should have—"

"I didn't want to disturb you."

"It wasn't that important. I was just trying to calm myself down and allow my brain to stop bouncing all over the place." He paused, then when she did not reply, he went on, "I'm worried about my wife and daughter."

"You too? I had trouble making my head stop with the 'busy mind' this morning. 'Course I did come down here to think and make a major decision in my life." Rorie reached for a pine cone that had fallen beside her with a clatter.

"Well, we could both be on the verge of cracking up, now couldn't we?" Clay laughed heartily, then changed the topic. "Are you able to sit for a while and visit?"

"Sure."

"Then let's go down by the river. It's cooler down there this time of day."

They sat in the shade of an old juniper near the pool that had two days earlier provided a bath for Clay. The ritual of their sharing moved deeper. Rorie had already noted some yet unnamed barely contained distress borne by Clay. She asked a few solicitous questions. Clay spoke at first in generalities about his wife's illness, but with evidence of Rorie's obvious concern, he sketched his story of the past four years. Their conversation became timeless, absorbed. He spoke forthrightly with no special pleading or implicit reach for sympathy, and she never interrupted him, only interjecting an occasional question or words of understanding.

"So here I am, like a kid running away from home." Clay concluded, remorsefully. He reached into his pack and drew out a small bag of wafers. They shared easily, like old friends.

"You're not running away," Rorie said, trying to comfort him.

To change the subject away from himself, Clay spoke, "I take it your trip is more than a vacation too?" He raised his eyes to meet hers, hoping she would not shy away this time.

"You can be sure of that!" She replied, nodding her head in affirmation.

"Okay. I've laid myself on the line. What's your story?" Clay gave Rorie an air-poke, to make his point.

Blushing at his insistence, Rorie wavered, then answered him, "Actually, your story makes mine seem silly and anemic."

"Everyone has a story, Rorie. Some are more difficult than others, that's all. None are more important than the other. So speak. I'm all ears."

Rorie turned to her own recitation of her relationship with Wil, his devoted but audaciously thoughtless way of proposing and her dilemma in trying to envision a future with him—or for that matter, any clear personal future for herself.

"So what's your problem with this proposal?"

"My fear is that if I say 'yes' to Wil's proposal, he will dramatically change my world—and I like my world just the way it is!" Rorie burst out defensively.

"Your world *will* change, Rorie. That's what marriage does—it changes us and our worlds, completely. For better or worse." His words caused a quick release of tears into his eyes and contorted his face. He turned away to regroup before going on. "Isn't everything perpetually changing anyway?"

Rorie was aware of the shift in the timbre of their discussion. "Well, I'm not against change, as such. That's one reason I'm here—to think about breaking out of my walls—to take an adventure of some kind. I'm too programmed in my current life. But is marriage the thing I want to do to create adventure in my life?" She sighed. "Surely, there are easier ways to shake up my world."

"When I married Mellie, everything changed for me. And for the better, I can I tell you. But now, for the past four years, we both are forced to deal with a situation never imagined in our vows to each other." He stared at the wild grasses, sweeping and swirling in the afternoon breeze, as if he could see into the very blades, before continuing, "Who could ever have guessed what we would face together?"

"That's what I mean." Rorie gestured to make her point.

"But," Clay stressed, "it was still the best choice for us, to be together, sharing life, a child, all of it. I know it sounds crazy and maybe even insulting to Mellie, but through everything, I still have to admit that this is somehow the way it is supposed to be—at least for us. I guess that sounds fatalistic, and that's not what I mean." He struggled on. "What I want to say is that it's better to be in this relationship even with this horrific trial we are suffering than not to have met and married at all. Though it may not be easy, it is better."

"That sounds very noble, Clay." Rorie halted, worried she might say something that would hurt his feelings. "Isn't life always about the risk? And that's what I am afraid of—the risk. I'm not sure I'm up to the trouble that marriage brings." Rorie shifted her eyes upward and Clay's eyes followed in the same direction. "Speaking of trouble," she quipped, "are we going to have another deluge this afternoon?" A chilly wind began to spin around them as the puffy clouds that had suddenly blown up over the rim of the canyon darkened and lowered.

"We could. After all, it's monsoon season here." He laughed. "But at least we've practiced the 'rain drill.'"

They retreated toward his camp shed. Soon the foreboding clouds teased them and began tumbling off into the distance. The sun conquered the cloud bank and once again began to warm the air.

The encounter with the almost-rainstorm had broken into their conversation. Rorie was about to bid Clay farewell for the day when Flame sprang into her territorial posture and barked. Rorie studied the direction Flame faced and saw a figure in the distance coming up-trail toward them. She called to Flame and held her. Clay stepped forward, taking a more-protective stance for all of them. The figure evolved into a young man, probably in his early 20s, smiling as he approached. "Hello," he mumbled, lowering his eyes before the two people in front of him.

"Hello," they replied, simultaneously.

The young man wore dingy cutoffs and a torn T-shirt, scruffy overrun boots and socks full of burrs in them sagging over his boots. He carried a disintegrating army bedroll slung over his left shoulder, while a faded blue backpack hugged his back. He apparently had not bathed recently. When he removed his faded and limp-brimmed hat, a line showed where the dust of travel ended on his forehead. Dirty blond dreadlocks fell out down his back. He appeared gaunt but not too thin.

The scraggly traveler was about to pass when he turned abruptly and exclaimed animatedly, "Dr. Jacobs! Is that you?"

Clay, even more confounded, responded with a carefully measured cadence, "Yes, my name is Jacobs."

"You teach at K. State? I was one of your students. Maybe two years back. I took the 'love course,' or at least that's what all of us called it. I had to do a lot of begging to get in because it was filled up, and I didn't have high enough grades." His breathless spin of words came laced with nervous agitation.

After pausing to assimilate the message, Clay acknowledged, "I must come clean and say that I only vaguely remember you, but—" The young man waved aside the need for further explanation.

"You've had so many students, I didn't expect you to remember me anyway," the former student interrupted.

Clay shifted the subject. "I never thought I'd find anyone down here that I knew, especially one of my students. . . ." An awkward silence fell upon the trio. Clay moved toward the young man, offering his hand, "Well, as they say. . . ."

"Yeah, I know: 'small world.'"

Turning toward Rorie, the scruffy hiker said, "You must be Mrs. Jacobs. I never met you. That's one of the weird things about college. Students seldom meet their professor's families. You were real sick, weren't you?"

Rorie, looking to Clay for a cue to her reply, confessed, "I'm not his wife. We only just met ourselves. My campsite is down the trail a mile or so."

"Yeah, I saw it. You have a really cool tent. Looks new? I'm hoping to have one like that someday," he said wistfully.

Clay, wanting to get the conversation moving, queried, "What brings you down into the gorge?"

"Man, all you have to do is look around, and you've got the answer." Clay and Rorie turned their heads in semicircles to affirm the vistas, and agreed by nodding. "What I'm trying to do is walk the gorge from below Taos, where it begins, to the other end, or at least into Colorado."

In consternation, Clay exclaimed, "You mean you're walking all the way?"

"Yep!" A broad smile filled the younger hiker's face.

"But there's no trail most of the way."

"You're tellin' me. I've been four days plus most of today coming this far. I probably ought to exit to the top, but I decided to go until the trail ends. It's the longest and best I've found."

"Are you carrying enough food?" Rorie wanted to know, noticing his slender build.

"Not really, but I thought I might do some fishing. No luck yet. Takes too long. Every once in a while, I buy stuff from folks. People along the trail are really nice. Most of 'em just give me some of whatever they have." Then, realizing that his words may have sounded like he wanted a handout, he stammered, "I didn't mean to. . . ."

Clay gave a dismissive wave to his former student. "Not to worry." The three of them stood on the trail for a while, continuing their conversation.

As the afternoon sun began its descent, Clay suggested they move toward his campsite, so he could begin preparing dinner for them. The three moved in unison back up the trail. When they arrived at the campsite, Clay turned his head toward the student, "What's your name again?"

"My real name's Edmund, but everybody calls me Eddie. I hate 'em both. On this trip, I decided I'm going by 'Coyote.' In an anthropology class, I learned about indigenous people takin' the name of the first animal they see after a vision quest. I don't know if this trip qualifies as a vision quest or not, but the first animal I saw when I began this walk was a coyote. Then later I saw three more. That's my sign for sure—Coyote! That's me for now."

Rorie chimed into the conversation, "Well, Coyote, it's a good thing you didn't see a skunk first, isn't it?" They all roared, and Coyote showed his good humor by holding his nose. "By the way, are we the first to call you by your new name?"

"Yep! That's good. I like the way you say it. And my former teacher is here to be part of my new identity. Can't beat that, huh?" He seemed pleased with himself.

Clay turned from his food preparation and requested, "Call me Clay. And this is Rorie." She nodded and gave a wave at Coyote.

"Who's that?" Coyote asked, pointing at the dog, who was closely watching every move the visitor made.

"She is the most important presence here. That's Flame, my dog." Coyote called the animal to him. She immediately bounded toward him to receive her expected pats and hugs.

With the dropping of the sun, twilight wrapped around them and stole the warmth of the day. The dinner was eaten with relish; cleanup was shared and took little time. Clay built a small fire in a cast iron grill on the ground near the shed. The three sat on logs talking, mostly of the grandeur and challenge of trying to survive in nature. Coyote explained that he had dropped out of school for lack of interest in his education. He wanted excitement and travel. His explanation was that he wanted to get away before he was forced into the 'rat race' by his father. When he said this, Rorie and Clay glanced at each other and nodded.

Coyote continued, his voice a bit surly, "I don't really want to settle down yet. Everything's too . . . you know what I mean? Well, too planned out—predictable. That's it." Finding the exact word he needed gave him the impetus to push on. "After this trip, I think I'll go to Europe and hike around. They have youth hostels over there and college kids stay in them." He spoke as if he had just discovered this reality for himself.

"What does your family think about all of this wandering you are doing?" Rorie intuited there was another story hidden in Coyote's words.

She was right, as Coyote vehemently responded, "None of their damn business. They don't know about what I'm doing, and I don't want them to know. They live like gods in their little made-up world, and they don't care about anybody else."

Coyote spoke with such heated hostility that it made Rorie uncomfortable. Clay made a mental note, *Coyote must have a load of unfinished business with his parents, like so many of my students do. Comes with the turf of being young.* Clay also picked up on Rorie's restlessness at Coyote's comments. She began to move about. He read this as her need to return to her own camp. He was about to suggest that they break up for the evening, when Coyote said, "You remember that discussion in the 'love course' where we talked about whether love is natural to us or we have to learn it?

"Yes, I do. That was a hot topic," Clay recalled.

"And you mostly held out for the 'learned' idea." After halting briefly to compose his thoughts, Coyote, staring into the fire, launched forth again. Rorie sat back down. "That other professor, that woman. She kept the argument going by sayin' over and over that love is just right there all the time in the heart from birth. Do you think she really believed that? I think she was throwin' fuel on the fire just to argue. She kept saying, 'Only wait for the occasion and you will see.' Man, she really fried my brain with that idea. I argued hard against her."

Not pausing for discussion, Coyote pushed on, leaning closer to the fire as the flames turned into embers. "Take parents, for instance. Everybody says you're supposed to love 'em. But what if your folks don't respect or honor you? Love doesn't just seem automatic. I mean, well, take my case. I might have got on with my old man when I was a little dude, but since I was a teen, I can't stand him anymore. And my mom just hangs around behind him and backs him up on everythin'." After stalling to focus his point, Coyote continued, "Love, to me, is learned, like you said, and they just didn't help me learn to love 'em enough."

Clay was about to ask Coyote whether and how he had learned about love, but Rorie surprised Clay with her own response, "When it comes to parents, the situation can be mixed. I learned about love, but I also learned about hate from the same people."

Coyote and Clay waited for her to resume her comments, thinking about what she said. Clay, however, sensed that Rorie did not wish to continue and rescued the moment by asking Coyote, "Do you believe you know how to love?"

"I'm still learnin'," he spoke pensively.

Clay, sensing a story about to unfold, asked, "What do you mean?"

Coyote shot back, "You!"

After stirring the embers with a stick to agitate them into a flame, Clay raised his head with a jerk. He was glad for the twilight because he turned crimson. Rorie, no less stunned by the comment, leaned forward to catch every word between the two men. She expected Clay to say something, but he only stared in dismay at Coyote.

To fill the silence floating between the characters in this summer's night drama playing itself out before canyon walls and the sounds of the rushing river as the stage and backdrop, Coyote explained, "You're the first, I mean, grown man I ever met who could talk about how he felt and then show it. In fact, you changed my life. I was about to become a business major and probably go into our family business. That's what my . . . my . . . Dad . . . ," he finally spat out the affectionate name as if it were poison. "You know, he kept saying, 'You have to study something you can *use*.' I hated this. Then in your course we studied people who thought about serious ideas, you know . . . like things about love. They took chances, and you took chances. Anyway, you helped me to break into a new way of thinkin.' That's why I said what I did . . . you know . . . about lovin' you."

More silence around the circle. Coyote, realizing that he might have disconcerted his former teacher, said in a soft voice, "I'm sorry if my talk embarrassed you, Dr. Jacobs—Clay. That wasn't my intention. I just never get to talk this way with anybody."

Clay cleared his throat, poked the fire again and spoke quietly, "Being loved by someone can be as big a burden as loving. It's a gratifying burden, but it can weigh on you. I appreciate your kind words." While he spoke to Coyote, images of Mellie lying flat and motionless in her distant bed engrossed him with the realization that he was surely being loved by her at the moment.

"See, that's what I mean," Coyote spoke mostly to Rorie. "He always says something like that. Everybody wants to be loved, but whoever thinks about what a burden it can be for the one being loved?"

Shadows from the glowing embers danced across Rorie's face, revealing her emotions as she confided to these two men in her new wilderness world, "I know exactly what Clay means right now. Sometimes I want to shrug until the love of the people who say they love me falls away. It's just too much." Wil's face slashed through her mind like an arrow.

The three "night farers" allowed the still of the creeping dusk to engulf them. No one spoke until Clay caught out of the corner of his eye that Rorie was stirring again, as if preparing to leave. That was his signal. He suggested that Coyote plan to spend the night at his campsite.

"Coyote, pitch your tent over there," Clay pointed toward a flat spot.

"I don't have a tent. I sleep in the open." Coyote grinned at them both.

Rorie, astonished, blurted out, "What about the rain?"

"Oh, I have some plastic bags and an emergency blanket. They work. I got caught yesterday, but I just wrapped up and sat it out beside a big boulder. I did fine."

Rorie, shaking her head in wonderment, said, "Good night, fellas," and then began her retreat back to the trail. Flame fell in beside her. Clay, seeing the situation, sprang to his feet, insisting on walking with her. She did not have her flashlight because she never expected the day to become a marathon mixture of strangers and conversations into the night. She protested that it was unnecessary. Clay offered his light, but he also wanted to talk with her alone just a while longer. Rorie acquiesced. They prepared to set off, when Coyote called out, "Good to meet ya, Rorie. I probably won't be around tomorrow." They both waved at him.

Clay nodded and said to the wanderer, "We'll talk more in the morning. I'll be back in about an hour."

They strode, one behind the other on the trail, following Flame, who seemed to be a beacon for them ahead on the pathway. They began to exchange stories of their most daring escapades, things they had done and things they wished they had done at Coyote's age. Their laughter rang into the darkness. Both wondered aloud if they could have done at his age what Coyote was undertaking so blithely.

Abruptly changing the subject, Clay stated, "You had some strong words about parents and love back there. And I want to check out the love-hate thing with you. That may be a conversation for tomorrow." With not-so-subtle words, Clay hinted that he wanted to get together the next day and continue their discussion.

Rorie shrugged, not missing his obvious plans for the next day. His expectations did not insult her. "I don't really have much to say except that parents are as much the cause of confusion and anxiety as they are the givers of love."

"Another story there, I wager," Clay retorted.

"Most likely," said Rorie, eluding him for now.

The change occurring as they walked and talked, however, had little to do with what they discussed. They fell toward familiarity, a pleasure in each other's presence that neither of them recognized at the time. They had become more than strangers, more than acquaintances, slipping into that nebulous space between encounter and friendship. The connection was not new. It was old, as old as the human habit of meeting other human beings and realizing the resonance of kinship. They entered into this mystery through the threshold of simply being together for an afternoon with decreasing pretense and protectiveness, though Clay was far more relaxed in the social arena than Rorie. Unwittingly they approached that place, in the dark wilds of human involvement, where coming together knows no distraction. Even Coyote added to their zest at being together for a stroll into the magic of the star-spackled night.

How to part? Neither of them hurried, but a certain awkwardness arose to urge them into a modest ritual of separating. He confessed to a great day, and she concurred. He offered an invitation, "Want to come up tomorrow? Or, I could come down here?" His voice was eager for a positive response from her.

"I'll come up in the morning. Flame can't wait to take to the trail."

"Good." He reached out and touched her arm, his fingers lingering on her skin. The skin of her arm turned warm where he had touched her. Clay's fingers tingled from the contact with Rorie. They parted with no more words. Enough had been said in this remarkable day for both of them.

Stillness settled like quilts over all of the pilgrims as each squirmed down into their camp beds. A lone owl hooted high above, reigning like a sentinel in the night.

Becoming

RORIE STOOD ON THE FRONT PORCH OF THE BROWNSTONE THAT had been her childhood home, gazing at the distant expanse of Lake Michigan. The shadow of her father darkened her face as he predictably followed her out the front door. Sean McDonough's red-bearded countenance, perspiring from his zeal, sought to block her movement. He even attempted to tower over her, as when she was a child, but was no longer able to do so. Backing up, he grabbed her arm, dropped into what remained of his Irish brogue, and tried pleading.

"Why do you want to throw your life away like this, girl?" He moaned. "You know what you're trained to do, what you're brilliant at. A mind like yours? You have sold your soul!" His face was red with frustration.

Pulling her arm away from her father's clutch, Rorie gave a heated response, "It's my own life, Dad. I'm going to follow my own path now. Just let me be!"

"But your education—that expensive education!" Her father roared this time.

"And my education taught me to make my own choices." Then she delivered the *coup de grâce*: "It taught me to be exactly like my father, who does whatever he pleases." This thrust stopped him briefly, and she took the opportunity to retreat further down the porch steps with one bag over her shoulder, pulling another behind her across the bumpy sidewalk. Managing to gain speed, Rorie rushed toward her car parked on the street on front of their home. She hated confrontation with her father, but on this issue she would not be convinced by him.

Sean turned to his only other tactic: "I won't come to see you there. I hate Texas. You are betraying your father and all that I've done for you." His words were spiteful, even as he loved her with a parental passion beyond explanation.

Rorie, already with her hand on the trunk of the car, waved and blew him a kiss. *Lucky I loaded most of my things last night or I'd never get away from him.* Recognizing that she truly intended to drive away, Sean stumbled across the lawn toward her, reaching out as if he could catch her with his sheer will. She thought at first that he was going to threaten her, but when she saw his face and the rare tears streaming from his eyes, she knew that she had, at least for the time being, won her victory. Dropping her bag into the trunk, she turned back to embrace her father. "I *am* leaving, Dad. I will call you when I arrive. And some day you might come to see me, even in Texas." Her voice was filled with emotion. She loved her father, though their personalities were too close most days, creating a constant bickering between them.

What Rorie wanted to leave behind, however, followed her, as the past always does. Her past continued shaping her attempts to start over, while breaking into her own sense of purpose and freedom. Prior to the move, she had lived all her life in one place, with the exception of college and her two years of study abroad in Spain. She and Sean resided in Hyde Park on Chicago's south side, where her father had taught anthropology at the University of Chicago since before she was born. Their life was urban and cultured. She lacked for little and had her father's full attention, whether she wanted it or not.

Rorie was a young child when her mother Dawn, whom she only dimly recollected, abandoned their family after a bitter divorce from Sean. The two were never a match, and finally Dawn had walked out of the house one day, never to see either of them again. With a child's memory, Rorie was imprinted by the day her father locked himself in his room and wailed all day, such horrible sounds coming through the door as he stomped and crashed his way through grief. A neighbor sat with Rorie in the living room trying to interest the child in various books and games, but nothing could hold her concentration, given the mournful and angry sounds filling the air.

Rorie could not distinguish between memories of her mother and what she knew from stories angrily recited by her father. The only time she ever asked about Dawn, her remaining parent shot an angry response into the air, like a javelin, "She couldn't get it in her head to stay with us, so she left." Rorie never asked again. Since that day, the two of them had never spoken of her mother again, yet her presence seemed to persistently loom in the corners of every room of their home. When Rorie was ten, they heard from a mutual friend that her mother had died of breast cancer. Sean refused to attend Dawn's funeral or allow her daughter to be taken to the funeral. It was as if he had dusted off his shoes from his marriage to Dawn and left everything behind, and he expected Rorie to do the same.

Doctor Professor Sean Donegal McDonough was, from the day her mother left, Rorie's confidante, chum, commander, and above all, nemesis. He both doted on her and made overweening demands, repeatedly reminding her of her "potential." His challenge to her, spoken and implied, required two things of her: that she be feminine in his Irish understanding of that ephemeral quality, and that she be tough and goal directed with the aim of "making a mark in the world." It never struck her father that his two messages to her, given his understanding of "feminine," were baldly at odds. And because he lived in the insulated confines of academia, he also assumed that Rorie would pursue an intellectual career. He could imagine no other option and considered this by far the best avenue to success for a woman. Furthermore, he was a purist and abhorred the idea of judging intellectual worth by dollars earned.

Sean devoted himself to only two things, a life of research and his daughter. Having come from a rough-hewn first-generation Irish American family, he possessed all of its attributes and deficits. A ponderously large man with thick, unkempt hair and a full beard, he filled any room he entered. He bore an earthy, swarthy brilliance that sharpened itself in the outdoors.

Through expeditions into America's "outback," as he called it, Sean took Rorie on many of his archaeological treks in order to teach her about nature as well as human civilization. Drawn to this side of her father, the young girl felt his strength, protection and his encouragement of her. But Sean had another side: a commitment to control and domination pressed upon him by spells of brooding darkness. He could demonstrate his true Irish heritage by drinking everyone under the bar at the little pub on Fifty-Third Street. He would stagger home in the waning hours of darkness, having left Rorie at home alone. She would rouse from sleep when she heard his shouts in the streets as he crooned Irish love songs, wobbling his way to the back door of their house.

Rorie's decision to avoid academia and pursue a career in the corporate world came as her decisive rebellion. Her father, no matter how much she resisted and plotted, tried to control her desires and decisions. He was her warden, even when they were apart. Their goodbyes were stilted and full of defiance on both sides. This would take a while to repair.

Rorie arrived in Dallas and competently settled herself into an apartment a few miles from her new office. Only after the novelty of these changes became her new normal did the rubble of her former life with her father begin to surface again in the registers of her mind. The line between Chicago and Dallas remained impotent for months as she recognized that her father was punishing her with his silence. *I can wait him out,* she told herself, her own stubbornness blocking her willingness to call the patriarch of her life.

After promotions and sufficient recognition of her work, Rorie adopted with confidence the trappings of her career. She bought a home, which she furnished precisely with her own lighter more feminine tastes to distinguish her abode from the heaviness of her father's dark wood and leathery choices, and his endless stacks of books. Her secret delight was a backyard that allowed her to fulfill one of her long-cherished dreams: to own a dog. Her father would never allow her to have a pet, since he believed they required too much attention. Purchasing a registered puppy, one with a coat quite close to the color of her own hair, Rorie found that the retriever gave her unexpected pleasure as she trained and fussed over it until they became inseparable companions.

Still, Rorie remained fundamentally alone, enjoying the peace and quiet of her own home as well as the professional ambiance of her days. This fact played relentlessly in her thoughts and always brought her back to her father and the muddle of emotions he incited in her. As this connection became clearer in her mind, she sought a friendship more substantial than the cordial but casual ones at work.

One afternoon after leaving work, Rorie chose a singles bar down the street from her office to expand her social horizons. Entering with some trepidation, she went straight to the bar and stood behind the only empty stool at the counter. On one side sat an older man with an attorney-look to him, suited with highly polished shoes. On the other side sat a petite woman with a boyish haircut, swept back on the sides. The woman's clothes were not particularly stylish for the Dallas urban scene, but were more colorful and comfortable.

The woman immediately turned to Rorie and said, "Hi, I'm Sara. Have a seat," as she pulled at the bar stool to indicate it was available. "I'll get this over right away and save us some time. I'm a therapist with my own practice, but I promise not to analyze you if you sit here. I'm married and a mother. My husband works down the street with an architectural firm, that building you see with all the funky glass on it. I need this martini in front of me so I can go home and face the various traumas of teen-aged boys, three of them!" Her words spilled out like marbles, each one bouncing separately with emphasis. She had a matter-of-fact demeanor, but humor lit up her face, marked with lines around her mouth that hinted at frequent laughter.

Rorie, not quite sure what to do next, and a bit overwhelmed at Sara's frankness, stammered, "Thank you, for the seat, I mean." She seated herself and then said, "That's quite a story you have. I thought this was a singles bar. Do married people come here too?"

Sara shot her an upward glance, "Most of the singles who come here are on the prowl for a mate. Are you one of those?"

Not yet used to Sarah's wit and impertinence, Rorie replied defensively, "No! I'm not looking to get married. Not at all. I had hoped to meet people who don't work in my office. My social world is rather small at the moment."

"I'm not sure a bar is the place to make a lifelong friend, but hey, who knows? We are just getting started here. So you aren't married and don't intend to get married? What else can you tell me about you that sets you apart from the crowd?"

Sara's questions disconcerted her, but Rorie wanted to join in the banter. This woman was, if nothing else, intriguing. "Well, I'm from Chicago, but making Dallas my new home. I don't particularly like the weather here, but Chicago isn't much better. My father is Irish, and I have a dog named Flame. Is this enough to get us started? Though my story is nothing like yours," Rorie said shyly. Ordering her drink, she used the distraction to recover from Sara's intensity.

"Good start!" Sara looked at her with respect.

"How long have you been married?" Rorie was curious that anyone would marry in the first place, much less for a lengthy amount of time.

"Oh, honey, I've been married since the Garden of Eden. But the trick is that I did not try to find the "right guy," nor was I desperate to be married. I just happened to be in the right place at the right time to meet a truly genuine human being. He makes me crazy from time to time, but we work it out and laugh about it later. See these gray hairs?" She bowed her head and pointed. "Marriage did not give these to me—those boys of mine caused every one of them. It's parenting that creates the madness in us all." She laughed at herself and then took a hearty drink, pushing the olive around with her tongue.

Rorie found in Sara a friend, mentor and something of the mother she had never known, all rolled into one. *This is going to work. What a delight she is! Good for me, if I can get used to her off-the-cuff comments. She's so bold, and I'm so reticent. One day. . . .*

Over the weeks after she met Sara, Rorie spent much time mulling over the conversation with her. Determining that she was happy as a single woman, Rorie became clear she was *not* searching for a romance in her life. She would remain single if she had anything to say about it!

The very next week, Wil, a recent addition to the management staff of another department on her floor, asked Rorie for a lunch date. Driving back to the office afterward, he invited her to a play the following Friday. With hardly a thought about her recent resolution, she accepted. Being single for her did not include cutting herself off from dating, or even intimacy, with men. It just meant staying out of the marriage trap. She made this resolution with no thought of what this might mean to any man who fell for her. Rorie's naiveté about romance kept her vulnerable.

Rorie's routine, while demanding, dropped steadily into a more comfortable and predictable tempo. Long days at the office created by her advancement in the company gave her a sense of pride. Evening jogs with Flame became her daily release from the tensions of her job, just as her home became a haven for her creative instincts for decorating and gardening. She enjoyed symphonies and plays in the arts district of Dallas, reminding her of good times with her father. Nights out at local clubs with friends provided her the social life she preferred, but required little commitment otherwise.

Regularly she met Sara for coffee, the bar long jettisoned for a quieter meeting place for their talks, where they spent time discussing everything from politics to their work, to their relationships. Her visits with Sara quickly became her most beloved encounters with another human being, mainly because their time together was genuine and open, something new to Rorie after years of learning how to speak cryptically with her father in order to keep her privacy.

Wil began to insert himself into her life but did not especially disturb it, at least not in the early days. Things began to change between Wil and Rorie one evening after they had gone dancing together. He walked her back to their table to share a drink and take a break from the vigorous salsa they had been doing. Both were panting and laughing. Wil took advantage of the levity of the moment and said abruptly, "What do you think about our moving in together?"

Confounded, Rorie asked over the din of the music, "Where did that come from? Do you believe we are ready for such a drastic decision?

"Why not?" Wil was puzzled at her reply. "We've been together for almost a year. We enjoy each other. We're not getting any younger, you know."

Rorie registered in her inner log that last statement. *Desperation.* Sara's words flowed into her head, "I'm not ready for that, Wil. At least not now."

"I can wait. I'm good at that," he responded.

"But I don't want to make promises. I don't even want to speculate about such a thing right now." Rorie was aggravated at being put in such a spot, but firm in her resolve.

Reading Wil's disappointment, she had to work to thwart something in herself that Sara had seen in her: a lifelong training in pleasing men, especially her father. From the night of their conversation about living together, Wil became more persistent in his pursuit of Rorie, and her resistance increased accordingly. The process was subtle, even gentle for the most part. But Wil's second attempt to urge their living together brought forth Rorie's intuitive sense of being invaded.

"It's that problem of control," Rorie told Sara over a girls-night-out dinner. "Why do men want to take charge of me?"

"Are you speaking of any man, about your father, or about Wil?" Sara asked, already knowing the answer.

"Right now, I'm talking about Wil, but I get your point. It might as well be all men, at least all the ones I know." Rorie was petulant now.

"Let's stay with Wil for now. You resist him, but you show clearly that you enjoy his company and even care for him. What are you resisting?"

Rorie fumbled at first, "Uh, you know . . . I've decided that I want to stay single. Well, I am single, and I like it that way, for now."

"But what about Wil himself?"

After scrutinizing her own feelings with care, knowing that Sara would detect any evasions, Rorie continued, "Wil is sharp, attentive and enjoys many of the things I do. He even likes Flame. And that's important, you know!" She added emphatically with a soft laugh. "And I think Flame must also give her approval. Still, there is something missing between us, and in Wil. It's something I don't know how to define. Does that make sense?"

"Make sense of it for me." Sara was clever at drawing Rorie out to detect her own issues.

"He wants to—I cannot think of a better way to put it—control me. Not like my father, so much because my father very blatantly intends to control me. No, Wil is ... he's crafty, even seductive, about it. Polished, that's it—he's polished at trying to control me. Yet every time he makes some move to force our relationship into being more committed than I want, I feel like I'm dealing with my father again." Rorie put her hands to her forehead.

Absentmindedly, Sara moved the saltshaker on the table from one side to the other before she spoke, "I can understand that. Most of the time this is what I hear you struggling over: control, yours or someone else's. Not that unusual, really. Power is an aphrodisiac to some people and a cause for great fear in others. But here's my question: What did you mean by saying that Wil has something missing? That's quite a statement to make about someone you spend that much time with."

Rorie sat up straighter in her chair, clutched her napkin in her lap for strength, and replied, "I don't have a word for this . . . feeling I have." She hastened to qualify. "I know that sounds trite, but all he does is work and talk about work. Everything we do, even all the events we attend together, seem to have something to do with "getting ahead," as he calls it. But I'm as interested in my own career as he is in his. I also like to do things outside of work that have nothing to do with my career. I want to explore more, take adventures that I haven't even dared to conjure yet." She squirmed in her chair. "I guess this all sounds silly to you. But I'm not ready to settle down with Wil, or any man for that matter. I feel like I'm just starting my own life."

Pausing to take a drink and take a mouthful of roast duck, Rorie continued, "What unnerves me is the feeling that he wants me to serve his plan, to be his . . . what . . . trophy wife? Or to fill some gap in his career planning. He has an image of a perfect life for himself, and somehow I feel that he thinks I am the "perfect wife" to fit that slot."

"Have you talked with him about this?"

"I tried, but only once. Nothing!"

"What do you mean, 'nothing?'"

"He didn't show any sign of comprehending my concerns," Rorie explained.

Sara looked solemnly at Rorie, and asked point-blank, "But you keep seeing him. Why?"

Rorie, oblivious to her point, replied, "He's great company, a lot of fun, and willing to do just about anything I want to do."

"Fills the gap, huh?" Sara zinged in on the truth.

Rorie caught her gist, and ducked her head, embarrassed. "I guess I have some thinking to do about all of this, don't I?"

"You said it, girl. If you plan to keep dating Wil, you might want to get honest with him, but first, you need to get honest with yourself."

Rorie sat and stared at Sara for a moment wondering how to solve this issue. *I want Wil in my life because he's good company, but does that mean I have to marry him? Why can't we simply be together and just enjoy things the way they are?* Her frustration with herself and Wil consumed her for the moment. As the evening passed, the two women shared their thoughts on the dinner as well as their high school antics. Laughter replaced the previous somberness, and their friendship became sealed in the camaraderie that only women can share.

"I need to get home to that mob of boys I'm the mother to," Sara patted Rorie's hand, "think we are done here for the evening?"

"Sure." Rorie, ready to leave and be alone with her own thoughts, agreed.

*　*　*

A year after she had bought her home, the phone rang and Rorie's father was on the line to remind her of their mutual birthdays. One of the surprising things that intensified their relationship during her childhood was the fact that she was born on his thirtieth birthday. He never let her forget it, and he proposed to fly down to celebrate.

"I thought you hated Texas," Rorie chided him.

"I do, but maybe I can rescue you."

"None of that! But it would be great to have you come." Her own words floated in ambivalence, but still, she wanted to see him. The difficulty for Rorie was that his visit would be so different from spending time with him in Chicago, when she could control her length of exposure to him.

Plans materialized into a flight that landed at Love Field. She met him there with a hug and nervous chatter about showing him her home and meeting her dog. As soon as they pulled up in front of her house, her father commented, "Not like Chicago. These suburban ranch houses have no personality."

"Now, Dad, don't start. I'm buying this house all by myself, and I don't want to hear one word of criticism about it from you!" Her words were sharper than she had intended.

"Okay. I'm sorry . . . you're right. It's your house. Show me around. And where's that dog you're so proud of?"

Right after the house tour and dog introductions, her doorbell rang. Not suspecting for a moment who it might be, Rorie left her father petting Flame, and strode off to the front door.

"Wil! What are you doing here?" Her voice showed her dismay. Wil knew her father had arrived and wanted to make sure he had a formal introduction to the man. Rorie suspected he may even be seeking an ally in some larger campaign to snare her into the male web.

The two men formed one of those bewildering male alliances so rapidly that Rorie would have admired it, had it not meant that she could hardly find a foothold in their threesome. When, after three arduous days, she drove her father back to the airport, he prepared to take his leave by rendering a blessing on virtually everything in her world, concluding, "Rorie, you've made your way pretty well, and I like that guy, Wil. My kinda' man." Rorie's antenna went up as she received his message loud and clear. No static.

"Wil is a fine person," she conceded from the driver's seat before exiting the car to embrace her father and help him with his luggage.

"What are you going to do about it, dearie? Got any plans?"

The vise closed around her. She felt its pressure. *Wil has put him up to this!* She issued herself a warning, not to fall into the trap she suspected had been set for her. "One thing is clear, Dad, I'm not going to be stampeded."

"Just asking, honey. No need to spill your whiskey." He convulsed with internal laughter and shook his head as he hugged Rorie farewell.

A month later, without telegraphing his intentions, Wil proposed. It should not have surprised her as dramatically as it did. Then she recalled how her father constantly behaved the same way, leaving her off-guard and often back-pedaling to locate herself in his schemes. *Damn, I'm dating my father!*

"Meet me at our coffee house, ASAP. Can you do it?" Rorie sounded urgent. It was early evening, and she had no idea how Sara was involved with her family for the evening.

"Sure, just give me some time. How about the bistro, so we can stay later? I'll see you in an hour."

They sat over cups of steaming coffee and coconut pie. Rorie asked, "What does possession have to do with love? That's what I want to know. Ever since Dad came, I've been thinking about this. It's not control that he or Wil wants. It's more than that. They want to possess me. Dad has finally learned he can't do this as if I were still a child. But now he's turning me over to another man to do the work for him." Rorie cried and laughed at the same time, full of anguish and rage. Her coming into her full self, her becoming, was about to be thwarted. She felt helpless.

"Whoa, Rorie. Things will be fine. Let's just talk through the situation like we always do." Sara poised herself for listening, her fork in the air as if waiting for a cue. Rorie struggled through her thoughts well enough to explain her concerns without the hysteria she felt inside erupting into the conversation. She gulped, then said, "Okay, let's start here. What's the difference between loving and possessing?"

"Everything, I hope." Sara rummaged to direct her thoughts carefully. Rorie noticed her furrowed brow and knew Sara was thoroughly considering her reply. "To my mind, possession is more like an enemy of love, a threat to it.'

"Do men have any clue about this?" asked Rorie.

"Let's not stereotype. Some men, maybe most men, do. My husband understands the difference."

"Could I send Wil on a mission to see your husband? And my father too?" Rorie said ruefully, wiping her eyes with her napkin. A jolt of caffeine hit her nerves and raised her energy level. "Wil, sometimes, not all the time, makes me feel like I did when my father would pressure me into whatever direction he wanted me to go. If anyone did that to Dad, he hated it. Yet he was quite comfortable controlling me. So why does he do that to me while claiming to 'love me more than anything in this whole world?'" Her voice rose to a higher pitch as she questioned the universe. "Dad is going so far as to pick out my husband! You should have seen him dote on Wil."

"Rorie. Rorie, calm down, okay?" Sara scolded. "This is one of the mysteries of male-female relationships: women and men who confuse love with ownership. It's possession driven by jealousy and insecurity. It's not love. This same emotion can even lead to murder, it's so powerful."

Relief came to Rorie in waves. Discovering the depth of her anxiety over the proposal rested in the possessiveness that shrouded it. She sat back in her seat, lifted her coffee mug to her lips and slurped down the now lukewarm beverage. "Well, I'm not sure what I'm going to do about all of this, but this much I've decided: I will take my time, and I will not be owned by anyone. Wil is a good man. Many would say he's a 'catch.' But I came to Dallas to get away from my father and to find my own life, not to live someone else's life."

Sara congratulated her, "Good for you! The only thing I can add is that love, the kind you'd give your life for, causes its own mess. Love of the sort you *would* marry for is not neat and tidy either. But this type of love invites you into the fray with excitement, anticipation for exploring the unknown mysteries of human love with someone else. It requires patience and endurance. It ties you up, but in a way that lets you go. Does any of this make sense, Rorie?"

"Not fully, but I believe that someday I'll understand what you've said to me."

Rorie heard Sara's strong words, but she knew she could not entirely grasp their meaning. About relationships she was not as mature as she wished she were. *I wonder if this comes from not having a mother and being raised by such a dominant father.* She had never known the kind of love that would swallow her whole and yet leave her free to be herself.

When she was standing in her bedroom, ready to settle down for the night, Flame curled on the floor beside her bed, Rorie pondered her conversation with Sara. A vague plan began forming in her mind, though at the moment it was shapeless and undefined.

Cleansing

LAY SLEPT FITFULLY, TURNING AND TWISTING IN HIS SLEEPING bag until the cocoon finally wrapped around his body, binding him, which roused him. Even though the remainder of the night engulfed him, he knew he would have trouble falling into further slumber. Something unnamable stirred him with anticipation as he scooted toward the flap of his tent to peer out at the panoply of fading stars and vague silhouettes surrounding him. His eyes adapted to the darkness, although he spied a thin band of light beginning to peek over the canyon rim. *Might as well start my day. Sleep isn't my friend at this point.* Crawling quietly out of the tent, Clay made his way through the dimness toward the shed.

The brisk morning chill suggested more clothes, but when he remembered Coyote, he postponed the noisy prospect of re-entering the tent. Walking gingerly toward where the young man slept, as a father tiptoes into a child's room to make sure they have enough cover, Clay looked down to see Coyote folded in a prenatal curl, lost in the dream world. Clay sneaked back to the shed, sat shivering briefly on the cold bench, then stood to begin a search for chips and twigs to build a fire. After he carefully laid a pyramid of tinder, the fire awoke with the first match. Sitting on a fallen log, he fed the flickers with larger and larger sticks of wood. Once the flames had cut through the chill, Clay brought his camp stove near the cordial little blaze, perching it on a nearby boulder. Within minutes he had brewed coffee to warm his insides.

Dawn's grayness began to mutate into streaks of color, slowly warming the early riser, creating an urge in him to take a morning hike and do some exploring. He banked the fire for Coyote. Moving toward the trail, mug in hand, Clay decided to walk up the mountainside to gain a better view of the coming dawn. This time of day perpetually thrilled him, providing not only the sense of privacy he rarely experienced any longer, but also an intimacy with his own thoughts. Returning to his tent, he reached in for his denim jacket, limp with age and faded from use. He shook himself into it as though it were an old friend, refilled his coffee cup and then took off to stroll the ribbon of trail before him.

Rorie played through his mind, her impish grin and capacity to show on her face whatever response she felt. Clay liked this about her. *A spontaneous woman! No calculations here, I suspect.* The day's allure rested mostly on the promise of her coming up later in the morning. Mellie hardly intruded, but rested in veiled remembrance behind all that now transpired. Clay could still feel a nagging sense of guilt over her injunction to him, "Go on with your life."

The coffee mug was now empty again. Clay placed it on the stump beside the trail and faced east. His eyes followed along the ridge of strewn boulders and rocks which he had climbed the day before. Light was now boldly marching over the rim into the gorge. He noticed a mist rising from among the display of rocks about forty yards up from where he stood. At first, he found this phenomenon curious, but after watching awhile, he was puzzled. *Is there hot water flowing under that rock fall?* The longer he observed, the more convinced he became that the steam rose from heated water beneath the lithic avalanche. Intrigued, he walked toward the mist to investigate.

Making his way cautiously, Clay reached the region of the mist after only a slight scrape to his shin from a rock he could not see due to the shadows still playing over the grey-green rocks. Immediately he felt warmth exiting through fissures between the stones and a dripping damp on their undersides. He moved along the craggy wall, looking for any opening through which he might search for the source of heat. Spotting a stash of smaller rocks above which vapor hung, he pulled them away and let them tumble down into an infant arroyo below. Removing his jacket, he tossed it across a spindly pinion limb and thrust his head into the opening between two sizable stones. A distinct acrid rush of foggy warmth greeted him. He cheered!

Clay probed, peered, and became an amateur excavator, until he located a cleft large enough for him to crawl through. He halted with half of his body inside, unable to see anything. *Should have brought my flashlight!* He backed out and surveyed the site, then retreated back to camp to retrieve his flashlight and a cap to protect his head.

By the time he reached his tent, Coyote, folding his bedroll, greeted him with a wave. "Man, you're up early. Where'd you find all that mud and grit?"

Clay ducked into his tent and brought out his flashlight and a cap, which he immediately planted on his head. Pointing up to the ridge, "Looks like there might be a hot spring up there. I'm headed back to check it out."

"Mind if I come?" Coyote was eagerly throwing on a wrinkled fleece jacket.

"Sure." Then, remembering he was playing host to his former student, Clay paused, turned around and said, "Do you want some coffee first, or something to eat, maybe?" He turned to check on the fire. "Or, you can sit here and get our fire going again until I get back."

"No way, Man!" Coyote scuffed more dirt over the dying embers and said, "Let's go!" Clay grinned and waved Coyote to follow him.

The two jogged up the trail like eager boys on a scavenger hunt, searching the horizon for a sign of the escaping mist. They periodically examined the terrain for the best path but mainly bushwhacked up to the location. Clay pointed out the opening he had created. "You're smaller. Crawl in there with my flashlight and check it out." Coyote fell to the task with the zeal of a hungry mountain lion stalking prey. He slipped easily inside, only his feet hanging out.

Moments passed. "Awesome!" echoed from the cavern. Clay winced at the use of that word. He hated the abuse of it by young people who knew little about what is truly awesome. But he decided to leave this judgmental thought for another time. "What do you see?"

Coyote continued, "It's like a little cave in here with water dripping from the ceiling. I'm goin' in further, but I have ta stay on my hands and knees."

Clay called out, "Do you see any running water?"

"No, but I can hear a trickle somewhere."

"How far can you go?"

"Hold it a minute. I see a kind a' pool, but I can't get to it from here. We'll have to go further down and try. I'm blocked here." He soon appeared head first, but he then turned around and backed out. His clothes where damp, clogged with grit. He beamed with enthusiasm.

Following Coyote's suggestion, the two explorers moved down the mountainside some fifteen feet and saw more mist escaping from a rift between large rocks. Tearing away at the smaller boulders, they found an opening. It was smaller. Coyote could squeeze through, but only about halfway. He turned the light to survey the dark space. "Man, this is some kind a' awesome!" Clay groaned to himself. *There's that word again!*

Coyote shouted with excitement. "There's a pond of water, about the size of two bathtubs!"

"How high's the ceiling?"

Coyote wriggled until he slipped through into the cavern. "Can almost stand up straight, but you have to watch your head."

"What's the bottom of the pool like?" Clay wanted to know, his excitement growing.

"Give me a minute," Coyote called back, crouching his way down to the pool to remove his shoe and feel the bottom. "Some rocks, mostly pebbles . . . and sandy grit, it feels like." Coyote exited with some effort, exclaiming, "Man, that place is a regular steam bath!"

Elated, they examined the area for a better entrance. Coyote spotted one large rock that appeared to stand free. The two spelunkers concluded that, if they could unseat the rock and make it fall, the opening would be large enough to use. Clay proposed going down for breakfast and coming back later to see what they could do. He could feel the need for nourishment, some water and a break for the two of them.

After hurriedly eating a light breakfast, Coyote began to search for substantial sticks for their project. He was successful. Clay sharpened them into tools for digging. They returned to the site and began poking their primitive instruments into the earth beneath the rock obstructions. The barrier they wanted to remove rested on smaller stones buried in the ground. Attacking these, the sweating pair managed to remove one or two rocks before a stick broke and had to be sharpened again. The two men became primal, hardly talking, scratching into the soft earth as if in search of treasure. Engrossed, silent effort gave way to gravel, pebbles and small bits of wood rolling into the arroyo, but the object of their intentions remained in place.

Again, reviewing the situation, Coyote ventured, "Maybe I can crawl far enough inside the cave to give it a push. He threw down his stick and wormed into the opening, finally clearing the wedge. "Hey, I'm in, but it's sure cramped in here. Hand me the light." Moments later, "All right. I'm gonna push with my legs." When he did, the stone at first sat defiantly, but on the second try Clay saw it wobble slightly.

"Hey, Coyote. Good try. Do that again!"

At first it only sagged into the hole they had dug, but with the force of Coyote's legs still pumping against the stone, it eased over the last lip, tumbled downward and crashed thunderously into a new resting place.

The two champions cheered their victory and surveyed the results. Before them some four feet behind the cavity left by the stone's departure lay a cauldron of water casting its fog toward the fresh opening. Coyote shone the light all around, and they could see a small den with an uneven cave-like roof not quite high enough for them to stand fully. Clay crawled inside and felt the water with his left hand. It was hot indeed—he yanked his hand back. Coyote laughed, "See, I told you it was hot."

Without words, they stared at each other briefly before ripping at their grubby clothing in unison, leaving them in rumpled piles as they began using their feet to feel their way into the steaming pool.

Though Clay's flashlight was all the illumination they had between them, it was enough, since a faint sliver of daylight peeked through the cave's opening.

"This is terrific! I've needed a bath for days. I tried to bathe in the river, but it was too cold."

Laughing at his young friend, Clay said jokingly, "Yeah, I knew you needed a bath. Hope this hits the spot," remembering his earlier bath by the river.

Nothing bonds males so quickly as working together, especially on a project outdoors. Clay and Coyote became comfortable enough to remain silent for a while, enjoying their new steam bath. Teacher and student were shrouded in a moist cocoon.

Coyote slipped out of the water and propped himself on a rock at the edge of the cave. "That stuff's hot," he stated bluntly. "Wish I could've brought Hannah here. She loves places like this. If she knew about it, she would've come with me for sure. Well, maybe. . . ." His last words were wistful.

"Who's Hannah?" Clay asked, with his eyes closed, lazy from the heat.

"She's, she *was*, my girlfriend. She said she was coming with me, but. . . ."

"Why didn't she? What happened?"

"Would you believe it? She ran across an old boyfriend at some party, and she dumped me."

Coyote gestured his agitation by kicking his feet at the water. "What a bummer. We'd even talked about getting married, not right away, but at some point, after we finished college and were ready to settle down. We were serious, at least I was."

"Did you ever meet this other guy?"

"No. That doesn't really matter because she dumped him too. She just ran away from both of us and joined some group hiking around Europe. Seemed like she was trying to escape everything."

Looking up at his newly found friend, Clay said wisely, "Maybe she was. Sounds to me like she wasn't ready for the serious stuff and was afraid of commitment."

"Sure seems like it, but it left me hangin' and wondering what to do. I've been thinkin' about all of this since I started my hike."

Clay prompted, "Lost love can drive a guy crazy."

"Yeah. I started to go out there to her school, it's in California, and at least ask her to consider staying together. Sure glad I didn't do that."

Clay ventured gingerly, "You don't seem very settled about Hannah's leaving you."

"I'm not over it, really. I still think about her all the time. But I'm doin' okay in spite of it. I mean, I keep swingin' back and forth between feelings for her, and then I get to where I'm passable again for a few days. Then it starts all over again. Gettin' over a broken heart is not very easy, Dr. Jac—Clay."

Clay sat rubbing his foot where it had rested on a stone too long. "Yours is a common story, about love and loss." As he said these words to Coyote, Clay realized he was talking to himself about Mellie's reality. *And someday I'll be the one trying to get over a broken heart. Is this just the way it is for everyone?*

"How do you think your current experience relates to your feelings about your parents, Coyote?" The young man sat bolt upright and stared at Clay. Even through the mist, he was able to meet Clay's eyes with his own.

"I'm not worried 'bout them. I told you I don't want to have anythin' to do with 'em."

"Do you actually *hate* your mother and father, Coyote?" Clay probed.

"I just don't care." His lips formed a pout.

"Indifferent?"

Crossing his arms over his bare chest, Coyote spat, "You got it!"

Clay went in for the kill at this point. "Well, here's my problem. You seem to have a lot of feelings where they're concerned."

"Nope!" Coyote interrupted, "Not on your life!"

"But you spent more of your energy on your parents in our discussion last night than anyone else." Coyote grew still and stared through the cave opening, this time wishing he were outside and away from this conversation.

"Here's my point," Clay softened toward the young man, "The one thing that I believe entirely cancels out love is indifference. When you really and totally don't care, then love is gone—absent." Clay waited for this idea to sink in. "If there's anything you are not, it is indifferent. I mean, toward your parents, at least."

Heatedly, Coyote snapped, "Then what do you think I have goin' with them?"

"You are entangled, I'd say. You're so wrapped up with them, this is strangling you."

Missing Clay's point, Coyote's youthful rebuttal stabbed back, "I'm not tangled up with them or anybody else, though I wish I was still tangled up with Hannah. My parents don't even know where I am."

"But you know exactly where they are. In fact, they're right here with you, following you around." Clay moved in the pool, ready to climb onto a rock to cool off, as if to emphasize his point. He lightly tapped Coyote on the forehead and added, "They're stuck right in there. That means they're as close to you as they can get." Clay spoke not like a mentor, but like a friend. "As long as they're that close, the one thing you will not be able to be is indifferent."

Coyote slid glumly back into the pool, silent until relieved to hear a remote voice waft into their cave. Asking, "Who's that?" he cautiously moved out of the pool again and felt his way to the opening and looked down. Seeing Rorie standing on the trail, he called out, "We're up here, but don't come up. Naked men on the scene! Turn around!"

Shocked at hearing Coyote shouting from the rocks above her, Rorie stared into the sun, saw a flash of skin, waved at him, and turned away to return to Clay's camp shed. Flame was already ahead of her, prancing through the grasses along the trail's edges. Rorie had left her wilderness nest mid-morning and started hiking toward Clay's campsite, ready to continue her interactions with him. She experienced a touch of disappointment when she realized Coyote was still on the premises. *What does that say about my expectations for the day with Clay? I better get ahold of myself!*

"Oh, I almost let the morning get away from me," Clay said, fretting about getting caught unprepared for Rorie's visit. "She said she would come up to our camp today." He was clearly overeager, and Coyote noticed.

"Take your time. She's not gonna run off," Coyote chided.

They dressed and made their way down the rocks, through to a faint path that some animal had made over time to the main trail. As they approached Rorie, they forgot their appearance, but she began to point at them, laughing, "What in blazes have you two been up to?" They both talked breathlessly about their find, until she stalled them, "One at a time, please," she begged.

When they finished with their tale of exploration and conquest, she insisted, "Well, I want to see it too!"

Clay spoke quickly, before Coyote had time to make a plan with her, "It's a surprise. I want to show it to you later." He caught Rorie's eyes and gave her a knowing nod. Coyote recognized the hint and remained silent.

Rorie smiled in agreement with Clay's little conspiracy but observed, "Not much of a surprise. You are both wearing the evidence all over you." She laughed again. Coyote and Clay decided to clean up, each taking fresh clothes from their packs and disappearing toward the falls near the river. Flame had run off with the two men to frolic in the water's edge while they bathed, leaving Rorie to wait for all of them to return.

Once they were all together again, Clay suggested they eat. Breakfast had long worn off for the two cave dwellers. Now they were ravenous. Rorie had brought some food with her, and between them a meal materialized on the table in the shed. While they ate, Coyote and Clay regaled Rorie with their exploits up the ridge. They dutifully embellished their accounts the way men do to impress women and each other. *It's a guy thing.* Rorie chuckled under her breath. She had picked up the phrase from Sara, who was a master at spotting such behaviors with three sons and a husband to teach her about masculine behavior every day of her life.

After lunch, Coyote went to his gear and came back shortly with his pack on his back. "I reckon I'd better head out. I have only a day left now." He started toward the trail.

Clay called out, "Aren't you going the wrong way? Colorado is north."

Coyote turned around, "No. I'm gonna hike out today and see if I can catch a ride back to my car."

Jumping up from the shed table, Clay ran toward Coyote. "Are you ending your hike?"

"Yeah. I have some other stuff to do now." After looking around as if trying to memorize the scene, he continued, "You helped me a lot, Clay. I think I musta come down here to find you, but just didn't know it."

"Some of the best moments in our lives are surprises, Coyote. You were as much a surprise to me as I have most likely been to you." Clay then thought immediately of Rorie.

"Well, this sure was a good one for me, but I've had some others I could do without."

"Where do you plan to go now?" Clay genuinely wanted to know about this young man and his welfare.

"Probably back to Wichita for a few days, and then. . . . Say, you goin' back home soon?"

"Oh, in a couple of days or so," Clay reported diffidently, still unsure of his itinerary. "I haven't decided just when. Why?"

"Maybe I could look you up back at school. Come to your office or somethin.'" Coyote spoke with hope.

"I trust you will. Just call the office and leave a message for me. I'll be on sabbatical next year, but I'll get the message and return your call. Hope to see you soon!" Clay waved to Coyote as the young pilgrim trotted back to the trail, slowly disappearing out of sight.

Rorie and Clay soon found their channel back to familiarity. They spent the afternoon in relaxed but animated conversation, hiking the trails with Flame running ahead of them as if this was old business for her. Each of them, recognizing the patterns of attraction growing between them, puzzled over the course their encounter was taking. Neither dared to speak about it. Still, each knew the gravitational pull was already at work, drawing them gently but firmly together. They were both aware that the only way for this temptation to continue was to locate themselves, not in the past or future, but in the moment at hand. They shared an evening meal over Clay's camp stove, working side by side as if by habit.

As the day waned, Rorie stirred nervously, wanting to unwrap the hours ahead. "Clay, when are you going to show me the surprise? I've waited all day. Now I'm mystified."

"Oh, it's better after dark. You know, cooler," Clay offered, remaining a touch secretive. As the dusky shadows began to climb the canyon walls, he went to his tent and returned with a small pack. "Ready to travel?" Rorie jumped up to follow. Flame cavorted between them, aware adventure was ahead. Carefully they negotiated the trail up to the ridge in the dimming twilight. When they reached the low drop below the opening to the hot spring, Clay pointed to a level spot outside the cavern and said to Flame, in an authoritative voice as if they had been buddies for years, "Stay, Flame." The dog dutifully obeyed and curled up to wait. Then Clay turned back to Rorie and warned, "You might get a little gritty, but I promise not as much as we did this morning. Go on and crawl in."

"That's reassuring," Rorie admitted with a grin, and began climbing around to the narrow shelf. Clay followed right behind her, shining his flashlight into the hollow spaces for them both.

"Cozy," she volunteered. "And warm, but I can't see very well." Clay dug into his daypack and drew out his lantern. Turning it on, they watched the cave fill with a soft light. As Rorie's eyes adjusted to the dim, steamy space, she looked around at her surroundings and saw the pool of water, exclaiming, "There's water in here!"

Without waiting on Clay, she started removing her boots. "I could use this for sure!" Dipping her feet in the pool, she jumped back, "This water is hot! How did you find this place?"

"Early this morning, I saw steam rising out of the rocks above my camp, so I came to check it out. Here's the result. Coyote helped me dig the entrance, so we could climb in here and bathe. Astonishing, huh?"

"Aren't you clever?" She wondered what his plans were for the pool. She had no swimsuit with her. Before she could study the problem any further, Clay lit a candle and placed it on a rock near the water, then turned off the lantern. Standing slightly crouched in the blurred flicker of light, he began to undress. Rorie sucked in her breath but made no other sound. No protest. *Well, I have seen him before, but it's not mutual. Now what?"*

Clay's shirt lay on his shoes, as he was about to remove his shorts. He stopped abruptly, "Had you rather I blow out the candle?"

"Uh . . . oh . . . I don't . . . I should be all right," she stuttered, fumbling with her blouse.

Clay's clothing removed, he stepped into the pool delicately to avoid any sharp stones and found a place to sit on the far side. The shadows of the candlelight leapt across his face. The water stirred, and more steam floated toward the entrance. "The bottom of the pool is mostly gravelly sand. It's comfortable enough to sit on once you wiggle into place. But you need to feel for the rocks with your feet." He heard no sound from her.

"You okay over there?" Rorie was still huddled against the wall closest to the entrance. He could detect that she was moving around, but was still concerned that she seemed quite uncomfortable.

Rorie looked at the outline of Clay sitting in the water, and then lost her anxiety. *This is Clay. He's fine. I don't have to assume anything here. Just go with it and enjoy yourself, Rorie!* She scolded herself, and immediately began to stand so she could strip. Taking off her shirt and shorts, she stood briefly in her bra and panties, allowing him to see her figure. *We are adults here. He doesn't seem worried about anything. Why should I be?* Taking a deep breath, she urged herself, *Relax. Rorie, It's okay!*

They sat, legs extended toward one another. The candle's flicker choreographed shadows on the walls and ceiling of the cave. Night intensified outside and left them nestled in an earth womb. Rorie confided, "After three days of sponge baths, this is heavenly." She sighed deeply.

"Yea, that's how I felt this morning when I found this place. I took a bath by the river the first day, but. . . ."

Before she could censor herself, Rorie confessed, "Yes, I know."

After an abbreviated silence, Clay asked, "What did you say?"

Rorie fumed at herself, and considered covering up her slip with an off-hand comment, but instead replied, "I guess I better come clean with you."

"Well?"

"You know that first day you came to the gorge? Well, that afternoon I hiked up the trail, not knowing anyone else was in the canyon. I saw you taking a shower at the falls." She ducked her head, wondering what his response would be.

Slapping the water with both hands, Clay guffawed. "You're a regular peeping, uh, what are you? A Peeping Rorie, I guess. You know, while I was taking that shower, I remember thinking that anyone could just walk up on me and catch me *au naturel.* Why didn't you say something?"

"I didn't want to interrupt the show," she quipped.

Clay pinched Rorie's leg, and she thrashed in the water. With this gesture of child's play, their relationship slipped into another level of intimacy. Their shared tranquility gave vent to an exchange of stories about catching someone else naked. Both had stories to share, but their fun was in telling of times when they were caught without clothes, both of them as teens, and the level of embarrassment this brought. "Why is that, do you think?" asked Rorie.

"We were exposed," Clay retorted, "caught off guard. It's against our nature to be caught out of control of our bodies."

"Like when you started to undress earlier, and I didn't quite know what to do?" Rorie teased.

"Yeah, something like that." Clay became pensive, thinking of Mellie for a moment, "But then, having no control over your body can be torture, as well as pleasure, I think."

Hearing the sadness in his voice, Rorie replied, softly "I never thought of it that way, Clay. Losing total control over my body is not really something I have experienced . . . at least not caused by something outside myself. And it's certainly something I don't think I want to experience, at least not right at the moment."

Feeling their talk becoming too painful for Clay, Rorie changed the subject and turned to ask a question about Coyote. "What do you think will happen to your former student now?"

"I have no idea, but I hope he will return to school. His heart is a bit battered from the breakup of a recent relationship." Clay, sensing Rorie's need to break the intimate talk they were having, told about Coyote's enthusiasm for digging and pushing the boulder away from the cave's opening. Then he told Rorie about the young rebel's experience with Hannah and its power over him. "He's had a hard lesson fairly early in life, a broken heart, broken from love. For one his age, that's a bit too much drama."

Nodding, Rorie concurred, and then said, "That's what I feel I need in my relationship with Wil; I just need to let go. And I need him to let go. Like Coyote, I don't want a broken heart and I don't want to hurt Wil, but I don't want to be so entangled that I am constantly trying to avoid promises for a future I cannot yet envision for us."

Clay stared at Rorie over the steam rising from the pool, sweat running down his face. He slipped from the water to sit on the edge, but left his feet playing in it. "My lowest point with Mellie came when I realized she would never make any progress toward health. Her progress is always toward death, toward loss for me, a daily broken heart for both of us. I need to let go, against all my best wishes. To see her like that every day, evaporating little by little, has been hard to tolerate. Coyote's loss was just as painful to him as my daily loss of Mellie is to me."

Rorie noticed the suffering on his face, feeling her own Waterloo so inadequate compared to what Clay was undergoing. She swallowed, "Clay, I really cannot imagine how the two of you do this." Her voice trailed off.

Clay became still and unresponsive for a while, causing Rorie to wonder how to handle the situation. Just as she was about to suggest they leave the cave and return to their separate camps, Clay spoke, "I was invited a couple of years ago to share teaching a course—the one Coyote mentioned—the course on love. I knew nothing technically or theoretically about love. Had never really thought about it, except on rare occasions. Love had just happened to me in my life, especially with my wife and daughter." He put his hands on his knees and laughed, "I do hope I know something about love now from experience, but until that course, the topic was just personal."

Rorie said nothing, so Clay continued. "What's always bothered me about Mellie's situation is that I could do nothing to make it better. Oh, I could take care of her, but I couldn't really *do* anything. Even love cannot fix her body. That's a true feeling of no control!" Clay turned to glance over at Rorie to see her reaction, but her face was turned toward the water and hidden in the shadows.

As she stared at the pool, Rorie's voice bounced over the cave walls, "Why is it that men I know go crazy when they can't *fix* things?"

"When you've been taught all your life that your responsibility is to take care of everything and fix things, then that's what you do." Clay, sounding too strident, immediately apologized, "I'm sorry—being a bit too defensive, aren't I?"

Rorie ignored his apology and moved on, "What a load to carry. Wil is the same way . . . always trying to get things *set* so life will be perfect." Rorie's temper flared as she shook her damp hair for emphasis. "Now, I'm the one who sounds too angry. This must be a tender topic for men and women to discuss. Do ya think?" she said, trying to lighten their mood and turn the conversation to something more congenial.

Picking up her clue, Clay followed, "After teaching that course, I felt like I had been somehow 'called'—is that a strange word to use?—to research and write on love, as if I was preparing for something ahead that I couldn't understand at the time." His voice broke with the timbre of his words.

Rorie allowed a silence to fall between them so Clay could become calmer. "So that's why all of your probing about love, huh?"

"That's part of it, but there's more. My concern is over the relation between love and loss. It's everywhere I turn these days. Even Coyote's story about his lost relationship with Hannah, or you, with your decision whether you will lose control if you agree to Wil's marriage proposal."

Slipping back into the liquid heat, Rorie nodded and admitted that part of her anxiety rested in what she would be giving up to marry Wil. Making a cup with her hands, she splashed for a moment to dribble some of the water down her back and over her neck. The water covered her, leaving only the curves of her breasts showing. In the flickering light she looked relaxed and at ease with herself, the tension lines on her face completely erased. Clay felt himself react to her loveliness without even a single word of encouragement from her. He moved back into the water to sit beside her this time, both of them with their backs to the wall of the pool, as if sitting in lounge chairs.

"What I'm learning is that you surely give up something if you love, and usually more than you imagine in advance." Clay moved slightly, his leg touching hers under the water. She didn't withdraw, so he stayed still. "Do you truly love this man—Wil?"

Rorie straightened herself, feeling slightly invaded, and almost blurted out that it was none of his business, but caught herself and recognized that Clay had detected her own earlier insight. If Clay was going to be this honest and open with her, she had some obligation to join him. She softened, "Clay, I really don't know. I *like* him, a lot really, but. . . ." Then, striving to be more precise, she fell back on a standard cliché. "Of course, well, sure, I love him, but I'm not sure I'm 'in love' with him."

Clay jabbed her foot with his. "That's what so many people say, especially women. But what does that statement mean exactly? It seems like a way of avoiding the issue." His foot rested on hers at this point, stroking it. Rorie noticed Clay's touch but did nothing to discourage him.

The woman knew she was under challenge. "There is a difference. Let me think for a minute." She paused, swirled her hands through the water, and then continued, "Yes, I can love many people, such as my friends and colleagues at work, but I'm not 'in love' with them, at least not in the same way we talk about romantic or intimate love."

Poking fun at her, Clay said, "That won't do. We got into this question in the love course. There *are* different kinds of love, that's true. You know, the love between a mother and child, or siblings, or even friends. But in a personal, romantic kind of situation, to say, "I love you, but I'm not *in love* with you is close to insulting. Don't you think?

Shaking her head, Rorie rebutted, "No! It's more honest, because both parties fully understand what is being said. One statement implies care for another person in the present moment. The 'in love' statement includes promise and future. In their most negative form, the words, 'I'm not in love with you' are surely a statement of intimate distance." She remembered her earlier decision about marriage and love. *Am I sinking here?*

Clay was astonished at her response, completely unprepared for what she had said.

"I do love Wil in a way, in the present moment. I really do have genuine feelings for him. But to say I'm *in love* with him implies that I am ready to build a future with him, and right now I am not."

"The great 'but.' I love you, *but*. . . ." Sitting next to her in the pool with the candlelight filling their space, Clay felt his body completely relaxing. Changing the subject of their conversation, he raised his hands to his face, allowing water to splash over him. "It's been such a long time since I have been this carefree with another person. Just to relax and talk, and this pool is. . . ." he stopped to look at Rorie's face. A subterranean emotion flowed beneath his words, deeper than he realized.

Rorie's senses went on high alert. She smiled at him but said nothing. She recognized the spark surging between the two of them. *This is not my game to call. He's married.*

In the cave, in the canyon, in the candlelight, these two people were fresh and new together. Innocent. The moment moved from awkward to sensual and back again. Clay rushed to stir up their conversation again, partially to protect both of them. "What do you have to say about 'falling in love'?"

"What do you mean?" Rorie asked, perplexed.

"'Falling in love' is often the way we describe the effects of moving into connection with another person when we intend romance and intimacy. But at some point, we must stop falling or love never becomes grounded in the real world. And when the falling is over, the true pressure of loving someone begins. I believe all this talk about being 'in love' can become a damaging fog of idealization. Love is tough work. And the toughest way of loving is when we acknowledge that, in the end, love will always mean loss."

"That's almost too depressing, but I can see what you mean." Rorie conceded. "I will leave this canyon with the understanding that I am either 'in love' with Wil, or I am not. If I am, I will promise a future to him. Otherwise, I go on my way." Pulling away, she stepped from the water, and reported, "Now we have to exit this pool before I become a prune."

Her teasing and obvious closure to their conversation caused Clay to sit up and move out of the pool. "Okay, agreed. But first I need to say one more thing. This may be pushing you too far, and if so, just forget what I have said. But Rorie, if you have to 'decide' whether you are in love with Wil or not, isn't that an answer of sorts?"

Clay's insight created instant chaos in her mind, but she refused to answer him before she had time to consider his words. Reaching for her clothes, she began to dress, signaling him to do the same. They donned their clothes over wet bodies. It somehow felt wickedly intoxicating. They still bore the surplus of the warmth from the bath as they crawled out of the hot cavern. The night air energized them. Flame rose from her nest as she heard their voices and greeted them vigorously, wagging her tail once she saw them exit the cave. On the way back down to the campsite, Clay asked again, "Do you really think you can solve your question by *deciding* whether you love Wil enough to marry him or not?"

Because Clay had the flashlight, Rorie was following closely behind him and could hear him pant in the night air, steam rising off his body. Dodging his question for the second time, she said wistfully, "I will not forget this place or this evening. It was truly an experience of paradise for aching bodies." Clay stopped on the trail, turned around and hugged her, allowing his question to default. "Good soaking, good conversation, good memories, Rorie. Thank you for your company and your insights. I truly needed some time like this in my life." They separated again and moved on down the trail.

Returning to his question on her own time, Rorie began to speak slowly, "Clay, I want to answer your question. Yes, I do believe that love is about decision, a commitment to another. Of course, there's more to it than that: emotion, passion. I'm not sure of myself at this point, but don't we have to say 'yes' to the attraction that comes to us if we want it to develop into love? And when we don't want that, don't we have to turn away and say, 'No, I won't respond.' We ignore the attraction. Don't married couples who want to remain faithful do this all the time?" And then she zinged him, "Didn't we do that tonight in that hot spring when we both felt a momentary attraction?"

Clay stopped dead still on the trail. "You are right! You have a most interesting turn of mind about these matters." He looked at her in wonder. "However, if I may challenge you, my thought is that you put your whole self, as it were, on the line. We have to take a risk with love, with other people. It's not enough to decide. Isn't that a control mechanism? Deciding? What about the urgency . . . the pull of love that is always ahead of us, drawing us?" By this time the pair was back to Clay's camp. He set the lantern on the table in the shed and turned it on to provide light for them. But they were too engrossed in their conversation to do much more at the moment. They plopped on the bench and continued talking, hardly missing a beat.

Rorie started again, pushing her agenda, "That's what I mean when I say, 'in love.' I may make decisions, but I do it from *inside* the love—the connection—that I have chosen." Rorie wasn't sure she made sense, but she felt that she spoke something that she had only just begun to understand by saying it.

Clay nodded, but said nothing in reply, his brow furrowed in thought. Shifting the winds between them, he mused to see how Rorie would respond, saying, "I had originally planned to leave tomorrow, but I think I'll stay another day. What about you? How long are you staying in this canyon?" Picking up his drift, she agreed she would stay another day too. Neither of them knew what this promise meant, only that it seemed pertinent to their separate ventures into Wild Rivers.

Clay fired up the stove and brewed hot chocolate. They drank standing, chatting with the calm reciprocity of life-long friends, but each knew that more was at stake than friendship. Finishing their drinks, they moved to the fire pit, where Clay turned the ashes into warmth, just as he had the previous evening with their young visitor. They sat by the fire until the canopy of the night sky filled with stars and planets, each telegraphing a message from light years away. Their easy talk continued, as the chill of the night settled around them, encouraging them to sit shoulder to shoulder, arm to arm, leg to leg for warmth. The fire died, and the embers glowed, mirroring the stars above. Only the sound of the rushing waters below could be heard echoing through the dark gorge. Rorie called to Flame. The animal came bounding up from her adventures into the underbrush, with an understanding that the day was about over for her and Rorie.

The three of them began the trek back to Little Arsenic. Rorie and Clay continued talking, confiding as they picked their way down the trail that they were stunned at how each day spent in the canyon drew them into a deeper desire to stay rather than leave. When they reached her tent, she vaguely wondered to herself, *Should I invite him to stay? Of course not,* she answered her own question. *He's married, obviously 'in love' with his wife. What am I thinking?* She compromised, "Want to come down for breakfast tomorrow?"

"Sure," he sounded relieved, not knowing how to keep their connection going. "Whatever you have to eat will be better than what I have left after feeding Coyote. He ate up quite a bit of my food and left me short." A half-moon had risen and shone on their faces. They grinned at each other. Without a further word they embraced, Clay drawing her close. For the briefest moment they melded, and he kissed her lightly on the cheek. Before either of them could assess the gesture, it was over. Clay walked away in a daze. Rorie stood rooted, touching her face where his lips had been. *How does one "decide" about such as this?*

Surrender

CLAY MOWED THROUGH FIVE DAYS OF FACIAL STUBBLE, USING the bottom of his cook kit as a rustic mirror, made dim by the early morning light. On the first day of his trip he had decided not to shave until he returned home, but the promise of this last day in the gorge prompted him to harvest his growth. Exactly what the promise might be remained unformed but enticing in his first thoughts of the day. By the time he sponged off and dressed, the sun peeped over the jagged edges far above and invited him to walk toward Little Arsenic. He had loaded his daypack with his rain gear and journal, throwing in a couple of granola bars. His supplies were growing thin at this point, he noticed. Grabbing his hiking stick from against a wind-twisted cedar, he began his tramp.

As Clay traversed the trail toward Rorie's campsite, images of Mellie played at the edge of his consciousness. She appeared like a well-polished stone, broken in the cutting. Beyond repair, she remained cherished but increasingly out of reach to him. Her force in his mind was diminishing as her frail body began to disappear before him. *What is she doing this morning? Very little, and that's the point!* He found himself wishing she had never sent him on this journey to discover how to let her go. Clay felt the conflict grip his chest. For a moment his breath came in gasps. *And yet her very wish is being granted almost without my ability to stop it. Mellie, you are my love.* He sent his thoughts winging to her through the bright morning air, knowing how much she would have delighted in this canyon and its beauty. He continued to walk, striding with determined steps toward an unforeseen destiny.

As usual, Flame served as an alarm clock, rousing Rorie much earlier than she preferred. Today she wanted to be awake and even momentarily domestic. Warming water for her "dry bath," she set out her toiletries to freshen up her body and hair. Her elation mixed with a faint sadness in anticipation of the emerging day. She hoped to spend all of it with Clay, but it would be their last. She finished her ablutions by brushing her shoulder-length hair with slow strokes, then with one quick twist and pull she fashioned its thickness into a ponytail. Absentmindedly, she watched Flame chase a frightened chipmunk back into its burrow. Done.

Rorie built a sturdy fire. Sitting on a log nearby, she waited for Clay to appear, keenly alert to the turbulence within herself, matching that of the tumbling surge of the river below. Nervous energy made her hop up again and begin to dig out their breakfast supplies, laying everything out on the shed table. Sitting down once more before the modest fire, she began poking at the burning logs with a stick that had fallen close by her tent. *Maybe some coffee.* Up again, she started their morning coffee brewing, listening for his footsteps on the trail while smelling the rich aroma of coffee made in open spaces. *This should bring him soon. Okay!* She scolded herself. *Enough of this. I need to be in charge of myself here. It's just another regular day . . . maybe we can take a longer hike today. Yes! That's the thing to do. Hike. I've got to settle down.* Just as she finished with her self-imposed monologue, Clay appeared around a turn in the trail.

"I don't know what you might have for breakfast, but I have little to add. I'm sorry."

"You fed all of us yesterday, so it's my turn. My supplies are scarce too, but we can have pancakes today. I brought a mix. I cannot promise what it will taste like, but it's food." She laughed as she saw the surprised look on his face.

"That sounds terrific! What do you need me to do?" Clay was already fussing around the supplies on the table searching for a task he could take on.

They grinned at each other and went to work. Clay stoked the stove while Rorie stirred water into the mix, excited to try out her new skillet. She marveled that social rules virtually evaporate in the wilderness. Here she could be more directly herself: strong, competent, efficient. *I like the "me" that I am in this setting. How can I take this home with me?* Rorie allowed herself to contemplate this new self-awareness. Once breakfast was ready, they sat across from each other, talking about everything and nothing all at once. Rorie rhapsodized about the hot spring, and Clay dwelt in her effusive mood.

"I almost went back to the hot spring this morning for a bath," Clay admitted, then grinning widely, he went on, "but I thought that might not be fair."

"Fair?" she echoed. "Certainly not!" Her grin matched his, as they both giggled at each other. "Do you think we could go up again later today?"

Clay caught the "we" in her sentence and realized he had also been thinking in terms of "we," but he chose not to answer her for the time being. Recognizing that this proposal put both of them in jeopardy, he let it drop for now.

Rorie recognized his hesitation and changed the subject. *Do not want to ruin this day.* "Hey, have you been to the point yet?"

"What point? No, where is it?"

"Where the rivers meet." She nodded her head toward the south. "It's called La Junta. I was thinking. . . ." She paused, unsure of herself again.

"How far is it from here?" Clay read her immediately and mentally began making plans.

"Not far, maybe a mile. I came into the canyon close to there and hiked on up here. Where the rivers come together is a sight to see, if you haven't. The rivers tumble into each other and race off in the same direction. From down here in the canyon you can have a closer view. Those waters are fierce when they join." She realized she was trying too hard to convince him to go with her, so she stopped.

Excitement showed on Clay's face. "Let's do it! Do you know exactly which two rivers come together? I don't have my maps with me. I assume the Rio Grande is one of them." Always the man with the maps, Clay wanted to know the details.

"The Red River and the Rio Grande. I know only because I went to the Visitor's Center when I first arrived. What about taking lunch with us?" She was ready to move into action and began picking up from their recent meal.

In concert, they cleared away the breakfast dishes and discussed the dwindling remnants of food. Clay proposed, "I'll head back to my camp and bring what I have."

Not wanting to waste any more time, Rorie offered, "Clay, I have enough to share for lunch. Let's just use this and go from here—it's closer to the point." Flame noticed all the sudden activity, jumped up from her resting place by the fire pit and began to do her usual dance of anticipation. She twirled around, tail flashing the signal that she was ready for adventure. Clay patted her on the head and turned to the trail.

While hiking, Rorie and Clay spoke little, but the silence marked their comfort and pleasure in walking through the morning stillness together. As they approached La Junta, the trail flattened, and Clay heard for the first time the rumble of the two rivers greeting. He turned to Rorie and threw his hands in the air in delight. He could hear Mellie calling to him from the river: *go on with your life*, as he began to trot toward the thunder of the converging waters.

Rorie caught the shift in Clay's face. She reminded herself once again, *He is married. He is here to remember times with his wife. Let him be. Wonder if I will ever be loved like this?* She was startled by how difficult it was to hold her emotions in check. She had not thought of crossing that boundary until now. She did not want, in any way, to be "the other woman," especially since Clay's wife was seriously ill and they were deeply in love. This idea did not suit her self-image at all!

Clay turned to look at Rorie, her face shining in the sun, her eyes glistening. His mood lightened. "Let's head on down," he said excitedly. Flame had long disappeared toward the water's edge, frolicking in the cold ripples. Clay's feet moved quickly down the path, and Rorie followed suit, hiking boots scuffing against the earth. When Clay stopped to make sure she was behind him, she almost bumped into him. They laughed with loud guffaws and turned to finish the jog to join Flame. Standing on a shore of pebbles and boulders, the two stared into the rushing opaque waters, arms around each other, without awareness that they had assumed such a stance.

Clay soon put down his pack, and then began picking up stones and putting them in his vest pocket.

"Are you planning to drown yourself with those rocks in your pocket?" Rorie teased.

"For later," he mocked her. Then, he moved to sit on a boulder and began removing his boots. When his feet touched the water, he declared, "That stuff's cold." Rorie followed his lead and soon waded into the shallows with screams announcing pained pleasure. Soon they were splashing about in the small bay of a quiet eddy, watching their steps carefully. Clay decided to move to another larger boulder in deeper water. He stepped on a submerged stone slick with invisible moss and fell instantly into the rushing water, creating a splash that bounced onto Rorie. Flame dashed in after him as if invited to join in the romp.

Rorie collapsed in peals of laughter on the tiny beach. "I'm beginning to suspect you might be a touch clumsy," she shouted at him over the sounds of the water.

"Sure seems that way!" he called back at her, wading farther into the river. Climbing onto a massive boulder jutting out of the water at least five feet, he shook his head, flinging water off his hair, and sat down to dry himself in the sun. Brushing through his hair with his hands, he said, "Okay . . . now that we've had a good laugh, let's lie here in the sun awhile. Come on over here and join me . . . and you might try not falling in like I did." Rorie worked her way over to him, and he pulled her up onto the rock. They basked in the brilliant light pouring upon them, like lizards sunbathing.

Eyes closed, both feeling lazy and at peace, they lay in pensive serenity, drenched with sun, dozing in and out for a while, content to be in that moment without any reminders that beyond the canyon walls resided their other lives, demanding and intense. Rorie spoke first, saying one word. "Surrender."

Clay's eyes shot open, "Surrender. Now that's a heavy word. Why did you think of this word at this moment?"

Rorie sighed, "This is probably what is at the bottom of my reluctance to marry Wil. What will I 'surrender' if I accept his proposal? Most women would be so excited, but I feel like I will suffocate. What does that say about me?"

"The act of surrender in love is *not* easy, Rorie. It's necessary, but not easy. So don't beat yourself up. Surrender, when applied to a relationship, sounds like one person must give in to another. And, sometimes it can feel like one person has 'won' some sort of invisible battle, like, 'I give up.' But, surrender inside of love can have another connotation."

Rorie pushed herself up, leaning on her elbow, face propped in her hand, "See those two rivers there, where they come together? As soon as they join, no one can tell the water of one from the other. At that point only one river exists, flowing on to the gulf, and that river should actually have a new name, or a blend of both names. But what happens? I'll tell you what happens! The most powerful river gets to keep the name." Rorie became heated and sat fully upright to talk to the river itself, "The Red River disappears, swallowed by the mighty Rio Grande. She 'surrenders' to the Rio Grande and is never heard from again! That's my image of what marrying Wil could do to me." Tears filled her throat and she choked. Then, turning again to face Clay, she continued, "If you go inside what people call love, it sure looks like a battleground for security to me—no, control—most of the time anyway. . . ." her voice trailed off until the wind drowned out her words.

"There you go preachin' again!"

Rorie looked across the water to the beach where Clay had dropped his pack with their food in it. Flame lay beside the pack as if guarding it, tongue hanging out in a pant from her energetic encounter with the rushing waters. Rorie bounded off the boulder on which they sat and tiptoed through the slippery rocks onto the beach. Clay admired the move. *Many women would have expected me to retrieve that pack. She's so different—a type of independence I'm not really used to, and if I'm honest, don't quite know what to do with.* While he spent the time in reverie, Rorie returned with their food.

As she strode toward him, Clay noticed her body. *She's really striking with that flaming hair and those long legs. I remember when I was so taken with Mellie's body. She was so shapely and petite . . . and that knockout smile of hers. I miss her body. I miss my body being with her body.*

Choking up, Clay began to fiddle with the bandana around his neck as a way to cover his tears. When Rorie made it to the rock, they spread his bandana and poured out their lunch fixings on the rock's surface in front of them. While they munched, Rorie prompted, "All right now, give your brilliant rebuttal to my comments," she demanded with a grin, biting into a dried apricot.

"Not sure I have a rebuttal, exactly. I was going to say that, although Mellie and I had our early struggles with control—who doesn't in a new marriage—we did overcome the, you know, the 'war of love.'"

"I'd like to hear *her* point of view on the matter!" Rorie challenged, wondering if Clay's relationship with Mellie was anything at all as he seemed to portray it. *I suspect it is, because he's obviously in love with his wife. She must be something else, or was before her illness!*

"Me too." Then he thought about how difficult that would be for Mellie now, to say anything, let alone express herself on something as complex and subtle as love and conflict. "What I came to see a little while ago is that even if our marriage was mutual? Reciprocal? Even if it was, it is not that way now."

"Your situation with your wife seems to me to be an exception, impossible, the ordinary rules would not apply." Rorie reached across and touched his arm in sympathy.

Clay raised his head to meet her eyes and replied, "We still claim to love each other. So why wouldn't the rules for love apply?"

"I don't know. I'm getting in over my head here, having never been married, but it seems that caring for someone and taking care of someone are different matters. When someone we love is in crisis, our duty is to take care of them until they recover. The balance shifts in terms of control. Right now you have more control than Mellie because you are the caregiver. She is forced to surrender to you because she needs your care. Seems lop-sided to me. How do you two deal with this, day in and day out?" Rorie's eyes were dark with concern.

Clay cleared his throat. "You've mentioned more than one subject here. First, Mellie is never going to get better. In fact, she is only going to get worse and eventually, she. . . ." Pain crossed his face and filled his eyes. "She will die, and until then she is entirely dependent on me. Which brings me to the second point: she has to 'surrender' every day to me, our daughter, the nurses. *Before she became ill I had no earthly idea how humiliating it would be to become helpless!* Surrender is very much a part of our lives, a part of the vows we took, 'in sickness and in health.'"

"It sounds like falling into a bottomless pit. You have no control!" Rorie slipped into the edge of her fears about marriage.

"Love, I guess, is the parachute," Clay ventured in an effort to use humor to take the conversation away from such heavy emotions for the two of them.

"Yes, but you are still in endless free-fall. Remember, the pit is *bottomless.*"

"Of course, there's death," he sighed. "All lovers lose in the end, Rorie. Loss is part of love. Someone dies or leaves. There's no security or control against this."

Clay stood on the boulder and stretched, slid carefully down from the boulder to land on a flat rock below which was sticking out of the water, pulled the handful of flat stones from his pocket, and began to sail them over the river. Looking up at Rorie still perched on the top of their resting place, said, "Your pit image doesn't do that much for me. I'm not sure that's helpful to the argument." The philosopher in him resurrected.

"But—" she pouted, "but that's how I *feel!* That's why I came here to Wild Rivers. You know, to see whether I can reach beyond my 'pit theory' of marriage. I'm sorry, but it just feels like a huge hole that I would fall into with no way ever to escape."

"You don't go into marriage trying to figure out how to escape," he said wryly.

After a frisky poke at his shoulder with her foot, she responded, "And I'm not sure you're helping all that much!" Rorie began to feel like the conversation was saturating her. Her feelings about Clay were becoming worrisome, and every time he mentioned his wife, she felt inadequate. Shrugging her shoulders as if she could wipe away her feelings, she turned her head away from watching Clay and stared downstream to the convergence. *Is that how I am feeling right now—like some merging is happening to me that I'm not prepared for? That I cannot control? This is not good!*

To cover, she challenged, "Hey, you're the expert on love—solve this for me." She wanted an easy way out of her dilemma for just a quick moment, but she realized that no one could sort out her problem except herself. Before she could speak again, Clay drew his arm back, threw another rock just as he tossed words back at her.

"Love is not about control, Rorie, or escape. If those are your feelings, I think you already have your answer. The real question for you may be: What is it that you wish to escape, and perhaps why?" He paused to let his words sink into her consciousness.

Flouncing about on the rock above him to distract herself from the shock of the question that coursed through her body, Rorie could not respond. *He sounds like Sara. They are both saying the same thing to me.* She waited to see if he would say more. He did.

"About all I can offer is that love keeps trying to bring balance or harmony with the beloved, not control or escape, even if balance is reached only rarely and even if we cannot maintain harmony all the time. That's still what love is about. It has to do with taking someone as seriously as I take myself, rather than running from them or trying to manage them. This type of love is truly tough work that utilizes every fiber of our being to participate." Pausing to strike himself on the forehead, Clay realized he wanted this insight for his manuscript. "Do I make sense to you with that thought?"

"Yes, well, maybe—I think so. This idea may be contradicting my own feelings about love and commitment because I haven't met the person yet that I'm willing to enter those waters with." Laughing at herself, she pointed at the river and the metaphor that had sprung from her mouth. Hopping down from the larger boulder to join him below, she pressed Clay, "Where does this leave our discussion of surrender? We dropped this along the way and I find the idea a block for me."

"All I can say for now is that I've had to learn to surrender my own expectations for how life will unfold. My best teacher is Mellie. She spends most of her days in surrender, but she does it in a way that is not weak or pitiful. She's not a martyr." He recounted Mellie's story of not being ready to die. Rorie listened quietly. *She's some kinda woman. No wonder Clay is so in love with her.*

The next couple of hours vanished, with their conversation, napping, and chatter about the scenery. They were easy together, these two.

A raven floated above them over the water, as Rorie squinted into the sun. "My arms are getting burned. We'd better move," she suggested. She gathered up their picnic remains and stuffed them into Clay's pack. Tossing him the pack, she slid back off their perch into the stream. Bobbing around the rocks, they began their trek back into the shallows, which rested in the shade of a huge ponderosa tree.

Rorie was not yet ready for their conversation to end. "It still takes trust, perhaps more than I am capable of, to hand someone my life forever and not fear being consumed by them." Wobbling over one wet rock onto another forced her to speak in phrases as she held her breath, hoping not to fall back into the river.

Clay was balanced ahead of her on the trail of rocks guiding them out of the river onto shore. His voice was determined as he said, "Love, the kind I want to write about and that I believe in, is the only antidote to that feeling of fear. That's why the old cliché, 'Love conquers fear' floats around on posters. And you have certainly introduced one of the key words in discussing love: trust. This could take us the rest of the year to hash out." Clay turned around and grabbed her shoulder as if he was going to push her off a rock on which she was precariously balanced. "How much do you trust me right now?" Her squeal made him laugh. Letting go of her shoulder, he grabbed her arm to steady her.

"I got your point—you don't have to push me into the water to prove it!" Rorie tottered, trying to rebalance herself on the wet stones so she could move forward and follow him.

Clay had been staring into the water as they hobbled over the rocks to come closer to the shore. Wading into the shallows, he reached down, probed the bottom briefly and rose with a small white object in his hand. He examined it intensely before turning to Rorie, "Would you look at that? A perfect, round, white marble, milled by the water. Astonishing."

Rorie waded over to him and stared at the oversized pearl of a rock on his palm. It glistened in the sunlight as Clay timidly offered it to her. She rolled the stone around in her hand, massaging her fingers with it.

"It's for you, Rorie," Clay spoke softly, " a memory stone."

"And what is the memory?"

"Wild Rivers—being here today." He wanted to add, "together," but didn't, chiding himself for his reticence.

"Thank you," she said simply, pocketing the sacred object in her vest. *He has no idea how much I will cherish this stone.*

A rumble of thunder turned their faces upward, "Ah, yes, the predictable afternoon shower," Rorie announced, "It never seems to miss. Think we can make it back?"

"I doubt it," Clay surmised, squinting at the panorama of piercing blue sky being swallowed up by a boiling dark intrusion of clouds.

Half a mile up the trail those large formidable drops started falling like pellets out of the sky, stinging them on their arms. "Uh, oh," shouted Clay, "New Mexico is doing its rain dance for us. Better run for it." Flame turned on the speed and charged up the trail, as if on cue. The couple ran about a hundred yards before locating the first camp shed. The rain was cold, showing no mercy in its intention to soak them through and through. Soon sheets of rain fell upon the metal roof, pounding away. Drenched, and cold, they breathed in gulps and abandoned themselves to fits of glee.

Rorie finally managed to ask, "Is history repeating itself here? Are we supposed to surrender to this deluge?" She grinned at him playfully, brushing her hands through her hair to loosen some of the drops trapped there.

"For sure!" Clay agreed, and without another word or even gesture of complicity, he swept her against him. They folded into an embrace, eyes locked, bodies melded, lips joined. The torrent swaddled them in a cocoon of reverberating sound and fury. The clatter on the roof proved no distraction to the fury of their immediacy.

When the rush of the rain dissipated into drizzle, and then into occasional rebellious drops from the trees, Rorie and Clay stood apart, ever so slightly. They stared into each other. No words. No movement. Stillness, together. Clutching hands, the two solitary people were no longer strangers; they converged into a pair for the next hours to come. Exiting the shed, they continued hiking toward Little Arsenic. Flame darted around them, delighted to be out from under the noisy clatter of the tin roof.

At her tent, Rorie excused herself and went into it. Clay ambled toward the river, staring in wonderment and repeating, *Go on with your life.* Clay sighed deep into his chest. *My dear Mellie . . . is this what you meant? Is this 'going on?' How can it be?* Yet, he knew with certainty that he was caught in an encounter from which he intended no retreat, though nothing felt connected to the rest of his life outside this rift in the earth.

When Clay saw Rorie's head emerge from the tent, he went toward her. She stood and reached back for her pack and handed him her sleeping bag. Her gesture announced more than Clay fully comprehended at the moment, but he joined, heart pounding.

The spell woven in the shed by the river subsided, but only barely, as they hiked toward Big Arsenic. Flame, knowing where the itinerant troop was headed, greeted them as they arrived. She was hungry and began to nudge her owner's knee, sending a clear message about her needs. Rorie deliberately and boldly threw her sleeping bag into Clay's tent. Then she set out Flame's bowl and fed her.

Clay started an early evening fire, while Rorie set out to prepare their meal, purchased as a celebration of sorts for her final night of camping. *What a surprise, to be sharing this meal with someone like*

Clay. I never dreamed that would happen! While they were each engrossed in their various tasks, Rorie spoke up, "I can hardly endure the thought of leaving tomorrow."

Unexpectedly, Clay ventured, "Let's not," turning to look at Rorie, wondering what her reaction might be to his bold suggestion. For a brief moment Clay imagined himself escaping his Kansas life.

Rorie posed, "Now, are you the one who's considering escaping?"

Suddenly ashamed, Clay replied, "Do you think we are escaping? I guess my idea does suggest that, doesn't it? Some things I cannot, at least I'm not willing to escape."

Bluntly, Rorie made the invisible, visible, "Like Mellie, I imagine."

"Exactly. When I fantasize about everything with her being different, having our former life back, I end up feeling worse." Clay stared into the fire, then sipped his drink, grateful Rorie had brought a small bottle of red wine with her. "This tastes so good out here in the wild. Thanks for bringing it even though you had no intention of sharing it with me, or anyone." His smile was tender, exposing his pleasure, in the wine and in her.

Clay stood, walked around to the camp table where the gourmet camp meal was ready to eat. Rorie had surprised him with her dinner, purchased to celebrate her final night on her self-imposed pilgrimage. Clearing his throat, Clay bursts out, "I have an idea. We both had planned to leave tomorrow, but what if we drove into Taos in the morning and stayed the night before heading back to the flatlands?"

Fully understanding his proposal, though it was not explicitly spelled out, Rorie paused—*Does this mean anything? What is this we're planning? Why am I excited about that idea and at the same time frightened of it?*

"Okay. Yes. That's a wonderful idea. I'll need to call Sara and let her know, but I'm game if you are." On the inside she was trembling. *I'm far more open to this plan than I should be. What am I thinking?*

"Who's Sara?"

"Oh, she's my closest friend—more like a mother really. I just need to let her know I'll be coming home a day later than planned."

They both knew they were trying to postpone the inevitable end to their interlude in this idyllic gorge. Even so, the proposal allowed them to return more fully to the present. They continued dining, enjoying each other's company, laughing at their banter as the wine took hold and relaxed the sexual tension between them. Clay observed that it would soon be dark. He lit his lantern and set it on the table between them, so they could clear away the dishes. Flame had settled once again near Rorie's feet, snoring lightly as the day's adventures caught up with her.

"Let's go up soon. Will you be ready?" Rorie jumped to her feet, rushed over to Clay's tent to grab her towel and hairbrush. Instructing Flame to lie down by Clay's tent, Rorie stood ready for him to guide them to their evening's destination.

The last gasp of daylight surrendered to the night skies as they reached the entrance to the spring. Warm moist air rushed from the opening to greet them. A burst of sound threw them into momentary panic, until they saw the silhouette of a deer prancing in leaps toward the river. "We must have startled him," Rorie whispered.

Clay crouched inside the warm grotto, stabilized his lantern and reached for Rorie, pulling her up to him. Startling her, he kissed her lightly on the lips and then bent over, making his way further back into the den, where he lit a candle and set it on the wisp of a ledge sticking out from the wall. He turned off the lamp. A comfortable glow filled the space for their ritual of undressing. Once Clay was naked, he stepped gingerly into the steaming water coming from the nether reaches of the earth. Rorie, with none of the discomfort she had felt the night before, undressed and was in the water moments after Clay. They sat facing each other.

Settling into the soothing luxury of a steaming bath, Rorie looked at Clay as if for the first time with a measure of surprise and said lightheartedly, "Why are we so fortunate as to be here in this hot spring? Can you believe this?"

He nodded his agreement, splashed water on his face and leaned back against the wall of the pool, fully relaxed, fully present. "There are no words for this."

Completely changing the subject, and ready to plunge into their dialogue again, Rorie posed her question, "What is the role of spontaneity in love, Clay?" She was genuinely beginning to feel that their connection was completely unscripted and almost wild. She felt safe enough with Clay to say what was really on her mind.

Her question caught him off guard. "Well, these three days have been pure improvisation for me, I can tell you. I never expected to run into one of my former students in this canyon or to meet you. This cave is an utter surprise, as well as our sitting here in it tonight. I don't think I'm clever enough to plan such occasions. Are you?" Then he realized he did not offer Rorie a particularly adequate response to her question. "Let me go at that one again. To be spontaneous in love, at least for me, is to be open, expectant, but without expectation. You allow emotion to be what it will be without contrivance or manipulation. To keep surprise in a love relationship is to keep the connection alive because it means we have not 'programmed' our beloved or ourselves." He stopped here to let his words sink in for both of them, resting his hand on her leg while she massaged his feet under the water. "Do you need me to say more?"

"Not at all. I need more time to consider what you have said, that's all. But I do wonder how our attraction to each other relates to your writing? Is this a spontaneous experience—right here, right now between us in this tub?" She looked at him quizzically.

"Are you asking if our attraction—good way to put it—is a kind of love?"

Rorie leaned forward, her breasts rising out of the water, giving her the look of a mermaid. "Or is it just about sex? What does sex have to do with love in your way of thinking? How are you going to write about that?" Her expression challenged him to face her thoughts.

"Maybe sex is a kind of love," Clay shot back at her without hesitation. "You know, the basic expression of it. I read a writer once who said that every word in Hebrew for love can be traced back to sexual love. Since I don't know Hebrew, I don't know if this is accurate, but the idea interests me."

Hesitantly, Rorie sat back again and let her eyes fall on him in a fresh, hungry way. An ache began between her legs, so that she squirmed, afraid he could read her expression. "What are we doing here, Clay? We both have other lives, and we *will* return to them soon. But tonight, I want to be with you, and you want to be with me . . . at least that's the feeling I'm receiving from you. So what's going on between us?"

Clay shifted as if to find a better posture for speaking on such a tricky subject. "Well, you're more than accurate. I'm sexually drawn to you. No doubt about that, but I didn't really face that fact until we were running in the rain together today."

"Really?" Rorie was stunned that it had taken him that long to realize feelings that she had owned up to in her own mind when she first saw him naked, taking a bath by the river.

"Keep in mind that I love my wife. I *love* Mellie. But I haven't had sex in too many years now. I've been preoccupied with her illness and decline. Sex had to be put on a shelf, out of sight, for both of us. I had to acknowledge that this part of our marriage was over. At this moment I'm learning that I am a normal man, capable of sexual feelings, and as ready as you are for an encounter between us."

"So for you this attraction is sexual only? Where is love in all of this for you?" She was confused herself at her own attraction to Clay, and what all of this had to do with Wil and herself and love. "You are writing a book on love. How do you plan to connect love to sex?"

"You are right! And you are helping me realize that the reason I hadn't faced the sex question is that my current reality doesn't include sex. As I said, I had put that aspect of my life on a back burner and have been 'in my head,' so to speak, about the topic of love. But Rorie, you are helping me to see that I cannot engage this project without discussing sex and love, because my feelings for you are *not* all about sex. These three days with you have been amazing and have included emotions long buried."

"But doesn't sex make love personal?" Rorie began to shift positions enough to crawl over to the edge of the pool closer to Clay. "Pardon me for splashing you but this water's too hot! I need to cool down."

"I think it might be the other way around, love urges sex to be personal. Don't you agree?" Clay was pondering hard now, mentally trying to keep up with her thought processes.

"I like that idea. Yeah, you may be right. But this leaves the door open for just sex by itself without love, just a type of release and enjoyment two people can have in each other. That seems healthier to me," she replied, thinking of her sexual relationship with Wil. *We have sex, but I'm definitely not in love with him. I have never felt about Wil the way I feel about this man sitting in this cave with me tonight. Never!*

Clay was riveted by the conversation at this point, "Sex can open the door to love, wouldn't you say? It's not automatic, but it can happen that way, and more often than not, probably does."

She nodded, wriggling her toes in the water close to his legs.

Clay spoke again, "Know what?"

"What?"

"I cannot ever remember talking about sex like this with another woman, at least not *before* sex."

Rorie blushed and was glad he could not see her face in the shadows of the cave. "In my experience men don't talk to women about sex. They talk to other men about it."

"There may be truth to that, but why do you think that is?" Clay was intrigued with where this was going.

Rorie leaned forward toward the pool, steam rising across her face and making her sweat. "Because they are terrified."

"Of what?"

"Perhaps of the relation between love and sex, or rejection . . . or maybe love and loss, as you put it. I don't know . . . this is your field, not mine. Are you trying to get me to do your work for you?" She teased and rubbed his leg with her foot. The touch sent an electric shock through her body. Moving slowly and sensuously, she slid back into the shallow water and kissed Clay fully on the mouth. She straddled him, and they were locked into one being. Too many years of abstinence melted into ecstasy for Clay. Rorie's knees buried into the sandy grit. Rocks made their movements awkward. But passion prevailed. One word pierced Clay's intensity: *Plunge!*

Rorie, her head thrown back and crushing Clay's face into her breasts, screamed from the well of her being. And again! And again! They rocked together in the water creating waves in the pool and in their bodies. Clay came inside her with a violent jolt and then broke into a hearty sweat, laughing and crying at the same time. Their bodies dripped from the steam and sweat that rolled off them. Rorie hugged him fiercely, declaring inwardly that she wished never to let him go. Her body trembled with pleasure. Slowly they pulled apart enough to look at each other's faces before they melded into a long, savory kiss.

"Ah, my knees!" she complained, as she tumbled into the water beside Clay. They laughed from their guts, hugging, kissing and stroking each other for several more minutes. "This water is boiling me alive! Any alternatives?" Rorie was gasping for air. Before she could inch back to her rock perch, Clay proposed they put on their shoes and run for the falls by the river to cool down.

They raced to see who could don shoes first and chased each other through the cool night air. Their bodies gleamed vaguely in the light of a partial moon—like two kids dashing with abandon toward a skinny dip, blundering their way through sex into love.

The falling stream greeted them with a rush of prickly cold water. They frolicked under the spouts and sprays until the heat of their bodies regained a normality, and they became cold. Rorie sat on the bathing stone where she had first seen Clay's bare body, and she delighted to watch him under the cascade of silver water bouncing around him. Flame had joined them in their play and was splashing through the water in her own private game.

When Clay emerged from the waterfall, Rorie had begun to shiver. He ran uphill to his tent to bring her a light blanket he always strapped onto the bottom of his pack. As soon as she was wrapped up inside of it, he tore off back to the hot spring to retrieve their clothing. "I'll run up and get our clothes. Be back soon. Don't freeze while I'm gone." She could see his body recede from her. *He's rather beautiful for a man,* she mused. *Sure have enjoyed this time with him. Wonder if I'll ever again be the same woman who came into this canyon?*

I doubt it. The sliver of moonlight that shone on her face highlighted her eyes in the darkness.

I think I now better understand love and being "in love" with someone in a way I never fathomed before tonight. And after this time with Clay, I know that I am not in love with Wil. I must not confuse sex with love, but somehow, it's all the same thing with Clay. This is the most erotic yet loving experience I have ever known. She recognized that the warp and woof of sex and love formed a tapestry for her tonight. She knew with impeccable clarity that this moment and this man would not fade away to oblivion for her. Clay had imprinted Rorie, in a way neither of them would ever fully understand or forget.

Inside the cave, Clay blew out their candle and put on his flashlight. *I'll leave this for future lovers. I am astonished at what just happened with Rorie. We are both being drawn into something larger than ourselves. The consequences could be devastating for both of us, yet we seem not to care. What is that feeling? It's so common in love and is the key ingredient in loss.*

Retrieving the lantern and their clothing, he skittered back down the hill to find Rorie. When he reached her, she stood, dropped the blanket and let him see her body in the moonlight. He dropped all their clothing. They met in an embrace that bound them together for longer than either of them could calculate. Even in the crisp night air, the warmth of their bodies allowed them to stand enmeshed, until any spectator would have thought them a frozen statue of lovers.

Back in Clay's tent, one sleeping bag served as a bed, and the other as their cover. Flame whimpered to gain entrance, but at Rorie's prompting, curled outside the tent close to the flap. Neither Rorie nor Clay really slept thoroughly that night. Between surges into the unbound reaches of bodily bliss, they spoke and stroked and touched lips in the dreaming innocence of the world's amniotic fluids. Surrender whispered between them, mutual. They became twins in a new womb, where they enjoyed the foretaste of birthings yet to come for each of them. Below them the river roared as they did, relentlessly meeting, greeting and entwining in their own roar of the heart. In the deep of the night Clay realized the full force of his release, this oasis after such an expansive desert of abstinence. He wept. Rorie consoled him with stroking and kisses. They held each other as if their very lives depended on it. Love and loss swept over them in the heat of their passion, both fully knowing the beginning and ending of love in one night.

Once in the night, Clay saw Mellie. She smiled and nodded, with tears in her eyes. Her sorrow choked him, yet her smile freed him.

Back in Kansas, Mellie lay restless, not sleeping. Cassandra was concerned and tried to find out what her mother needed. When Mellie's face streaked with tears, Cassandra panicked and decided to call the doctor. Mellie was able, with urgency in her eyes, to dissuade her daughter. Using her alphabet board, Cassandra deciphered that her mother was all right, only thinking of Clay and how happy she was for him. Cassandra could not make sense of this sudden, tearful joy, and she pondered over her mother's last labored statement: *He's alive, on his way. I am free.* Mellie finally rested.

With the first utterings of dawn Rorie and Clay dropped, entangled, into the borderland of a fatigued sleep, clinging to each other. Their night of convergence would pass with the coming light of day.

Gone

FLAME PAWED AT THE TENT FLAP TO AWAKEN RORIE, WHO SAT up groggily and muttered, "Darn it, Flame, couldn't you at least wait until the sun is up?" Leaning over Clay to unzip the tent, Rorie peeked out at her dog, who looked at her with expectant eyes. The sun was beginning its morning creep around the edges of the canyon rim. "Down, Flame. Sit back down," she lovingly scolded her dog, rolling back under the warm down bedroll cover.

Clay rotated toward Rorie, encircling her bare waist with his arm. "What's with Flame?" he asked in a thick voice.

"Oh, she's hungry. And I totally forgot to bring her food with me for the morning," Rorie muttered, her head buried under the cover. "Still sleepy," she mumbled as she turned her back to spoon with Clay's curled form.

Whispering in her ear, Clay stroked her body, "Why don't we hike down to your tent and feed her?" Trying to stir himself awake, he fell back down and answered himself, "Later, maybe."

When Rorie wriggled to rise again, he leaned over and kissed her lightly on the lips, only to utter, "You taste good. Let's do that again." This time he kissed her soundly, long and deep.

"Before I have brushed my teeth? You are a bit on the crazy side, aren't you professor?" She teased him and snuggled closer to him. This roused Clay once again, and this time he was more insistent with her, craving her touch and his body against her body. They made love with a fury, both recognizing the impending coming apart that lay ahead. Rorie had never known such passion, had never felt this side of herself awakened. His intensity both frightened her and thrilled her. Her physical satisfaction at their union came in waves, engulfing her entire body. Her fingers dug into the bedroll as she muffled a deep cry from within. Touch became electric between them as they stroked and pulled at each other. Their eyes locked, his blue, hers green, seeking a fierce connection so as to memorize the moment. Clay, allowing the past months to fade away, sinking into Rorie with renewed vigor, cried out when he came inside her with a bellow like a wounded beast. He dropped onto her, heavy, panting, and whole again.

For a long time, they lay together, holding, caressing, no words flowing . . . just a comfortable silence between them, hearts beating in rhythm. Slowly, Clay slid onto his side, so he could see Rorie's eyes and gaze into them. She smiled at him, touching his lips, ears and hair, then simply went limp in his arms. *Here is where I could live for the rest of my life. How sad that this cannot happen.* Rousing to sit up again, Rorie pushed gently at Clay to signal they needed to leave the tent. "Hey, it's time to get this day rollin'," she teased. He acquiesced to her suggestion without speaking and moved so that she could begin putting on her clothes.

Sliding into their wrinkled hiking clothes, hair askew and bodies stiff from having hugged the ground all night, the new lovers giggled as they bumped into each other during the dressing ritual. Crawling from the tent, they embraced tightly, exchanging light kisses. Then Rorie began gathering up her things, saying, "I'm taking this gear back to my camp so when it's time to pack up, everything will be ready. That plan okay with you?" Clay nodded his agreement, turning to locate the coffee pot and start a fire.

She methodically stuffed her bedding and clothing into her pack, then turned toward the trail with Flame bounding ahead of her, food in the forecast. Rorie's last words to Clay were, "I need to feed Flame. You rustle coffee and pull out whatever you have to eat. I'll bring back the last of my food for us. It might be an interesting breakfast at this point. See you in a bit." She waved airily over her shoulder and faded from view. Clay stood watching his canyon lover and her dog evaporate into a wedge of trees. *She has disappeared too soon,* he whispered to himself.

After standing with a paralyzed gaze toward the point where he had last seen Rorie's scrambled, flaming hair wafting as she walked,

Clay brought himself to the current moment and trudged over to the table to start the stove. Lighting the tiny circle of fire on the camp stove, he placed the pot of water atop it and soon had a mug of coffee in hand. For the next half-hour he stood, then sat and finally walked down toward the river. *Rorie,* he repeated to himself several times, and marveled at the magnificence of the past few days. She had come to him as an emissary from a region of fresh anticipation from which he had long been banished. She introduced him to "possibility" through her presence. *This whole situation is the most real and at the same time the most surreal occurrence I've ever experienced. I couldn't have planned even a minute of it.*

Abruptly looking up to see the angle of the sun that had planted itself squarely in the stunning blue sky, Clay's awareness rose enough to realize that Rorie had been gone for perhaps an hour and a half. He grew restive. Reheating the pot of coffee to have it ready when she returned, he gave himself a lecture about patience. Time passed. Still no sign of her. Sighing, he decided to go ahead and break camp, but deliberately wasted time folding his tent, stuffing his sleeping bag and pad, and placing everything strategically in the pack. Throughout the process he halted repeatedly to search the terrain for Rorie and Flame.

When Clay finished packing everything except his cooking gear, he wandered down the trail several yards and sat on the trunk of a fallen white fir, a slain giant in repose. He became a sentinel: waiting, watching, wondering. Surmising that she must have been gone for more than two hours, Clay reviewed their agreement for possible misunderstandings, even walking to a high point on the trail to see if he might spot her. Finally, the wait got the best of him, so he decided to load up and hike out to meet her. Within the next half hour, he left his camp without so much as a wave.

When Rorie's campsite at Little Arsenic came into view, Clay saw only the shed. He could not find either Rorie or Flame, and then he noticed that her gray and blue tent was gone. *Ah, she must have taken time to pack her gear, but why did it take so long?* Now, he was completely puzzled. *And where is she now . . . no Flame—what's up?* He started walking faster to reach the site only to find it abandoned. Not a trace of her remained. In a daze he rushed back to the trail and scanned to the south. Leaning his pack against a tree, he scurried toward the river to see if she was taking one last dip before her time in this stunning gorge passed. He scrutinized the vista for any sign of her. Nothing. Rorie had vanished. She was gone.

Clay walked back to her campsite, despondent, and a bit worried. He could not fathom why she left or why he had not met her on the trail. He entered the camp shed to sit on the table bench and regroup his thoughts. As he sat down he spied a small white object in the middle of the table. It was the marble stone he had taken from the river and offered to her as a token between them. Beneath it lay a scrap of paper. He picked up the stone in one hand and the paper in the other. The stone felt warm in his palm, as if her fingers had only recently been on it. Dreading what he would find written, he looked at the bit of paper. He barely made out the words scrawled on it: *Perfection never lasts, except in memory.* He convulsed into tears. He knew what she meant and that she was right. All he could muster was a muffled plea, *But one more day!*

For the flit of an instant, Clay considered chasing after Rorie, but he knew that would be, if not futile, terribly unfair. Her breaking away bore the weight of finality. He composed himself with consoling thoughts. *Whatever we had, whatever it was is too good to spoil. She has her life, and she must go on.* Clay's own life outside the idyll of the gorge surged to his attention. *Mellie!* He called her name with a jumble of guilt and longing that he could not continue to suppress.

The faces of Mellie and Rorie merged and separated and merged again in Clay's mind, but they never competed. Clay's eyes wandered to the scenes outside the shed, pulling him to inch from the shed into the natural world of the canyon. The sky spanned the horizon in unsurpassed radiance. Winds stirred through the swaying trees to comfort him in the growing warmth of the day. The first muted signs of autumn played in the change of the breezes. Most of all, the ceaseless play of the Rio Grande below him and his memory of Rorie in the eddies of its flow assured him that *all goes on.* Life is in process of a vibrant *going on. So this is my lesson: learning to move on. Mellie was right, after all. So be it.*

Returning to his pack and swinging it onto his back, Clay hiked toward the trail that would take him to the rim of the gorge, the La Junta trail. His mood swung between melancholy at leaving and Rorie's departure, and euphoria at having found something yet to be named that allowed him to imagine a future stronger than death. As the trail ascended, he made periodic checks of the receding canyon floor and the narrowing, now silent river. About halfway up, he perched on an overlook where the trail down toward La Junta came into view. He strained to see the point where the rivers met. *Those wild rivers never stop churning, like my mind and heart.*

By early afternoon, when the sun beamed down on his head, he reached the rim and began walking the long hike from La Junta to the Big Arsenic campground where his motorcycle was parked. He saw it sitting under the pine tree like a faithful horse awaiting its rider. The only marks were splotches where raindrops disturbed the thin coating of dust on the seat, the gas tank and the windshield. The seat had a smudge across it as if someone had sat on it. The camper truck that had been parked nearby when he entered the canyon, sat in the same place. Clay detected no tire marks suggested by any movement. He wondered whether it might be abandoned. *Abandoned! That's how I feel,* but he censored that invitation to self-pity.

He sat down at the camp table, his journal lying before him, staring at it and wondering where and whether he could even start to record what he now knew. After wrestling with himself whether to call home, he decided to wait until the next morning. Clay forced himself to open the journal and find the first blank page. He took a pen from his vest pocket and wrote, *These last four days have been. . . .*

He scratched through the sentence fragment. Not dramatic enough. Although he was writing to himself and no one else would ever likely read it, he wanted to write as though shouting to the world. He started again:

I love two women! They are Mellie, companion in suffering, beloved in life, and Rorie, the bearer of elusive passion, a reminder that the future exists. With Mellie I find my grounding. With Rorie I soar. Four days ago, I loved only one woman and could not even imagine loving another. Today I write here on this ridge above the Rio Grande gorge in honor and pledge to both of these souls. How can this be?

Before I left on this trip—no, this pilgrimage, if one can go on a pilgrimage without knowing until afterward—Mellie said that I must go on with my life, but I had no idea what she meant. Perhaps she didn't either, but she did want me to stay alive and not move so close to her dying. I left Kansas not knowing what lay ahead and entered shamanic depths here in the Wild Rivers canyon only to discover another living, loving soul. Or did she find me? Or did we find each other? Truthfully, we were both on a search. This interplay of love and loss is as confusing as anything I've ever faced before. I feel this exotic encounter is somehow more than an accident or coincidence. It was at least a synchronicity, if not destiny, although I'm not supposed to countenance such possibilities in my field of study.

Rorie, even if she has disappeared, is still so palpable. I can almost grasp her, even now. She is love embodied, not an idea of love, but its presence. The enigma—yes, that's it—of her simply coming up the bank from the river and appearing before me is enough of a riddle, but I could not see any of its future. I thought I was immune, due to my love for and commitment to Mellie. But Mellie is leaving me too, and I must prepare for this unspeakable reality.

I do know my experience with Rorie holds a deep secret about the mystifying fact and force of love. Love only grows more expansive when allowed. Yet, love at this ethereal level must be handled carefully, otherwise it becomes an excuse for shallowness and betrayal. Either I betrayed both women or neither of them. All I can speak to is that I love them both with all the devotion I can muster. How is this possible? If I can penetrate this truth, a door will open. I do wish we could have explored some of this together. Mellie somehow knows, but is unable to speak.

"How ya doin' there?" The sound of a human voice made the pen leap from his hand. Clay looked up to see an aging man standing before him in baggy khaki pants, a faded denim shirt, a slouched western hat and a full faded beard. "Didn't mean to startle ya. Just thought I'd say a friendly hello. I'm over at that camper there. You must a been down in the canyon for a while."

"Yep. I camped down there for a few days."

"I knew you was in there 'cause I kept watch on your motor scooter."

Clay grinned. "Thanks!"

"I see you're stayin' the night? Wanna eat over there with me? Heck, I almost never have anybody to eat with."

"How long have you been out here?" Curiosity about the old man began to cover Clay's face, even though at first he was irritated at the interruption of his mental work.

"Oh, close t' a month now, I reckon. I been waitin' for the ranger to come an' run me off, but this time o' year they don't seem ta mind. Nobody much comes 'round, 'cept for some day folk pokin' about and takin' pitchers."

"Where do you live?" Clay grilled him further, wondering when the man would find him too nosy.

"Right there," the old man said, pointing to the worn truck. "Nobody can tell me what ta do when I live like this. I been doin' it since my wife died last year, just ta hide out from th' loneliness of it. She was a good woman. Puttin' up with me's enough to prove that." He looked over the lip of the bluff into the canyon, where the Rio Grande became a silver string unwinding from an invisible spool, and nodded, "Man, I envy you."

"Why?" Clay queried.

"Cuz you can go down in there, stomp around and see everything. I can't make it down and back any more. My bad back'd give out on me if I started in. How was it?" His eyes were dark pools of loneliness.

Clay wondered how to dismiss this incarnate sadness in order to be alone with his thoughts and the journal, but he recognized that his intruder was at least a fellow traveler in the province of love and loss. *These strange encounters keep happening to me in this place. Maybe I better respect this and listen up.* Closing the journal, he answered, "It was the finest four days I ever spent camping." His eyes had a faraway look in them, as the stranger faded before him.

"My, my. That's sayin' something,' unless you never been campin' before," he responded with a crackling chuckle.

Clay came back to the moment with a jump. "No, I've been camping plenty, but I needed this one. And Wild Rivers was the right place, I can tell you."

By this time the man with the camper was emboldened enough to advance to Clay's table. Clay invited him to sit. "I'm Bedford Randall," he offered as he thrust a gnarled, vein-laced hand toward Clay.

"Uh, Clay . . . Clayton Jacobs." They shook.

The sage continued, "Most everybody calls me 'Spark.' I always hated my name . . . Bedford. Who would name a kid that anyway? Belonged to my mother's grandfather, way back."

"Spark. That's a good one!" Clay's eyebrows raised in surprise at the name of his new acquaintance.

"Emma always called me 'Sparky.' She was the only one to do that, and I sure miss bein' called that sometimes."

"Who's Emma?" Clay guessed who she was but wanted to hear Spark's explanation.

"My wife," he replied, but suspected Clay had another agenda. "Your wife die on you too? That why you're in here alone?"

"Not exactly. She's been sick a long, long time, and someday she will . . ." his voice gave out.

Spark jumped on Clay's response, "Not quite the same, I'd say. Emma just left me all of a sudden. Just up and left. I never had a chance ta tell her anythin'."

"Yeah, that's different, but I don't know which is worse." Clay's interest in the conversation began to rise. *This could be helpful . . . wonder where he is going with this?*

"Both seem worse to me. It took all I had ta put up with her dyin' like that. I mean th' way she went." Spark snapped his fingers to illustrate. "Heck-fire, I been mad about it ever since."

Even more confidently, he continued, "I'll tell you somethin' I ain't never told nobody." He looked around as though expecting to find someone eavesdropping on them. "The day she died, we had breakfast like we always did, and I left ta tend th' stock with her cleanin' up th' kitchen. When I come back to th' house, she was lyin' in a lump on th' floor. I didn't have th' least notion what was wrong with her. So I didn't know what t' do. I just picked her right up. I been pickin' up hundred-pound bags of feed since I was a kid, and I laid her easy on our bed. She was alive 'cause I could hear her groanin.' I kept saying to her, "You hang on now, Emma. I'm right here. You hang on—I'll get some help." Spark wiped his mouth where spit had gathered in his beard and raced on.

"I called th' emergency number. When an amb'lance came, they commenced ta work on 'er. I was fit to be tied. So I just went to th' barn and screamed at God to help her. I kinda went crazy for a spell, then I thought about Emma in th' house, so I ran back ta see what was goin' on.

Clay suspected Spark had been sent by some cosmic force to make him feel as bad as he could possibly feel. Mellie lay before him, quiet and placid. Dwindling. He regretted with a sting of guilt, or was it shame, that he had postponed calling her until the next day. He regretted ever leaving her alone—like he felt right now. But then there was Rorie, the days spent with her that healed his broken places. "You must miss her terribly," Clay commented lamely in an effort to regain focus.

"Right! Right! And I ain't ashamed of it. Still, her leavin' me like that made me mad an' sad. I'm still mad—and sad. I been drivin' 'round th' country like I wuz runnin' away from a burning fire." Spark shook his head from side to side, trying to clear his thoughts. He looked away in the direction of infinity, as if he might catch a glimpse of Emma. "Then I start feelin' bad about feelin' mad at her for dyin' like she did, and I try to find somethin' that lets me feel glad again. But it only lasts a little bit. Then I start all over again. I'm in some kinda crazy circle. Life's a heavy weight, but death is worse!" Spark said nothing more for some time. Then he looked at Clay, and the gloomy cloud on his face disappeared. "Well, you sure didn't come up here ta listen to an old codger carry on. Want some food?" It ain't all that much, but it'll keep you from havin' to cook." He stood and beckoned Clay to follow him. "It's in the pot. I eat early, farm hours, ya know. Is it too soon for ya?"

Clay jumped to his feet, stretched out his tired, cramping legs, and moved to put away his things. "No, sounds just right. I don't have all that much food left anyway, and come to think of it, I've not eaten much today. What's cookin'?"

"No sense starvin' yo'self now. Stew, my homegrown stew."

Shortly they were eating a tasty but unidentifiable stew. "Want some bread?" Spark offered. "It's a bit stale, but if you dunk it in your stew there, you won't know the diff'rence." He guffawed. Clay took two pieces and laid them beside his steaming bowl. Glancing up at the sun's afternoon tilt, he wondered where Rorie might be at this point. *This time yesterday with her we were. . . .* He jerked his attention back to Spark slurping his stew. For the briefest interlude, Clay knew consolation in this human encounter, one man to another, both in mourning, both sating their hunger.

After their meal, Spark resumed his questioning of Clay, "Hey, you say your wife's sick? What's wrong with her?"

"Yes, yes she is," Clay evaded the question about Mellie, feeling it was too complicated to explain in his current mood.

"Long time now?"

"Almost four years." Clay opened the candy bar Spark had tossed him and crunched down on it.

"Like you said, I don't know what's worse, sudden death or lingerin'.

Clay sighed, realizing this curious old rancher was far more intelligent than Clay was giving him credit for. His questioning was relentless and pertinent. *Might as well plunge in there with him.* "Well, it seems to me that one way leaves *you* suffering and the other way, you suffer together."

"Not much of a choice, I'd say. I guess I did have the good luck if I can say that, to not watch Emma suffer for long."

"That's what I mean when I said 'we're suffering together.' Of course, my wife has by far the worst of it, but to watch her go through this is another kind of suffering; it's wrenching." He did not want to tell Spark that the reason he was in the canyon was from the fatigue he had experienced from watching Mellie suffer.

Spark turned his chair sideways to the table to lay his elbow and arm across it and asked with concentration, as if solving his own problem: "All right. Let's give it a vote. Which d'ya think's worse, sudden or slow death? I mean, if it's somebody ya care about?"

"Huh. I don't like the choice, Spark, but after watching my wife, Mellie, suffer for so long, I'm tempted to vote for sudden." Then after giving the horrific options further consideration, Clay added, "But then having her with me and being able to be with her through all of it has changed my life. And we do talk a lot, about living and dying, you know. In a way, her illness woke me up, or it's trying to wake me up, to living. But then, does she have to suffer just so I can become less of a fool? That doesn't sound right. . . . I don't know, Spark, I just don't know. It's a tough call." Clay's head dropped to his chest.

"Indeedy. Your wife is givin' you somethin' special. Like me, for instance. I keep thinkin' about having just a little bit more time with my Emma. Maybe an hour or so, just so I could tell her a bunch of stuff I never told her. Now you tell me—why do we put off telling our loved ones stuff we know they want us to say—why do we do that? Like I said, I always planned on tellin' her, but I didn't, and she up and died."

Spark, getting no response from Clay, slapped his knee. "If I could, I'd vote against being the one left behind." He stood up, walked over to the stove, and placed his blue-speckled, metal coffee pot on one of the burners. "Death's such a devil, but what're we gonna do about it? In th' end, you lose every blessed thing you love, then eventually we die an' someone else loses us." Clay's mind flashed instantly to Cassandra, realizing that at some point, she would also lose him, and go through her own grief again. With his back turned, Spark did not notice Clay's face had changed, so he went on, "What kinda deal is that?"

Turning back around with two cups of hot coffee held in one gnarly hand, Spark sat back down at the table, shoved one cup at Clay, and then abruptly changed the subject. "You down in that canyon by yourself all that time?" His words were sly but friendly.

"Well, I went in there by myself, but I did meet a couple of people. . . ." Clay drew the hot liquid to his lips, hoping Spark wouldn't see his expression.

"One of 'em a woman?" Spark persisted.

"As a matter of fact, yes."

"You musta sure upset her over somethin'," Spark pronounced, this time searching for an honest answer in Clay's eyes. The wizened old man was not stupid, nor was he vicious.

"Well, what do you mean, Spark?" Clay sat up and leaned forward with interest in Spark's line of questioning.

"Well, this morning, I reckon it was, this woman come plowin' in here in a white car . . . one of them car-truck things all the young-uns are driving these days. . . ."

"What did she look like?"

"Oh, I don't know. Tall. Not skinny but not heavy. Her hair was kinda reddish . . . but what I really noticed was the dog with her . . . pretty and red-colored. She kept tellin' it to stay in th' car."

"Did you talk to her?" Clay's intensity caught Spark's attention, and he became more concentrated and curious.

"Not at first. Her drivin' woke me up from my mornin' nap. She jumped outta her car, left the motor runnin' and th' door open. She went over ta your motor scooter there an' set down on it. She set there runnin' her hands over it like she just found somethin' she lost. I thought for sure, she was thinkin' a takin' it, but I couldn't make out how she planned to do that. She kept looking 'round like she was expectin' somebody and worryin' that they'd come. Then she commenced to cryin.' I was a fair ways off, but I could tell she was upset. So I decided I better check on her.

Clay nodded and then pressed his elder, "What did she say?"

"Well, I asked her if I could help out. She said, 'No.' Said she was all right, though she didn't *look* all right. I told her I could listen if need be. She nodded at me but didn't say much else. She got off your scooter—almost knocked it over, but I caught it with her—said, 'Thank you' real nice, and drove off in a hurry."

All of the mending Clay had done throughout the day unraveled. He could not leave Rorie in that deep valley of tears, and he could not escape Mellie's ordeal. Both women pressed upon his heart, one gone, the other going. He could rescue neither, a feeling, as a male, he was not used to having. He thanked Spark for telling him the tale and then sat quietly drinking the rest of his coffee.

Spark took Clay's cup, put it on the tailgate, and said, "It's about time for my evenin' walk. Wanna go with me?" His voice was laced with hope that he would have company today.

"Sure. Sounds good . . . I need to stretch my legs and clear my head. This country is so grand. I hate to think about leaving here tomorrow." Walking back to his own campsite, Clay grabbed his cap, pulled it over his unruly hair, and shouted to Spark, "Let's go!"

Once they were on the trail, Clay resumed their talk. "You said that you wish you'd said things to your wife. What sort of things?"

The old man stopped on the trail and looked straight into Clay's eyes, "That's kinda personal, but seein' it's just us fellas, I guess it's okay."

"I don't mean to pry into your personal life, Spark," Clay apologized.

Spark waved his hand dismissively, "It don't matter now. It's just between you and me anyhow."

"Maybe if you can tell me what you would like to say to her, you'll help me know what I should say to Mellie before she's gone too. See what I'm getting at with my question?" Clay's eyes pleaded his case.

"Probably won't be th' same, but what I'd say first off is that she made up half o' me an' that I'm only half a person with her gone. Course, she wouldn't believe me. She never took herself very serious." He waved his walking stick with frustrated exuberance. "Took me a long time ta learn how close we was stuck together!"

Clay entered into Spark's intensity, "What else would you say?"

Spark didn't answer for a while, rubbing his chin full of whiskers. Then he confessed, "You know what? Now that you put me on th' spot, I see that I can't say it. Puttin' your closest feelings into words . . . that's purty near impossible."

After pondering the matter, Spark speculated, "If Emma was to show up, walkin' right up this trail, know what I'd do? I'd just hug her 'til I wore smack out, and then I'd look at her 'til I went blind. But my tongue'd just go blab-blab-blab! Even if I said somethin', it'd be nothing against what I wanted ta say. When I think of all the times I just took her fer granted, when she—well, and them three kids—was all I ever felt really connected to in this world!"

Clay thought about Mellie's long ordeal and how his bouts of rage served to cover his deeper passions. Spark now allowed his heart to express itself freely. Clay wanted to tap those same depths in himself and let them sing before Mellie died.

"What I might say ta her?" Spark returned to Clay's query, "Is that lovin' somebody is almost always sad, when you think how it's gonna turn out. Somebody always goes away—either they run off or die. That's th' way of it. And we have ta live with this our entire time together, but usually we don't until it's too late. Then the end's too big a surprise. That's what I did." His foggy gray eyes blinked.

"It might be better not to ever love anybody too much," ventured Clay, just to test Spark's logic.

"Easier, I reckon, but not better. Besides, you can't help yourself. Love ain't planned out like buildin' a house. It comes at you like a. . . ." He paused, searching for the right word.

Clay waited, "Like what?"

"I was gonna say, like a heart attack, or some other tragedy, but that don't sound right. Still, that's how close it gets, love does. It takes you over and you have to just let it be, pain an' all."

"Even if you know how it's going to turn out?" Clay continued to press the old man.

"Yep. You bet! So when you let love in, and everybody's tryin', even if they make a mess of it, you have to agree to the sadness that goes along with it. It all goes together."

Clay stared, stupefied, into the sage along the edge of the trail, realizing this old man had a grip on the whole business Clay had struggled to comprehend. *Love is inherently tragic. Yet, the tragedy itself is bonded to the highest ideal of human happiness. The paradox of it all. This creates both the pain and the ecstasy, the suffering and the freedom. The endless search for love.*

Clay and Spark turned back toward camp, the end of the day announcing its arrival in the heavens, drawing them toward their transient homes. The sky blazed with one of the loveliest sunsets Clay had seen on his journey into the wildness of this isolated place. Suddenly the fact that Clay had not slept much the night before struck his body full force. His brain was tired from the intense conversations with Spark. He body was tired from the night of love with Rorie and his climb out of the gorge. His heart was tired from the relentless battle of loving two women. As earth drew him down, his eyes closed and sleep took over.

Realization

RORIE WATCHED FLAME DEVOUR THE LAST OF THE DOG FOOD she had brought into the canyon. The dog knew nothing of the drama playing out in her owner's mind, but Rorie had just traversed the proverbial "valley of decision" and began dismantling her camp with an almost frantic zeal.

A half-hour later, she checked about her campsite for any overlooked remnants of having been there. After hurriedly scratching out a note with an impossible stub of pencil, she placed it on the camp table in the shed and weighted it with the small sphere of white stone she had carried in her pocket for less than a day. She did not want to leave the fetish of her time with Clay, but she knew she must. It would be the only thing that would speak sufficiently of her decision to leave.

Rorie called to Flame, and they hiked in a haste that suggested the whole canyon might soon flood. The wonders of nature surrounding her no longer registered. She was bound, as if on a mission, back to her familiar world. At the junction of the trail leading in two directions, to La Junta and to the top of the gorge, she halted and stared longingly toward the point, but she dared not take the time. Perhaps another time. *But when? Will I ever be able to come back here and see all of this again?* A sadness filled her heart at the prospect that this lovely place might not fit into her life again. Nonetheless, her determination prevailed; she turned left and ascended rapidly up the trail. Though it was early morning and the sun had not yet reached the trail, Rorie perspired under the weight of her pack and the steady climb.

Reaching the top of the mesa, winded and panting, she gazed over the lookout facing La Junta more than a mile below, while

Flame stood patiently beside her. Unexpected tears filled her eyes. *How can I be doing this?* Staring at the convergence where the Red River rushed headlong to meet the Rio Grande, Rorie felt a cavalcade of pain surge through her body. *There it is—merging, meeting. But only for a while.*

When Rorie opened the rear door to the Jeep Cherokee, Flame bounded through. She tossed in her gear with no regard to its care, looked over her shoulder to be sure she was alone, jumped into the vehicle and drove toward the pavement. Her resolution grew stronger.

The sign to Big Arsenic pointed to the left. Rorie drove past, then backed up to the gravel road. *What if he's already out by now? Why am I trembling?* But she decided to dare, and turned down the road to the campground. She drove too fast, throwing gravel, as she wound through the camp roads in search of Clay's motorcycle. When she saw it, she stopped, ordered Flame to stay in the car and jumped out, leaving her door wide open. Rushing to the dust-covered black machine, she straddled it. *Clay will soon be riding all the way back to Kansas on this cycle. Away from me, away from us.* She looked furtively around, sensing his absence and feeling for his presence.

Searching again for her courage, Rorie found herself caught by another rush of tears. An old man appeared. At first, she though he might be Clay when she heard his feet scuffling over the gravel. The man came closer and then tried to console her, but how could he possibly understand? *Tears invariably attract males who wish to fix the problem so that the tears go away since, in the male world, they are quite inconvenient.* She was not quite sure what her tears even meant at this point. Climbing off the motorcycle, almost knocking it over in her hurry to escape, she dusted herself off, brushed her hand over her face, walked briskly back to her car and jumped in to rejoin Flame, who had watched her every move. She sped away with the old man standing in the gravel road waving as if he had known her all his life.

Rorie approached Taos with a foreboding that puzzled her. Then she knew. Had she stayed in the canyon and returned to Clay, they would have been together that night, here in this quaint town. This thought sent her once again into a wail. She set about to convince her wounded heart that she would survive. *I had to do this. Clay must return to Mellie. There's no good outcome if we had spent the night in Taos. It would just be the same wretched separation again tomorrow. Better to let it go now.* Choking off her lament, she focused on the road ahead.

Below Taos, Rorie abruptly made yet another decision, not to go through the mountains to Las Vegas but to continue south toward Santa Fe. That town had long infatuated her. When she reached the edge of town, she stopped for gas. As she stepped out of the car, a mysterious feeling of belonging here swept through her. Such an experience was new, because Rorie had never felt strongly that she belonged to any particular place. The fragrance of pinion and pine in the air, the billowing clouds playing across a deep blue sky, the sand-colored adobe buildings looking ancient and unique, stirred her blood. She relaxed, breathed in the mountain air and realized she was being invited by this place to claim a deeper sense of origin here. When she finished filling the car with gas, she stopped to call Sara. To her surprise, Sara answered.

"You're there!"

"You did call me, you know," Sara said mischievously. "Say, where are you?"

"Just drove into Santa Fe."

"You're not going to try to make it back today, are you?" Sara's tone was stern.

"No. I'll be back tomorrow."

"Wil isn't going to like this—he's on pins and needles."

Rorie sighed into the phone. "Maybe I'll just stay here." She laughed to mask her frustration.

"Well, are you going to tell me—your best friend—what you've decided?" Sara was beyond curious at this point.

"Yes, but not on the phone. It's a real corker of a story. I'll say that much." Rorie grinned, though Sara couldn't see her face.

"But. . . ."

"I'll talk to you tomorrow when I get back."

"You'd better see Wil first. He'll probably be waiting on your porch," Sara challenged her. "Drive safe."

"Keep him at bay, will ya? See you later." Rorie ended the conversation with a modest wave of dejection clouding her spirits. *Wil! How I dread that encounter. Maybe I should take the long way home.*

Rorie stopped for the night in Amarillo. After a quick evening meal and a long-deserved hot shower, she piled her hair into a towel and plopped onto the white fluffy bed to ruminate over the events of the past few days. No television, no phone, just her own thoughts to keep her company. She wanted to feel Clay's presence once again, if she could conjure such an experience. She allowed her mind to wander over his body, shivering from his imagined touch. Her skin tingled as she thought of their night together, and she decided to allow herself to bask in those memories one last time while she was still alone. *Life in Dallas will steal all of this from me, so I'd better enjoy these remaining hours by myself—to remember Clay and our time together. After this, I have to let him go.*

She wrote in her journal about every detail she could recall. At times there were tears dropping on the pages. Flame would stand up and come over to her, nudging her arm to offer sympathy. At other times, as she wrote, there was soft laughter when she recalled some of his quips and teasing. She wrote as much about their conversations on love and loss as she could, cheering on their dialogues with flares of her pen. Finally, she savored the details of their night of lovemaking, leaving out nothing. Her feelings were vibrant and full of passion, causing her body to tremble with desire. To Rorie such responses of her body were unfamiliar, leaving her confused and aching. When she finished her reverie, she rolled over and turned off the light, patting her dog on the head by way of saying "good night." Her final thoughts before sleep consumed her were of Clay. *I'm not sure, but I think I fell in love with him, beginning with that naked wilderness shower. How is that possible in such a short time?*

A day later, the skyline of Dallas greeted Rorie in the distance, drawing her back into the vortex of the life she had left behind and the challenge of her own future. In her encounter with Clay rested a mystery of liberation she did not yet fathom. A window had opened within her, and she now saw sheer possibility in a way formerly denied her. Every mile between Amarillo and home had allowed her fledgling confidence to flourish. She wanted to drive directly to Sara and tell her everything, but she knew instinctively that Wil was her first order of business. She was tired from the drive, and Flame was restless to exit the car as she pulled up to her house.

Rorie heard her phone machine beeping as soon as she walked into the house. She had turned her cell phone off when she entered the canyon and had not turned it back on again, except to call Sara from Santa Fe. She wanted no one to find her during her adventure, much less on the drive back to Dallas. A constant red light flashed on the answering machine. Eight messages. The last five calls revealed Wil's anxiety. From the first, "Call me when you get home. I'm waiting" to "Excited to have you back" to the last call, "I'm still waiting," his disappointment mounting with each message. Rorie wanted to unpack, take a shower and reorient herself before reaching out to him, but she also wanted to take the initiative with Wil. Once her pack lay on the living room floor, and Flame had been tended to, she dialed.

"It's me, Rorie."

"Hey, I've had a time waiting on you to call me. Glad you're here. When can I see you?" Wil's voice was a mixture of consternation and excitement.

Rorie offered him only excuses.

Brushing those aside, Wil responded, "I know, it's okay, you're here now. When can I see you?" he asked again, impatiently this time.

"Wil, I have driven most of the day. I'm tired and hungry. I just walked in the door a few minutes ago. Let me have some time to change clothes." She desperately wanted to postpone their meeting until the next day but found herself offering to meet the anxious man at their favorite Mexican restaurant for a late dinner. Wil agreed but with a muffled plea in his voice that increased her emotional resistance to their meeting.

"What if I pick you up?" Wil begged.

"That's out of your way. It'll be quicker if I meet you there." Although Rorie was more distant than she wanted to be, she also did not want to fake her feelings. More importantly, she wanted to be in charge of the evening.

At the restaurant, Wil was already seated at a table when she arrived. Jumping up to greet her, he kissed her on the cheek and hugged her tightly. When her response was one of restraint, she saw tension rising in his face. *I want to get the worst of this over as quickly as possible, but not here in front of everyone. I hate this! And only two days ago I was in romantic bliss.*

Once they were seated and reading menus, Wil observed, "I see you're not wearing your ring. Afraid you'd lose it in the back country?" His voice revealed his desperation for this to be the reason Rorie's finger was naked.

Rorie looked at her left hand as if she did not realize the ring was missing. She saw this was her opening to speak. Still staring at her hand, she opened the conversation she knew she must have. "No, Wil, I removed the ring before I left because I wanted to make a decision about whether I should wear it or not."

"What? What are you talking about, Rorie?" Wil interjected as he laid aside his menu, panic rising in his voice.

Rorie raised her hand, as she often did in response to interruptions by Wil. "I'm quite clear, Wil, that I am not going to marry you." Though her voice trembled slightly with nervousness, she did not lack clarity. "Nor, for that matter, anyone else."

Wil said nothing but sat and stared past her left ear. When he finally mustered a response, he spoke incoherently. "But what, I mean, why? Did I do some—I was only—" He grabbed her hand at this point and held on as though she might escape.

Rorie unconsciously pulled her hand away from his and said, "This is not a rejection of you. I just need—"

"Sure feels like it." Wil's head sagged, and he clasped his arms across his chest.

"I can understand that." Pausing as she retrieved her napkin from the floor where it had fallen, Rorie then continued, "But I did not take this time away to decide whether to marry *you*." She pointed toward him to make her words personal. "I went away to decide whether to marry at all." She reflected, as she spoke, that this was only partly true. She did not want to marry Wil, that was certain, and she knew why. His gestures toward her seemed forced, often stiff and formal. She picked up the message in his behavior: *desperation.*

Rorie could not move past her suspicion that Wil simply wanted to be married, and she was the most available candidate. He was always deferential, even solicitous, toward her, but she did not want to be a token wife. She wanted someone who could and would meet her on shared ground and with a zeal and ease that Wil had seldom expressed toward her. She had decided on the drive home, *If I cannot have what I found with Clay, I'll stay single.* She could imagine no reasonable way to explain all of this to Wil.

The waiter came, and they ordered distractedly, indifferently. The intrusion left them awkward and increased the strain between them.

"You mean you want to be single *for the rest of your life?*" Wil's voice became shrill as he asked his question.

"Yes." Rorie answered bluntly, but she retained one reservation to herself. Only if she met someone who challenged her beyond herself, joined her in mutual capitulation, and took her seriously when she spoke, might she ever consent to a sustained intimacy or perhaps even marriage. Rorie admitted to herself, *I'll probably spend the rest of my life searching for another incarnation of Clay.* She sighed and gathered her flagging energy as best she could. "Wil, I've decided that I cannot settle for a conventional life. This is what you seem to want. At least everything you talk about sounds that way to me." Wil started to challenge her, but again Rorie raised her hand.

"Since my college days, I have been under constant pressure to settle into life and to become, oh, regular. I had three choices, according to my father. I could settle down by marrying, or I could find a career, or do both. I went for career. Then you came along and threw everything into confusion for me. While I was away last week, I came to see that I am not bound to live out only my father's options. I have *real* life choices." She stressed "real" to emphasize that she faced possibilities she had never before entertained. "I'm not sure exactly what they are or what I will do, but I will not settle for the "programmed" life. I will not be seduced into that life by you, by my father, or by anyone."

As though Wil had heard nothing Rorie said, he posed the inevitable question, "Is there someone else?"

"No." Rorie answered firmly. But she realized one more time that her response was only to some extent true. She had indeed met someone else, and that meeting changed everything for her. But Wil would never see it as more than a diversion away from her proper affection for him, and he would surely try to woo her back. She puzzled over her series of half-truths offered to Wil with all the honesty she could muster.

When their food came, they both picked at it. Silence reigned, until Wil dropped his fork onto his plate, to announce his rising anger. "Here I've waited patiently, faithfully, for over a month. I even let you go off on that crazy jaunt to, to—what? 'Find yourself,' I guess?" He spoke with a blend of sarcasm and only slightly suppressed fury. Rorie spotted that one word "let" as further confirmation of her decision. Wil continued with a low-key diatribe about fickle women, but every word came to her as reassurance of her decision. Unwittingly, Wil constructed a wall further separating them. He only gradually recognized by the look on her face what he had done, and shifted from attack to bargaining. "I'll do anything to make us work, Rorie. You must believe me."

"Actually, I do believe you, Wil, in that I believe you will do whatever you can to change my mind. But I also believe that any permanent relationship between us will not be what I seek for marriage."

"What is it that you want? Try me. I'll do it! I want you that much." Although seated, Wil took a barely-managed stridently masculine posture that said, "Give me a problem, and I'll solve it."

"I am not a problem to be solved, Wil. I am a woman with desires and choices." Rorie was becoming exasperated.

"Then what is it that you want?"

"There's nothing you can *fix*, Wil" she spoke with emphasis. "There is no problem here to solve. The issue is simply the complications of love. That's what I am talking about. Love is not a puzzle to be put together and completed." Rorie halted. "It's, love is, about connection, but in a way that includes vows and sacrifice, patience and. . . ." she searched for the word. Her eyes lit up as she blurted out, "Surrender." Clay's words bubbled up inside her, and she spoke as she never had to anyone, much less to Wil.

Wil, his forehead furrowed with puzzlement, leaned forward now in a pleading mode, "I know. Happy. You want to be happy. Isn't that what this is all about? Isn't that what you are saying? But I could make you happy."

Rorie sharply interrupted him. "Please don't say that you will 'make me happy.' No one can 'make' me happy!" She had long ago heard Sara say, "If a man ever promises to make you happy, the best thing to do is run. No one can be the source of someone else's happiness."

Wil's body sank back in his seat in defeat. She made one more attempt to clarify herself to him, feeling helpless that her explanations seemed inadequate to him. "Wil. You are a good man, and there's nothing wrong with you. But I know what you want because you keep telling me. I cannot fulfill my piece of your dream. It's nothing personal."

"Rorie!" He shouted at her, "Don't hand me that line." Then noticing that other patrons were watching them with furtive glances, he lowered his voice again. "I hate that phrase, 'not personal.' This *is* personal. I am a person. Your decision hurts me, and I don't like it. Does this make sense to you?"

"You're right, and I'm sorry. That was a trite thing to say. What I wish I had said is this: you deserve to be loved in the way you need, and to have someone who loves you the way you wish to love them in return. I'm not that person. Can you accept this?"

Wil did not immediately answer Rorie's question. Taking a deliberate drink of his beer to calm down, he created a space in the heat of their discussion. Setting his glass down slowly, he asked that most forlorn but predictable question: "Then you really don't love me?"

That word! Rorie reached to place her hand on his arm by way of comfort for what she was about to say to him. "No, Wil, I do love you, but I'm not in. . . ." Her conversation with Clay on this very distinction came thundering back to her. She stumbled for more adequate words. "I . . . I believe there are different kinds or levels of love, and I do love you as a person, and as a friend."

His face was stricken. "A friend! That won't do. I want to marry you!" He yanked his arm away from her and pushed himself away from the table.

"Friendship will have to do for us, Wil. And I do hope that because we work in the same building, we might be able to be friends and enjoy each other's company. Just let's don't expect this to turn into marriage. Is that possible for you?" Although Rorie meant these words, she could see in Wil's eyes that the idea remained out of his reach.

The evening proved to be long and tedious. Rorie ended the engagement to Wil by slipping the distinctive velvet box out of her purse onto the table between them. He reached out, grabbed it and stuffed it into his coat pocket, embarrassed. Walking to their cars, Wil marched stiffly behind her, and continued what he believed was his obligation by opening her car door for her. Once she was behind the wheel, he turned without a word and walked away.

An unexpected loneliness merged with her sense of relief. *It's over! Thank goodness. Guess I'm on my own now.* She drove past Wil standing beside his black sedan and waved to him. He did not wave back. She drove away wondering why anyone would drive a black car in the Texas heat.

From her bathtub filled with soothing oils, and candles lighted around the rim of the tub, she called Sara.

"Well, the deed is done. If possible, I want to see you tomorrow," Rorie insisted to Sara.

"Are you calling from home?"

"Yes, relaxing in my tub, trying to soak off the grime of breaking up a relationship."

"You've done the deed, I guess."

"Sure have. How did you know that?"

"He just called me. He's incoherent and threatens to come apart. You must've let him down hard." Sara's voice had a twinge of judgment in it.

Rorie came back at her friend in defense of a newly minted self-confidence, "Not at all. I just tried to be clear, as clear as I could be under the circumstances. I don't want him to misunderstand me or try to put us back together again. He may have dropped hard when he saw he could not convince me to change my mind. I didn't want to hurt him beyond repair, but neither did I want any openings for reconsideration." As she spoke, Rorie was certain of her decision and wanted Sara to hear her resolution.

"What circumstances?" Forgetting about Wil, Sara was now prying into Rorie's hints.

Rorie smiled to herself in the candlelight. "That's what I need to talk about."

"Did you meet someone?" Sara's intuition was in overdrive.

"Well, yes and no." Rorie did meet someone, but this particular someone could never belong to her. The pain of this thought crossed her face and made the tears stream again. She muffled her voice, so Sara could not hear her anguish. "I promise to explain everything. When can we meet?"

"How about tomorrow night? Todd can cover for me at home." Sara was completely intrigued at this point.

"My place?" Rorie was ready to leave her tub and head for a desperately needed night's sleep in her own bed. "See you at 6:30. I'll have munchies and wine. Bye for now." Rorie ended the call before Sara could ask more questions.

Sara hung up, mystified. *What's that girl gone and done now?*

Home

WITH A HAND TOWEL, CLAY WIPED THE EARLY MORNING DEW from his tent just before kneeling on the ground to fold and stuff his canyon home into a bag for travel. Spark walked up behind him bearing a cup of coffee in each hand, steam drifting upward from the cups. "Brought ya some mornin' brew," he announced.

"Thanks, I need something for a kick start," Clay responded as he took the proffered cup. They posed together for no one, two men standing side by side, weight on one leg, brooding in the mist at the edge of another brilliant day. A friendly stillness lodged between them. The day had dawned clear enough that Clay knew the heat would bear down on him on his ride back to Kansas.

While Clay finished packing and lashing his gear to his BMW, Spark watched as if taking lessons from a master. They bade each other farewell, as Clay handed his empty cup back to his new friend, patting him on the back by way of saying thanks. Spark stood on the edge of the gravel road, waving at the receding motorcycle. The old man looked forlorn as his image danced in Clay's rear view mirror. Clay waved over his shoulder. *I'll miss that guy. What serendipity to meet him!*

In Questa, Clay pulled over to consider whether to make the loop into Taos, a nod to former haunts with Mellie and a lost promise with Rorie. He had not visited the high desert town in several years, not since his wife fell ill. *It's out of my way, and I can't hang around here that long. Next time.* He turned east and drove up to Red River, where he ate breakfast at a local diner whose owners seemed to come and go, while the restaurant perpetually remained open for business. It was still too early to call home.

Riding over Bobcat Pass, Clay became melancholy, as he realized he was slowly leaving the beauty of this spectacular land behind. At

Cimarron, he pulled into a station for gas and to check his phone for reception. Dialing Cassandra, he waited. She did not answer for so long that he began to panic.

"Hello," came her voice across the space between them.

With relief, Clay replied, "Hey, Honey, it's Dad. How are things there with you and your mother?"

"I was beginning to wonder if you were okay," she replied a touch petulantly, "I'm fine. Mom's good too. We both miss you."

"Tell me about Mellie first," Clay insisted.

"She's about the same but seems really happy for some reason. It's strange. I can't get enough out of her to know what's actually on her mind, but I like seeing her this way. She smiles every time I come into the room. . . . She's sure ready to see you. That's probably why her eyes are so frisky—she knows you're coming home." Cassandra interrupted herself, "When will you be back?"

"Tonight, but it may be after dark," Clay said with caution, "so, don't wait up for me if I'm too late getting in."

Clay could hear Cassandra announce to Mellie that he would be home that night. "She's beaming now," Cassandra confided to Clay as if to draw him homeward more quickly.

"You tell her that I love her more than ever and can't wait to see you both." His voice broke.

"Why don't you tell her yourself?" Cassandra held the phone to her mother's ear and Clay whispered his pet words of greeting to her. "Mom's smiling and has tears in her eyes. Come home as soon as you can." Then with a hesitant tone, she asked, "Dad?"

"What is it?"

"I have some really great news to tell you."

"Do I need to sit down? Go ahead." Clay suspected he knew what was coming but wanted to give his daughter the chance to tell him by herself.

"Not now. Not on the phone. Tonight. When you get in, I, we'll tell you."

Clay laughed into the phone, "Is this your way of making sure I arrive tonight?"

"Well, more like preparing you, but that's a good idea if it makes you return faster." Her voice was light and excited.

"That sounds enticing but okay. I'll wait." Clay was now ready to get off the phone and back on the road home. "I'll see you both this evening. Love to Mellie, and give yourself a hug for me."

The lone rider continued east, the mountains receding behind him. He headed across the plains of eastern Colorado, bound for the rolling tall grasses of Kansas. Mile stretched into mile as the day spun itself out in sun, wind and vibration. The open road suspended him in memories and dreams.

Clay ruminated between the still-vibrant recollection of Rorie in Wild Rivers and his sober anticipation of finding Mellie lying motionless as when he last saw her. These two loves rode with him, one as passionate as it was fleeting, and the other substantial and dense with demand, promising to take leave. The theme of his study, love and loss, stirred freshly as he rode. *The possibility of loss, as much as the fact of its inevitability, accompanies every promise love holds.*

Arriving after dark, Clay traversed the familiar web of streets leading to his family sanctuary. As he pulled onto his street, he saw that his home was blazing with lights, as if a desire to make sure he could find the house was the driving force. Cassandra, listening for the drone and crackle of the motorcycle, heard her father turn the corner, and burst through the front door. Before he could cut the engine, her arms wrapped around him, welcoming him through the waft of road smells from his long ride.

Stepping from the cycle and wobbling uncertainly, Clay and Cassandra moved up the walk toward the house, arms entwined. He looked up to see Justin standing on the porch, waving his own warm reception.

"Is the whole town showing up to greet me?" Clay teased his junior colleague from the university. Even though Justin was almost young enough to be his son, they had become academic, and then personal friends over the past four years. Clay enjoyed the bright and enthusiastic young thinker. During the past year and a half Justin showed up at the house with increasing frequency for long stays. It took Clay a while to realize that his colleague came more for the chance to see Cassandra than to visit with him. More recently the pair had spent most of their free time together, and when Cassandra took care of Mellie, Justin hovered in the background, waiting for any chance to help. Clay stepped onto the porch and reached an arm around him in a half-embrace.

Clay insisted on going at once to greet Mellie. She could not turn to look at him but stared straight ahead with one of the few gestures still under her control, a ready smile. He crouched beside the bed and gave her motionless form a delicate hug, while kissing her forehead, cheeks and mouth. Mellie's moist eyes revealed her heart to him.

As was the family custom, all social activity took place in Mellie's room, a sun porch on the side of the house which had been reconfigured for her. Everyone wanted to know about the trip. Three chairs formed a semicircle at the foot of Mellie's bed while Justin cranked it up so that she could see. Clay offered a spare outline of his adventure, concentrating on Wild Rivers and its grandeur. He then asked questions about Mellie's care and routine during the past week. Abruptly he turned to Cassandra with jest in his voice, "Okay, I've done my part to get here and fill you in. So what's the big surprise?"

Cassandra looked up sharply, a touch apprehensively toward Justin, who fidgeted immediately with the ball cap in his hand. He cleared his throat more than once before saying in measured words, "You know, Clay, that Cassandra and I have been seeing each other for more than a year?"

Clay posed as if he possessed no foreknowledge of what was about to happen and decided not to scoop the story. He teased, "Justin, are you in trouble?"

"Probably," Justin confessed, and Cassandra, pretending to be insulted, slapped him on the arm. "But we—Cassandra and I—are engaged. Well, we want to marry, of course, with your and Mellie's approval." He dropped his eyes, as his face flushed with hope.

Mellie, wide-eyed, radiated her confirmation, and Clay could tell that she already knew and waited to share the moment with him. Clay's mind stirred with so much more than he could express that he felt utterly inept. He found himself sandwiched between his own daughter, sparkling with life, and his languishing mate. Behind the array of emotions that stirred in him rested the memory of the days before. He wished his family had given him time to re-enter his world, but he recognized also Cassandra and Justin's enthusiasm at having promised themselves to each other. He longed to urge them to rush out, waste no time and do as they wished. Yet, he also longed to warn them of the uncertainty and fragility of the whole enterprise of love. He refrained and settled for a deep embrace of his daughter and of the man who would become his son. Moving to Mellie's bed, he grasped her hand, and the parents beamed proudly at the youngsters, remembering how their own love story began.

Although the hour was growing late, the excited group discussed plans for the wedding, everyone talking at once. Mellie even signaled with her eyes that she had something to offer. Cassandra helped her spell out the word *H-e-r-e*, and they all knew that she wanted the wedding to be held in her presence. Both Justin and Cassandra agreed instantly, declaring that they had already decided to have the wedding on the lawn with friends standing at open windows outside the sun porch, where Mellie could see and hear.

As exhaustion settled over Clay, he announced that the day was spent for him, and he excused himself to unload his motorcycle and take a long soaking shower. He kept remembering the hot spring and the bewitching bath of only two evenings before. It seemed like a half-remembered dream or something he once read. He concentrated to bring it more sharply to mind.

When Clay returned to the sun porch, Cassandra and Justin stood to leave. "I'll take over from here." Clay chuckled to his daughter, "Go celebrate!" The couple left, and he turned to Mellie as if for the first time. Being away for a week in the sun-drenched climes of New Mexico left him alien to the paleness of his wife. Reality and illusion played tricks on him.

Pulling his chair up close to Mellie, he took her slack hand in his and rested for a time. She signaled for the alphabet board and spelled out, *T-e-l-l m-e.* He understood she wanted to hear every detail of the trip. His adventure was her only excitement. *Sure wish we could do this tomorrow when I am rested and I have my wits about me, but Mellie was never one to wait to hear all the news.* Despite his fatigue, he struggled to tell his story without turning it into sheer fabrication, and he knew this would never succeed in any case. Mellie, as debilitated as she was, possessed acute, even uncanny, awareness of what took place in the lives of those closest to her. And deceit was not part of their connection to each other.

Clay told his story, including the encounter with Rorie and Coyote, and their finding the hot spring. Mellie's eyes spoke elation at every detail. When Clay finished, she signaled for the board again and gave him one more word, *H-e-r.* He nodded acknowledgement and obliged by giving Rorie's background and some details she had shared from her life. He included her struggle over her engagement and whether she should marry. He talked about the walks they took and some of their conversation.

Mellie lay as patient as a stone, waiting but not satisfied with Clay's recitation. She signaled again and asked, *Y-o-u a-n-d h-e-r?* He wanted to wait, to excuse himself on grounds that he was bone tired, but they slept in the same room every night. He knew he could not rest so long as she remained dissatisfied with his story. *Dammit, she knows. She knows. She always knows everything.*

In carefully chosen words, mixed with fathomless anguish, Clay told Mellie about his relationship with Rorie. He told the story simply and clearly, while censoring the details of his intimacy with another woman. When he told of their bathing naked in the hot spring, Mellie became exuberant, though she had no resources for showing it except her face. She insisted on the board again, signaled, *F-u-n,* and beamed when he read the word aloud. *This woman is beyond comprehension, pure mystery.*

Although Clay spoke in veiled references to his intimacy with Rorie, he knew that Mellie understood what had happened in the deep river chasm, and he knew also that she embraced this potentially devastating truth, as though she had conjured the encounter herself. Tears flooded her face and drenched the lace of her nightgown. But when he showed concern for her, she gave her unmistak-able sign that he must continue. He remembered how, when she had cried so desperately during the discussion of her own funeral plans, she nevertheless commanded them to proceed. *This beloved woman of mine is astonishing. I wonder if it is possible to love her as deeply as she deserves for the quality of human being she is?* Mellie's strength, framed now within such overwhelming fragility, left him inwardly raging against her enemy and raving over her invincible heart. He wanted to scream at the universe about the injustice in her dying.

Clay crawled onto the bed beside his withering mate and lay em-bracing her voiceless, motionless body. He knew her body so well, from its vibrancy before her affliction to its steady dwindling. Few days had passed in the last four years that he did not bathe and care for a body he had once adored, from which he had drawn such de-light and rest of soul. Much of their love came through his constant touching of her. And now Mellie seemed to be turning him over to another, a proxy, to keep alive the vitality which they had once known. No longer able herself to cling to him in body, she sought to release him and turn him outward toward the world.

Lying beside Mellie, he heard heavy breathing. She slept but did not move. *Love is letting go. Mellie is letting go, and so am I, but not yet, not while she hangs so tenaciously to life.* He then recalled the long discussion with Rorie and whispered, as if speaking to Mellie, "Sur-render." *It's all about surrender, taking the leap. Here is where I belong until this ordeal is over. Mellie, I love you. You are the Light that has given me love and taught me how to live my life. You are free. Rorie, you changed my heart from bitterness to hope. You taught me I will survive losing Mellie. Love for you has planted itself in my heart. Two remarkable women have now become my teachers. All I feel tonight is gratitude.*

Clay slept soundly much of the night in the close confines of Mellie's bed, holding her curled fingers in his hand.

Discovery

Rorie's first day back at the office dragged on with an inability to concentrate. Throughout the day she was vague with her colleagues and inattentive in the weekly staff meeting, longing for the hours to pass. As soon as possible, she rushed home to prepare for the evening with Sara. On a dark hardwood coffee table, she placed colorful dishes filled with tomatoes and avocado slices. A basket of handmade chips sat beside a rich smooth queso dip that Rorie had learned to make with expertise. A variety of hard cheeses and summer sausages fanned out on a cutting board lined with large, red grapes and cracked pepper crackers. A bottle of Pinot Grigio and two stemmed glasses finished the scene. *Now, I'm ready to talk. I really need Sara to help me make sense of the muddle in my mind.* The doorbell rang at the same time Sara shoved open the door and let herself into Rorie's cozy home.

Surveying the room, she exclaimed, "Oh, I see! We're going to have one of *those* talks. My kind. Can't wait!" She hugged Rorie warmly, holding her a moment longer than usual. As she stepped away, Sara began removing her shoes and slipped onto the floor to occupy one of the plush cushions carefully placed in front of the table filled with food. Taking her time to enter an alternate universe of female familiarity, Sara astutely said nothing, waiting for the right moment to open the passage into that sanctuary of conversation between two close friends. Sara could tell from signals Rorie was sending that the evening ahead would be intense. Rorie joined her friend on the floor, grabbing for a blue tweed cushion and tucking her legs under her. Both women leaned back against the sofa, sitting close to one another, as the soul sisters they were.

Glancing over her glass of wine, Sara said nonchalantly, "Sure glad you came back and took Wil off my hands. He was crazy while you were gone. He actually threatened to drive out there and look for you. I told him New Mexico was more than a spot on the map, and he would just have to wait. No patience." After hesitating, she continued slyly, "Seems as if he's now also off your hands."

Rorie sighed, took a hearty gulp of her wine and spoke softly. "Well, the ending wasn't exactly the way I wanted it to be. But when are such things as breakups ever tidy? The way he reacted all evening confirmed that I did the right thing." Rorie shifted her body so she could see more of Sara's face and speak directly to her. "Sara, I believe Wil is a good man, for whatever my judgment may be worth. For some woman, he will be a 'catch,' as they say. But my affection for him cannot stretch beyond friendship. Let me ask, do you believe we'd have been a fit—over the long haul, I mean?"

"So you brought me here for interrogation?" They smiled warmly at each other, and Rorie assured Sara that she only wanted her assessment for comfort's sake. Sara continued, "You two are definitely different people. Almost anyone can see that. Wil is the stable, settled type, and. . . ."

"That's exactly what I tried to explain to him!" Rorie exploded.

"Honey, he can't hear that. He's smitten, or thinks he is. Actually, from some of my own experiences with clients, I offer this opinion: He is drawn to something in you that's missing in himself. Maybe that's the way it is with most romantic mergers, but in your case, it lies on the surface. Marrying him would most likely squelch you, not him." Sara squirmed around on her cushion, propped her elbow on the sofa and moved her legs to a more comfortable position.

Staring Rorie in the face, her eyes flashed determination as she continued to share her thoughts. "Wil would be comfortable with you, Rorie, but not likely to grow much more beyond where he is now, at least in terms of understanding who you truly are. He wants to fill the 'wife slot' in his life and you are, to his way of thinking, a prime candidate for this. He's looking for security and stability. For some strange reason, he believes you could give this to him, which also says he doesn't really know you at all. And he would be totally bewildered as you began to change over the course of your own life."

Sara searched Rorie's eyes to see if she has caught the meaning of her statement. "Are you hearing me, Hon?" Rorie nodded while crunching on a cracker.

"On the other hand, my dear," Sara said as she reached over to pat Rorie on the thigh, "you would never be challenged enough by a marriage to Wil, to continue to grow and become more fully the person you have the potential to be. There are aspects of yourself that have yet to be explored. I'm about to say something important, and I want you to listen to me carefully." Sara grabbed Rorie's hand and held it firmly in her own. "Your father spent much of his parenting efforts working hard to contain you. Wil is a man who would likely do the same—attempt to control you. Do you understand this connection?"

Rorie marveled at Sara's consistent wisdom. "Yeah, you're right," Rorie conceded. "I felt caught, but I hated letting him down like that. He walked away like a deflated balloon caught in the wind." She grimaced at the image.

"Can't rescue him, Rorie. He's a big boy now. Besides, I think he already knew. He does have some savvy. He just wanted to make it work, push the river if he could. He is kinda nuts about you, in an odd sort of way." Sara moved her arm, reached for a chip and plunged it into the cheesy dip. "You feelin' all right about giving the ring back?" she asked, munching on her chip, holding her hand under it to catch the drips. Changing the subject, she made a sound, "Yum, Rorie. This dip is delish!" She finished by popping the rest into her mouth, wiping her lips with her napkin. "Go on."

"Relieved, mostly."

"And free!" Sara clapped her hands together smartly to create a pop. "Letting go of something holding you back, even if you make a mess of it, can be deliverance."

"That's coming, but I've been through so much in the past week, Sara. On the way home, I could almost feel the liberation. Yesterday I drove like an escaped convict with no one chasing me. But last night, Wil tested my sense of release and freedom. I need you to help me unravel something." Rorie paused to see if Sara caught the hint of more to come.

"Why do you think I came over here? Besides for the food, of course!" As they resettled themselves on the cushions, Rorie topped off their wine, and Sara built a stack of cheese on a cracker.

"To make a long story short. . . ."

"Make it long. I've got all night!" Sara retorted with glee, eyes bright with anticipation.

Pulling in a long breath, Rorie began, wistfully at first. "By accident, I found the most magnificent place to spend the week. There is this deep, long canyon gorge cut by the Rio Grande, in northern New Mexico, close to Red River, a little ski village up there." Her eyes drifted away to focus on a painting hung on her living room wall depicting aspen trees, golden and shimmering in the fall winds. "I met a man."

Sara slapped Rorie's leg again with a chuckle, "I knew it! Even the sound of your voice when you called from Santa Fe gave it away. So what's the story?" She was leaning forward now, all eyes and ears to hear Rorie's story as it unfolded.

Rorie revealed the tale of Clay, with Sara repeatedly slowing her down for details. Every nuance of the relationship with Clay surfaced through the channel of her memory, and Sara went back with her through it all. Rorie told of first seeing Clay naked awhile bathing and her feelings about his body there in the wilderness, natural and beautiful. Sara exuded, "I can't top that! When I brought a boyfriend home to meet my family once, Dad said, 'He's a handsome boy, but you know, beauty's only skin deep.'" He didn't like my rebuttal. 'Yeah, Dad, but I do love that skin!'" She giggled as laughter crackled between them.

At Rorie's report of Clay and Coyote creating the hot spring bath and of bathing in it with Clay, Sara threw her head back and howled. Then she sobered, "Todd and I used to take candlelight baths together, when we were first married, but not so much once the kids came. Did this just drive you wild?"

"Yep. Into the void—but you haven't heard the best part." When Rorie tried to explain the experience of surrender, of actually going beyond herself, her words became pitiful.

But Sara caught her meaning and nodded. "Did the earth move?"

"Oh, yeah. It moved!" They fell together in a duet of gaiety.

Sara straightened up, took a sip of her drink, cocked her head and thoughtfully replied, "A roommate from my graduate school days used to call it 'oceanic.' Was it like that? Never mind, I can see the answer on your face."

"I've never quite heard it put that way, but the word is perfect," Rorie agreed. "Vast, flowing and running deep . . . like Wild Rivers," she said softly, her voice trailing off.

"That's good enough for me. The only problem is, sounds like it ended. Hard to tolerate too much of a good thing?" Both women sighed deeply, in unison, allowing the wine to smooth the edges of the unanswered questions ahead of them. "Now we need to go further. Are you ready?" Sara was on her turf now and primed for the conversation ahead.

"What do you mean?"

"The sex part. How was it? Was he sex-starved? With the sick wife and all?"

Rorie, swallowing at the bluntness of Sara's questions, was not quite sure where her inquisitor was going. "Maybe at first. He kept crying and talking about how long it had been, and he was kind of awkward at first. I couldn't tell whether he worried about being with another woman or what, but before the night was over, he came through in fine style. He was gentle and sweet, and fierce and thorough." Smiling to herself, she asked, "Is that the way to describe such an encounter? I don't really know . . . this was my first time."

"I know this was not your first time to sleep with a man. There's at least Wil, after all. So you must mean your first time to experience what lovemaking can really be all about. Is that what you are saying?"

Her mind drifted before continuing. "I don't even know how to describe what happened to my body next to his body. I don't have words for those feelings, Sara. I just know that I can never settle for less than this again, with any man."

Sara said, "You know how they used to say that marriage was or was not 'consummated?' I always wondered why they used that word to describe the first time a couple had sex. Sounds like sex brings everything to an end, rather than a beginning. Sex, if it really 'moves the earth' between two people. . . ."

"Yes, that's exactly what happened to me. And for the first time ever. We dissolved into each other for hours. And nothing *ended.* Everything started! I feel like I became a human being, a woman, a person, all at once that night." She sat up straighter, as if to emphasize her words, "I came alive during this encounter with Clay and realized I could never go back to the person I had been before I met him. Something has changed inside me, Sara." Her eyes pled to be understood.

Sara noticed the glisten in Rorie's eyes and reached over to pat her face. "Dearie, this kind of sex is not consummation at all. It is an initiation into something greater than sex. This kind of lovemaking becomes a threshold, an opening up."

Rorie sat up on her knees, radiating enthusiasm. "Now you're coming closer to what I've puzzled over since I met Clay. More went on in that canyon than a sexual *tête-à-tête*. It was all about love and lonely people and the complications of life and death. It was about a whole unexplored region of relationship, at least for me, from our first conversation until I left. But at the same time our encounter concerned what we think and fuss over every minute we are awake. Since those talks, I have never felt so . . . so excited or passionate about life . . . about everything. Where is that coming from? What is this, Sara? Tell me!"

Sara nodded knowingly, "Rorie, you have awakened to the other side of life."

"What are you talking about?" Rorie queried a bit defensively, not understanding her advisor's words at all.

Sara replied easily and slowly, "That feeling you have described with Clay. That is what's called consciousness."

"Everybody's conscious. Conscious about what?" Rorie was fully perplexed and exasperated at this point.

Sara paused to compose her most earnest thoughts. "There's conscious, then there's consciousness, Rorie. Most people are walking in their sleep, doing what comes next, paying as little attention to life as they can get away with. But they still consider themselves conscious. To wake up from that, from ordinary vague stupor, is more like . . . well . . . like really seeing the world for the first time. It's being truly alert, aware and alive."

Rorie brushed her fingers through her hair, then bowed her head and dropped it into her hands. "Seeing what?" She muttered in frustration.

"Seeing that everything is connected. Seeing everything as an expression of love. It's all right there in front of us, but we keep looking past the moment. It's paying attention, Rorie—to life, to everything around you, taking nothing for granted. I bet Clay knows a lot about that, these days."

The new ideas were confusing to Rorie, but she trusted Sara enough to know she was hearing wisdom first-hand. "Yes . . . yes, he does. Losing his wife as he's doing has created a very soulful man . . . is that the right word? That's not a word I've ever used before in my life, but somehow it seems to fit this conversation."

Uncrossing her legs and moving closer, Sara grabbed Rorie's arms and shook her, "Now you have it! You saw his soul, and he likely saw yours, because you were both in the space to be open to each other and the moment. Nothing was binding either of you in that canyon, so you were able to be yourselves—to be awake, aware, alive!"

A splash of joy fell across Rorie's face. "When you put it that way, I do feel like I've been asleep most of my life. This is probably what made it okay to date Wil," she said wryly. "But now, after time with Clay, I've somehow walked through an invisible veil that I cannot see, but I can sense exists. I've been trying to become aware so that I can find the essence that makes me . . . my own self . . . to connect to something that is not me but makes me—what? More real, more vital, more myself. That's what happened in the canyon, Sara. Even with Coyote! If that is what you mean by 'waking up,' then I'm ready. I want my life to hold those days forever, not just in my mind or heart, but in my body, as part of me."

Grinning at her mentee, Sara reached for some grapes, sat back against the sofa, popped one into her mouth and said, "Tell me how you feel right now, about all of this."

Rorie grew pensive and responded carefully, "Ecstatically disoriented. Unsteady."

"Oh, my. Right. Like a newborn opening her eyes for the first time to the world outside the womb, perhaps?"

Rorie lifted her glass and gestured for Sara to do the same. They toasted to no particular thing, but to everything, "You've been living this way, in this 'consciousness' for a long time, haven't you? Since we first met, I could tell that you knew something I could not begin to fathom. And you kept trying to drag me along, but I never understood much of what you said. I decided to humor you, like the time you took me to that workshop on meditation and consciousness. I didn't understand most of what I heard, but I do now. This is what you are talking about, isn't it?"

"Can't really awaken anyone. I learned that. I can only make some pointing gestures and try to be there if and when anything comes of it." Sara jabbed her fingers into the air to express her words.

"Is this 'awakening' usually tied to sex?" Rorie was now curious.

"No. Not necessarily, but. . . ."

"But the sex was really, really good, not like anything I've experienced before. I don't want to leave that out of the equation."

"You're not supposed to. Just don't stop there. Like I said, the time with Clay was an initiation point for you. If you stay there, it's a trap and you'll keep starting over, mostly by craving sex until you have slept with so many men you can't remember them all. This happens to more people than you can imagine. When we have that 'wakeup' moment, those of us who do, it begins with something that is a shock to our psyche, usually a new experience, and it can be something sad or something joyful, something shocking or something soothing. Do you get my drift?" Sara draped her long skirt over her knees and straightened her legs, so they stretched under the table. "There, I was getting sore from sitting on the floor." Reaching for her wine glass again, Sara pushed on ahead, "Let's say, you fall in love. . . ."

Interrupting her, Rorie broke in to say, "Clay and I discussed that very phrase."

"Everyone needs to experience that sensation at least once. But you must remember, this is a jumping-off place. Literally. When you land, then what?" Sara poked Rorie's leg with her forefinger.

"But what's wrong with falling in. . . ."

"Nothing, really. Romance is hard to imagine without some sort of 'fall.' You just don't want to be hung up there and keep falling in love over and over just for that initial adrenaline rush. In fact, you can't stay there for long. Reality sets in. Soon the bills come due, the car needs repair, a child is on the way, your boss overlooks you for a promotion. Whatever it is, life takes over and romance is shoved aside. Soon, the couple discovers each other in new ways that are often not all too pleasant, if you keep hanging on to the romantic binge you were on when you first met. By the way, how did you and Clay leave things after this romantic orgy you two had?" Sara teased as she asked her question.

Rorie stood to stretch, walked across the room and turned the thermostat to a cooler temperature. Then, with no explanation she strode into the kitchen and put food in Flame's bowl. Her dog ambled over to see what was available to her for dinner. Rorie returned to the living room and plopped herself into a curved, blue armchair. "I'm ready to sit here for a while," she announced unceremoniously.

"You are avoiding my question, Missy!" Sara scolded her friend.

"I may be," Rorie agreed, "but here goes. I left the last morning without saying goodbye to him."

"You what?" Sara sprang up to sit on the sofa behind her, adjusting her height to match Rorie's, even though she was several inches shorter, then leaned forward and urged, "You mean after all that time together and the intimacy, you just disappeared? What's wrong with you, Girlfriend?"

"Look, Sara, the man is married to a wife with an awful disease. She is dying. He has a life in another state, a long way from Dallas. He loves her too, very much. There's absolutely no future for us." Tears formed in Rorie's eyes once again, as she slumped deeper into her chair.

"Rorie, things change. You don't own a crystal ball. And you can move, you know. Or, he can. . . ."

"But I didn't want to color what we did have with some maudlin departure. You know, one of those romantic farewells that actually means nothing, like in the movies." At this point her tears were streaming down her cheeks, making tracks through her make-up. Then she added, defiantly, "And I don't want to be the 'other woman' in his life distracting him from his dying wife! I'm *not* that person." At this point she was sobbing.

Sara waited for Rorie to regain her composure, then pressed, "Do you mean you have no plans to stay in contact with Clay?"

Wiping her nose, Rorie responded with thick, teary words, while shaking her head, "No. I haven't really thought about that. It seems quite over to me, Sara. A beautiful moment in time that has no future."

As if speaking to someone else in the room, Sara calls out, "My friend here's gone 'round the bend." Then turning back to Rorie, "Do you think about him, or miss him?"

"Hourly, moment by moment. There's so much to think about, so much to remember. Clay and I actually talked hours upon hours for almost four days, you know, and we discussed love more than anything else. He's writing a book on the subject, but mostly because we both went into that canyon with our own personal projects: to find out for ourselves what love actually means . . . what the mystery is inside this emotion. Me, because I had no idea what to do with Wil's proposal, and Clay because he's in love with his wife and she's dying."

"What did you two discover? Anything useful to the rest of us?" Sara jibed at her.

"One thing I know: There is more to the subject that anyone can possibly figure out. You know what astonished me most about that trip? I had never thought much about the word 'love' before. But I notice it now and it's all we humans seem to talk about. This thought hit me as I was driving home from Santa Fe listening to the endless parade of songs on the radio. They all talk about love, love, love. Can't escape it." She smirked.

"Are you trying to escape love, Rorie?" Sara's intuition was on high alert now.

"I was when I left town, but now I'm trying to come to grips with the fact that love is, not only everywhere around me, but is in every encounter we have. For instance, right here, right now, I love you for being my friend and for talking with me. I've never had that thought one time since we met. I just took it for granted that we cared about each other and were loyal to each other . . . you know, as friends. But now as I say this to you, I can hear that I react to those whom I love as my father reacted to me: with loyalty and caring, not affection or intimacy. Humph!"

Rorie stopped to take a deep breath, and then rushed on, "This feeling of love, since my time with Clay, just seems to cover everything from those syrupy love songs to this 'consciousness' you talked about. I've always thought love was an emotion that happened in a particular experience, in a given moment in time, not a constant in all things, all around me. I'm so confused and a bit sad—that I may not have this experience again. Help me, Sara. Help me figure out what comes next for me." Rorie spoke plaintively and her face crinkled with distress.

Sara grasped the anguish in Rorie's eyes and knew her response needed to be pertinent. "The most important thing I've learned in twenty-five years of marriage is that the toughest kind of love is not romance, the 'falling' you felt with Clay, but the ordinary kind, where you have to deal with day-to-day issues with other human beings placed in your path. It's always easier to put someone on a pedestal and worship them, than it is to learn how to love them when they argue with you or ignore you or leave you out of their plans. And when it's all said and done, you don't really choose who shows up in your world, only whether you're going to honor the connection and how you're going to relate to them. Your situation with Clay does not allow you to take the next step, Rorie. Relationships have stages; yours with Clay has been thwarted. This is why you have so much pain over the ending. You cannot complete the connection and see it to its rightful end. You left. He left. There's loss before the love can blossom and become steady and true." Sara paused, brushed a crumb off her blouse, twisted the stem of her wine glass in her fingers, and sat quietly so Rorie could absorb what she had just heard.

Rorie rose and strode across the room to sit next to her mentor. "While I was driving back here, I kept thinking, 'I have new options. I have to release Wil. I also have to release my feelings for Clay. I have to start over. I have changed and now I need to make new choices for my future.' But I have no idea where this leads me, Sara. No idea whatsoever."

"Yep," Sara chuckled, "you can't wake up and stay the same. That's unfortunately, how this consciousness thing works."

Rorie sat speechless, flooded with feelings that bound her to the gorge and those two merging rivers. The meeting, not only with the natural world, but with the human world through Clay and Coyote bonded her forever in time to love and loss. She was now an "insider" to this milieu.

"So that's why I say it's not necessarily or usually sex that wakes up a person. This can be the beginning point, but for most people sex seems to help them fall asleep, rather than waking them up. You were one of the lucky ones that sex was your entry point into consciousness." Sara halted to take a breath and then continued with a furrowed brow. "Coming alive always begins with some kind of meeting, a connection."

Rorie's voice deepened with fatigue, but she persisted, "Sara, what is the key to this new level of understanding for all of us, in particular for me, right here, right now?"

Sara looked into her lap and said nothing for so long that Rorie wondered whether she had fallen asleep. The hour was growing late, and their conversation had been intense for most of the evening. Sara's life with her family began calling to her. Then she raised her head. "I could put the answer in so many ways, that I cannot work my way through them all. It might do to simply say that what you've discovered about love is that it is dense, with multiple layers of complexity, enough to keep us busy for a lifetime, if we allow ourselves to participate in the circus of it all. Love has a constant pull on us, if only we allow for this to occur. Welcome to the arena, my friend!"

The two women, friends at a new depth, stood and walked to the front door, arm in arm. Flame followed them, in dog fashion, and while Sara stroked the animal, Rorie remembered something else. "Clay asked me the first day we met whether I love Flame or not."

"What did you say?"

"I said I do love Flame but only as much as she can be loved. This impressed him, I think."

"You gave the right answer. You saw the connection between yourself and your pet." Sighing, Sara begged, "Can we please stop this for now? This could go on forever, and I have to work tomorrow."

"Okay, but I do wonder, if everything is so bound up together, why do I keep leaving the men in my life: Dad, Wil, Clay?"

Opening the front door, Sara turned and answered, "Oh, you're still connected to all of them and always will be. You don't have to share time and space with someone to be connected to them once the connection is made."

"Even Wil?" Rorie's voice echoed her alarm.

"Most certainly. Without Wil you would never have met Clay. Wil's done his part for you, and he will forever belong to the cast in your life drama, same as you are part of him. Be grateful!"

The two weary friends grabbed each other for a hug. Rorie ushering Sara through the door, returning to host mode, saying, "Go now. Rest well. Call me tomorrow. I love you!" She grinned with her words.

"You too . . . rest well." Sara yawned as she spoke.

"Not sure I'll get much sleep tonight," Rorie commented wryly.

"Why not?"

"Consciousness . . . love . . . connections . . . my brain's whirling."

Rorie's life did not return to normal. She turned over every new leaf possible, including clearing her garage, refurbishing rooms in her house and creating a special space in one bedroom for "reading and pondering," as her father called it. She developed a routine of running with Flame in the nearby park, took walks with Sara, attended plays and concerts, and began planning her next solo trip. But her newest gain was to start keeping a journal as she had witnessed Clay doing, in order to explore her own thoughts and dreams.

At times she did not have much to say, but on other days she found she could write for an hour or so. *I don't know how much good this is doing me, but the process keeps me connected to Clay in some strange way.*

Wil could hardly look at Rorie at first, but gradually he moderated and then softened to the point of actual conversation. Rorie even thought of inviting him out for dinner together, but decided it might be better to wait for him to acknowledge the shift from a romantic tie to a friendship. She was unsure of his ability to do this.

Through her low-key euphoria, prospects of more far-reaching choices and changes stirred in the eddies of her mind. No sure message or directive came, but Rorie delighted in the patience and awareness she found to enjoy her daily activities. She began a meditation course, going out on Tuesday evenings with a friend from work who had noticed the changes in Rorie's demeanor and invited her to attend. Awareness began to blossom in her mind and her days. *I can do this.*

In the evenings, Rorie began to notice she was more fatigued than usual, but chalked it up to the perpetual emotional stirring she had experienced since her return from Wild Rivers. Getting over Clay was not easy—too many thoughts of him absorbed her mind. No matter how she worked to distract herself, moments of time she had shared with him in the canyon would creep through, leaving her breathless and then exhausted. Her dreams were swirls of bathing with him and walking the trails with him. She would often wake shivering, as if she had felt his touch in the night. Some nights, sleep was elusive as she wrestled with her covers and pillows. *It isn't as easy to fall out of love as it is to fall into love. Why is that?* Her realization of this truth kept Rorie agitated on some days, unable to move on past her attachment to the memories of their time together. *Will I ever be free from this obsession?* She longed for another conversation with Clay. She was convinced that his thoughts on the subject of love and letting go could help her with this same troubling dilemma. The days passed as the smells and colors of early autumn began to permeate her daily world.

While talking on the phone to Sara one evening, Rorie suddenly interrupted their conversation. "I need to go—will call you back." She hung up before Sara could reply and drove immediately to a pharmacy. Much later that evening she called Sara again, waking her up. Her voice trembled on the verge of fear and shock. "Sara. . . ."

"What's the matter, Rorie? You just hung up on me earlier. I didn't know whether to be concerned or not." Sara sounded puzzled.

"I'm pregnant."

"Are you sure?" Sara gasped.

"Yes. I did one of those pregnancy tests . . . actually three of them." Rorie's voice was full of emotion, on the edge of breaking.

"I'll be right there."

Crisis

O N A QUIET FALL EVENING WITH THE WINDOWS OF THE SUN porch open and the crème-colored gauze curtains doing ghost dances in the room, Clay roused from a catnap to the sound of Mellie choking. He bolted from his chair and rushed to her, where he performed the procedures he had been taught by her visiting nurse. She continued to strangle. Desperately he called for emergency help and after a whirl of lights, voices and scurrying, Mellie stabilized and lay resting in a hospital room. She was not out of immediate danger.

"Mrs. Jacobs has lost the ability to swallow—paralysis of the esophagus. Most likely she will not regain this capacity." The doctor stated his diagnosis with antiseptic precision.

"What can we do?" Clay asked urgently.

"A tracheotomy is the only remedy, and of course, that is probably short term."

"I know, but how will she eat?"

"She will be fed intravenously." The doctor could not meet Clay's eyes as he gave this report.

Clay first thought of their daily feeding ritual and how he would miss it; then recounted to himself the agreement Mellie had extracted from him early in her illness. He was to allow no 'extraordinary means' to prolong her life. But he couldn't be sure whether this was "extraordinary" and if so, whether he could go through with it. *What would Mellie want?* He kept asking himself, over and over, as the doctor laid out the options.

When Mellie began violently choking again the next morning, nurses rushed to her aid. Clay watched, feeling more helpless than at any other point in his life. He saw the frantic look on Mellie's face and decided to act. He grabbed the alphabet board that always went with her and asked whether she wanted to allow a tracheotomy, so the choking would end. She began in desperate concentration to spell out a word beginning with 'H.' When she reached the second 'R,' he blurted, "Hurry? Is this the word?" Mellie blinked affirmatively, and Clay shouted to the doctor who had arrived. "Proceed. Now!" Within moments Mellie disappeared on a gurney down the hall.

A week later Mellie was back in her sunny room at home, but now with machines attached to her. One fed into her veins and another helped her breathe through the wound in her throat. At first Clay had difficulty with the mechanical invasion of his wife. The equipment distanced him even further from her. He especially missed feeding her. The closeness of this process had consoled him, but now these machines replaced his ability to physically express his love to her. Still, the devices kept her alive and present to him. He shortly mastered keeping them maintained.

Once again life returned, not to normal, but at least to routine. Cassandra took over in the mornings while Clay went to his university office and worked on his manuscript. At mid-afternoon, Clay returned and usually remained with Mellie the rest of the day, except for tasks in the home that needed his attention. Justin relieved him three evenings a week, while Clay went to the gym for a round of racquetball with a colleague. Only gradually, imperceptible to anyone but those closest to her, did Mellie's condition deteriorate further.

One afternoon, when Clay came home to relieve Cassandra, she met him outside the door of Mellie's room. They spoke softly about Mellie, Cassandra whispering that she and Justin wondered whether they should speed up their wedding plans before Mellie became worse. Clay agreed, and together they entered the room.

Mellie signaled for her board and laboriously spelled out, *N-o w-h-i-s-p*. . . . Clay responded, "Okay, you don't want us to whisper." She affirmed his guess, flashing her eyes. Mellie always chided them when they whispered. Her spunk remained, shining through the prison of her condition.

"Okay, but what if we were making plans to give you a wonderful surprise?" he teased.

Clay and Cassandra both knew that Mellie could not tolerate anyone talking about her as if she was not there, so Cassandra revealed the decision she and Justin had made to have their wedding within two weeks. Mellie smiled her agreement. Everyone knew the real reason for the change in dates but ignored this forewarning as they focused on the upcoming celebration.

Every plan for the ceremony went through Mellie. Cassandra insisted that her mother be at the center of the details. Mellie mostly winked out her concurrence but occasionally offered suggestions, which Cassandra meticulously followed. Justin and a friend groomed the yard outside the sun porch. Cassandra decorated the entire house, rendering Mellie's room particularly elegant. Mellie struggled with a constant attempt to smile as she watched the transformation of her tiny habitat.

On the day of the wedding, a sunny October day, a friend of Cassandra's tied back the curtains over Mellie's bed and opened all the windows to expose the crisp sparkle of ideal weather. The pastor of the Lutheran church came to visit Mellie and assured her that he had counseled the young couple and found them exceptionally mature and ready for "this day of days," as he put it. Clay stood by Mellie's bed, listening as parents who adore their offspring do when someone is offering compliments about their children. The pastor seemed uncomfortable in Mellie's presence and scurried out of her room as soon as he completed his pastoral duties with her. Clay wondered whether it was Mellie's condition that made the man nervous, or the proximity of death in the room. *Funny how some people cannot handle illness, debilitation and death. And he's a man of the cloth!* Clay would have been amused except that he could not tolerate anyone who seemed to be condescending or dismissive of Mellie.

As guests gathered in the yard, Clay and Justin raised Mellie's bed so that she could see everything that went on outside her window. Then they disappeared and within minutes Justin stood beside the minister under the window. Down an aisle composed of friends and flowers came Cassandra on her father's arm, walking across the recently mown lawn to join her future with Justin. *What a bizarre thing we do, to marry.* Clay mused to himself as the strains of music from a violin quartet drew them into another web of life. Mellie appeared impassive during most of the ceremony, but tears came with a poetic reading by Cassandra's college roommate and maid of honor. The couple spoke their own carefully crafted vows, looking straight into each other's eyes. Clay heard their promises, and tears filled his own eyes as he remembered the words he and Mellie had spoken so many years before. *Such innocence at this stage! How easily we make our vows, all the while eventually love becomes loss. They have no idea what can happen to all this love and beauty. Thank goodness we don't really understand, or none of us would ever marry!* Clay suffered a moment of bitterness as he glanced up at Mellie through the window but let it go, turning his attention to his daughter's face as joy spread across her cheeks. *I will not be morbid on my daughter's wedding day!* He chided himself.

The wedding over and the reception dismantled, Clay sat with Mellie at the window, a light breeze blowing over them. It was late afternoon at this point and the sun was dipping behind the trees. Virtually all their friends had come by the open window to wave at Mellie as she lay like a statue in her bed.

Cassandra and Justin bustled into the room to bid the parents farewell before leaving on their brief honeymoon trip. They had planned nothing extensive because Cassandra was emotionally incapable of being away from her mother at the current stage of her disease. Both hugged Mellie as best they could. She smiled and blinked her blessing on them. Clay was about to wish them off, when he caught Mellie's stare and realized that she wanted to say something. He took up the alphabet board and held it for her. She blinked out, *L-o-v-e . . . i-s . . . p-a-t-i-e-n-t.* When Clay repeated the phrase, she winked her concurrence. Clay turned to the young couple, "Mellie wants you to know that 'Love is patient.'"

They nodded in agreement, but without the experience to understand what she meant. If they learned how to love each other deeply over the years to come, they would eventually discover this heavy truth. Clay gave his blessing as he ushered them from the room, walking with them to the front door. "If anyone is qualified to make that statement, it is Mellie. Now, turn your attention to each other. Have a wonderful trip and don't worry about things back here. This is your time to be together. Enjoy it!" Clapping Justin on the back, he shook hands with his new son-in-law, and then turned to hug Cassandra with a tight embrace.

Clay slowly returned to the brightly lit room as the sky outside was dimming into twilight, his shoulders slumped from the weight of the day's events. *How can one day include such deep joy and such painful sorrow, both at once and for all of us?* Brushing his eyes with the sleeve of his suit coat, he controlled his weeping just enough to keep it from Mellie. "*Love is patient,*" huh? He whispered to himself. Of all things she might have said to Cassandra and Justin, this was perfect. That statement, thought Clay, was everything Mellie embodied. He wanted so desperately to converse with her, feeling trapped in the bondage of monologue. Yet, he acknowledged that her few words, forced upon her by the theft of her voice, bore into the heart of the matter.

Clay sat, and Mellie laid, as they often did, in sustained quiet. At other times he talked or read to her. She periodically offered fragments for him to decipher, but for the most part she remained, day in and day out, silent. Listening. But now, with their own child off to her new life, they both listened. Clay paid close attention to the monitors clicking, sustaining his wife's life. He knew their every sound. At the same time, he listened to the astuteness of her one sentence, chosen from all the possible sentences: *love is patient.* He longed for her to unveil the massive wisdom that lay behind her choice of words but realized that he would be forced to plumb it for himself.

The room cooled with the drop of the sun, and Clay asked Mellie if she wanted her bed moved back into its usual place. She gave a negative signal. He covered her with a light blanket, turned on the lamp near her bed and sat again, holding her hand. He was not sure what made this brief interlude so compelling, but he chose, almost without recognizing what he was doing, to seize the moment.

"Mellie," he said quietly, while placing his face so that she could see him, "your words about patience are powerfully and painfully true, but I fear that only a few can know what you mean by them. I'm not even sure that I know . . . that I am patient enough to love. I am sure of only this much. Whatever I do know of the patience that comes from love, or that is demanded by love, I learned from you." For a while he could not continue but sat staring into the reduced face that remained his wife's only point of contact with him or anyone else. *Damn!* He screamed inside. *Is this the way one must learn love? What a beautiful . . . what a sordid deal it is, if this is true.*

Catching him by surprise, the thought of Rorie and their dizzying collapse into each other dropped into his mind. He thought of this because the lightness of those days in the canyon lay in his heart in such contrast to the ponderous weight of devotion he now felt for Mellie. Before he could monitor himself, he began voicing his thoughts. Mellie's eyes grew wide, not in surprise, but as if to take into herself everything he spoke. He recalled the passion he and Mellie had known before her illness, of how this passion had not disappeared, but had been transmuted into this more substantial truth, about love and patience. He mentioned Rorie, what he had discovered with her and how that understanding reassured him of the lighter and more uplifting aspects of love. "You and I no longer have much of that," he confessed, "but we do have something far more crucial." He puzzled how best to say it. "Bedrock. That's what it is. We've spent years boring for bedrock, for what undergirds and holds up everything we value in our relationship. What drives me to distraction is that it takes so long."

Mellie signaled for the board and smiled so broadly that she could hardly blink her word:

P–a–t–i–e–n–c–e.

Clay, catching his wife's tricky humor, poked her lightly. She offered a rare attempt at a smirk, and he laughed. He noted to himself that she had never lost her capacity for jest, particularly her readiness to make fun of herself. He said, "That's another thing. Your humor. It's kept us both going. Maybe humor is the link between love and patience." He jumped to his feet in playful enthusiasm. "What do you think?" he asked. "The test of love is patience, but we can stand the test . . . through humor." Clay paused to check her machines and then resumed sharing his thoughts with her, standing at the foot of her bed, massaging her feet. "Do you ever ponder 'endurance' in all of this madness?" He looked to her for support and response. Mellie offered a frown of rejection, but Clay knew that look and recognized that she was teasing him. He embraced her with the delicate touch that years of care had taught him. "I'll be back."

Clay left the room, then returned with a glass of tea and a chicken salad sandwich. He had eaten nothing at the reception, partly due to excitement and partially due to playing host for both himself and Mellie, which had been a daunting task. Asking Mellie once again if she wanted her bed moved, this time she blinked, "Yes." He obliged her needs. She signaled for the board and offered him two words, *N-e-v-e-r e-n-d-s*. Puzzled, he asked, "What never ends?"

L-o-v-e. Her intention shone through her eyes.

After further deciphering, Clay recalled the final phrase in the love hymn that had been read for Cassandra and Justin during their ceremony. *Love never ends.* Mellie's visage charged with emotion, and he knew she sought to convey her most serious feelings. "Yes," he agreed, "love is supposed to last, but that's what I've been thinking about for months now. I love you, but we both know that I'm going to lose you. This is the unbearable burden of loving you. I *will* lose you." His voice choked as he continued, "How can I tolerate that?"

Again, Clay held up the board, and Mellie signed, *N-o f-o-r-g-e-t*. She used 'no' for all negative references. "Do you mean, 'don't forget?'" She signed agreement, and he asked, "Don't forget you?" She again agreed. Her words dumbfounded him. He wanted once again to scream. *How could I ever forget you? How could that possibly happen?* But he controlled himself by sitting quietly beside her bed, until he could form words of reassurance.

"You live in every thought I have, Mellie. You are an imprint inside me." He struck his chest forcefully with one hand. "Forgetting is out of the question. If that is how 'love never ends,' then this love is safe." He locked his eyes onto hers and held on for dear life.

Mellie signaled, *M-e t-o-o.*

Clay stroked her hands and withered arms, amazed at her continued intensity in the face of her ordeal. Then he suddenly remembered a passage written by Joseph Campbell about marriage: *Marriage is not a love affair; it is an ordeal.* Certainly, within the relationship between Clay and Mellie, Campbell's statement applied. Though theirs was a love affair, her illness had clearly cast them into an ordeal neither of them could ever have imagined when they married. Today, on Cassandra's wedding day, the love between her parents was more endearing and demanding than ever before.

Clay surmised that Mellie struggled with the encounter he had shared with Rorie. After the years of their patterned sketchy dialogue, Clay had begun to know her thoughts beyond what she uttered. He admitted openly to her, "The thing that perplexes me most of all is that my devotion to you continues undiminished, but meeting Rorie gave me a sense that I will have a future . . . a difficult idea to believe in without you in the picture."

Squeezing her fingers gently, Clay went on, "Mellie, I know you offered me the gift of my future by accepting the story of my time in the canyon. I know that story causes you to suffer. Yet, we both recognize that you will leave me, and that I will need to continue my life. I want you to know that I am aware you have given me hope for life after I lose you. You have given the ultimate in our relationship; you surrendered your own desires for mine. Though this hurts right now—to imagine a future without you, I know that someday I will fully recognize your sacrifice. I will always be grateful to you, my beloved Mellie. You will *never* be forgotten."

Mellie cried as her way of participating, tears streaming down her lined face onto her clothing. Clay knew that such expressions of emotion were especially difficult for her now that she could not swallow. Her tears frightened him. "Is this talk between us too hard for you? Should we stop?"

She indicated with a roll of her eyes that he must continue. Clay saw in a flash that they had to have this conversation before Mellie could be free. *I understand this now. Mellie, I understand.*

She finally managed, despite her pitch of emotion, to spell out the same phrase she had offered before his trip into Wild Rivers. *G-o o-n.* He was not sure whether she wanted him to continue talking or meant that he must go on with his life. He chose the latter, and she confirmed it. "It's not easy to talk about or even think about life without you," he confided in a soft voice, saturated in agony. "It's easier to believe that I won't forget you. Remembering you will hold me together, I believe, as long as I don't drown in anger over losing you." After waiting to summon his inner rage into obedience, Clay added, "You do realize that all of this makes me livid, don't you?"

Through her stream of tears Mellie grimaced acknowledgement. On her board she signed, *R-e-l-e-a-s-e.* Clay leaned carefully across the bed to hold her. A sentiment overwhelmed him that this halting conversation might be the seal on their life together. Last words. He lay down beside her, cradling, until he felt a shared sense of peace with her. She indicated that she wanted to sleep. He slipped off her bed, made sure she was covered, and lowered the lights before leaving the room.

Wandering into his study, Clay, emotionally exhausted and still angry at the universe for tormenting his beloved, dropped into his reading chair. He brooded for some time, dozed, then thought of Mellie's face. For most of his adult life he had been a man of words, but she stalled and limited his words by her own spare communication. She forced him to know her face, to read her eyes, her lids, her lips, even the way she made her nose crinkle or twitch. Her heart began to live in her face, and he had learned ever so gradually and painfully to read it.

Clay spotted his journal resting on a shelf beside his chair. He had not written in it since the trip to New Mexico. Picking up the book, he rubbed his fingers over the embossed cover, opened it to a passage and read the first sentence: *I love two women!* The declaration, so blatantly true when he wrote it, bewildered him now. *Can that be so,* he wondered, *if love never ends? Do I endlessly love both?*

Turning to a blank page, recording the date in the upper right-hand corner, and after logging the wedding and his feelings about it, Clay scrawled:

Mellie knows so much more than she has the energy to speak. How cruel that this disease is teaching her such potent lessons that she is unable to communicate to us. She wants my assurance that our love is not lost, even in her death, but she loves me enough to want my life to continue. This is the great pain of love: Death! Mellie can die, if she knows she will not simply disappear without a trace, but her own love for me still wants me to continue living, even now. Death makes love, and life, feel so tenuous. I cannot solve this tension. All I can do is assure her now and remember when she's gone. What an irony if she were to outlive me?

Clay placed the journal on a book-laden side table and fretted over his conversation with Mellie. Their understanding, that unending love means remembering, failed to satisfy him. It wasn't enough. *If love never, never, ends, then it is larger than my own memory of my own beloved. I too will dissolve into death. Where does memory go then? Does it cease? That's not possible either. Love has to be larger than any one soul.* The thought came flooding to him that never-ending love had to be larger than the love between him and Mellie, more encompassing, or between any two or more people. Reaching quickly again for his journal, he wrote feverishly:

I recall that startling passage in one of Gabriel Marcel's books, where he confessed that even though his wife was dead and had been gone for several years, he still loved her. At the time I read it, I thought him romantic or sentimental, but now I begin to see what he meant. If this is not true, then love is a temporary stopgap measure to take our attention away from death. The problem is that death will not stay at bay, not for long. It is so damn real! I can feel it hovering around that sun porch.

Clay's concentration broke as he thought of Mellie sleeping but a few feet away. The word "bondage" came to his mind again to describe her situation, and he recalled another statement from Marcel. He wrote:

Marcel also said somewhere that marriage is a bond that sets us free. The paradox of this has obsessed me since graduate school days. Mellie may be in bondage to her body, but if Marcel is right, the bond between us still liberates her. But into what? What good is such freedom?

As fatigued as he was, Clay could not stop his thoughts from pouring through his beleaguered mind. They came to him in an overwhelming jumble. He recollected another book he read years earlier, *The Denial of Death*. At the time, Clay had thought that Becker's basic idea, that humans live by strategies which deny death and that they thus live violently, seemed overdrawn. Clay confessed to himself, *Now I can finally grasp what Becker is saying*. Clay added his own insight that because death is the supreme enemy of love, we seek a love that never ends.

Picking up the journal for the third time, Clay scribbled rapidly:

That's it! Love is not the name for a particular relationship. It is more like a universal force, loose in the cosmos. It is what holds everything together, and our "little loves" are only expressions of this greater truth, like moments of participation in the stream of love. We step into the stream at birth and continue in it until death. Even if we spend our lives denying this love, railing against it, we are saturated with it all along. The strength of love holds us, contains us. It is more than remembering, as important as that may be. It is a matter of undergoing a "shock of recognition." If we awaken to the depths and reaches of love, even once, we join the vast flow of it. This is what never ends.

Clay flopped back in his chair, as exhilarated as he was weary. In a mystical slice of time, he saw the drama of life with Mellie more fully for what it was. For a moment he enjoyed a release from the melodramatic way he had endured love and the rage of this sure march toward death. He knew he probably would not be able to sustain this luminous emancipation for long, but it marked him, and he could hardly wait to share his insight with Mellie. *I've lectured for years on life, love, death and the words of great minds, but this thought has never become clear or personally compelling until now. We are so dense in the face of our own mortality. Or is it rebellious?*

Clay pored over his own thoughts and this moment of lucidity. He wondered whether he was confessing more than his hard-nosed philosophical bias could digest. He sounded nearly religious and wondered what that meant? But what he had mentally created through his own anguish mixed with joy possessed a ring of truth he refused to deny.

After he again set the journal aside, the new ideas dominated his reflections, especially that he and Mellie and Rorie and everyone else belonged to a grand sea of love and connection. They were all in this vast ocean together. Standing, he felt the stiffness of the day fall upon him and stretched to unlock his muscles. He walked back to Mellie's room, checked her breathing and then lay down on his own bed for a fitful night filled with a groggy brew of images: Mellie, love, death, Rorie, merging rivers. . . .

After the return of the newlyweds, Mellie's decline continued, gradual and grueling to the point of cruelty. The family waited. So did she. Patience.

Ending

DEATH CAME IN THE NIGHT.

Clay awoke starkly and sensed a presence in the room. His eyes searched, but he saw nothing. The only sound came from the low hum of a monitor attached to his wife's body. He was accustomed to punctuating his sleep by rising to check on her, but he realized he had slept longer than usual.

Stretching and allowing his mind to clear, Clay still sensed something alien and anomalous but pervasive around him. He stood awkwardly out of his recliner chair, where he had often slept beside Mellie's bed in these last few weeks, taking a moment to regain his balance and come fully awake. Moving closer, he saw her face from the dim light of a lamp always kept on in the corner of the room. In the grim, rigid cheekbones he read her death. Her last remaining means of being present to him had vanished. Her lower jaw sagged. Her eyes, half open, were fixed on infinity. Without examining her body for vital signs, Clay knew, but he performed the tests anyway, as taught him by the hospice nurse a few weeks earlier. Once he had confirmed her departure, he sat down beside Mellie's still form, numb.

Duty prompted him to phone Cassandra and Justin, but when the numbers on the face of the clock spoke of deep night, he refrained and settled back into the recliner, taking Mellie's limp hand in his, as he had done with daily regularity for several years now. He decided at that moment not to call the hospice nurse until morning. Clay did not want to be robbed of the remaining few hours alone with this woman whom he had known and loved since they were a young couple. He claimed this right to be together in the stillness of this final night. He had endured a deathwatch of well over five years and now found it difficult to do anything else but sit with her. As long as the vigil had been, her departure still struck him with its abruptness. Death, he discovered, is rude, impertinent. Its presence in the room replaced her absence.

Clay had long feared he would mark Mellie's passing with relief, and he did not want to experience that. Far too dismissive. After all they had endured together, that would never do. To his surprise, however, he did not feel relief at all. He felt lost, bereft of her presence. He murmured to her, as if she might hear him. *It is not the loss of you, Mellie, but it is my sense of being lost without you that I didn't expect.* Having grieved gradually and for so long, he assumed that the actual end of her life might bring a closure to his mourning and her suffering. Instead, the separation itself proved more daunting than he had imagined.

Mellie lay in state before Clay until dawn. He watched over her. He washed her body in ritual fashion, just so he could view all of her one final time, remembering how he had caressed and stroked her over the years. A chaos of memories and images of her filled his mind, a pending uncertainty invaded his soul. The incomprehensible fact of her death passed before him like a phantom. In this final dissolution of their oneness he loved her more than ever, but this love felt set and inflexible—a separate reality. *Was Rorie right? Mellie can only be loved in as much as she can return my love because the truth of love is that it reaches for reciprocity . . . that door is closed to both of us. Our love is now frozen in time. We will never witness our love fulfilling the normal stages of life. I do love you Mellie, but now I have lost you. Our love rests in the memories we made together.*

He sat down again, for one more hour, reading love poems to the woman who had filled his life, day in and day out. This was Clay's intimate and private farewell, offered for the both of them before the world would entangle them in bittersweet details.

A shaft of light sliced through the room from the window next to Mellie's deathbed and drew Clay from his chair. He rested Mellie's hand on the cover, her favorite quilt, and reached for his phone to call his daughter. Cassandra and Justin arrived in what seemed like seconds, and the house pulsated with their anguish. The hospice nurse arrived immediately after and began her routine. The three family members stood about Mellie's bed, watching the nurse perform her duties, and then, with sparse words, asked for moments alone with Mellie. They turned back to face her body and share their goodbyes with her lifeless form, speaking haltingly and with reverence, each taking a turn to voice their personal grief and gratitude for this woman. Memories. Appreciation.

Cassandra removed a necklace that she had worn constantly during Mellie's illness and placed it over her mother's folded hands. After an interlude of silence, the three weeping figures interlocked their fingers, and Clay spoke softly, "And may flights of angels bear thee to thy rest." Clay removed Mellie's wedding band, and his mind flashed to the day he had placed it on her finger and promised, "'til death do us part." Aloud he said, "I never dreamed on our wedding day that our parting would come so soon." His voice was gravelly and wrought with misery. Once again, the three of them huddled tightly just as the official world entered the room, led by the nurse, to efficiently arrange the death details as they had been dictated long ago by Mellie herself.

Every wish Mellie had uttered became a reality over the next four days, ending with a memorial service in a garden at the university. Clay, sitting awkwardly in his rarely worn dark suit, marveled at the crowd that gathered on a partly cloudy morning in late April, the sun peeping through just enough to warm the gathering. At the center of the circle of humanity a blue urn rested on a table draped with a white cloth. Surrounding the urn rested the artifacts of Mellie's life, including a photo of her in robust health. A second photo showed her emaciation attended by her notorious smile. She had insisted on just that juxtaposition. She said this would be a "statement," but Clay could not quite comprehend her intention. *Whatever she wanted to make known remains mysterious to many of us, yet it's so like Mellie to insist on such a metaphor.*

A music student stood on a stone wall, guitar in hand, and sang in slow haunting echoes, *Morning Has Broken.* Then Mellie's pastor, the same one who had performed Cassandra's wedding just a few months before, said the requested and required words. Daniel, Mellie's counselor, sat with the family, melding his grief with theirs. Mellie's closest friend, Dana, gave her eulogy. Neither Cassandra nor Clay felt up to the task, unable to compose themselves for this ritual of heartache. The family duty had fallen to Justin. As he stood to speak, Clay felt a lump swell in his throat, grateful this young man could bring some semblance of clarity to the event.

Justin said to the audience, "Near the end of his life, Plato was asked what all of his writings taught, and he answered, 'They teach us to practice dying.'" Clay immediately felt Mellie's presence close by. *She certainly put in her practice hours on that one. I've never known anyone to be so faithful at this formidable task.*

Clay broke down upon hearing Justin's words, now staring fixedly at the blue urn. A choir assembled inconspicuously within the circle and sang, *Ode to Joy*. Cassandra joined her father's tears as they grasped each other's hands tightly between their chairs. The minister pronounced the final benediction and the service ended quietly. A light breeze stirred the air and vanished. Clay shivered in his suit. *Goodbye, Mellie. You are loved. You will be remembered. I promise to go on, just as you instructed . . . but I don't promise that it will be very soon, my love. I will miss you greatly.* Although others were rising, Clay continued to sit, holding onto his daughter's hand, quaking inside, his face drawn and full of sadness. He leaned over and whispered in Cassandra's ear, "Here comes the hard part." She nodded, understanding that they were both now expected to present themselves to others and receive their condolences. The pair stood up in unison, repaired their tear-streaked faces and began the awkward ritual of accepting sympathy.

Familiar faces began to mill around Clay and Cassandra, shaking hands and patting Clay on the shoulder. He was numb to the words of his colleagues and friends but gave the appropriate smile and response. One particular face in the crowd puzzled him. A young man, clean shaven and dressed beyond the care usually taken by students, called him by his given name, embraced him and passed into the dwindling crowd. When only a few people remained, a woman, dressed in a severely tailored dark suit, moved toward Clay with conspicuous professional propriety, handed him the urn, and offered her services if he needed anything else. As Clay accepted the container of the remains of his wife, he spotted the young man leaning against an elm tree at the edge of the garden. Unable to quell his curiosity, he walked toward the stranger who appeared to be waiting for someone else.

Approaching tentatively, Clay asked, "Do I know you?"

"Yes, sir, you sure do," the stranger spoke quietly, reverently.

"Are you one of my students?" Clay felt embarrassed and irritated all at once.

"Yes, I have been. But there is more to our story than that, Dr. Jacobs."

Clay, vaguely recognizing the familiar voice but unable to make the connection in the fog of loss, finally asked, "What's your name?"

"My official name is 'Edmund,' but . . . that's not the name you would recognize. I go by Eddie now." The young man teased, and then suddenly erased the smile from his face as he realized he was speaking with a man in grief. He hastened to add, "You probably remember me as Coyote."

Clay's mind spun into gear, and he was immediately back at Wild Rivers meeting a scruffy, ill-clad virtual waif with long, unkempt hair and a straggly beard. "Coyote!" Clay greeted his young friend with too much enthusiasm, relieved to have a break from the agony of the previous couple of hours. "You sure have changed your appearance!" he exclaimed, stroking his chin to symbolize Coyote's missing beard. He then grabbed Coyote—now Eddie, and hugged him awkwardly, the urn bumping between them.

"It's a story I'd love to tell you, Man. I can swear to that," Eddie said, shaking his head in disbelief at what he had to share with his mentor.

This sudden appearance of his young friend thrust a host of memories upon Clay. He stood under the aging elm, holding the ashes of his wife and conjuring the week with Rorie and Coyote. This reverie somehow felt irreverent, though not unfaithful. He had from time to time thought intensely about Rorie, more in fantasy than remembrance. Now these memories came to the fore with unexpected force. Coyote stood before Clay like a trickster.

"I can see this is not the time," Eddie acknowledged, "but I sure would like to talk with you at some point . . . when you're ready. I'm back here in school, about to finish my degree."

Clay stared at the student, noticing that he had matured in stature and in his demeanor. "No," he agreed, "this is not the right time. But I would enjoy a visit with you. I need to process what has happened to me and hear your story. Let's meet. Just give me some time. Right now, my head is not really very clear." Clay shook his head from side to side as if to demonstrate his point.

Eddie and Clay agreed to meet for breakfast two weeks later. They parted ways, and Clay returned home with a commitment to begin the exorcism of his pain. He by no means wanted to rid himself of the vestiges of Mellie, but he did want to sanitize the entire house and clear it of her disease. All of the paraphernalia that had sustained her seemed to him like mighty anchors, holding him and their house at bay. Now she was delivered of them, so could he become free.

Over the next few days, Clay did purge all the things reminding him of Mellie's suffering and her death. Out went the hospital bed, the machines of sustenance, the wheelchair she had used earlier, and all of the bottles and boxes representing her great enemy. Consulting with Cassandra, he decided to paint the whole place, inside and out. He wanted the color of Mellie's life around him, not the scent of her death. They chose light, bright colors to fill the rooms, splashing pillows and throws around to create a space that drew one into an embrace of warmth and welcome.

Three photos were placed on a table under the window where her bed had been for the past few years. A picture of Clay and Mellie standing before a minister, her long white gown trailing behind her, displayed their faces glowing with excitement and anticipation. The second photo was a snapshot Clay had surreptitiously taken of Mellie sitting on their patio one summer when she was in her thirties, reading. She did not know he had taken the picture. Thus, her face was not posed, but pensive and open. He loved this image of her, having placed it in a simple frame many years earlier. Taken by a photographer friend, a family photo completed the trio, with Cassandra as a young teen, tightly held by her parents on each side. *Memories, silent images, reflecting times that are no more.* Clay stared at the photos and wondered how long it would be before they would be removed and replaced.

Clay reached the café ahead of Eddie and ordered himself a coffee, dark roasted and steamy hot. When Coyote breezed through the door into the quaint local student hangout, he searched the room for Clay's familiar face. The two men were in the place early, before most students had spilled out of bed and headed for their caffeine fix of the day. Eddie dropped his book pack on the floor and scooted into the booth to join Clay,

During the two-hour conversation that ensued, Clay learned that Eddie's father had died. Their grief gave them a new common ground, even more intense than digging into the hot spring had offered them. Eddie shared with Clay that the woman he had lost, Hannah, had returned to Kansas, and they were both back at the university, resuming their relationship, at first tentatively, but now in the full blossom of love. Before long Hannah appeared through the door of the café, her eyes focused on her love. Eddie waved to her, calling across the room,

"Hey, come over here. I want you to meet somebody."

She maneuvered through the randomly positioned tables to the booth where Coyote reached up from his seat and put his arm around her waist as she stood beside him. Studying the young woman, Clay noticed that she had a sprinkle of freckles across her nose, with wide striking green eyes that stared at him with curiosity. She was a bit too slender for her choice of clothing, which seemed baggy around her waist and legs. He noticed a small tattoo on her wrist. Yet something about her seemed to exude confidence. He easily grasped why Coyote was attracted to her.

After the usual greetings, Hannah said nonchalantly, "We need to head to class now, Eddie. Okay?" Coyote nodded and stood up to leave, turning back to Clay one more time, "I hope we can talk some more. I'd like to talk like we did in Wild Rivers." Suddenly he was shy again, hoping his former professor and now friend would see him as a man with whom he could talk about the more serious matters of life.

Standing up, Clay waved the two off to their class. Sighing deeply, the grief-filled professor dropped back into the booth, melancholy filling his mind. *I remember how it feels to be in love like those two. Will that feeling ever be part of my life again? Why do I feel so empty?* Unable to determine his next move, he did not want to return to the office. His book was in disarray, not the manuscript, but its counterpart in his mind. He was muddled and weary these days. He did not want to go home either, and face all the signs of unfinished business waiting his attention. While Mellie lived, he at least had well-worn grooves in which his days played out. Now everything was smooth but trackless. No familiar ruts to comfort him, to keep him plodding.

Desperation

CLAY LEFT THE COFFEE SHOP AND DID SOMETHING HE HAD NOT done since high school. He slid into his green Ford pickup and drove all afternoon, cruising the streets and then the outlying roads around the town. He considered driving the three hundred miles into Nebraska to spend time with his father, now in a nursing home and unable to recognize him or anyone else. At least he would be company of a sort. He and his father had been close, but in a traditional, manly way. The old man had too much of the sediment of years on the farm and all that went with that way of life to do better than treat Clay with distant kindness. But it was enough, for the most part, because Clay's mother had brought balance to the equation of his childhood. She had died far too young, but not before leaving him the imprint of her constant quiet affection. His childhood had been stable, predictable and comfortable.

But now that lost feeling pressed him from all sides. Cassandra remained his only orienting beacon, but she bore her own grief and needed to find solace in her new marriage. Clay chose not to intrude, even though they would have granted him sanctuary without reservation.

Having exhausted his meager options for company, Clay dissolved toward desolation. He stopped at a roadside park on the opposite side of town from where he and Mellie had shared relaxed hours together. He sat on a bench, wishing he could cry, or write, or scream. *How do you write down one long howling scream?* Everything was too close, too immediate. He wanted to escape, but realized he would only take his raging grief with him everywhere he went.

Thoughts of Coyote's story—*he still seems like Coyote to me,* he ruminated—revived him and invited him back into all the events at

Wild Rivers. And to Rorie. *Not even a picture. All I have of her is one small white stone. What did, does, she look like? How can these thoughts fill my head when Mellie just. . . ?* The whole business was far more bewildering than he dared examine.

Weeks . . . months passed in a blur of sleepless nights, lethargy, a feeling of drowning in sorrow. He woke at night for weeks on end, hearing Mellie's voice. He raged and stormed about the house before collapsing into the chair where he had sat holding his dead wife's slender hand, tears running down his face. *I have to get my act together,* Clay would scold himself. *But I really cannot imagine living every day for the rest of my life without her.*

September arrived in a blaze of warm days that announced summer was not yet finished. Then, toward the end of the month, with leaves beginning to color, cooler temperatures propelled Clay to another park where he and Mellie had often met for more serious conversations. He needed to be close to her, to find closure on the trails and tracks of their lives. Simultaneously, he wanted to savor memories of her and release the sadness. His heart and mind were fatigued from the daily onslaught of grief.

After he had spent an hour of wallowing in the morass of his sorrow over his loss of Mellie, Rorie once again came to Clay's mind. Afternoon dwindled into twilight and early evening. Street lamps in the park came on, shedding halos of light around him. While Mellie lived, he dared not take even the memory of Rorie seriously, but now. . . .

Deciding to find something more substantial to ground his memories of the phantom woman he had known in the canyon, Clay drove back to his house. After preparing himself a light supper, he settled into the leather chair in his office. Before long, his attention turned to the telephone on his desk. He kept telling himself this was ridiculous, that she was surely married by now and living under another name. He remembered her full name but was not sure of the spelling. He tried three variations and then, to his amazement, there was a listing for 'Rorie McDonough.' Just as he was ready to dial, Cassandra called to him from the living room where she had entered the house.

Clay fell into embarrassment bordering on chagrin. Cassandra intuited him, but did not press. She attributed everything these days to their shared pain. They visited only briefly. She begged him not to change everything in his life too quickly. He assured her he was only trying to make some basic changes to rid the house of death, and to acknowledge that he was single again, though not happily so.

"Justin and I want to get away for a few days, for fall break."

"Good idea. Where are you going?"

"To the beach, in Georgia. But we don't want to leave you stranded." Her face showed her concern for Clay.

"Don't worry about me. I need some time anyway. Say, are you going where we used to vacation as a family?" Clay's demeanor perked up at the rush of memories from the times he and Mellie had spent on St. Simon's Island with their small daughter playing in the sand.

"Yes. Justin has never been there, and I need to walk the beaches and think about Mom. This seemed like a good time to do it—but only if you are okay?" Her forehead wrinkled with concern for her father. "When we return, Dad, promise me that we can have a real talk about everything."

Clay walked over to her, and they embraced. "Yes," he agreed, "I will sure need that, probably as much as you do." *Well,* Clay mused, *I'm sure not ready yet to discuss everything.*

Cassandra retreated, and the screen door squeaked shut behind her. Pulling his phone from his pocket, Clay pondered whether to call Rorie. He knew rationally that such a move might score against his sanity, but the vacuity within him did not currently respond well to reasonable options. He stalked through the house, randomly moving things from one location to another, looking into the refrigerator, throwing trivial items in the trash bin by the cabinet. He felt an implosive pull at his gut, unrelated to anything he could grasp, let alone explain.

The brewing outrage of his isolation continued to heat until late in the evening. On the one hand, he knew everything he did. On the other, he sought some folly to express his outrage, something deliberately mad. Nothing sufficient rose to consciousness. He staggered back into his study, closed the door, a thing he had not done since Mellie's illness, and sat on the floor. At first, the rage was undirected. Then tears. Then a moan rising into a cry. The volume and length grew into a full scream that lasted as long as his breath, followed by another more focused and welling from his diaphragm. In the back of his mind he did think of the neighbors, but he did not care. His screams continued, increasing and subsiding, in a steady rhythm of cathartic exorcism. It was as if he needed to release some inner demon that threatened to take him over or to occupy a vast vacuum that filled him with an utter void. His cries continued but gradually dissolved into brief, panting grunts and finally whimpers. He lay on the floor, curled into a prenatal position, and fell asleep.

In the night, he was not sure just when, Clay awoke, still sweating from the ordeal and stiff from tensing his body. He sat up, lightheaded, and returned to the familiar world that ordinarily protected him from such dashes into psychic chaos. He felt a certain release but no deep gratification of soul. He still wanted desperately to do something of consequence, not simply going on as always, but something that tore an opening into his future.

Clay stood uncertainly in the middle of the kitchen. Reaching for a bottle of wine, he poured himself a glass and toasted the air. *To doing something different!* He pulled the phone from his pocket again but saw that it was far too late to call Rorie. *I need to let this idea go for now,* he instructed himself. Then, moving toward his bedroom, he began preparing for bed. *Later. I'll call later . . . right now is not the time.* His eyes closed, and he fell into the first dreamless sleep since Mellie's death had begun robbing him of his rest.

After Cassandra and Justin left on their trip, Clay saw his opportunity to once again try to contact Rorie. It was a Friday evening. Because fall break had begun, the town was quieter than usual. Most of his friends were away or were with their families. Clay had made no plans for himself when his mind began to churn with a sense of urgency. But this time the idea was wild, completely unlike anything he had ever done before. He filled his toilet kit, grabbed an extra shirt and jeans, then plowed through his dresser for underwear and socks. Within an hour, before better judgment could prevail, Clay drove out of the driveway, headed out of town. He plotted his course along a southern route.

Through the waning night into the dawn Clay drove. Once he found I-35, he drove faster. Kansas granted permission. By early morning he entered Oklahoma, and well before noon he left the red land for the grand landscape of Texas. In the afternoon he reached Dallas. He had located Rorie's address in his search for her phone number. He wound through a complex of highways, avenues and streets until he located her neighborhood.

Only when he spotted the sign marking Rorie's street did Clay finally stop and sober sufficiently to reflect on his actions. *What in the world do I do? Go up and knock on her door? What was I thinking? I must be crazy!* He felt suspended between folly and utter disconnection, neither one attractive. *If I could only see her,* he concluded. *That's what I need. To be sure she's real.* This flash of insight gave him enough confidence to drive, ever so slowly, down the street of upscale manicured homes, until he came to her address: 3208.

He drove past and came back, stopping across and slightly down the street but still within sight of her front door. He rolled down the truck windows for fresh air and waited, but he did not know for what or for how long. By then it was close to dinnertime. After sitting for more than an hour, he realized that he had not eaten a meal since he left Kansas. He vacated his stakeout and drove to a nearby shopping plaza, where he resigned himself to food designed for cardiac trauma.

Taking his time to eat, he wanted to reenter Rorie's neighborhood in the dark. When he drove back to her street, traffic had settled down and houses were lit up for the evening. He returned to his lookout station and did not have to wait long before he saw lights come on in various rooms in her home. Then they would shut off as she moved through the house. He fell asleep watching her home.

Rubbing his eyes, Clay startled awake as early morning light struck the windows of his truck, covered with condensation from his breathing all night. He started the engine, praying that the neighborhood did not notice him, and slipped out to a local twenty-four-hour gas station with a fast food eatery attached. He went inside for the restroom, sustenance and a hot coffee to warm himself up. Having met his needs, he drove once again back into Rorie's neighborhood, vowing to knock on her door when it seemed reasonable to do so. After parking the truck again in his usual spot, he sipped his coffee and studied the houses scattered down the street. *She's done well for herself. Nice neighborhood. Good place to. . . .* Just as Clay was about to turn on the radio for the sound of a human voice, he noticed her front porch door swing open. Rorie emerged, with a small child on her hip, bent over to retrieve the newspaper, looked up and down the street, paused, stared at his truck, and then entered her house again, closing the door behind her.

Clay's emotions vacillated between elation at seeing Rorie and utter devastation at her carrying a child. He concluded without reflection that she had chosen Wil and that she now enjoyed marriage and motherhood.

After Rorie retreated through the doorway, Clay sat staring as if to memorize her appearance and what she wore. He even tried to conjure the child's face but had no luck at this. Although from a distance and incognito, he found consolation in being this close to her and having her reality confirmed. Rorie had, for a moment, gazed in his direction, creating a bewildering panic in his chest. He started the truck and glided past her house as quickly as he could. He wanted to look toward where she had stood, but he dared not. His chest was pounding, and a light sweat had broken out across his forehead.

With no further thought of intruding, Clay drove funereally down the street and turned into increasingly heavier traffic, bending toward home. *I sure pushed the limit here*, he admitted with recovered composure. *She left me in that canyon and came back to her life here. Why should I expect her to have done differently? She would not have been pleased to see me. Ugh. I'm tired.* He drove into a huge parking lot attached to a Walmart and slept deeply and soundly through the morning until noon, when the sun was straight overhead and the cab of his truck had become too warm. Once he had fed himself, gassed the truck and bought a strong coffee for the road ahead, he left Rorie and her world behind. Driving into the night, Clay used every strategy he could summon to release himself from his fixation on this elusive woman. She persisted in his thoughts. He fought with all his mental fortitude to turn his mind from her face. When he could no longer stay awake, he pulled over to a rest stop and slept again.

The following morning, unable to believe his own behavior, Clay drove sheepishly, slipping into his hometown like a wayward teenager returning from an all-night beer bust. He wanted to see no one, nor to be seen by anyone. He entered the house he had still not fully accepted as home once Mellie's presence no longer lingered there.

Although Clay could not yet give the inner voice his full attention, he heard a whispering deep within, urging him to surrender this place and to plot another course for his life. Looking about him, he felt the panicked need to run away flash through him again, shaking his body. He wanted out, out of the house and out of himself. If it were not for Cassandra and Justin, he might have bolted at that moment.

Steadying himself, Clay once again trudged through the rooms, inspecting signs of disorder all around him. Somewhere in the wellspring of his being he realized that, given the choice between facing up or fleeing, he must begin with the former. The fever of his anguish subsided, but desperation remained within him, a goad.

Beginning

Sara insisted on going with Rorie to her visit with the obstetrician. The earlier pregnancy tests were confirmed. Pregnant. Returning to the waiting room, Rorie whispered to Sara, "As I suspected, I am—what did they used to say? A 'lady in waiting.'" With a fist full of prenatal pamphlets, brochures and sample vitamins, Rorie and Sara exited the colorful room where they would spend much time over the coming months. Rorie giggled nervously, spouting, "Let's go have lunch. I'm already exhausted and starving, and this baby isn't any larger than a tadpole yet."

As they headed to their car, Sara noticed a restaurant across the street. "Let's walk over there for a quick bite?" Rorie nodded absentmindedly.

As they sat down over cool raspberry iced teas, Rorie whimpered, "Sara, what am I going to do?"

"Knowing you, Rorie, you have probably considered all the options and then gone over them again and again," Sara replied, shooting Rorie a wry grin.

"Every possibility I can imagine: adoption, abortion, talking Wil into marrying me, calling Clay, doing nothing. I've thought of it all. None of these ideas are options, at least not for me!"

Baiting her friend, Sara mischievously asked, "What about Wil? Is he an option?"

"No! He most certainly is not!" Rorie answered heatedly. "I don't want to trick him, nor do I want to spend my life with him. That's off the table, Sara!"

"Whoa, friend—I was teasing. Didn't expect such a reaction from you. I'm sorry." Sara grabbed Rorie's hand and squeezed it. "I can see you are more upset than you are letting on. So I'll be serious for now. What do you truly feel about this pregnancy, Rorie? In your heart of hearts?"

"Actually, I have not seriously thought about anything but keeping this . . . uh . . . baby?" Rorie blinked away the sudden burst of tears that filled her eyes. "Raising a child without a father does not sound easy and I am scared to death. But this is also Clay's child, and I cannot imagine doing anything but raising him . . . her . . . it. It's all I have left of my time with him. This baby is the only connection between us."

"Think you'll ever tell Clay?"

"Probably not. But I have wondered if I should, and if I do, when? His wife is ill and dying—what a terrible time to learn such news. Would he even want to know? He should be told, but I cannot imagine how I could tell him without sounding like strings were attached. For now, I think I just have to leave this situation to myself alone. Maybe later."

Sara spun around to squarely face her friend, "Rorie McDonough! You are *not* alone in this. I will be with you every step of the way. So take that idea and erase it from your mind right now!" Sara's face had flushed with righteous indignation.

"Thanks, Sara. I know I can count on you. I was just referring to the 'long haul'—the years without Clay while I raise his child. Right now, that sounds formidable. Yet that's the right decision, at least for the time being." Rorie slapped the table in affirmation, feeling much more vulnerable than her words sounded.

Sara asked out of the blue, "Does Clay have any children?"

Rorie sighed, "Yes. He has a daughter. And now I realize my child belongs not only to Clay but to his daughter." Dropping her head into her hands, she groaned, "This is so complicated, Sara. I cannot sort it out in my mind at the moment."

Finally, she looked up at Sara, "But some secrets should probably stay that way, out of sight. Right?"

Shaking her head, Sara replied, "I'm not one to appreciate secrets so much. Why do we have to be so secretive about such important matters, especially when the details of our stories connect us to one another? I won't be one to urge you to keep your pregnancy secret from Clay. I understand your reluctance to tell him, but at the same time, he deserves to know."

"Knowing is a burden, Sara." Rorie spoke clearly, "Clay is then forced to carry this news around with him and try to respond. Do I want to put that pressure on him? I'm not sure. And now, I'm one of those stories, with strings hidden beneath the surface. I'm not ignorant of what you are working hard to say to me without judging me, Sara. And I love you for this. For now, I just have to go with my gut in this situation." Rorie squirmed in her seat and shuffled her feet under the table. Then she continued her thoughts.

"Ever since I suspected the pregnancy, I've gone over every conceivable possibility in my mind, day and night. If I ever have the least suspicion that telling Clay might. . .you know . . . benefit him, I'll do it in an instant. But for now, the most . . . I don't have a better word for it . . . compassionate thing I can think to do is give birth to this child and take care of it. When and where to let the father know that he is a father has to be left to the future. I cannot worry about that right now. This is my burden."

Sara concluded, "So I see you are in this for the duration. I'm happy for you. It's your decision, and I know you can and will live it out. You are strong, Rorie. You have your father to thank for that strength. I was worried about having this conversation with you because I thought it might be about which option to take. But I can see you have made up your mind and you feel clear."

"I'm sure about it," Rorie acknowledged, "but that does not mean I'm not afraid. Even when I called you the other night, I knew what I would do. But I'm also living in daily panic about the enormous burden of what is ahead for me." She shook her hands in the air to demonstrate her fears. "Sometimes I have these tiny ecstatic moments, now and then, at the very idea of carrying this other life wrapped up in my body. Having children was all right for other women but not for me. I never gave being a mother much thought, probably because I didn't have a mother, so I know nothing about whether it is important to have a mother in one's life or not. I survived without a mother. But now, with the fact of the pregnancy dawning on me I'm excited, worried, yes! But also thrilled. Does this make any sense?"

Sara grabbed Rorie's hands on top of the table, patted them and grinned, "Yes, it does. You are going to be a terrific mom, Rorie. Don't you worry."

The following months of Rorie's pregnancy flowed through the routine markers: occasional morning nausea, exercise, diet, larger clothes, backaches, tight leg muscles. When her belly began to show that she was obviously pregnant, Wil came into her office one morning in near hysteria. He punctuated his entrance by slamming the door closed.

"Is that . . . uh . . . a baby?" He stuttered, pointing at her midsection as though it were a poisonous snake.

Rorie almost laughed out loud but decided this would only make Wil angrier. "Yes."

"Is it mine?" He stomped his foot for emphasis.

"No, it's mine."

"That's not what I mean, and you know it!"

"Think about it, Wil. It is highly unlikely, at this stage, that this baby is yours."

Wil responded like a sleuth who has uncovered a decisive clue, "Then you *are* involved with someone else."

Rorie sighed deeply, "It's a long and impossible story, Wil, but I offer you this assurance. The baby is not yours, and I'm thrilled to be carrying it."

Wil turned solemn. "You're not doing one of those surrogate things, are you?"

"Hardly. But I am making a decision to be a single mother."

Wil snickered, "Oh, that new thing women are doing. . . ."

"I don't know or care about some 'new thing.' This is a deeply personal matter to me, and I really don't. . . ."

"Okay, okay. I'm not trying to nose into your business, but I sure didn't . . . don't want a paternity suit out of this. I'm about to. . . ."

"No chance of that. You're safe." Rorie reassured him as she ushered him out of her office.

Wil turned back toward Rorie. "Have you told your father about this?" He knew exactly Rorie's weak spot and how to gouge her emotions.

Exasperated, Rorie snapped, "Wil, you have my permission to stay out of this." She closed the door with a sharp click. "Whew! Glad that's over!" she mumbled to herself. Then Rorie began to stew over how and when to approach her father with her news.

Rorie's pregnancy and planning for the coming of her baby fanned into a flame of smoldering dissatisfaction with her career. Good pay, great benefits, maternity leave, chances for advancement. These lures hung constantly before her and everyone working for the company. Such treats kept the employees in the groove. But since the gorge and her encounter with Clay, to say nothing of the life throbbing below her diaphragm, the domain of her living options had expanded. She considered specifically searching for a position closer to her original love: literature. Since coming to Dallas, she had perceived her work and her life there to be an adventure of privilege and pursuit. But the upcoming advent of a child had thrown her into hidden desires for a less intense lifestyle, closer to her own sense of purpose.

When Rorie learned through office gossip a few weeks later that Wil had announced his engagement to a woman in another department, she inwardly delighted at her own decision against marriage. *Ugh! As I suspected. He only wanted some woman to fill a missing square in his portfolio. Better her than me.* A more perverse thought encroached: *Can't wait to tell Dad. He needs to know this.*

Wil's announcement only added to her incentive to consider other options for her livelihood. Within days she collected and reviewed job descriptions, ranging from teaching to editing journals to editing for publishers. Most of them represented a considerable comedown from her metropolitan lifestyle. Some she rejected, because of where and how she would have to live. What guided her more than anything was the possible consequences for the baby.

In one of their "girl talks," Sara shared that when she was pregnant, she repeatedly dreamed of the baby and what it might look like. Rorie confessed that she seldom remembered her dreams, but two nights later. . . .

Clay walks toward her. He approaches from the other side of a river. Rorie calls to him but worries that he will not be able to cross the expanse of water. Clay begins leaping from stone to stone in the river, great ballet leaps. Rorie rushes to meet him, but when she reaches the river's edge, Clay is a baby, laughing at her and reaching its arms toward her ready to be taken up and held.

Rorie sprang awake at first light, reviewed the dream repeatedly, and when enough time had crept by, she called Sara to share the story. Sara responded with a hoarse morning chuckle, "They merged."

"What?" Rorie had no understanding of Sara's esoteric interpretation.

"Clay and the baby. They became one."

Again, Rorie tried. "What does that mean?"

"Oh, Rorie. I'm no dream analyst, but I do believe dreams show us things we miss when we are awake. In your mind Clay and the baby are so tangled together that you see them as one being. The baby carries Clay for you. Or within you."

"Oh, my! I hadn't thought of that. I kept trying to get him across the river to come get me. But instead, he became my baby."

"Well, our dreams tell us truths about ourselves that we don't yet know. Just keep working on it and thinking about it. Soon you will understand the dream."

Rorie plopped into her favorite bedroom chair and threw an afghan over her legs. "All right then. What is the truth in this dream?"

"You are the only one who can decide that, but for starters, if I were to guess, I'd say that much of your investment in the baby has to do with your continuing interest in Clay. You haven't yet let go of him."

"You mean 'my obsession' with him?" Rorie snapped back.

"No. I didn't say that." Sara answered quietly.

"No, you didn't," Rorie said contritely, "I said it. Sometimes I do find myself chasing around that canyon looking for him and for what we had there. He's a difficult fantasy to surrender."

Sara breathed into the phone, "And your baby is a way of finding . . . or actually keeping Clay close to you, or at least what you had with him."

"That doesn't sound healthy, Sara, having the baby all mixed up with my lover. I have a lot of work to do on myself before this little one comes into my life, don't I?" She sought Sara's confirmation of her conclusion.

But Sara did not want to take the bait. "Well, eventually maybe you'll need to separate the two, for the child's sake. The baby will have a right to its own life, not yours or Clay's. Still, they are connected, both biologically and emotionally for you." Sara paused, her own thoughts diverting to her sons and their connection to her. "That's the hardest part of being a mother. At least it is for me. You make this bond with your children, and then you have to unravel the cords and untie the knots, so they can have some kind of life separate from yours. But then you don't want it all simply to come undone. You'll find once this happens to you that it's the strangest connection."

Rorie mulled over Sara's comments in her own mind. *That's what Dad has not been able to do with me . . . unravel.* Then, mumbling to herself, Rorie muttered, "So that's the trick love plays on us . . . we still have to surrender, even our own children, if love is to stay alive and healthy."

Sara replied, "Now you're catching on—love ya."

The two women rang off, resuming their daily routines, Sara with her family, Rorie with her preparations to create a family. The following week, Rorie went for her ultrasound. She had debated whether she wanted to know the baby's gender but decided in favor of the information. *A boy. It fits,* she told herself, recalling her dream. Dashing home, she called Sara on her cell, then her father, with the news.

The fact that she would bear a son gave her the opening she needed to tell Sean, and he handled the news in a rare fashion, calmly with a tinge of excitement but only after besieging her with questions about the paternity. "Is this Wil's baby? Are you involved with someone? Why didn't you tell me about all of this, Rorie?"

Rorie stayed quiet through his interrogation, until he finally relented, "I guess you aren't going to answer me, are you?"

"No, Dad. I'm not. It's none of your business really. Suffice to say, I'm not with the father of my baby and likely never will be. This baby is mine and if you are nice to me, I'll share him with you." She hoped her levity would get her father off her back for the moment and allow him to move along into the joy of the news. Sean's attitude changed when he heard the determination in Rorie's voice. "Okay. Let's go from here. What's your due date?"

The day passed quickly after this, Rorie returning to work and then concluding by taking Flame on a long walk. That evening she sat in her living room, flipping through parenting magazines, studying hints on how to get babies to sleep along with how to choose a name. *I will be the mother of a son. Me! A boy who will become a man. And I have to raise him alone. Can I do this?* Panic crept back into her body, causing her to shiver. *Yes. Yes, I can.* She assured herself. She fell into a free-flowing fantasy about how they would be together, how she would take him into the woods for walks and allow him the pleasure of all that she had known from a childhood spent along Lake Michigan. For Rorie, to invite any male creature into her life involved the calming vitality of nature. She had long suspected this, but the days with Clay along the Rio Grande had sealed suspicion into fact.

Stirring from her flight of imagination, Rorie made her way through the darkened rooms of her house, leaving the lights off. She entered her ample, rather cozy bathroom, began filling the elevated oval tub, and sank into the swirling water.

Her mind flashed immediately to the hot spring in the gorge, to the exotic and intoxicating grotto, where she had found herself in that fateful meshing of body and soul with Clay. After lying back, a towel folded beneath her head, and dozing to the gurgle of water and oils around her, she awoke and stared down at her abdomen. Her veins stood as clear as state roads on a travel map, covering the tight distended curve that reminded her of a world globe. She supposed that all the roads led toward her son, and she was traveling to meet him.

Don't worry . . . She began talking to the mound beneath her breasts encircled by water. Suddenly Rorie realized the life within her had no name. *What am I going to call you?* She began exploring for his name. *You will have a name. Your very own.* Her hands clasped the sides of her burgeoning womb, and she entered upon her first conversation with this life which was only briefly one with her own. *I don't really know you yet, and you don't know me. But we will soon meet, and nothing will ever be the same again. I will show you the world, and you can help me see it again through your eyes, new eyes. I will tell you everything I know, and you will teach me how life feels as a boy, and then as a man.* Suddenly she thought of Clay. *Will I ever tell you about your father, or your father about you? When? How? Will you want to find your father and know him?*

The rush of questions drew Rorie away from the quiet intimacy with her son-in-waiting. She drained the tub as she toweled dry. For the first time, she faced the stark fact that her son would have his own personal connection to Clay, a connection that did not simply rest with her alone. *Am I robbing my own child of his chance to know his father?* She felt like a thief in that moment, stealing away treasure after taking it from the one person she least wanted ever to offend.

Draping a light robe around her shoulders and walking to her bedroom, her bare feet massaged by the soft carpet, Rorie felt her way to a small writing desk where she turned on the lamp, sat down and began to frame a letter. She wrote on her best stationery, a mauve parchment with scrolled edges.

Dear Clay,

Although I should apologize for the abrupt way I parted from you, I do believe that you, more than anyone I have ever known, will understand. The problem for me that last morning was simple but disastrous: I loved you instantly, from the moment you fell sprawling in the rain, but I knew this attraction could never be fulfilled. Given what you were facing, my presence could only contaminate and complicate your situation with Mellie. I also knew that in your own way you loved me, and I vowed to save both you and me the hurt of separation. If I used poor judgment, please forgive me. No day passes without my thinking of you and wishing desperately that our connection could have been otherwise. We were both in that gorge on a mission, and the result became that we were caught in an improbable love story. Surely not the best of outcomes for either of us.

But now I find the separation and ending of our love is not fully possible. This will no doubt come to you as a great surprise, perhaps a shock, but when I returned home, I soon discovered that I was pregnant. You are the father. Please know that I have no intention of making demands on you. You have entirely too much to face without this new dilemma causing you more grief. On the other hand, I am not comfortable keeping this information from you. You have the right to know about the baby and to choose your own response to this news.

Today I went for my examination and learned that I—we—are to have a son. I promise to raise him with the best ideals of love we discussed during our days in Wild Rivers. You must know this much: in some fashion he will bear your name. I do hope that our child will come to know love in a way we both knew it for those few precious days in the canyon.

Tears gushed as she wrote, and she overwhelmed the nearby tissue box with her demand. The letter proved cathartic beyond any expectation she could have conjured. She was at last speaking with Clay, even if indirectly and only within herself. She longed to pour out her soul, to do all in her power to draw him nearer to her. Yet, she knew she must keep distance, remain steady in her resolve not to intrude beyond this one clarifying note.

Our time in Wild Rivers has changed my life forever, not only in my understanding of what love truly is, but in the reality that our connection will give life to another human being. For this, I am forever grateful to you.

With love, as you made it possible, Rorie

Rorie slumped against the back of her chair, as if she had given another kind of birth. The letter lay before her as perhaps the most honest single utterance she had ever made. Reaching into her desk drawer for an envelope, she folded the letter, inserted it and folded over the flap. Only then did she realize she had no address for Clay. She would have to snoop for it. She wrote only his name on the envelope and slipped it into the drawer.

During Rorie's last weeks before the birth, she invited Sara to serve as her coach. They attended sessions together. Sara called herself "the midwife." On the night when Rorie's contractions gained rhythm and frequency, she called Sara, who rushed her friend to the hospital. By this time, Rorie had undertaken every gesture of nesting, like a bird or a beast preparing an extended womb for a new life. The nursery was prepared and waiting, with blue blankets and other soft touches for the arrival of a baby boy. Tiny pastel clothes were stacked in baskets, and diapers were folded and ready beside the changing table. A stuffed toy bear with a turquoise bow around its neck rested in a rocker where Rorie looked forward to spending many hours in the months to come.

Ushering the expectant mother into the birthing suite, the nurses tried to block Sara from entering. But Rorie insisted, "This is my helper. She's the baby's Godmother." When the nurse still did not budge, Rorie said more emphatically, "This is my birthing coach. Please let her come with me."

"Certainly," the nurse said officiously.

Birth. The drama and pace of the process stunned Rorie, even though she had read every book possible on the topic.

"There's no other way to get into the world," a fleshy nurse announced as she began to prep and attend to Rorie. Sara, only slightly uncomfortable, sat near her friend's head, as they visited between contractions and procedures. During a lull in her labor, Rorie rushed through a litany of thoughts. *I am now a channel—a conduit—for this small creature, this boy, to come into the world and join us. What an astonishing process!*

When the tension in her body returned, she fought to reduce the pain and agony. Sara whispered instructions to her about breathing, relaxing and pushing. Rorie concentrated through the spasms contorting the lower half of her body. As the tension subsided again, Rorie imagined the face of her own mother, who was actually only a vague spirit to her. Feelings for her mother intensified for the first time in years and left her longing to look into the face of the woman who had made her own life possible. *My own mother went through all of this to bring me here.*

I have never once before now given this a thought. How I wish she were here to share this with me, to hold my hand and tell me things will be all right. I've never really missed my mother before, but now I am so aware that she is not with me. She tried to share her feelings with Sara, but the sentences would not come out without groans surrounding them.

Rorie entered another spasm, and groaned out, "I think . . . it's . . . time . . . Ugh! Ask for the nurse, quick!" Sara jumped up and ran to call for assistance.

When it came time for Rorie to push down, everyone in the room focused on the opening of her body, the yielding. Through her rapid panting breaths, she urged Sara to look at the delivery so that later she could describe the baby's first appearance to her. A round convex mirror hung from the ceiling, but the doctor and nurses kept blocking Rorie's view of herself exploding with life. Sara, despite having birthed three children, stood transfixed at the marvel of this most universal human event.

"Except for death, nothing matches this. It's pure mystery." Sara whispered to Rorie.

The baby first coughed, then squalled its way into the room, announcing his presence with momentary authority. Rorie's sense of release came instantly, and her subdued euphoria gave way to tears of fatigue and relief. Then a large, bustling nurse brought the infant to its mother, nudging her to try to suckle her son. Through the fog of dulled consciousness, Rorie uttered the child's name for the first time: Donegal Clayton McDonough.

"Well, that's a mouthful, I must say. Not a very modern name. He's not big enough to be called something like that, is he?" The nurse made her declaration with authority. "Where'd it come from?"

Before Rorie could answer, Sara said protectively, "From his grandfather . . . Irish." Then she stared into Rorie's sweat-lined face, and said, "And we won't forget it!" The nurse chuckled and turned to attend to Rorie's needs. The moment was sweet and tender, as Rorie looked into her son's face for the first time. *My, he's wrinkled and so tiny. He has Clay's eyes and my nose. I'll have to explain that to him some day, I suspect. Well, little fella, here we go. Are you ready?*

Rorie had promised to call her father after the birth. Sara stood in for her and made the call. Sean answered in Chicago, and upon hearing the news crowed like a rooster in the barnyard. Then Sara held the phone for Rorie. "Hi, Dad. It's a boy, like I promised."

"What'd you name him?"

When Rorie told him, Sean said, "Ah yes, I like Donegal. Had a cousin. Remember? Killed in the war. But it's a fine Irish tag, I'd say." He repeated the name to himself several times, then spilled his emotions into the moment. "I'm pleased the family name continues. If you'd married that fellow Wil, he'd have robbed me!" He bellowed into the phone, and Rorie felt as though she had finally done something to deeply satisfy this demanding father. He then asked, "Where'd you come up with that middle name?"

"Oh, I just like the way it sounds . . . especially if he wants another choice when he is older." Then to divert Sean she added, "I plan to call him Donie. Dad, I'm tired . . . I need to let you go for now." She handed the phone back to Sara, saying nothing more, but thinking, *Someday, he may choose to call himself Clay. That would be just fine by me!* She thought of the letter tucked away in her desk drawer. Rorie's eyes blinked and she realized she needed a thorough sleep. Handing her son over to Sara, she yawned as her head dropped onto her chest.

During her six weeks of leave from work, Rorie and Donie bonded as she negotiated the rituals of learning to mother. Her own sense of affection for her tiny charge grew and changed daily, astounding her, even fatiguing her. *How is it possible to love something this small so much?* Recalling the impact of those conversations with Clay about love, she longed to reexamine the topic with him. "Nothing," she confided to Sara, "can match loving this baby. Nothing! How come no one tells you this?"

"It just happens to you—or it doesn't. There's no way to describe what it is like to fall in love with your own child." Sara grinned at Rorie, as she took the swaddled baby from her and held him close before laying him down.

Rorie sobered up and reported her immediate thoughts to Sara, "I'm learning quickly that mothering is paying attention, constantly paying attention. Loving anyone at all requires paying attention, but being a mother seems to make extra demands." The two women sat surrounding the infant as he lay on the sofa between them, arms flailing in the air.

By the time Rorie had integrated her life with Donie's and returned to work, she once again concentrated on her options for the future. She wasn't in a rush, but was definite that she wanted a change for the two of them. The first two years of Donie's life were spent very much in a routine of expanding the world for him and adapting to parenting for Rorie. They were a compatible pair, and Donie was an easy baby to nurture. He ate and slept well, with only a minor rash here and there. He learned to sit up, walk and form basic words easily, clapping his chubby hands when he realized he had delighted Rorie with some new accomplishment. The only part that Rorie found challenging was being a single parent: there was never a break. All responsibilities and decisions fell to her. At times she was so fatigued she wondered if she could do it all. But then, she would look into her son's bright eyes, and the burden lifted immediately in the rush of love she felt for him.

The day finally came when Rorie was ready to move on her desires to create a new life for the two of them. Leafing through a publishing trade journal one evening while listening to the baby's soft breathing from his crib, she spotted an inconspicuous advertisement. It sought an editor for a flourishing publishing firm. But it was the location that engrossed her: Santa Fe, New Mexico. Negotiating for an interview, Rorie asked Sara to keep Donie for her while she made the trip. Donie was a precocious toddler at this point, and it would not be good to take him with her.

Rorie spent two days in the heart of New Mexico, saturated in memories of her brief time in the land that had offered her love at one point. Before she left Santa Fe, the company offered her a position as one of two editors. She asked for three days to consider their offer, and then called Sara to check on Donie. "I think I am going to accept the job. I'm ready for a change and this will put us in new spaces. I can see myself raising Donie out here. What do you think? I trust your feedback on this."

"You've said for quite a while that you want to move, Rorie. And I know how much you love New Mexico. I will miss you terribly—I'm not happy about that part at all. But I would never try to stop you from living out your dreams. So go for it, girl!"

As she resigned her job, sold her house, said her farewells, and packed to leave, Rorie's days whirled with feverish details, chasing Donie, and packing boxes. She took the child on daily outings along with Flame to a park close by, just to give them both a break from the madness of moving.

The evening after her last day at work, with its official rituals of separation, Rorie tucked Donie into his crib and then retreated to her own bedroom. At first, she felt the sadness that attends endings, but looking about her almost-bare room, stripped of its décor at this point, she realized it was time to pack her most intimate artifacts: photos, books, gifts connecting her to other people. She reached into her desk and cleared the drawer quickly, throwing away things that she no longer needed. She groaned at the chaos of papers and began riffling through them. Hearing something fall to the floor, she reached down and saw her letter with "Clayton Jacobs" written in her hand. All focus on the move vanished, and she sank to the floor. *I never mailed this.*

The earlier questions about whether to tell Clay pervaded her thoughts again, and she yearned for wisdom. Torn between protecting Donie and preparing the way for his own life, she turned to the man who continued to occupy her imagination. *What would you do, Clay? I mean, with all your talk of love. Tell me, what is the loving thing to do here? Would you really want to know given what you are going through?* No answer came to her, but she sensed him, that he was in turmoil and that she was in his mind and part of his tumult.

Rorie did no more packing that night, but continued to sit beside her bed, ransacking her mind for memories to caress. Leaving this house would mean her final goodbye to Clay. Starting a new life, she realized, really meant letting go and moving forward. The night was spent in tears and reflection. She slept only briefly, curled on top of her covers, in her clothes. Donie stirred and cried out in the early dawn, as if sensing his mother's angst. She scurried to his room and picked him up. He was feverish. This gave her the perfect excuse to extend her nightlong brooding into and throughout the day ahead. She kept telling herself that she should be packing, but she also felt the pull of another need, to stall long enough for her own inner goodbye in preparation for the dimly imagined future. She moved through the day in slow motion, picking up Donie to hold him, checking on him, then putting him back down to rest. She had called the doctor, who had instructed her to come in if the boy's fever reached a certain point, which it never did.

While caring for her sick child, she handled things around her house, decided whether to rid herself of them or take them, puttering with boxes and tape. In the afternoon, the teen-aged girl next door came over to watch Donie so Rorie could run to a nearby shopping center for food and a prescription for her son. The kitchen had been packed, so she was eating out at this stage.

The night brought relief for mother and son, both sleeping soundly until their usual rising time. Rorie awoke and ran into Donie's room to check on him. Relieved, she found him playing with the stuffed and tattered toy bear that had lain in his crib since birth. Looking up into her face with a grin, he called out to her, "Mama." She grabbed him up for a resounding kiss and hug. "How about some breakfast, young man?" She crooned over the boy. About that time, she heard the newspaper hit the front porch, reminding her to cancel her subscription. Going to the door in her robe, holding Donie on her hip in his pajamas, the two greeted the sunny morning. She stepped out to retrieve the paper, then stood watching a pickup truck start up and move down the street. It had an out-of-state tag but was too far away to read. She wondered why the driver would be in her neighborhood. *A wayward soul, looking for a friend or family*, she mused.

Three days later, Rorie bade Sara adieu, the only seriously sad separation marking her departure. The last thing she packed was her letter to Clay, just before the movers hauled her desk down to the truck. She stuffed the troublesome note into her personal satchel. At this point Rorie had decided not to mail it, not yet. *It's not time. I don't know why, but I'm not ready.* She put Donie in his car seat in the rear of her car. Flame lay on the seat beside him, guarding Donie as if he was the most precious item in the car. Boy and dog were well bonded.

Rorie backed out of the drive and began the long, two-day journey to Santa Fe.

Leaving

WHEN THE SCREEN DOOR BANGED SHUT, CLAY TURNED TO SEE Cassandra standing inside with two bags from their favorite deli. "Thought it might be time for some sustenance," she explained as she walked past the clutter of boxes into the kitchen. Clay followed her, washed his hands and pulled a chair up to the kitchen table.

"You read my mind, and I didn't even realize I was hungry," Clay cheered. "You must be clairvoyant."

"Wish I was. Then maybe I could understand why you are packing up and leaving. Isn't this your home, Dad?" Cassandra set their food out on paper plates, as his dishes were already packed. She waited for her father to respond, but he only stared at her while he bit a plug out of his sandwich, chewing slowly. "Remember what the counselor said, that you . . . none of us . . . should make any major decisions while we're grieving."

"Then I might not make a decision for the rest of my life, Cassie." Before Cassandra could retort, Clay gestured, as if surrendering. "I know, I know. I recognize that I've been mourning ever since your mother's diagnosis. But now that she's actually gone. . . ." He did not pursue this line of discussion; he didn't want to repeat again what he had said so many times already. "This is the fact of the matter for me right now: I must do something, and I need to do it somewhere else. It's been two years, my dear daughter. I need to make a move forward for a change. I've been in a pit of grief for what feels like an eternity."

"But your family, Justin and I, we're here. And friends, colleagues. Don't we matter to you? What about the grief you will put us through when you leave. I've already lost Mother. Now I'm losing you too." Tears formed in her eyes as a storm cloud gathered on her face. "This is the worst possible time. If Grandpa Jacobs hadn't died on top of everything else . . . I just feel like our family is falling apart." This time the tears streamed down her face as she pushed her plate forward, unable to join him in their impromptu lunch. "You used to be close to Grandpa. You always talked about him and. . . ."

"But Dad didn't know me at the end, Cassandra. I'm not mourning him in the same way I feel sad about your mother's death. The timing is uncanny, for sure: a year to the day after Mellie died, I lost my own father." Clay hesitated, disturbed by the words he was about to say. "But in a way, Grandpa's death actually helps to bring to closure another chapter in our family story. It was hard enough to lose your mother, and then to add my father's death to our already difficult grief was a bit too much. Yet, because of his dementia, there is relief, unlike what I felt when I lost your mom. I need to seek a new life path now. Could you please try to understand this?" His mind shot back to Mellie. "Your mother kept saying to me that I had to 'go on.' I hated to hear her say this, but as usual, she got the picture long before I did."

"Hey, remember me? I'm still here. I'm part of your. . . ." Cassandra was pouting at this point.

"Yes, you are not only part of my family, you are part of me. You are the future, not my past."

"But I am here in the present, Dad." She spoke defiantly.

"And I need to build a new present, Cassandra. My days are empty, habituated, without excitement or passion. I can no longer live this way—and your mother didn't want me to!"

Father and daughter stared at each other, both afraid of saying something that would take months or even years to heal. Clay reached for Cassandra and she reluctantly placed her hand in his. "Cassandra, I know you think I am running away from all of this. And I cannot actually say you are wrong. But that's not how I feel. I actually feel like I am moving toward something. Everything that happens here in this house, in this town, keeps me stuck in the past and feeling useless. I want courage and inspiration. I need to explore what it means to live without Mellie and see if I can rebuild my life. And, most of all, I need your support."

Releasing a huge breath, Cassandra slumped in defeat. "Okay, Daddy, then, tell me exactly what you're after. Maybe then I can understand all of this."

Clay took a drink of his lemonade, and then gulped out a reply, "Perhaps this sounds hokey, but I'm after a new life. I can taste it, but I don't have words or a picture for it yet. Only the book that I am writing is my continuity. It will go with me and perhaps if I leave here, I can actually finish it now. The rest of what might happen to me will just have to be a surprise."

"That book hangs over your head like an avalanche waiting to happen. How long have you worked on it and muddled with it? I'll bet—" She was about to make an exaggerated guess, but Clay interrupted her.

"I know that's what it must seem to you. But what I know is that I could not have finished the darn thing before now. Mellie's death inspires what remains to be written. I am doing this for her now. Something of her needs to be left for the world as a way to know her. And Grandpa's death only adds to the script." His eyes wandered as he tried to explain to his daughter thoughts that he had not yet formed until this moment.

"I get it, Dad, but you can finish the book anywhere, including right here in Kansas!" Cassandra felt now that she had her father at checkmate.

"It's more complicated than that," Clay replied, not sure how to outwit her maneuvering at this point. All he could do was confirm his decision and stay the course, even if she failed to grasp his explanations.

"You're the one that's complicated. You!" Cassandra stood up from the table and stomped over to the kitchen cabinet with her paper plate, her sandwich only half eaten. She gathered the remainder of the lunch into one of the bags and shoved the remnants into the trash bin by the back door. "Look, this is probably not going anywhere. You've almost finished packing. I don't know why I keep bringing it up, but if Mom were here. . . ." She halted abruptly, not wanting to use her mother against her father. Her resolve crumbled.

"Justin will come back here with me tonight, and we'll help you finish packing." Her concession was granted grudgingly, but Cassandra loved her father and wanted no quarrel with him right before he went away.

"You don't have to do that, you know." Clay was grateful for her offer but did not want to push his frustrated daughter any further.

"I know that," Cassandra shot back over her shoulder as the slam of the screen door marked her departure.

A lot of her mother in that young woman, Clay surmised as he looked to find where he had left off packing. *Except Mellie would have encouraged me. She was more adventuresome. She always wanted to go, go, go.* He stood as fixed as a statue. *That's what made her disease so bizarre. She couldn't go anywhere.* Turning to a group of boxes with their mouths wide open, Clay began to pitch towels and linens into one of them, slowly dismantling his world.

Then the thought that had repeatedly crept along the back edges of his mind and surfaced at his most vulnerable moments, spoke itself through him again. He said to himself, "Where, where is she? She must be somewhere in this universe. I just don't know how to reach her." On the most unexpected occasions her absence continued to hang, almost palpable, before him. And just as he was at his worst, the image of Rorie with the child on her hip would flash through his mind. *Gone, both of them gone.* This thought stole his energy and forced him to move toward a bookshelf that needed to be packed. Sometimes Clay distracted himself from this absurd interrogation of no one, but his heart never let go of the oppressive sense of her absence . . . their absence, the two women he loved.

I've done this long enough. It's time to close all of this down. All along I thought I was preparing for her to leave me. Now I must leave her . . . both of them. I must put the past behind me. It's time! He scolded himself until he turned and grabbed an empty box, staring at the books in front of him. He needed to concentrate on a task to break this freakishly persistent obsession over Mellie and then Rorie, back and forth his mind would go. When thinking of Mellie, he would tell himself that she no longer suffered.

Since the failed attempt to contact Rorie, Clay dismissed her as a source of consolation, and added her loss to his list of grievances. He told himself that it was really not fair anyway. *Too much like an escape. I don't want to do that. How would I know if I was running from my grief over Mellie if I connected to Rorie right now? I would never know. Not a good plan. Besides, she's married now and with a baby. Enough's enough.* Still, Rorie's image remained, a sliver of light, splitting him away from the clarity he needed right now to plow through his anxiety about the "new life" that he threw so carelessly at Cassandra. *Ugh*, he mumbled to himself, picking up a spool of tape to seal the first box of books he had dared to pack. *Why am I packing all of these? Shouldn't I cull some of them? How much of my past do I want to take with me?* Clay ripped more tape from the spool with a vengeance and slapped it on the box.

Because the packing consisted mostly of mindless details, Clay fell to reviewing the past two years: the death of Mellie, closure with Rorie after his hurried trip to Dallas, the loss of his father, the complications of the estate, along with medical, funeral and other debts, the endless bits and pieces demanding attention. With special relish he recalled the very day when the last of the paper work had dropped into the appropriate file, and he saw that he was more than solvent.

His father had left Clay and his sister with hefty inheritances, which had the potential to change their lives quite dramatically. Clay still regretted selling the farm, and when he thought of that expanse of fertile Nebraska land that had been in the family for three generations, he moved through nostalgia to melancholy. His sister, who had soon moved to Vermont after their father's death, did not want the land. Since she was twelve years older than Clay, they had never been particularly close. As adults they had hardly seen each other. She had no children and had never been interested in Cassandra, who likewise did not feel the absence of her strange, rather reclusive aunt. Clay felt like thanking the land for at least opening external possibilities at the time of his most bewildering internal disorientation. He could make decisions now that allowed him to move on with his life, even without his teaching position.

After turning in his resignation, Clay exited the department chair's office with a sense of having cut a tether from an imaginary dock and floating out toward an open sea. The sea was not calm, but its horizon beckoned him. *I think I shocked him, but this decision is exactly what I need to move on. Amazing what extra coins buy. They buy time! About the most elusive purchase I can imagine, but I'll take it.*

A week later Clay told Cassandra and Justin about the resignation, and that he was giving them the house and moving away. "Where on earth will you go?" Cassandra's voice was shrill, with only barely controlled panic and a flash of anger stirring in her eyes.

"West. Not sure just where at the moment, but it will be in that direction for sure. It has to do with time. Kansas is the past for me. Out there," he pointed through the window toward the distant, barely visible rolling country side, "Out there lies tomorrow, and I'm buyin' in!"

From that day forward Cassandra pulled every strategy she could conjure to keep her father from leaving. As the end of the semester approached, Clay's resolve to move away only strengthened. During the final week before Clay was to leave, when the house was in disarray with his boxes, most of them bound for storage, Cassandra relented. By that time, Clay knew where he planned to live: Taos. "I should have known," Cassandra nodded. "That's where you and Mom spent your best times, wasn't it?"

"No doubt about that," Clay noted wryly. "Too bad she. . . ." *Not going there!*

"At least we will want to come and visit you there." Cassandra sought to help him, sensing his struggle with memories.

It worked. Clay joined her playfulness. "Oh, and if I'd decided to move to Oregon or Louisiana, you wouldn't come see me?"

"Sorry. You'd be on your own in those places," she giggled.

Clay had sorted and packed for weeks, both his work office and his home. Final exams intervened during the last week of the semester. *That's my last time to grade papers. I wonder if I will miss doing that onerous task,* he thought ironically. *Actually, I will miss my students, watching them learn and grow up right before my eyes.* He thought about Coyote, now Eddie, and his experience of watching the disheveled pilgrim become a man bent on living his own story. On his final day, Clay quickly finished sorting out the living room and most of the dining area. He was done by noon with this part of the house. Feeling the urge for lightness, he had decided to leave most of the furniture and artifacts to Cassandra and Justin, though he did want to keep his desk and a small curio cabinet that he and Mellie had chosen when they were first married. *I want a fresh start. Not taking this household with me . . . too loaded with memories.*

The sun beckoned him into what had been his study, slanting just above its setting and shafting through the west windows. He walked into the room for a final check. An echo bounced off the wooden floor as he crossed over it to sit one last time in his desk chair.

Spinning around to face the window, Clay looked down at the windowsill. An object resting there caught his eye. It appeared to be a tight wad of paper, but when he reached for it, its solid form became a revelation. It was a white stone. *Rorie!* He had kept the rock on the shelf behind his desk chair and could not fathom how the stone had ended up next to the window ledge. Picking up the burnished pebble and rolling it in his palm, Clay allowed his mind free rein. *One thing about her . . . she is persistent, even if she did bolt and run. Can't shed her, either in my mind or my house.* The discussion with Mellie about his encounter with Rorie charged again into his mind. He still could not grasp the capacity of his dying wife to so much as face the reality, let alone accept it and encourage him. He discerned that both women, each in her own way, had marked him for life, and the loss of them did not allow him to slough off either of them. Shoving the stone into his pocket, Clay turned off the ceiling light, exited the room and closed the door.

Still sweaty and grimy from stuffing boxes all day, Clay plundered the house for paper. In recent days, while planning his move, every thought of Rorie or Mellie inspired more attention to his book. Rescuing used sheets of paper from a small table in the hall that would stay with the house, he sat down at the kitchen table, holding the solid round stone in his hand as though it were Rorie's heart, and wrote feverishly on the backs of the pages.

Once we have loved, truly loved—and that is our purpose, to reach that highest state of human emotion—we can never really lose this love or the beloved. If we can discover this for ourselves, then loss becomes bearable.

Clay asked himself whether he really believed this and added, *I want to believe this is true. If it is, I don't know how to make it real. How do I allow love to grace my life again and ward off this unutterable absence? This longing.* Then he wrote, as if in his journal: *This is probably why I'm writing the book, to find out what love is worth in the face of loss. I want to show that loss is actually part of love (probably its most definitive part), belongs to it and can't be separate from it. When we buy into love, we buy into loss. Love is the only thing that actually survives loss. The human heart urges toward love.* Clay shook his head, running his hands through his hair, searching for clarity to continue. *Love is the essence—the core—of the human story. All we have in the end is our urge to love—and our ache to be loved. It's all we are left with when everything else is gone. And it's quite enough.* Clay reflected for some time, watching through the kitchen window an afterglow in the sky, as day spread itself along the undulating horizon to become one with the impending night.

When Justin called from the living room, Clay stood, crammed the sheets into a folder that needed to be packed and hoped he would remember later how to retrieve the papers. He answered hoarsely. "Yeah, I'm still packing." His son-in-law complimented him on how much work he had accomplished. Clay, offhandedly, replied, "Tryin' to finish something, at least somethin' positive for a change." He did not want to sound depressed, because he wasn't. He then regretted his remark.

Justin only nodded and continued, "Well, you've sure pulled it off."

Clay appreciated Justin's cheer. Cassandra joined them, and the three threw themselves into the final push. Before midnight everything to be stored was in the dining room, and everything for the rental truck dominated the living room, neatly stacked.

Clay spent the night at Cassandra and Justin's apartment, itself in disarray from their own pending move back into Cassandra's childhood home. The achingly long day ended as Clay cleared a space for himself in the back bedroom. Cassandra peered into the room, asked her father if he needed anything and said, "It'll be odd—I guess that's the word—to move back into the house where I grew up. All those. . . ."

"Memories?" Clay guessed.

Cassandra nodded an affirmation, then offered her testimony. "Dad, I've lived in this town most of my life. I've seldom been separated from you. Mother is gone and now you are leaving. I've been thinking that I guess this means I'm truly sailing on my own now."

Clay moved to hug her. "Well, Taos is not the end of the earth if you really need me. But yes, you are launching your own ship now honey, you and Justin. It's called growing up." He grinned at her as he embraced the one living thing that remained of him and Mellie.

"I can think of nothing more comforting to me than knowing you and Justin will care for that house. I hope it comes to mean home to you two the same way it was for your mother and me. It was our sanctuary, a safe place to be. Let's hope at some point that your own child will know that feeling growing up there." He winked at her, knowing she hated to be teased about having a baby. "For me this house became a place of dying, but you and Justin will make it a home of life and joy again."

At the moment neither of them knew that Cassandra was pregnant with her first child, his grandchild.

Late the next morning Justin and Clay pushed the last items onto the rental truck. The final task was to load his motorcycle and close the doors. His pick-up truck would be hitched behind the van, on a special trailer. The whole thing looked like a miniature train. The three of them stood on the front porch, looking at what Clay would be driving to Taos. "Drive safely, Dad . . . I guess." Cassandra said with a query on her face as she stared at the rental truck being chased by the pick-up. Justin and Clay embraced, clapping each other on the back. Clay turned to his daughter with tears in his eyes, "I love you, Cassie. I'm just a phone call away, you know. I'll let you know when I arrive, so you won't worry." He turned, stepped off the porch, then waved back at both of them. The sluggish vehicle chugged and groaned as it lurched into motion. *Well, here we go. Mellie, we had a grand adventure together here in Kansas. Now, I'm going to take you home.*

The blue urn sat in a box on the seat beside him, waiting to be safely enshrined in his new home.

Arriving

As Clay lumbered westward, he entered a euphoria unlike any since the gorge, where the two wild rivers splashed into one. It had to do with release, those feelings that began the day he resigned from the university, of having broken binding constraints while yet belonging to everything. Light spurs of guilt briefly nudged his conscience when he considered all that had to take place for him to take this enticing gamble. But he looked at those events, none of which he caused or could have prevented, and declared aloud, "So be it. I hope someday my own demise will let someone else enter free-fall." And he laughed above the roar of the diesel engine.

Weaving and groaning through the stunning heights of the Sangre de Cristo Mountains between Angel Fire and Taos, the ton-and-a-half GMC truck channeled its way through dense pine timber sprinkled with aspen. In the autumn, those leaves would splash yellow and drop like chips of gold onto the mountain floor. *I'll actually be living here this year to watch this happen!* His heart skipped a beat with excitement.

Rounding a hairpin bend, Clay saw the vista open into a broad meadow where a small herd of elk clustered on the far side near the forest. Clay sensed that he had crossed a boundary and entered, not just another land, but another dimension. He shed old skins as he drove. He rolled down the window of the truck. Even the air smelled different, crisp and cool and clean. He let his left arm rest on the window's edge and felt the brisk air swirl into the cab of the truck. *I'm going to like living out here, just the weather alone is enough.*

Clay had rented a small house sight unseen. As the traveler pulled into Taos, skirting its dense summer traffic by turning south on a bypass, he drove the winding roads until he passed through the final signal light, which took him out onto the high mesa. Within ten minutes he located his new home, a tan adobe sitting in spare isolation on the high plain southeast of town, back from a gravel road. On one side, at a distance, a faded blue dilapidated trailer home flanked his; on the other side was a large expanse sporting only an abandoned school bus surrounded by bales of hay. The mountains loomed in the distance. The smell of sage engulfed him. "This isn't Kansas anymore, that's for sure!" He shouted as he bounced along the unpaved road into what was supposed to represent a driveway.

After opening the front door and exploring through the quaint house, Clay pronounced it a perfect fit. Old adobe walls, thick and cracked here and there, decorated with two tiny windows on the north side and a large picture window facing the south. The interior and exterior wooden doors were rustic, heavy with metal hardware. Worn Saltillo tile floors were uneven, drooping in the corners, with low ceilings, which added charm to the place. The kitchen was nothing to speak of, a nondescript grouping of cabinets stuck on the wall over a chipped ceramic sink. An apartment-sized stove sat primly next to one wall, and an out-of-date refrigerator stood in the corner, door slightly ajar. *So much for a kitchen. But it will do. I'll need a small table. There's just me to feed for now.* The living room was a larger open space, the one attraction being a woodstove set in the corner next to the south wall with some pieces of pinion pine stacked beside it. A black stovepipe ran into the ceiling and out the roof. *Perhaps I could send up smoke signals if I ever need help,* Clay mused.

Retreating to the rental truck, Clay retrieved the sacred container from the front seat. He carried the package into the house, and entered his bedroom, a cozy room with a petite kiva fireplace nestled in one corner of the room. A full set of windows facing the mountains allowed the day's waning light to filter across the walls. *What a view,* he thought as he studied the room to see where he would place his bed. Setting the box down on the floor, Clay opened it and carefully lifted a spackled blue urn from it. He then gingerly placed the vessel on the white mantel above the fireplace and stepped back to stare intently at it. This initial ritual marked the place as his, proclaiming his remembrance of Mellie, as he whispered reverently, "We're here, Mellie." This is where you always wanted to be. I've brought you home to your beloved New Mexico." Struggling to keep tears from ruining the moment, Clay turned immediately to return to the truck for enough gear to spend the night in his new home. He had prepared for this first night with a sleeping bag, a change of clothes and enough food to make it through until he could hire some help to unload his motorcycle and the contents of the van.

Days later, after the house became more habitable, Clay pulled the small round stone from his pocket where he had been carrying it since he left Kansas, placing it ceremoniously on the window sill that overlooked his writing desk. "Rorie," he whispered, noticing the disproportion between this emblem and the blue urn. The bleached stone, offering a resounding contrast to the urn, lay visible to his eye. He was now officially moved and ready to call Taos his home.

Already familiar with the historical New Mexico town and the surrounding country, Clay made his way easily in the environs, but even after several months he still felt as though he were on an extended vacation. When he passed places where he and Mellie had been together, he remembered them and her. This fact did not disturb him as it had in Kansas, but rather it consoled him. They had been happiest in their hiking, camping and backpacking days, tromping all over the mountains in the area. These memories slowly began to erase the thoughts of her agonizing last days and her dying that had been etched into his psyche. Mellie came fresh to life again as he walked some of the trails they had hiked together. He could feel his heart beginning to heal, and his mind awakened again to his project. *This move to Taos was certainly the right decision for me. I feel alive again! I am moving on!*

Clay acknowledged to himself one Friday morning staring out the windows at the mountains that he had subconsciously avoided driving over to Wild Rivers to peer over the railing above the gorge and reminisce about Rorie. *Although I sometimes still feel her presence, I'm not ready for that yet.* And then he wondered why.

After Clay finished his morning ablutions, he entered into this "studio," as he named the cramped room off the short hall to his bedroom, to begin reading and taking notes, composing and revising his manuscript. He luxuriated in the daily freedom of writing, editing and reflecting on the subject that had clung to him and moved through his synapses for well over four years. For the first time, he seriously envisioned its completion and began to consider what he might want to explore for his next book. *I have not had that sensation in a very long time . . . of imagining a future with a project beyond this one. That raging grief I have felt for so long must be waning. Finally!*

He could actually begin to feel his shoulders lifting from the slump that had lain on him the past few years. He woke naturally in the mornings, not feeling groggy or drugged. On his daily walks on the desert floor, his steps were lighter, and his eyes focused on the horizon rather than the ground. He tuned his days to watch the stunning sunsets and stood outside his house each evening to spy on the stars and planets as they began to rise in the darkening skies. He would then go back in to light a fire in the woodstove and settle down to read in a comfortable large leather chair he had secured from a local consignment store. Bit by bit, Clay sank more deeply into himself, tension and stress falling away. *Thank you, Mellie, for inspiring me to come here. I am slowly coming back to life. I owe you this, for telling me to go on with my life.* Clay began to feel gratitude as his daily touchstone.

The phone rang. Clay reached for it noting Cassandra's number on the screen. He gave a hearty, "Hey, there, Daughter. What's up?"

"Dad, Justin and I have something to tell you," she replied getting straight to the point. "Are you ready?" Clay heard her soft giggle through the line.

His skin prickling, he replied, "Of course!"

"You are about to become a grandfather. How 'bout that?" Cassandra's voice was filled with excitement.

Clay gulped and breathed deeply before responding, "Cassie, I could not be more thrilled. How wonderful to have a new life join our family after all we've been through. How's Justin with the news?" He could hear them switching the phone.

"Hey, Clay. I'm thrilled. I'm going to be a dad. A bit nervous, but also excited that it's our time now. You gave us this house just in time!"

When Cassandra took over the phone again, she jabbed at her dad, "Now don't you regret moving away from us?"

"Now, Cassie. . . ."

"I'm teasing, Dad. We're doing fine. It will all be okay, as long as you come immediately after the baby is born. Since mother isn't here now, you have to take her place, you know. We'll just want you to come visit us more often now. That's all." She conceded to his scolding tone.

The three continued their conversation for another twenty minutes and then rang off, each vowing to spoil the baby immediately upon its arrival.

Well, what do you know, Clay mused, *I'm to be a grandfather. On the one hand, I am so happy for my daughter. On the other hand, my heart aches because this news would have thrilled Mellie beyond words. How can life be so cruel?* Shaking his head as if to rid his mind of such debilitating thoughts, Clay stood up from his chair and walked to the kitchen to make a hot drink for himself. *I will not allow my grief to ruin this moment with my daughter. Mellie, you will just have to be here in spirit with us. This baby is still ours, and we will find a way to share stories of you with him? Her? Oh, now that will be the fun part—learning what the gender is.* He began to hum under his breath as he brewed a cup of tea.

Inspiration had increased following Clay's decision to make his book less academic and more personal. He found it possible to write a seriously intelligent book without its being as abstract as the university or his own academic training required. And a book about love, about his own loves, especially challenged him in this direction.

After completing his revision of the first chapter, designed to quicken the reader's anticipation, Clay boldly titled the second chapter, "The Love of Two Women." He began with a journal entry made the day Rorie and he left the gorge, quoting the passage in full. After fleshing out the stories of his relationships with Mellie and Rorie, he raised two questions: Is it possible to love two women at the same time, and what is the greatest test of love?

The first question he wrote as confession:

Before I met Rorie in the canyon, I would have insisted that no man can love two women at the same time, not with the same depth of which I spoke in the first chapter. Now, however, I am confronted through my own experience with this truth: I love two women. Yes, the loves are different, but not lacking in depth or intention. Experience has a way of canceling our presumption and our generalizations, and my experience is that these two women claimed my heart. One might wonder whether this could ever be a legitimate love without one of them, my wife in this case, actually being terminal. Perhaps the way this is possible is that Mellie was "on the way out," as horrific as that sounds now, and Rorie was all potential—life as it might be possible. The love I experience is "love on the cusp," and this is probably the only *place deep, intentional romantic love is possible for both of them. All I can say is that I loved and still love two women, and my love for one does not cancel out the other.*

Clay's central message, however, lay in the inevitable test for this depth of love: loss. In the baffling fact that love is bound up with loss lay the puzzle he most wanted to solve. Thus, he began the next paragraph: *I love two women, and I lost both of them.* In spite of all his reading and thinking on the subject, this sentence stalled him for days.

One night, engrossed in composing his most intense thinking on the subject, he became so frustrated that, on impulse, he called Cassandra. The phone rang several times before she answered with a groggy mumble, "Hello?"

"Were you asleep?" Clay glanced as his wrist and noticed that it was close to midnight in Kansas. "Oh, dear. I'm sorry. I forgot the time difference. I'll call back tomorrow," he said apologetically.

"No . . . it's all right, Dad. Don't hang up . . . I'll talk a few minutes. Is everything okay?" Her voice was thick with sleep.

"Things are great out here, honey, except that I'm in the most critical part of my book, and I need you to talk with me about it."

"Not sure I can help that much. You know I'm not the philosopher in the family." Cassandra yawned into the phone. "Hang on, I'll wake Justin."

"I don't need to talk to Justin. I have a question only you can answer. I'll give it to you, and we can deal with it tomorrow." Clay's words were crisp and determined.

"No. Go ahead, Dad. I'm awake now. What's the question?"

"Do you still love your mother?"

"What?" Cassandra was fully awake now, her voice rising in pitch betraying her astonishment at Clay's question.

"I mean right now, this minute. Do you still *love* Mellie?" He placed a hard emphasis on the word love, so she could distinguish the meaning of his question.

"Heavens, yes! I think about her every day, Dad. Some days it's all day. Last week I went through a tough spot because I drove past the little pastry shop where we used to go for coffee on special occasions. I could hardly look at it without crying. Yes, I still love my mother, very much. Why are you asking me such a question in the middle of the night?"

Clay walked out of his studio room where he had been working on his manuscript and began to wander around the house as he talked. Cassandra's father continued his response, "I've had the same thought. All I have is this vase of her ashes, and it doesn't do anything for me at all." He stood before the urn in the shadows of his bedroom, lit only by a small lamp. He reached up to caress the vase, rubbing his thumb over the embossed flowers on the front. "The other night I found myself talking to the darn thing, wanting to say something to it, to her, but the distance proved to be too much. Felt like trying to scream across the Grand Canyon." Clay's body felt heavy as he allowed himself to wander into the living room and sink into his chair next to the woodstove, still warm though the embers were dying.

"I know that feeling, for sure. Same here." Cassandra's voice was despondent.

"Hey, I didn't call to make you sad. What I need, Cassie, is your experience of continuing to love your mother in the face of your loss of her. How does the loss . . . no, let me ask it another way. When did you give up hope for your mother? I believe that's part of the riddle I'm wrestling with here."

Clay could hear Cassandra crying into the phone at this point, and he regretted calling her. *This subject is still too tender for her. What in the world made me call my pregnant daughter only to torment her like this? Ugh.* On the other hand, Cassandra was his link to Mellie now. If anyone understood what he asked, she did. There was no sound for so long that Clay asked, "Cassandra?"

Her voice broke as she replied to him, "Well, in a way I never did give up hope. Even when I knew better . . . you know . . . all those books and brochures we read. None of them ever gave us a shred of hope, but. . . ."

"Yes. I kept dreaming of miracle cures too. I had a fantasy that one day we'd walk into that sun room and she'd be sitting up in her chair laughing at us."

"I think Mom might have died sooner if we'd let her go. I believe she kept trying so hard to stay alive because we didn't give her permission to go."

"Yes, you may be right. And hope was all that kept us going too." Clay's voice was full of resignation.

"Dad, she was terminal. You know what that means. She sure did." Cassandra allowed her words to take effect before asking, "When did you . . . uh . . . surrender to the facts?"

Clay sat in a stupor. The whole encounter with Rorie streaked through his mind, and he wondered whether she had been the agent for his willingness to release Mellie to her fate. He recalled, with a surge of anxiety binding his chest, those hours late into the night, when the machines attached to Mellie bleeped and whirred. As he lay in his bed near her and listened, thoughts about the outcome and his place in the ordeal assailed his urge to sleep. He knew, as well as he knew anything, that she would die, and as the months spilled into years, he wished, against his sharpest desire, that she might easily slip away from her paralyzing agony. But he could not stand himself for having those thoughts. He even tried to blame them on Rorie—*If I had never met her*—but that never worked either. He covered his turmoil by ever more strident efforts to express to his wife encouragement and vague hope. He played the optimist against the buried darker desire that it all end before she became bitter with defeat. Watching Mellie suffer in such a debilitating way was the worst situation imaginable, day after day. Now Cassandra's question called to the surface this concealed vein in him which he fought even yet to deny.

Finally, Clay startled himself with his own words, "I suppose I did resist the facts too much. Those last months she probably did stay against her own wishes—for us," and his voice choked. "Letting go is surely the hardest part of loving. That's so obvious, it's cliché. But I'm realizing that when we let go, we also agree to the loss that's coming our way."

Cassandra shifted the conversation back to Clay's original question. "In a way I love her even more, you know, desperately, now that she's finally and really gone from us. It's different, but not less. Does that make sense?"

"Good. Stop right there," Clay interrupted. "I've been thinking about that very idea. How is it 'different'?"

Cassandra was quiet for a moment, then spoke, "For me it has to do with loving her and at the same time feeling like she's not as real. Like she is . . . I can't explain it very well . . . a phantom? It's as if my memory of her is stuck in time—I have no new ways to love her. We can't go anywhere from here in our love for Mother, because we have no new experiences to help the love continue to grow. I do continue to love her, but my love for her has been forced to stop expanding. There's no place to move forward with this love, forever, for the rest of my life."

Clay listened intently. His daughter had deftly circled around the point for which he had sought clarity and could find none. *What is the difference between concrete, lived love after the loss of our beloved, and the love that is left ethereal and vague after loss?* Before he could solve his own riddle, Cassandra continued, "What I miss, the lost ingredient is touching her. I also miss the future we will never have. For instance, she will never know my coming child, her grandchild, so I will never experience her as a grandmother, which would expand my love for her even more. Know what I mean?"

A sharp pain plunged into Clay's heart from Cassandra's words. He recalled with laser vividness the contrast between the slack skin-on-bone of Mellie's body and the ample, pliable feel of Rorie. Touch. *What do I do when there's no skin to touch—Mellie is gone. Rorie is gone.* Clay had fallen silent, drifting into his inner world, leaving Cassandra wondering if the connection had been broken.

"Dad? Are you there?"

"Sorry. Just remembering the feel of your mother, wandered into territory I should not go at this point."

With sympathy in her voice, Cassandra replied, "Dad. I'm so sorry. As your daughter, I forget sometimes to visualize you and Mom as a loving couple who had an intimate life. Normally children don't like to think about that part of their parents' relationship, but I can hear from your voice how difficult losing the fact of touch is for you too."

"You've helped me with my thinking about this, Cassie. Realizing that touch is so central to intimate love and how we express it. There's something wrong with the way I've been working on this issue."

Cassandra suspected that her father's comment might reflect his loneliness. She had worried about this for weeks and weeks, so she decided to probe. "Dad, are you beginning to want a personal life, I guess that's the word, for yourself?"

"My life *is* personal, Cassie." Clay knew this retort would drive his daughter crazy. He chuckled under his breath.

"Evasion! Evasion!" Cassandra blasted back at him.

"Actually, I have gone out a couple of times, sort of. . . ." Clay admitted sheepishly.

"That doesn't sound like you know what you are doing. How do you 'sorta' date?" Cassandra asked in a sassy tone.

"Well, I was with a group of people. Mostly chitchat over dinner. A friend 'paired' us for that dinner. It was casual, relaxed, but leaned a bit toward boring. Probably for both of us, because I kept wanting to get back home to write."

"There's more to life than writing, Dad." Cassandra said dryly, as she had reminded him hundreds of times in the previous years.

"Right. Like more than talking to your old man in the dark of the night? Go back to bed. You've helped me immensely. On another note, are you taking care of yourself? How are you feeling?"

"I'm truly doing well. Don't you worry. Okay?" His daughter showed her concern for him in these comments.

"Talk to you later this week. Okay, hon? Love you." Clay hung up, grinning as he thought about Cassandra. *She sure is developing into a highly intuitive young woman. More and more like her mother every day. Maybe this is the way Mellie stays with me—through our daughter.*

When Clay returned to his studio, he scribbled hastily on a pad by his computer. *Two orders of love, the real and the ideal, and the difference is touch—presence.* Not yet ready to write any further, he walked through the house again, exploring his fledgling insight. His love for Mellie, he saw, had not diminished. It had become another sort of love. It was indeed fixed, as Cassandra had said, and now bordered on perfect.

What an odd term to label my love for Mellie, but I realize that this is what happens once the person is gone. What we had every day was real, lived, flawed. Now our love is perfect because it's frozen in time. All the negative memories and experiences are washed out of the cloth and what is left is a beautiful pristine lacy shroud of love—not real, but ideal. Our love is set by her death. I've lost her physical, palpable presence. Her flesh. When she was here, I could at least touch, kiss, stroke her frail arms. This faded when she died. Clay returned swiftly to his studio, ready to write.

We are creatures who write poetry and sing to the gods. But we are also incarnated spirits who lust, defecate and die. We keep trying to hold apart these great forces within us, naming the higher one good and the lower one base, visceral, if not evil. No. The evil lies in splitting them asunder. The two must meet, and they meet in the touch, in the encounter of flesh. It is not a curse to be embodied. It is our very dwelling, the habitat of our humanity, and when we touch, more than through any other medium, we come home. This is why the experience with Rorie was so potent—we touched!

Chills raced through his body as he wrote. He found the seam of precious ore running through the long struggle to comprehend love and loss. Time and touch.

Loss in love begins with the actual or even symbolic loss of touch. When fleshly presence goes, we may love ever so passionately, but the constant urge and longing is for the reunion that overcomes the separation from touch—which death interrupts. Time stands still when one is lost from the relationship, however that occurs. With the severing of the possibility of that connection, especially in death, love moves from the real to the ideal. Love lives in the everyday reality, the present, or it moves into the ideal, eternity. There is nothing wrong with idealized love, but it is not the same as real love. Idealized love sits gently, or intensely, in the memory or in our imagination. Real love is immediate, earthy, laden with the concrete presence of the Other. And the Other makes claims on us that cannot or dare not be ignored. Otherwise, it is not love. Yet this real love never achieves the ideal. It can only strive for perfection while paradoxically striving to remain real, and in the present.

Clay hammered at the keyboard until dawn. The night slipped by him. He did not notice. He wrote of the two kinds of loss he had endured, in death and in separation, and how each became the end of real love, but the continuation of this other more elusive yet demanding love. The ideal. He reflected on the relation between touch and time, and the importance of the latter for the pursuit of earthly love, which has to take place within the authentic present. In touch the physical relationship can blossom, regardless of whether this includes friends and family, where pats and hugs are employed, or a romantic relationship that includes intimacy and sex.

As fatigue set in, he wrote the last paragraph before turning off his brain:

Ideal love retains an echo of desire. It is called longing. But this longing, like my ache for Mellie, remains empty and without possibility. Desire is different, full and overflowing, drawn toward touch, like my passion for

Rorie. Desire belongs to this embodied, incarnate existence. It is not a curse, but our great blessing as human beings.

Shortly before sunrise, Clay abandoned his project and drove into town for breakfast at a diner that opened early each day. He wished to acknowledge his breakthrough with a one-man, jubilant celebration. He kept muttering to himself about his insight, which had released his confidence, allowing him to forge ahead in his project. The coffee kindled his energy again, allowing him to continue writing in his pocket notebook that he was never without these days. As he completed eating, a wave of fatigue swept over him again, and he realized he needed to return home and sleep. Driving back to his house, he noticed the morning cascade of light rushing over the mountains and onto the plain. *When I finish this book, Cassandra's going to read it. How in the world do I explain Rorie?* Clay headed straight for the bed, falling across it with his clothes on. He was asleep almost before his head dropped on the blue and yellow quilted cover.

Reaching

Sara grabbed Donie's hand to help him navigate the flight of stairs of the parking garage to the street. The steps were still quite a stretch for the three-year-old, but he was also doggedly independent. He yanked his hand away from Sara to climb down on his own. "Young man, you must hold my hand on these steps, but here, I'll let you go ahead of me. How about that?" After raising her own three boys, Sara knew how to convince the child to get him to do as she wished. Once at the bottom, the three meandered with a relaxed gait toward the downtown plaza of Santa Fe. Flame was on her leash guarding Donie with protective attention, walking beside him.

Sara observed, "Flame doesn't leave his side, does she?"

"That animal believes she's Donie's mother!" Rorie exclaimed. "I'm only the nanny." The two friends laughed heartily, causing a tourist couple ahead of them on the sidewalk to glance over their shoulders.

Sara stopped periodically to take in the view of the mountains rising to the north and east, dotted with adobe homes. The crisp dry atmosphere, a respite from the humidity and heat of Texas, caught her attention. "I can see why you'd want to move here. This weather is luxurious after the summer we have just suffered through in Dallas."

"I've fallen in love with this place. Starting over on everything: my home—if you can call that postage stamp condominium I live in a house—my job, Donie, new friends. Still working to create new friendships, but I find I'm actually not in a hurry. I've really enjoyed just getting acquainted with the town and its peculiarities. Santa Fe is, I have learned, quite a unique little city." Rorie's eyes swept over the plaza, the shops surrounding the center of town, the visitors strolling the sidewalks. A scent rose from a vendor grilling chicken for a handheld burrito. On the bandstand, a singer and a guitarist were carrying on, their music wafting over the grassy green.

"So after a year here, you find yourself settling into the place?"

"Yes. I do delight in living here. It's a bit too crowded in the heart of town during the summer months, but tourist season is our livelihood, so we don't complain." Sara noticed Rorie's use of 'we' and realized her friend had made this quaint town her home.

As they left the plaza area, they strolled down the street toward the cathedral, looming large over the landscape with its twin bell towers, leaving the displays of endless shops and galleries behind them. A surge of people drove them off the sidewalk because they were walking slower with a child and dog in tow. Sara suggested they head to the church to get a closer look. Rorie stayed outside, holding onto Flame, while Sara entered with Donie to stare at the windows and elegant altar. When Sara returned, she reported, "There's a lot of people in there, but it still seems to have a serenity about it. The windows are striking."

Sara pointed to a grassy retreat near the side of the church and proposed they sit and rest for a while. They spread a blanket and watched Donie run around, playing in his imaginary child's world. Flame watched over the boy with unwavering focus. Rorie and Sara talked.

"Rorie, you do seem more at home now, relaxed, even happy," Sara commented, observing her friend.

"It's been a tough year. I've always gone it alone to a great extent, but this one was a challenge. Donie is so much more important to my life than I ever expected. I love my job, I really do, but Donie is never away from my thoughts. Never thought of myself as 'the mother type,' but I have turned out to be one. I feel like I never have quite enough time with him. Being a single mother of a young child is not the easiest thing in the world."

"What about Brent?" Sara queried slyly.

"We went out for a while, but I think my having Donie gave him pause. He's actually become more like a best friend, than a . . ."

"Lover?" Sara teased.

"Well, we were never much of that . . . I think we are too much alike. And I could never get sitters worked out on nights when Brent was free. It just faded away. And I haven't thought about it much since. Actually, I've felt relief." Rorie surprised herself at her own confession.

Sara took up her mantra, "Well, you have had the one who 'made the earth move' and after that it's hard to find an encore." Rorie sat pensive and distant, while Sara corralled Donie and Flame.

Rorie straightened up and said with purpose, "Sara. I need to tell you something." Sara glanced at her with alarm. Rorie didn't say such things unless something dramatic was ahead.

"Ye-ah?" Sara was attentive as she drew out the word.

"I wrote Clay a letter." Rorie ducked her head, wondering how her friend would react.

"You did? When?"

"Back in Dallas, when I was pregnant."

"Did he answer? What did you tell him? What did he say? Why didn't you tell me?" Sara was on her knees, crowding Rorie like a reporter hot on the scent of a juicy news story.

"I never mailed it." Rorie stared at her friend, waiting for a reaction. She received it.

Sara fell back and sat down. "Never mailed it! What good's that?"

"Oh, given all that he was going through at the time, I couldn't bring myself to add another burden to his life."

"Then why'd you write it?" Sara was now peering curiously at her friend, wondering what in the world Rorie was thinking.

"Probably to relieve my mind. At the time I thought he deserved to know that he had a son in the world, but then I got cold feet. Just before I left Dallas I almost mailed it. I even located his address, but then I lost my nerve." Reaching for Donie, Rorie pulled the child onto her lap and handed him a cup of water to drink. She stroked his thick brown curly hair as he drank, hugging him as closely as the squirming child would allow.

"Rorie, why are you bringing this up now?" She smiled at Rorie's cuddling with her son and continued, "What's not done is not done."

"But I still have the letter. I keep it in my desk drawer. Someday I will show it to Donie . . . he has the right to know how this all happened. But I wonder what you think I should do?" Rorie was asking for genuine advice from her friend and mentor.

Sara recognized her friend's need but answered evasively, "It's been years now. What do you want to happen?"

"I want him to know he has a son. That's all I've ever wanted really, and for him to know that, of course, Donie is safe with me."

"I don't think your motives have changed, Rorie. I just think your circumstances are different. Here in Santa Fe you have a home and a life with your son, one that you have created all by yourself. You are probably experiencing some loneliness at this point, wishing the father of this child could share what you are experiencing with him every day."

"Yes! Yes I am, but. . . ."

"But Clay doesn't live here and doesn't even know about his son. You still have a decision to make, and that decision is yours and yours alone." Sara spoke quietly, making sure Rorie understood that she would not tell her friend what to do.

Rorie sat still, as Donie wiggled free from her lap and climbed over her to get to Flame. "Say, are you two hungry? I know a fabulous place to eat down here. It's only three blocks away. Wanna try it?"

Recognizing Rorie's avoidance tactics, Sara replied, "Sure. I can always eat New Mexican food, and this boy looks like he's getting hungry himself," she said as she tickled Donie until he fell on the blanket giggling and kicking. "Where are we going?" She glanced up at Rorie for an answer.

"Pasqual's. My favorite restaurant here in town."

"What do we do about Flame?" Sara wondered.

"Oh, that's easy. It's Santa Fe. We just tie her up close to the fountain across the street, with a bowl of water. It's shady there. No one will bother her. She'll be fine until we're done." Rorie grinned and lifted the blanket, shook off the grassy tidbits and stuffed it into her bag.

The four of them, two women, a little boy and his dog, strolled over to the restaurant, a landmark in the city bearing its full charm. To

Rorie's shock, it was not especially crowded. Inside they found a table for three. Donie, easily occupied, played with the condiments on the table while munching on crackers that Rorie had brought for him.

The two women lost themselves in conversation, until Rorie heard her name rise from across the restaurant, "Hey, Rorie!" She surveyed the quarter of the colorful room from which the call came but saw no one she recognized. A young man stood and waved as he looked directly at her. "Rorie, is that you?"

Rorie whispered to Sara that she had never seen this person before, but as he called out, he was maneuvering his way around tables and chairs until he stood before them.

Noticing that her expression was puzzled, he said, "Isn't your name Rorie?"

"Yes, yes, it is, but I don't know. . . ." She spoke hesitantly.

"I met you in that gorge up above Taos, where the rivers join. You and Dr. Jacobs. You know. He was my professor at. . . " The young man was smiling and gesturing at her.

Rorie blanched with recognition, but he looked so different. No straggling hair, worn-out clothing, or youthful manner. And she couldn't recall his name.

"No wonder you didn't recognize me. I've cleaned up a bit. You may remember that I went by 'Coyote' in those days." He waited for her sign of recognition.

Rorie's memories awakened: exotic memories, never really buried, but lying dormant. *This person is connected to Clay. Am I ready for all of that to reignite?* She sputtered out an introduction of the young man to Sara, calling him "Coyote" and motioning him to sit down.

Coyote sat in the available chair, and looked fixedly at Donie, before he turned his glance back to Rorie. "I don't call myself 'Coyote' anymore. It was a phase I was in. My name's Edmund, but I go by Eddie." Sensing Rorie's hesitation, he went on, "Say, I don't want to disturb you two. Maybe I'd better rejoin my fiance." He waved to her across the room. An attractive young woman with her hair in a single long braid down her back smiled back at him, signaling that she could also come over to join them. Eddie nodded negatively.

Rorie, trying hard to recover her composure, stammered, "What . . . what . . . why are you here in Santa Fe? I thought you were from Kansas." Blushing deeply, she wished there was some way to disguise her discomfort.

"I guess that's a fair question. I brought Hannah here to see this country that I stomped around in after she had dumped me. I want her to understand how being out here changed me, so she could trust me again. Our wedding is next spring. Well, that's a long story I won't go into right now." Bobbing his head up and down, Eddie rushed on, "And then, fancy this, meeting you here—part of my story out here. Isn't that something?"

Rorie could only nod in agreement at this point, still shaking from the encounter.

"Say did you ever hear again from Dr. Jacobs?"

Rorie, rushing to pursue the conversation but trying to remain composed, urged Eddie to stay for a moment. Sara supported her invitation, curious at what was about to unfold. Rorie told him, "Actually, I have not seen or heard from him at all since we three met in the gorge."

Eddie poked a finger at Donie, who grabbed his hand, afraid of being tickled by the stranger. Eddie pulled back, "Yeah, that's how it goes. Meet someone and then they vanish. That's why I was so surprised to see you here. Are you on vacation? I remember you live in Dallas."

Rorie felt his questions were too close for comfort, so she hesitated, "Well, I like Santa Fe. Actually I live here now. Coyote, Eddie. Have you seen Cla—Dr. Jacobs?"

"Yes, after my own dad died. He was sick with a brain tumor when I went home after my trip into Wild Rivers. He lived about a year. Then I went back to school. All of that was a tough time for me, then I ran into Dr. Jacobs on campus. His wife had died, and I went to the funeral, hoping I could see him again and reconnect. We talked a bit after the service. My own dad's death helped me understand what Dr. Jacobs was going through, you know?

Rorie, stunned by the news, caught Sara's intense glance, a wordless message only women can deliver and read instantly. Eddie noticed nothing but continued talking about his conversation with Clay. He handed Donie a spoon to see if the child would accept it. He did. Rorie hung onto every word Eddie uttered, her heart beating so rapidly she suspected everyone could hear it. She tried desperately to sort through a twist of mixed feelings: concern for Clay's loss, elation he was no longer bound, confused because she had no idea what the news of Mellie's death had to do with her. As the conversation waned, Eddie stated matter-of-factly, "I've graduated now, so I haven't been on campus for a while."

At this point, Rorie wanted Eddie to leave the table so she could process all of this with Sara. She made the appropriate comments and gestures that sent such directives. Hannah was also growing restless, and signaled him that it was time to return to their table. Rorie did not introduce Eddie to Donie but left the two to tease with each other. When Eddie studied the boy's face, Rorie took a napkin to wipe the crumbs from his chin and then directed the conversation away from Donie. The former pilgrim finally took the cue and departed with a friendly wave.

Rorie grabbed a menu and stared at it, avoiding Sara's gaze. She signaled a waiter to come and take their order. Once these details were handled, she sucked in her breath, as Sara said, "Well, that's what you get for asking the universe a question like that!"

Looking up at her friend totally puzzled, Rorie, quipped, "I have no idea what you are talking about!"

"Rorie! Don't be dense. You wanted to know if you should send the letter to Clay. There's your answer, right in your lap!"

"But maybe it's been too long now." She was avoiding the obvious at this point. "She must have died well over a year ago. No telling what he's doing now. What if he's in another. . . ?"

"You cannot calculate *everything*, Rorie. He's a grown man. Let him take care of the news when he receives it. You won't know until you've mailed the darn letter. You might be able to go on with your own life once you at least have done that." Sara's words showed her exasperation.

Rorie defended herself, "But I am going on with. . . ."

Sara interrupted, "Then why are you allowing that unmailed letter to stalk you?" Sara stared at Rorie across the food that sat in front of them, steaming and ready to be eaten. "Mail it," she concluded with a growl of insistence.

Later that night in the sanctuary of her own room, Rorie pulled the letter out of her desk drawer. It was modestly rumpled at this point from being carried and moved around. All it needed was an envelope and a stamp. She gazed at the missive as if conjuring advice from it. Every conceivable scenario sauntered through her imagination. She played the "what if" game late into the night. Only when she remembered the desire she had long held tightly in her heart did she resolve to mail the letter the next morning.

After brushing her teeth and nestling into her bed, covers piled around her, Rorie still could not settle her mind. Her resolution sank. She battled with whether she should send this letter or compose another one that would include recognition that Mellie had died. Sleep did not come. She turned on the bedside lamp, sat up again, threw her legs off the edge of the bed, and argued heatedly with herself. Standing up, Rorie strode determinedly to her desk to write another letter. She picked up her pen, put it down again. *Why would I do that? I said in the first letter what I want him to know. What am I afraid of at this point?* Rubbing her eyes and feeling a slight headache forming, Rorie realized she must act. Indecision was not her friend at the moment. She decided to rewrite the letter on fresh stationary, leaving the words as she had first penned them. *I'll decide later what to do with the original,* Rorie proposed to herself, unwilling to abandon her earliest letter to Clay. Stuffing the paper back into her desk drawer, she confessed to herself, *For some reason, this letter draws me closer to Clay. Why do I still miss him so much?* Shaking her head to stall her thoughts from becoming morose, she finally climbed back into her bed. The clock read 4:17 a.m. Exhaustion made her sleep fitfully until her alarm went off.

Donie had crawled out of his bed and was playing in the living room with his toys when she joined him. In the light of day, though she was groggy, Rorie realized her letter was adequate and should be mailed. *I will do this today. Sara is right—it's time to act. Clay has the right to know about Donie.* Looking down at her son, as his bright blue eyes stared into hers, she felt a sense of peace. *It's time. He should know about our beautiful boy.*

Sara strode into the living room to find her host, house shoes making whooshing sounds on the wood floors. After breakfast, Sara drove Rorie to the post office on the edge of downtown Santa Fe. Rorie went inside to buy a stamp while Sara held their parking spot. She walked stoically to the mail slot in the wall, paused as she pulled down the lid, held the letter for a moment, then finally allowed it to slide into the bin. The letter disappeared toward Kansas.

After another day and night, Rorie drove Sara to Albuquerque for her flight back to Dallas. Melancholy prevailed on the journey back to Santa Fe. Her dearest companion and friend had departed. Donie was asleep in his car seat behind her. She returned home to wait. She had sent forth her message. *Now it's his turn.*

Shock

CASSANDRA RACED TO REACH HOME BEFORE JUSTIN. IT WAS ONE of their games, to see who could get the wine glasses down, an appetizer prepared and set on the patio table before the other arrived. They were tied. Cassandra set to work and had things ready when she heard Justin's steps on the front porch.

When her husband rushed through the door with their daughter in his arms, a colorful cartoon tie strung over his shoulder, he brought a fistful of mail in with him. "Hey, not fair! You didn't pick up the mail before you came in. That's one of the rules. Remember?" He laughed at her dismayed expression, knowing he had scored a point with her.

"You're right—I cheated." She grinned, "But I won today. I beat you home. I've had a rough day. How's that baby of ours?" She took the baby from his arms, hugged her and began walking toward the patio while Justin carried out the glasses and food. This was a special time of day for the little family, the parents cherishing this time with their new daughter after being away from her all day. Cassandra had recently returned to her career, and the couple was learning how to include an infant in their lives while managing two highly demanding schedules. Cassandra stroked her daughter's plump cheeks and stared into her blue eyes. Becca cooed in soft tones at her mother's touch. *She looks like Dad in a way. I like that.*

The early evening passed in a flurry of feeding Becca, bathing her and putting her down for sleep, the parents each doing their assigned chores. Finally, the time came to tend to their own needs for catching up with each other. Cassandra picked up the mail Justin had tossed on the island counter while he started their dinner. "Junk, junk, junk," Cassandra announced as she sorted through the pieces of nondescript paper, tossing them into the waste bin beside the cabinet. "Ah, here's one from the IRS—just kidding," as she noticed the alarm on Justin's face. "Let's see, here's a note from your sister, must be important to cause her actually to write something. And a bank statement, who wants that, right?" At the bottom of the stack rested a personal letter, addressed by hand, a woman's handwriting. "Hey here's something for Dad. Someone who doesn't know he's moved away, I guess. Looks like it's from a woman. What do you think?" She leaned over to Justin to show him the mauve envelope, obviously good stationary.

"Well, I guess you should forward that to him," Justin said offhandedly. "Would you refill my wine glass? That's a terrific Cab. Where'd you find it?" Their habit was to take turns cooking their evening meals, so Justin turned back to his cutting board to slice vegetables.

Cassandra, not to be distracted, replied, "But don't you think I should at least open it to see if it's important enough to send on to Dad?" Her curiosity was evident.

"Not on your life, Cassie. Don't you dare. It's none of your business," Justin admonished.

Cassandra stood up from the bar stool, walked down the hall and laid the letter on an antique table near the front door, but she kept its presence in her mind. Her intuition was working overtime as she and Justin prepared their dinner. They ate in the kitchen at the breakfast table, enjoying their closeness and sharing the events of their day. Then Cassandra announced, as if out of nowhere, "It came from Santa Fe. That's strange. Since he lives in Taos, who would mail him a letter here?"

Justin, caught off guard, asked, "What? Who are you talking about?"

Cassandra replied sheepishly, knowing Justin would be displeased, "That letter. . . ."

"Leave that letter alone. It should be forwarded to him tomorrow!" He spoke more sternly than usual. In order to justify his tone, Justin continued, "Clay does live in Taos, you know. Not that far away from Santa Fe. And he hasn't lived in Taos all that long. It's just an address mistake."

Her husband's statement made no sense, "Yes, but then why would someone he met out there send a letter to him back here, in Kansas?" Justin, recognizing her logic, shrugged.

More than once during the evening, Cassandra wandered into the hall, as if to make sure the mysterious piece of correspondence had not vanished. Its magnetic pull inserted itself into her psyche. She fretted often about her father and his social life. Her intuitive hunch persisted, and when she tried to ignore it, she became only more agitated. Shortly before heading upstairs to bed she mused aloud, only half intending Justin to hear, "I wonder whether I should open the thing and call Dad to let him know what it says. Save him having to wait."

"Cassandra Renai Benson, don't you even think about it!"

"It's only an idea," she teased.

"That letter's not yours. It's your dad's. And it's really none of your business, is it?" Justin worked hard to reason with his wife." He looked up at her, exasperated. "What's with you and that letter anyway? Why does it disturb you so much that your dad has a piece of mail?"

"Someone has to watch out for him," she replied defensively. "There is a woman's name on the envelope. I think I have a right to be snoopy on this one." Justin's heavy breathing and scowl told her not to push things any further. Capitulating to his arguments, Cassandra surrendered, "Okay, I'll go brush my teeth and leave the darn thing alone."

The next day Cassandra did not have to go to the lab until after lunch because new equipment was being installed. As she stood by the front door holding their baby in her arms, she lifted Becca's tiny hand to wave goodbye to her daddy. Justin glanced at the letter on the table and said dryly, "Better put that in the mail today." He kissed Cassandra and Becca each on the cheek and then turned to skip down the steps of the porch.

"At least there's no perfume on it," Cassandra yelled at her retreating mate. Staring at the missive on the table, she paused, wondering what to do, as the baby made noises that it was time for her morning feeding and nap.

While indulging in a tuna salad lunch, Cassandra went again to the hall, picked up the letter and took it with her into the living room. She noticed how thin the stationary appeared, simple yet from quality stock. *What does this say about the woman who wrote it?* She placed the envelope in front of her plate on the table. The silent epistle resting inside taunted her, until she could no longer tolerate the mystery of it. In a fit bordering on temporary insanity, she tore open the envelope, like a child snatching an extra dessert just before someone sees. Her breath came in bursts. She held the contents but did not read immediately. The secret remained safe. She could still redeem herself if she reinserted the letter into the envelope.

But Cassandra plummeted beyond redemption into misbehavior and read feverishly, driven to a strangling disturbance by the revelations unfolding through the lines of the script. She finished reading the letter and reached for the disabled envelope to seek its date. It had been sent only days earlier. Her first assumption was that her father had, indeed, met someone and that he now faced more than he surely wanted. She wished desperately that she had not read it and began to explore ways to cover her crime and forward the letter.

Seeking to make sense of it all, Cassandra read the letter again, ploddingly, word for word. The passion of the writing and the possibility that she herself might soon have a half-brother drew her more intimately into the bombshell. As she laid the two spare pages on the table, the date at the head of the first page caught her attention. "Holy. . . !" she exclaimed. "This is over three years old." Grasping again at the envelope to compare dates, she noticed for the first time the words "finally mailed on" jotted on the back flap. The enigma grew and her perplexity with it.

An attorney's barrage of questions assailed Cassandra. *Who is Rorie? How did Dad meet her? How could he even know a woman from that far back, when he was always here with Mother? Is that woman telling the truth, or is this a trick she's playing on him? Why would she mail such an old letter now? Why from Santa Fe? What will he do with this information—that he's a father again? Is it really his child? I'd better warn him!*

Questions drowned her ability to think clearly, and then the answer thundered into Cassandra's mind, "That trip! To New Mexico!" She said the words aloud. "He must have met her there." Once the evidence formed in her mind, she retold the story to herself. She saw exactly why the woman's revelation had been dated well before her mother's death. If true, this meant that her own father, the noble Clayton Edward Jacobs had philandered on her mother. Vivid images charged into her mind at once: her mother lying prostrate and helpless on that torturous bed, the victim of deceit and betrayal.

Cassandra reviewed her memory of her parents' marriage. To her, their relationship was exemplary. She stumbled through predictable questions, *How could Dad do this? How was I fooled by him all those years? How was mother fooled by him? How can I ever accept this?* She slowly arrived at the most critical question of all: *How will I ever trust my father again?*

Reaching for the phone, she called work and told them she would not be coming in for the day. Then she called Justin, "Come home now!" Her breath was ragged and barely audible.

Rushing headlong into the house, Justin called to her in panic, "What? What's the matter? Is Becca okay?" He saw Cassandra sitting at the table, morose and staring blankly at the telltale papers in front of her. She did not move, but when he reached her, she pointed to the open sheets of paper. He started to scold her, "Damn it, Cassandra! I told you. . . ." Her face was ashen.

"Read it!" she insisted. He sat down at the table, picked up the letter and began to read.

"Well, he's created a fine mess, hasn't he?" Justin concluded as he tossed the document back onto the table. "My question is why did you—?"

"Compare the date on the letter and the one on the envelope" Cassandra spoke crisply, as tears streamed down her face.

Justin complied, "Whoa. . . ."

He did not return to work that afternoon. They called a friend to come pick up Becca for a few hours, so they could process the news and sort out a plan for how to handle things. The couple spent the afternoon reviewing every possible explanation. No scenario they could summon relieved Clay of the charges his daughter made against him. Although Justin still fumed at her for opening the letter, he joined in her distress. All he could muster was a feeble defense of his former colleague and now father-in-law. "We really don't know the full story, Cassie. Maybe there's an explanation. Things like this do happen. Shouldn't we give him a fair chance to explain?"

"Things happen?" She screamed at her best friend and husband. "Things like this don't just happen!" She rebelled at easy platitudes. Her deep loyalty to both parents lay broken in two.

Justin fumbled for words that might ease his wife's anguish. "Cassandra, your father was under a burden neither of us could possibly fathom." She started to interrupt, but he persisted, "You and I were here through your mother's death, but when it's your spouse. . . ."

"Yes! Tell me about it. His wife!" She sobbed uncontrollably, falling into his arms. "And my mother!"

Seeing that no conjectured explanation would assuage Cassandra's growing rage, Justin chose to hold and comfort his wife. Soon her anger dissolved into a pain unfelt since her mother's last days and death. The energy produced by the shock of her discovery gradually evaporated into exhaustion. She slept, and then they slept. The doorbell rang, waking them both. A friend handed them their child, chattering about how good she had been all afternoon. They clutched the baby as if her life were in danger, thanked the friend kindly and closed the door on their grief. The family huddled together throughout the evening, Becca having no idea why her parents were so subdued. The evening passed, and the house grew quiet.

The next morning the couple fell into their usual routines, dressing the baby to be taken to day care and getting themselves ready for work. "I've got to call him today," Cassandra announced at breakfast.

"Wouldn't it be better just to send him the letter with a note that you want to talk to him as soon as he receives it?"

Cassandra snapped back, "You are being so practical!" She stamped her foot as her eyes flashed Justin a warning signal.

"I'm sorry . . . you are still raw. But Clay has a story too. He deserves to be heard. That's all I'm trying to say." He reached over to wipe the baby's mouth and hand her a bottle.

"Can't wait to hear it." Sarcasm dripped from Cassandra's mouth. "I may go to work for only half a day. I need time to think about all of this. Why don't you take Becca to the sitter and go on to work? I'll go in later this afternoon." Cassandra spun around to leave the room, dejected. Then turning back around she offered her apology, "I'm sorry, Justin. I'm not being fair to you because I'm mad at my wayward father. I promise I'll regroup. Just give me some time." She walked over, hugged him and Becca, and left the room.

Sitting in a chair in their bedroom, Cassandra felt drained, remembering a recent conversation with her father and how he spoke of Mellie's death and his loss. It all seemed so phony now, such a fraud. Her only concession lay in waiting and hoping her hostility would moderate. She took a shower, dried her hair, put on her make-up and sat once again in the chair by the window. It was time to head to work, but she could not bring herself to follow through. Calling her boss, she feigned an illness and asked off for the rest of the day.

When Justin came home, he laid Becca in her crib for a few moments. The house was quiet. Walking into the kitchen, he saw the envelope and letter sitting on the table where it had been that morning. He found Cassandra upstairs, under an afghan her mother had given her and asked tentatively, "Did you call your dad?"

"No. I'm not ready for that. How's Becca? It's all so outrageous, confusing—I need more time." She sat up and added, "All I keep thinking about is what I suppose everyone thinks in a situation like this. I never really knew my parents. They must have had another life or something. . . ." Tears, uncensored, rushed down her face, making trails in her make-up. "Let's go downstairs. I want to hug the baby and fix our dinner. I want our lives back to normal."

Cassandra held her father's letter for over a month, using her free time to probe her memory, talk to a therapist, process with Justin and hug her baby. From a box in the garage, she took scraps of writing from her mother's past and read these, along with some love letters between her parents when they were young. Nothing revealed information that would unravel the searing pain of betrayal that she felt.

Returning home from work early on a Friday afternoon, before Justin and Becca, Cassandra sat once again, holding the offending letter. *This thing has already taken far too much of my life. Why am I so obsessed with it? It's time to act.* She thought of taking a last desperate risk and calling Rorie herself, but she knew that would cross a boundary she dared not violate. Then the most perverse thought of all came to her: *I could destroy the letter. Dad would never know and that would be the end of it.* Again, she delved into every ramification of the possibility. It gave her momentary power to realize what this could do, what would end this horrific pain she felt.

Then Cassandra's thoughts penetrated to a more profound level. She wanted to understand how love and honesty related. *Does love inevitably require dishonesty?* That possibility sounded utterly contradictory to her own feelings about her family, and especially about Justin and Becca. She reviewed her bond with the two of them. She recalled things left unsaid with her husband, withheld, though not designed to deliberately deceive him. She could not imagine wanting to be with anyone where dishonesty and deceit defined the relationship. *No*, she concluded, *Love must be a way of revealing ourselves, not a way of hiding. Deceit is hiding.* Cassandra pondered the issue further, *What if this is why the woman sent the letter in the first place, to be honest with Dad?* And with that insight Cassandra determined to mail her father what was surely his own. Her only remaining question was when to send it.

Cassandra woke early on Saturday morning, the house still dim with a gray morning light filtering into the bedroom. She was plagued with a clear memory. Slipping from their bed she left Justin sound asleep, his mouth open and hair rumpled. The baby had not yet awakened, so Cassandra was free to explore her suspicions. Her father had given her a file folder just before leaving for New Mexico, explaining to her that it was full of letters her mother had dictated for the two of them throughout her illness. He was taking his with him to Taos, but he wanted to leave behind Cassandra's letters for her. However, his daughter did not wish to read the letters so soon after her mother's death. The thought hurt too much.

"Someday when it's not so painful, you may find these letters worth reading. They were dictated for you," Clay had told her with a husky voice. "You will know when to start reading them, but don't rush." So Cassandra had put them away. Only as her life began to unfold did she venture into the box, but only one letter at a time. There were still plenty she had not yet seen or opened. She read them only as she felt the need for wisdom from her mother. With the birth of the baby and going back to work, she had promptly forgotten about them. Only now, in this situation with her dad, did she crave some explanation, hoping a clue was in the letters Mellie left for her.

Padding her way into her father's former study which now served as a combination library and workspace for Justin, Cassandra began a systematic scavenger hunt for the folder. After a half-hour search and a littered floor, she found what she sought: the portfolio of a loose collection of papers, different sizes and colors. Clearing a space on Justin's work desk stacked high with papers to grade, she eventually began sorting through the notes to find the ones that applied to where she currently found herself—lost and feeling betrayed. The project turned into renewed mourning. None of the letters hinted at conflict between her parents or infidelity.

Finally, just as she came almost to the bottom of the pile, there was a letter to Cassandra that exploded with pathos and hope, both at once.

My dearest daughter,

If you are reading this, then I assume your father has told you about his escapades in Wild Rivers gorge with another woman. Women don't ordinarily appreciate being betrayed by their husbands or lovers, but in this case—my dying—there is an explanation. Please read on. I know you so well that I know you are angry at your father, and perhaps at me because you feel betrayed by our marriage. I know you are struggling right now and are probably very confused. I wish I could spare you those feelings, but I am not there with you any longer. So please allow me to explain.

I am the one who pushed your father to go on that trip. Remember? I knew he was tired from my illness, and sad so deep down that he was no longer truly living his own life. I knew he was suffering more than I was. So I made a plan—to send him away from me to our favorite place: New Mexico. I don't know that I deliberately hoped he would meet someone or have a liaison while he was away. But I knew I was also not opposed to this happening for him. I love your father more than life itself, but I am dying. I want Clay to know life again, even love again, however painful that is for me to say and think about. I do not want him climbing into the grave with me. His life is here. You are here. And his happiness with someone else is a possibility that I wish for him because he deserves to be loved and allowed to love again

When Clay returned from his journey west, he told me he had met a woman and they had a brief encounter, one that was important to both of them. She needed rescuing as much as he did. As far as I know, he has never seen her again, or even spoken to her. But he did come back with an understanding that he must go on with his life after I am gone. You must allow him this and support him when it happens. You will never have another mother, but your dad will likely have another wife. Please find it in your heart to love her and appreciate your dad's efforts to rebuild his life. This is how strong our marriage is, Cassandra—strong enough to wish love and happiness for each other no matter what the price of the loss might be.

Your mother

Tears streamed down Cassandra's face onto her robe. Her nose turned red and ran. She could not stop the deluge. Grabbing a pillow off the loveseat she hugged it to herself and buried her head in the soft cloth, sobbing loudly. As soon as the typhoon stopped, she looked at the letter in her hands, thinking, *Guess that was Mom's own way of being honest. One thing she did teach me: if honesty doesn't fit with anything else, it fits with dying.* A chill ransacked her body as she groped to stand up and return to her sleeping family.

Justin had awakened and entered the nursery. She found him changing Becca's diaper and cuddling with her. Hearing Cassandra enter the room behind him, he asked, "Wanna take a morning stroller walk with the babe?" Then he noticed his wife's red nose and eyes. "What's the matter, Cassie?" Grabbing her, he hugged them both, mashing Becca between them as the baby whimpered.

"I just read a letter my mother left me explaining this mess with Dad. I'll tell you about it. Let's go for a walk. I need to get outside for a while. Give me time to change my clothes."

As they left their home pushing the stroller together and holding hands, Cassandra told Justin about the letter her mother had written. Then she stated firmly, "I'm not going to call Dad. This secret needs to stay buried for now. I'll save the letter and then someday maybe I'll give it to him. Right now, he's found a good life and is happy. I need to let that be what it can be. Mother wanted this for him." She smiled at her baby and hugged Justin, peace returning to her heart and mind. *I can live with this decision and let Dad be. He's suffered enough.*

"Tell me what changed your mind." Justin spoke gently to his wife, anxious to hear her story and understand her change of heart. "Your dad hasn't called us in a while now. Should we check on him?"

"Probably. We can call this afternoon. I'm ready to talk to him, not about the letter, but simply to talk to him. I miss my dad, and I know losing Mom was tough on him. It's time for us to really connect again."

A sparkling Saturday morning took Justin, Cassandra and Becca to a local park where they played among other young families, all with stories to share about raising babies. Clay spent the day hiking with a woman he had met in Taos, Victoria, who preferred to be called Vickie. They walked into the ski basin with daypacks and dreams.

Rorie's day included taking Donie to have his hair cut in preparation for Sean McDonough to arrive the next day from Chicago. Distances between all of them created the divide none were able to cross.

Release

THE PICKUP GROANED INTO REVERSE, AND CLAY GUIDED IT BY mirrors down the drive and onto the gravel road. Beside him on the seat lay a package. He rested his hand on it to hold it in place as he trundled toward town. The sun's slant accentuated his squint and his crow's feet creases. After being up most of the night in the final surge to send his manuscript to his publisher before the imposed deadline, he drove groggily.

Clay reached the post office only minutes after it opened for the day. A line had already queued in front of him. He had imagined some modest ritual to mark the delivery of his five-year effort, but fatigue and relief overwhelmed the moment. He found quite enough solace in simply handing over his work to the spry, chatty representative of the postal service.

Returning home, elated and relieved, Clay fell asleep to catch up from his all-night marathon. Befuddled by deep slumber and unaware of how long he had slept, he slowly roused as he rubbed his neck from a crick that had formed while he slept. When his thoughts first took shape, he enjoyed the thrill of knowing his work, now out of his hands, was on its way to his publisher. *I've written a good book,* he told himself. *It honors Mellie. That's enough. But I hope someday Rorie might read it and know. . . .* He thought no further about the matter as he sat up on the sofa, then ambled over to his stereo system and punched buttons to play his favorite music by John Lennon. Time for a late breakfast. *Amazing how ravenous I am now that I've finished that manuscript. Time to move on with my life—that chapter's over.* He began to prepare a bowl of oatmeal and fruit, toast and black coffee. The day lay ahead of him, empty yet full of promise.

Clay had for weeks formed a plan for this day following the completion of his book. Clearing off the table, he reached for his daypack on the top shelf of his tiny storage closet, prepared a lunch and two bottles of water, along with other incidentals, for a day hike. He walked with deliberation into the bedroom, where he took the blue urn from the mantle. Then he returned to his studio and retrieved the white stone and brought them back to his kitchen table, where he loaded his daypack. He wrapped the blue urn in a towel and placed it in the bottom of the pack, adding other gear around it for security. He snuggled the stone into the pocket of his hiking vest, the one that had retained Rorie's imagined touch after their meeting at Wild Rivers.

In the dilapidated garage behind Clay's house, his motorcycle rested upright, always ready, like a favorite horse, to bear him forth. He checked the machine with a sharp eye before strapping the pack to the rear carrier. Straddling the seat, he turned the key and the engine hummed above its internal explosions with a rhythm that relaxed Clay. He wheeled sharply out of the detached garage and drove down the familiar road to the highway.

Heading north out of Taos, the cycle glided between expanses of sage on either side. The mountains rose on the horizon, thrusting themselves effortlessly into the sky. He could see Mount Wheeler to the right, snowcapped and dominating the range surrounding it. The highway dropped and curved, rose and swerved, as he moved through the Hispanic hamlets and clusters of adobe homes that dotted the desert plains. He passed a sign pointing to the D.H. Lawrence home, where the novelist had lived early in the century. Clay thought about how he would have enjoyed a conversation with Lawrence about love, since the story with his wife was quite entrancing. *Some lessons to be contemplated there. . . .*

North of Questa, Clay saw the sign that he had seen only once before: Rio Grande Wild Rivers Recreation Area. Sensations borne of all the memories now recorded in his book swept him along. He turned west into the village of Cerro. *How familiar this is, yet how distant at this point in my life. This very road drew me to love in one direction and returned me to loss in another.*

Clay slowed the cycle as he crossed into the preserve itself. Sage waved at him, then cedars, and the saw-tooth edges of the rim of the gorge began to greet him. He slacked his pace even more, to savor and relive. The whole place appeared petrified in time, as if nothing at all had occurred since his departure, as though everything here waited for his return.

Clay had no detailed plan for the day. He wanted it to unfold and to draw him into the environs. At the sign Big Arsenic he drew to a stop and sat, while a lizard darted across the asphalt road in front of him. Turning onto the slightly rutted gravel road, he progressed to the campsites bordering the lip of the massive rift. To his astonishment a pick-up camper sat perched in the very site where he had encountered Spark. For an instant Clay dwelt on the possibility that the old man had come back. Or perhaps stayed all of this time? He told himself that such a coincidence was too incredible to entertain, and when he saw a young couple come around the vehicle, the man carrying a child in his arms, relief and disappointment merged inside him. *No such luck. . . . I'd love to hug that old man.*

Staring into the depths below at the silver thread of the river lying across the distant floor, Clay decided to hike down the same trail he had taken before. He unstrapped his daypack, locked the cycle and found the trailhead. Half an hour later he rested on a tree stump and drank as he distinguished the scents of pinions and ponderosas around him. At one prominence he could see the roof of the very camp shed where he had stayed before, and he laughed out loud, recalling his shower under the falls and the fact that Rorie had spied on him there.

When Clay reached the bottom of the canyon, signs pointed up and down the trail. He halted to decide which way to turn. Memories of the hot spring tempted him, but he decided to turn down-trail, where he would pass Rorie's former campsite.

Reaching the place where her tent had stood, he saw the table that once held the stone. His reaction surprised him. Although the warmth of the sun on his back and the eternal flow of the river welcomed him, feelings for Rorie did not intensify as he had anticipated. The whole place spoke loudly of her absence, not only from that particular space, but from within him. Their relationship had never found closure, and he longed for a conversation that might grant completion—for them both.

After sitting at the camp table, munching on trail mix and sipping water, Clay drew his worn journal from the pack, the same one he had brought with him on his first trip into these depths. He had almost filled it, but with everything that had happened, the process had gone slowly. Only brief notes, a page or less at a time. Three pages remained blank. *Perhaps*, he thought, *I can gain some finality with a one-way conversation.* He found the blank pages, dated his entry and began:

Hello, Rorie.

You'll never believe where I am as I write this. After you left, I never returned to Wild Rivers until now. Too many memories. I didn't want to spoil anything. But here I am, and I must report that, no matter how hard I search for you, not even a whiff of you remains in this place. All I can find are images of you scattered across this gorge and in the waters of the river. We have been erased by time, you and I.

In case you wonder why I came back, I'll tell you. I didn't really expect to find you here; I only <u>wanted</u> to find you here. I really came to finish this thing we began, but I only realized this today. I had to come down to this idyllic place, this rift in the earth, to discover why I came. I want to say goodbye to you. It must have been difficult for you back then, because you chose not to attempt to say goodbye to me. This might have been the best for both of us, but I still feel incomplete. So I'll say goodbye now. You gave me a new and fresh image of love. And now I release that gift back to the earth and water here where we found it. It will always be here if you wish to return and say goodbye too.

Clay closed the journal, stood and walked down the same path Rorie had ascended to meet him for the first time. At the river's edge he sat on the grass and chunked pebbles into the dashing water. He remembered poetry that spoke of such sights and the often-repeated images of eternal flow and endless movement. *Nothing lasts, but still it all continues*, he reminded himself. Clay had tried in his manuscript to capture the relevance of this truth for the meaning and force of love, especially after Mellie's death. Now the truth comforted him with an assurance that, while life and all its agonies and marvels do end, especially the joy of human sharing, the unparalleled gift of participating remains. *That has to be enough*, he said to himself, *and if I can stay mindful of this, it is enough.*

Striding back to the table, Rorie's table, Clay opened his journal one more time and wrote a final entry:

You may never know, unless I send you a copy, that I have written about you in my book. It says all that I can put into words about how important you were, and are, to me. I hope you don't mind that I used your name. There's no way to improve on "Rorie."

Today I shall close the book on our brief encounter. The quality overwhelms the brevity, at least for me. But as you have gone on with your life, so I must now find my way into the rest of mine. Mellie is now gone. You are living another story. I must create a new future for myself without either of you, the two women I loved with my full heart. My life will be all the more profound for having known the two of you.

Clay ended the journal entry with his initials and closed the volume. He noticed a tiny crevice high in the nearest pinon tree, its limbs shading the area where Rorie once slept. Reaching up into the opening, Clay placed the round stone from his pocket, as if placing his whole relationship with Rorie there. A private monument.

Swinging his pack over his shoulders, Clay continued down-trail onto the bending, rising and falling path until he reached La Junta. He could see people staring down from the lookout at the rim, but no one appeared at the point where the Red River flowed into the Rio Grande. He spied a mammoth boulder, tossed into place by the force of a long-stilled volcano, and clamored up on it to lunch in the sun. A peanut butter sandwich complemented by fresh plums and a granola bar nourished him. He lay back on the dark solid surface, heated by the sun and became lost in a brief, cleansing sleep.

Roused by the cry of a raven overhead, Clay donned his pack again, slid off the gray boulder and picked his way among the splay of basalt and tuff, decorated with dying clusters of Indian rice grass, broom snakeweed, and even a narrow-leaf yucca, to the exact juncture of the two rivers. In the water rested more stones, and he plotted a way of jumping from one to another, until he reached the most stirring turbulence. There the two rivers became indissoluble. He sat for some time, luxuriating in the magnificence of that one spot. "A convergence," he said out loud, but not above the roar of the two clashing bodies of water. *Why do we always seek these points of union? I still haven't answered that question for myself—except love. Love must be the reason.*

Standing on the farthest rock from shore, Clay removed the blue urn from his pack. It glinted in the sun as he held it high, like a Native elder holds high the medicine pipe. After offering prayer words to Mellie and on her behalf, he lowered the urn and removed the top, waiting for the spinning wind to name its course. He cast the contents before him and down the river. Sediment dropped instantly into the torrent, but the lighter dust lifted on the breeze and formed a cloud dissolving in brief episodes.

That's not really her, Clay assured himself as he watched until the barest remnants of his wife's body disappeared. The release he expected did not come until he raised again the thick-glassed urn. Lifting it high above his head, he brought it crashing down on the boulder on which he stood. Its pieces sprayed into the tumbling river, bits of glass refracting the sun as it spread and fell. Only then did the enormity of his gesture dawn on him. He cried out to overcome the sense of dreaded loss, and in doing so came his release. She had finally and fully released him. Now both were free to move on.

The climb back to the rim, the sterling blue-sky day, the hike to his motorcycle, all conspired to invigorate Clay. He rode back into Taos like a man recently freed from torture. Stopping at Orlando's for his favorite meal of enchiladas and posole, he ate heartily. He finished his meal, satisfied and prepared to turn an invisible corner into the rest of his life.

As Clay opened his front door, the phone was ringing. He bolted to catch it.

"Hello, Dad. It's Cassandra. . . ."

"Hey, honey, how are you? Perfect timing! You won't believe where I have been. Yesterday I finished the book and this morning sent it off to the publisher. Then, I went to a place called Wild Rivers to scatter your mother's ashes. She never saw this place, but I know she would have loved it. When you are out here again, I want to show you." He stopped to catch his breath, "Say, I didn't mean to go on about that. So much has happened, and I could hardly wait to share it with you. How's my granddaughter doing?"

Cassandra listened to her father's enthusiasm and replied appropriately, all the while wondering about what she knew that he didn't know—that he had a son by a woman he once loved. "She's terrific, Dad. I never knew being a parent could be so complicated, or so much fun." The secret would stay buried for now.

Passages

THE WAIT WAS EXCRUCIATING. EACH DAY, RORIE FOUND HERSELF rushing home to see if a message awaited her. Although she had not put her cell phone number in the letter, she never let the phone out of her sight in case he decided to call. Her landline telephone sat on her desk, and she found herself often staring at it, willing it to ring. How she longed to hear his voice on the other end, exclaiming over their son and giving her a promise to come to meet him as soon as possible. Visions, fantasies, stories filled her head. *Surely I will hear soon.* At work, her colleagues found Rorie absentminded, distracted and inattentive. Days turned into a month. As she watched the days tick off the calendar, her spirits drooped. *He has the letter now and he's choosing not to respond. I never expected this. Maybe he wasn't the man I thought he was all along. Or, perhaps he has moved on with his life and the idea of a child is too complicated. Or, maybe he's on his way to me. I'll give him a few more days.*

Rorie's hopes were unrealistic but she kept them alive, determined not to falter in her trust that Clay would contact her. Six weeks passed. Two months dragged by. She finally surrendered late one night and wept until she had no tears left. *This is the end. I must finally let him go.* Turning off the light beside her bed, she fell into a dreamless sleep, aching in her soul for a love like she would never know again, lost in the mists of time.

After she mailed the letter and realized no response was forthcoming, the months slowly righted themselves and the memory of Clay began to recede into her innermost parts. Rorie finally found that days could pass without a single thought of him crossing her mind. She began to date again, finding herself often with a crush on one man or another from time to time. Nothing replaced the passion she had felt for Clay, but she accepted this reality and moved on.

As Rorie picked herself back up and returned to her daily routines, she became even more attentive to Donie. A new author turned in a book to her publishing company, and she was assigned to be the reader. She enjoyed becoming involved in her work again. Rorie was skilled at what she did, and she loved the lifestyle that working for her publishing company allowed her. When he was a child, Donie and Rorie often spent weekends on outings in the local park or up in the mountains at a picnic spot along Hyde Park Road. As the boy grew into a chatty teen, they hiked together, or prowled around art galleries in various Hispanic towns scattered about the state. He loved concerts and she loved plays, so they took turns choosing their entertainment. She taught Donie how to cook. He taught her how to appreciate the music of kids his age. The two loved to ski together. In the winter months they could often be found on the slopes at the Santa Fe Ski Basin racing downhill with each other. Their lives together were easy, compatible with little stress between them.

In her 40s, Rorie had a close call when she met a man named Russell through a mutual friend. He was a writer, and for almost a year he enchanted her with his ability to discuss just about anything. He loved theater as well as sitting on her sofa on quiet evenings reading a book, rubbing her feet while he read. He asked Rorie to move in with him, but she refused, concerned about the effect this would have on Donie. Then he asked her to marry him. It took Rorie a month to decide, but over a dinner in a restaurant just off the Plaza she finally confessed to Russell that she liked her life the way it was. She was quite comfortable dating him but felt that she was not particularly good marriage material, at least in her mind. Rather than continue to pursue her, hoping she would change her mind, Russell left Santa Fe, and she never heard from him again. *I don't have a very good record with guys,* she told herself in the shower one night. *They want to get married, and I don't, or they can't get married, and I want to. Obviously, I need a new pattern here. Oh well, such is life.*

Time passed as Donie grew from a boy into a teen-ager and then a college student. Rorie and Sara kept their friendship intact with visits back and forth between Dallas and Santa Fe, sometimes interlaced with what they liked to call "girl trips" to Tucson, Denver, San Francisco, even once to London on a whim. The years seemed to fly by, and she turned fifty with little fanfare. Rorie had not lost her natural beauty and had transformed into a striking woman, full of confidence and poise. She still grew her auburn hair long, and she let it fall in soft waves around her neck and face. Living in Santa Fe, she shifted her fashion sense from the stylish clothing of her past in Dallas to casual, non-descript soft shirts and jeans, with the occasional long flowing skirts and boots worn to the summer opera performances.

Upon reflection, Rorie considered herself to be content with her life. Donie's leaving for college created grief in her at the loss of his daily presence. But she loved to hear his enthusiasm for leaving home to make new friends and to develop skills in his mind. Though she missed him terribly, he returned often enough during school breaks to keep her from growing too melancholy. Their talks over a beer around the fireplace were deep and interesting, unlike what most of her friends were experiencing with their college-aged offspring. But the two of them, Rorie and Donie, had long ago learned the art of conversation between them, and most enjoyed times alone with a juicy topic to wrangle and mangle. Rorie still had a habit of running her fingers through Donie's thick hair just before he went to bed, and he had come to tolerate this after years of resisting his mother's gesture of love. *He's a good kid,* she thought one evening when he was home for spring break. *I'm the lucky one here.*

In Taos, the story was similar. Clay continued with his writing, completing two more books on philosophy and then penning three novels he had long imagined. After his second novel, he had begun to gather a base of readers who enjoyed his style of writing: creative philosophy, he called it. He was enjoying a measure of success in his writing, thus his days felt meaningful and pleasant. Life flowed with little disruption.

Becoming a grandfather had changed him considerably in terms of his ability to simply stop work and pay attention to Becca. Watching her grow up was so different from what he had experienced with Cassandra, which had seemed far more like worry and work. Grandparenting was so much fun. When she turned eight, Clay began taking Becca on "joy jaunts" as he called their little road trips. He took her back to Nebraska to see the farm where he grew up. When she was ten, he took her to New York City to see the sights and sounds of the Big Apple. She was especially taken with Times Square at midnight, simply because he allowed her to stay up and see the garish colors and hear the noise in the middle of the night. When she was twelve, he had taken her to canoe the Snake River. They almost fell into the cold water watching a moose grazing on the river's edge while they were trying to take photos. Laughing loud and hard, the two bonded such that throughout Becca's teen years, it was often her Granddad Clay she called to talk to when her parents were entirely too much trouble. The youthful years with Becca thrilled Clay and kept him involved with his Kansas family.

His social life in Taos was simple, with good friends and local events to keep him interested in life in his adopted town. In the meantime, Clay and Vicki developed a comfortable companionship that suited both of them. This charismatic middle-aged woman possessed jet-black hair, brown eyes, and stood lean and lanky. She wasn't beautiful, but she caught one's attention with her smile. Clay was drawn to her upon first meeting at a local gathering of authors. Vicki was also widowed so the pair shared stories of how difficult it had been to regroup their lives after the loss of their spouses. Though she would hike the mountains with Clay from time to time, Vicki preferred to show him a side of Taos he had not known before meeting her. She was well known in the film crowd, a social participant in the film festivals that occurred each year in both Taos and Santa Fe. She knew many of the celebrities who lived in and around New Mexico, taking a teasing delight in dropping names to Clay about who she had shared dinner with or had talked to on the phone.

Once she discovered that Clay was not easily impressed with fame, she began to set up quiet dinners at her beautiful adobe home with one celebrity or another who had interests similar to Clay's. Slowly he began to trust that she genuinely liked people, regardless of their status and came to enjoy these occasions. They engaged in a sexual liaison after a period of seeing each other that became comfortable for them both. Neither put pressure on the other to marry or even become monogamous. This just happened. They considered themselves a couple, as did most of their friends, and left it at that.

The years passed in an easy rhythm as Clay watched Becca become a teen and then head off to art school in Chicago. His relationship with Justin and Cassandra was close. They still talked about Mellie in loving terms, though occasionally Cassandra seemed to have an edge to her voice about his relationship with her mother. Clay never asked, assuming that Cassandra was still uncomfortable with his dating Victoria and feeling protective of the memory of her mother.

On a cold and cloudy Thursday morning following the Christmas holidays, a knock came on his front door. As he opened the door, a student who wished to interview Clay for his college senior thesis project in philosophy stood in the whipping wind, asking to see him. Since Clay had been away from teaching for several years now, the encounter with this student had delighted him, reminding him of the years when he had students swirling around him. Their meeting in his living room had been slightly awkward, yet they planned a second meeting. Clay met the young man at Michael's Kitchen two days later. Clay had thoroughly enjoyed their first encounter and was looking forward to continuing the dialogue. During the discussion Donie had dropped two pieces of information that so stunned Clay, he could hardly participate in the rest of their meeting. *His mother is named Rorie. He never knew his father.* Clay immediately became suspicious but did not want to grill the young man.

Donie had continued talking, intensely, finally looking straight into Clay's eyes and asked, "Dr. . . . uh, Clay, what made you choose this particular topic, for a book in philosophy?" *His eyes. It's in the eyes. He has my eyes.*

Clay swallowed nervously, paused for a moment, and then replied, "At one time in my life I loved two women, and I lost both of them, as you know from reading the book. I saw during that time that love and loss are always connected, can never be separated. Therein lies our human dilemma, our agony and our joy. When we agree to love; we agree to loss." He stopped, waiting for Donie to respond.

"Sorta tragic, isn't it?"

"Yes. Yet, something in the human spirit desperately seeks to live with joy rather than the tragedy. It's a choice we end up making, each of us, for ourselves." Clay, spurred on by his new revelation, asks pointedly, "Which are you choosing, Donie?"

Donie, surprised by the intensity of the Clay's tone, stuttered, "Well, I—I'm not sure yet. I prefer to be happy, of course, but sometimes I find myself anxious or upset or just plain mad." He grimaced at the professor. "Do I have to make a choice right now? I don't think I'm ready."

Chuckling, Clay popped back at the young man, "You probably aren't ready for such a question at your age. It's all right. You'll know one day. You can call me and tell me."

The breakfast meeting came to an end with the two men agreeing to stay in touch. Clay walked Donie outside, shook hands with him, and turned abruptly to walk back to his truck. *Now what do I do with that information? Why didn't she call me, find me, tell me? Why would Rorie keep this information from me all these years? Why would this woman I have loved for so long do that?*

Truth

THE SKY FILLED WITH DARK, HEAVY, GRAY CLOUDS JUST AS CLAY turned into his driveway. Snow was on its way. His mind spun in whirling dervish circles from his realization that most assuredly Donie was his son, not Wil's, as he had supposed all those years ago. Rorie had never married. Donie did not know his father. The boy was the right age if one did the math. Climbing out of his truck, Clay staggered into the cabin, stoked the fire and fell into his leather chair. Memories flooded into his head, filling his eyes with tears. *I have a son. Imagine that! All those years lost.* Then a rage filled his heart at the years he had missed with Donie. *How could Rorie have done this to me, to Donie, to us? There has to be a reason. Surely there is an explanation.* Pounding his fist on the arm of the chair, Clay then brushed his hair out of his eyes, wiped his face and stood up, resolute.

"Cassandra?" He called her name clearly as she answered the phone. "I want to come to visit with you and Justin. I need to talk to you about something important."

"What's the matter, Dad?" Alarm sounded in her voice.

"Not gonna share over the phone, Cassie. I'd like to start driving tomorrow. That okay with you? Are you two available for a couple of days or so?" Clay's tone was urgent.

"Sure, Dad. Come on. We'll be waiting for you. I wish you'd tell me what's going on, but I'll wait if I have to." Cassandra was dreading the visit because she assumed Clay was coming to tell her that he and Victoria were engaged to be married, or even worse, already married. Though she liked the woman well enough, Clay's daughter still had trouble imagining her father being married to anyone besides Mellie. "I'll have your favorite soup cooking and the porch light on." She hung up the phone with a sigh. *Oh dear, I need to get ready for what he has to tell me. Put on your happy face, Cassandra Benson.*

Early the next morning before light invaded the cabin, Clay packed quickly, throwing an extra pair of jeans and shirt into his duffle, grabbing his jacket, keys, phone and glasses as the last tasks before shutting down the woodstove. As Clay locked the front door, Flame ran in front of him to the truck, sensing a road trip ahead. He opened the passenger door, instructing his companion to jump into the truck while he tossed his duffle behind the seat. Into Taos to gas up and soon on the road, Clay turned on the radio for music to drown out the clamoring noises in his head. He made himself promise to ask no more fruitless questions for the time being. "Let's just make this trip without any drama, huh, Flame?" He spoke to the dog as he would a human being.

After several years alone, having learned how to live beyond grief and sadness, Clay had finally settled into his life in Taos enough to call this unique place his home. In order to mark the change in his psyche, he'd decided it was time to get a dog. Naming the male golden retriever puppy "Flame," to honor his memories with Rorie, he and the dog formed an immediate connection, becoming inseparable.

Pulling up to the house he and Mellie used to own and inhabit, Clay stepped out of the truck, stiff and tired. The drive had taken over ten hours, with frequent stops for Flame and himself to stretch. Justin reached the porch first, greeting his father-in-law with a warm handshake and hug. Cassandra followed her husband to the front door and stepped outside, shivering in the night air, "Come on in, Dad. It's cold out here! Soup's on! You hungry?" She loved to feed her father, who always appreciated any meal she made for him. It gave her a way to fuss over him that he would tolerate.

The three chatted easily throughout the meal and then moved into the family room for steaming hot cups of chamomile tea and some of Cassandra's freshly baked apple cake. "What did you want to talk about, Dad?" Cassandra's curiosity was about to eat her alive. Even though the hour was growing too late to start a serious conversation, she urged her father to answer her question.

"Cassandra, I'm not trying to avoid talking to you—truly I'm not, but it's late tonight, and I'm exhausted from the drive." Flame had already fallen asleep, her head propped on Clay's socked foot. "Could we agree to meet over the breakfast table in the morning and I promise, I'll tell you everything?" Clay's voice broke with his plea to his daughter.

Recognizing that she would get nothing else out of her father and that he needed rest, she reluctantly agreed, "Sure dad. You had a long drive. I'm sorry I pushed you. That's fine. I have planned a yummy breakfast for all of us. Justin and I are both free for most of the day tomorrow. I have a quick meeting in the afternoon, but other than that, we are here with you for the weekend. Let's just enjoy each other. I'm sorry you are missing your granddaughter on this trip. Becca is away at an art festival in Colorado this weekend."

"Me too. That girl is something else! I'll see her when I come back. It won't be too long." After he had eaten, the warm food exaggerated his need for sleep. Clay sighed and then yawned, stretching his arms in front of him. "What I really need right now is a bed. I'm assuming I'm in my usual room upstairs?" Justin nodded to him. "See you two in the morning." Clay called Flame to the back door, and sent her out for her nightly duty before they retired, then the two of them wandered upstairs, Flame crowding Clay on the way up to the room. Even the dog knew where to make her own bed for the night.

The pungent smell of coffee woke Clay the next morning. Glancing at the clock beside his bed, he sprang up from the covers, looked around the room, disoriented for a moment. *I don't usually sleep this late!* Even Flame had disappeared. Before long he descended into the kitchen and saw his daughter working at the stove as his dog rushed over to give him a morning greeting. "You beat me up, Girl," he said to the creature while patting her on the head.

"Good morning, Dad. You sure slept in this morning. Haven't known you to do that in years!" She grinned at him and walked over to give her father a warm hug. "I love having you here with us. You ready to move back yet?" She knew she was skating on thin ice to ask Clay this question because he had made it clear over and over that Taos was home for him.

Giving her "that look", Clay responded, "Now Cassie. . . ."

"I know. I know . . . Taos is home! I was just teasing you." She turned back to the bacon frying in the pan. "Anyway, it's always good when you are here."

Once breakfast was cleared away, Cassandra poured coffee into hefty mugs for the three of them, sat down and waited. She was determined not to press her father again, though the look on her face was a clear message that she was ready to learn what this trip was about.

Clearing his voice, Clay began hesitantly, "Cassandra, Justin, I do have something important to share with you. It's not an easy matter to discuss, nor is this something that can be taken lightly. I wanted to tell you face to face, not over the phone. It's that important." He paused to make sure he had their attention. The couple was now staring at Clay, eyes wide, puzzlement on their faces.

"I need to tell you a story first in order to bring you up to the present. It will take me a while. That okay?" They nodded their heads, still wondering, a bit fearful.

"Cassandra, when your mother was ill toward the end of her life, she sent me on a trip to New Mexico. Do you remember that?" Cassandra swallowed. *He's not going to share anything about Victoria at all! He's going to tell us about Rorie! Oh, my God!* "Yes, I do, Dad." Fear permeated her face.

"Well, when I went on that trip, I chose to go into a place called the Wild Rivers gorge just north of Taos. Remember?" Cassandra nodded. "Please keep in mind that I had not wanted to go on that trip. Mellie insisted. So I went. She was right. I did need a break. I needed to think about what was ahead of me—losing her, and about how I could possibly go on without her." He glanced at Cassandra to see if she was accepting his words. The look on her face was oddly strained. He continued. "While I was in the canyon, I met a woman. Her name was Rorie." Clay did not know how to state the next part of the story, so he pointed to his mug and asked for more coffee.

Once Cassandra had given him a refill and reseated herself, Clay went on with his story. "We had an affair, a three-day rendezvous, if you will." Pausing to see their reaction, Clay was shocked that neither Justin nor Cassandra said anything. *That's odd. Why isn't she reacting to this story?* "I never saw Rorie again. I learned from that experience that I would be able to survive your mother's death, Cassie, but that I also loved your mother more than I had imagined possible. I came to realize that losing her would be the most difficult thing I would ever face. The experience with Rorie was life affirming, for sure, and it gave me hope that I would someday be able to rebuild my life. That encounter taught me that I might even love again. But it also made my situation painfully clear to me, that even though I loved your mother, her death would force me to learn to live without her whether I wanted to or not."

"Go on, Dad," Cassandra whispered, clutching her coffee mug as if it were a lifeline.

"As you know, I moved to Taos and have rebuilt my life there. I have even met someone who is a good companion for me. You've met her several times over the years. I'm aware that you prefer that I not marry her. Be that as it may, in the end it will be my decision whether I do that or not. But marriage to Victoria is *not* the reason I am here." He noticed that Cassandra let out a sigh of relief, and saw her face soften as she heard his words. "What I want understood right at this moment is that I did manage to learn to live without so much grief. I like my life in Taos—I feel normal there. Whole again." Justin and Cassandra clasped each other's hands and smiled at Clay.

"A week ago, a young man came to see me, a student who is using my book on love and loss for his senior project. This is the story I have come to tell you."

Cassandra blanched. *Here we go. He knows! What on earth am I going to tell him now?*

"I met with this kid, at least he seems like a kid to me—his name is Donie—a couple of times, first time at my house when he just showed up to talk. Then the second time we met for breakfast to finish our discussion of his project. In the middle of our talk he revealed to me that his mother's name was Rorie and that he did not know his father." Clay stopped to see if Cassandra was following him. She was.

"At one point I looked into his face and realized he has my eyes. He also confessed he had grown up with a dog named 'Flame,' which was the name of Rorie's dog that she had with her in the canyon. When I put his age together with all the details he was dropping on me, I knew immediately that this was my son."

Cassandra was full of questions at this point but held back and allowed Clay to finish his story. Clay went on, "I wanted to come here and tell you both before I go any further with this information. I have not spoken to Donie about what I have put together. . . ."

Cassandra interrupted him, "Have you spoken to Rorie about this?"

"No. I have not. You come first in my mind. You have the right to know before I act on any of this and get things stirred up. So I have come here not really knowing if Donie is aware that I am his father. I don't believe Rorie knows that I now know her secret."

"She did not mean for this to be a secret, Dad." Cassandra confessed, tears welling in her eyes.

Startled, Clay turned in his chair to face his daughter directly, "What do you mean?"

Here we go, Cassandra, thought. *The truth has to come out. I hope my father can forgive me for what I've done.*

"I'll be right back." Abruptly, Cassandra stood up and left the room. Justin just stared at Clay, not knowing what to say or do. He knew that Cassandra was retrieving the letter, long buried in the family trunk upstairs. Years ago, she had hidden the letter in the box of letters from her mother, placing it safely away from prying eyes. The two men just sat there, fixated on their cups of coffee as an uncomfortable silence rose between them. Clay began to wonder what was going on.

Soon Cassandra returned to the kitchen with a rumpled mauve envelope in her hand. "Dad. I have no explanation or excuse that will seem appropriate to you. But it seems now that you know about Donie, I need to give you the letter that Rorie sent you after she moved to Santa Fe. She did not keep the news from you. There was no intentional secret." Cassandra handed the envelope over to her father, sank into the chair beside him, and began to cry softly.

Clay was astonished. "What? I don't understand, Cassie. Rorie wrote me? You have her letter? What? How?" He opened the envelope and began to read the delicate sheets of paper. As he finished Rorie's final words, he sat stunned, unable to speak. All three of them were in shock, not quite sure what should come next. Finally, Clay spoke, sensing the tension in his chest, and holding his face rigid so he would not explode. "Cassandra, you owe me an explanation, don't you? Tell me how this letter came to be in your hands. And then you know the next question I will ask, I suspect."

Cassandra was sobbing at this point and could hardly answer her father, "Look at the envelope, Dad. It came here. She thought you still lived here."

Clay turned the envelope over and saw his address in Rorie's handwriting. "So why did you keep the letter from me?" Clay spoke quietly, but firmly, knowing that if he were too intense with his daughter, she would crumble.

"At the time, it just seemed like the right thing to do. Mother had died. You had moved to Taos. You seemed happy for the first time in years. I just did not want to interrupt any of that."

Clay waited for her continue, not ready to speak.

"And, yes, now that I am older, I realize that my motives were not pure. I did not want you loving someone else after Mother. I didn't want a brother. We had Becca, and I wanted your attention on her. I was angry that you had made love to another woman while you were married to my mother, as she lay dying. I was full of rage and fear and frustration at you. I was confused, so I just hid the letter. Justin wanted me to send it to you, but I just couldn't." Cassandra was hunched over her crossed arms, as if in pain in her gut. Her words tumbled out, ragged and soggy.

"Dad, after I saw the dedication page in your book, along with the chapter on Mother and Rorie, I realized that you had done the best you could with what was a horrific situation. I could hear your struggle, your pain, and your clarity as you came to understand what had happened to you. I was hurt and angry. I was selfish to hold the letter, I know. At that point in your healing process, I just felt it was too late to mail the letter. You had moved on with your life, and you seemed ready to put all of it behind you, both Mother and Rorie." She reached out to touch her father's arm, desperate for his forgiveness.

"Well, this now explains why you never said anything to me about my book other than you liked it, which wasn't actually honest, was it? Did you even read the entire book? I just assumed the truth was too painful for you and you never wanted to discuss any of it. I had no idea you didn't speak to me about the book because you knew I had a son by Rorie. This is just a bit much to swallow, Cassandra. Do you understand that?"

"I just didn't know what to do. I can see how my actions are completely unacceptable to you." Her wet eyes pleaded with him to understand. "I don't know if you will ever forgive me for this. Now I know I made the wrong decision—it was not my decision to make. I let you down and deprived you of your son." Her crying turned to wails at this point. Justin put his arms around her, cradling her head in his shoulder.

At this point Justin decided it was important to defend his wife. "Clay, Cassandra did wrestle with this decision for weeks on end. She knew it wasn't right to keep the letter, but she didn't feel it was right to send it on to you at that stage in your recovery. We were both pretty miserable for weeks around here. I am sorry. We are both sorry. This was not a mistake; this was a gigantic wrong done to you, and to Donie."

Clay sat very still, staring into his empty cup. Feeling dejected, his shoulders slumped, and his hands fell to his sides. "I need to go for a drive, if you don't mind. I need to think. I don't know what to feel or say right now. Please don't be upset, but I need some space right now. I promise, we will sort this out. You two and Becca are my family, and I will not leave town before we have come to an understanding. But for now, I need to absorb this information. I need to think. Okay?"

They both nodded, mutely, as Clay stood, reached for his coat on the hook by the back door, called for Flame to join him and left the house. Without even thinking much about it, he turned his truck toward the park where he and Mellie had solved many of their more difficult issues when they were married.

Revelation

DONIE HEARD HIS MOTHER EXIT THE SHOWER. WAITING FOR her to dress and join him, he sat in shock, clenching the letter until it was imprinted with crinkled edges. The news that Dr. Jacobs—Clay—was his father was too much to grasp for the moment. *How is that even possible? And why didn't he say anything to me when I mentioned Mom? And why didn't Mom ever tell me the story of my father? I don't understand!* Rorie padded into the room in her best-loved sweats and leather moccasins, her favorite attire for movie nights with her son. "Rorie, what in the world!" Donie's voice was pitched high. Rorie knew he never called her by her given name unless he was angry with her or in a crisis. This was a trick he learned when he was a child to gain his mother's immediate attention. She stared at the expression on his face and realized he was furious.

"What's wrong, Donie? What's the matter?" She then spotted the paper in his hands and the book on the floor that he had dropped once he saw the letter. *Oh, dear. What a terrible way for my son to find out about his father. I really blew that one.* She scolded herself for not handling this earlier in his life. *Too late now.* "Oh. I see you found my letter. I'll explain, Donie, okay?" Her heart began to beat rapidly.

"You better!" Donie screamed at her, which was seldom his usual behavior. "You have no idea how I spent my day—this is preposterous. Tell me! Tell me now!" Her son was lashing out at her, arms flailing, the letter flying through the air. He was on his feet, his face close to hers, eyes flashing.

"Donie, this is not how I wanted to tell you the story of your birth father. Please try to calm down. Could you? I am sorry, hon—very sorry for the way this happened. But it's done, so let's talk. Will you?"

Rorie reached out for her son, but Donie yanked his arm to the side and moved away from her.

"I don't want to talk to you right now, but I want you to tell me the story. How could you?" Her son was irrational at the moment. Donie still had not revealed that he had met Clay that very day; his mother had no idea the source of his anger. The young man stomped around the room, slamming his fist into the furniture. Rorie tried to calm him down, but nothing worked. She finally sat on one end of their worn leather sofa and waited.

The last time she had seen Donie like this, he was a teen-ager of fifteen. She had grounded him for breaking his curfew and this caused him to miss a concert he had waited months to attend. The evening of the concert he stormed around their home, lashing out at her, kicking the air, and yelling behind his closed bedroom door after she sent him to his room for his disruptive behavior. His teen tantrums had been few and far between, but that one had been a doozy. Rorie knew she had to wait out the storm for him to be able to talk with her. *He doesn't use it often, but he has my father's temper when he needs it!* As she sat waiting for her son to recover his sensibilities, Rorie pondered the situation. *Why did I let it happen this way? This truly is my fault. He has a right to be angry.* She felt chagrined at her son's suffering. *I caused this. I'm so sorry, Donie. I'm so very sorry.*

Finally, Donie's energy was spent and he collapsed on the rug in front of their fireplace. He did not want to be close to his mother at the moment, but he did want to hear the story. Hugging his knees close to his body as if to protect himself from any more assault, he spouted out the words, "Okay, so go ahead and tell me your story." His forehead was riddled with angry creases, his mouth set in a straight, determined line of grimness.

Rorie told Donie about her encounter with Clay Jacobs in the Wild Rivers gorge. She spared him no detail. He was old enough to hear the entire story, she felt. At first the story seemed awkward to share, and Rorie found herself embarrassed for the actions of her younger, naïve self. But soon she began to open up to her son, sharing her own desires and feelings at that time of her life, using this as a moment to teach him that life can be pell-mell even for the best, and that such crises would happen to him too. No excuses. People make decisions and have experiences that change their lives forever. This had happened to her and was now a part of her story. When she finished sharing her tale of failed love, Rorie felt a burden lift from her heart.

"Donie, I don't know why I did not tell you this story earlier in your life, except that I just didn't. Somehow, we seemed complete, you and I, and after a few years passed, I didn't want to interrupt our lives with all of this. You never seemed particularly curious about your father, so I just let it ride. Perhaps I was wrong, but that's how I handled it. I thought you would ask when you truly wanted to know, maybe when you became a parent yourself. I don't know—it was just easier not to talk about it with you. I took the easy way out. I am sorry."

Rorie waited for Donie to engage. His silence filled the room. She noticed he had unfolded his legs, and his body posture had softened. But the boy's eyes glistened with emotion as she urged him to tell her his thoughts. "I need to tell you something, Mom." *Finally, I am Mom again! Thank goodness!*

"Okay. Shoot." Rorie sat forward to listen carefully to his words.

"I met Clay—in Taos."

"You what? How did that happen?" Rorie was shocked.

"I met him, for breakfast just this morning. I am working on my senior thesis paper, and I wanted to interview this professor who had written that book right over there," Donie said, pointing to Clay's book still lying on the floor where he had dropped it. "So I contacted him and set up this meeting. I had no idea I was meeting with my father." Pouting at her, he resumed his defensive posture.

"Does he know who you are?" Rorie asked fearfully.

"No. How could he? I didn't know to tell him." Donie's eyes were still flashing with anger at his mother. Yet, he could see her distress at his news. *Serves her right!* He thought to himself. Then regretted it. Donie was close to his mother and such feelings were not normal between them. They loved each other and their relationship had always been based on trust. This situation was providing both of them with new experiences of each other, mostly negative and unwelcome.

Leaning back on the sofa, Rorie put her hand over her mouth and sucked in deep breaths. "I've really made a mess of things here, haven't I?"

"You sure have!" Donie exclaimed, giving her no mercy. "It's bad enough you never told me about my father, but why didn't you tell him? Why did you never contact him to tell him about me?" The hurt in his eyes was palpable.

"Donie, I don't know what to say. I don't know what to do next, really. But I do need to share one more thing with you that could explain some of this to you. Do you want to hear me out, or are you still too mad at me right now?"

By this time, Donie was curled up in a fetal position on the floor, hugging a pillow to his body. Then, as if he had been prodded, he rose and came to sit beside Rorie on the sofa. "I'm listening. I need to hear anything that will make sense of this because right now none of it does."

"That letter you read. I mailed the original to Clay when you were three years old. I sent it to him, and he never responded. I had just learned that his wife had died the year before. I felt like maybe it was the right time to tell him, so I sent the letter."

"Then why. . . ?" Donie's face wrinkled into a huge question mark.

"I don't know, Son. I don't know . . . he never responded to me. I never knew why, only that I never heard from him again. I had no idea that he had moved to Taos or when he moved there. I have assumed all these years that he was living in Kansas, close to his daughter, and that he had created another life. He certainly never tried to contact me after his wife passed away, so I just figured we were never going to meet again." Her green eyes shimmered as she shared her pain.

Wiping her hand across her lips, Rorie grimaced at Donie, "I know this does not explain why I never told you about your father, except maybe that moving on with my own life gave me a way to forget so that when he didn't contact me, I could bear the pain. You see, Donie. I loved Clay. I know it sounds silly to say you love some-one after only three days together, but I fell deeply in love with him. I've never really gotten over him. I guess you can see that now. I never married and never had another deeply serious relationship. None of this is an excuse for my behavior as a mother to you. But perhaps my story will help you understand my behaviors even if you cannot forgive them."

Donie spontaneously grabbed Rorie and hugged her. "I can see how much this hurt you, Mom. But I have other questions right now. Do you think he knew all this time and didn't reach out for us? And now I wonder if he knew who I was when we met this morning. He did have an odd look on his face when I mentioned your name to him." A look of sleuthing passed across Donie's face. "What if he knew and said nothing to me? What does that make him? A jerk . . . that's what!" Donie was exploding again. Rorie grabbed his hand and urged, "Let's don't go there, Donie. Shouldn't we give him the benefit of the doubt? The man I knew would never have met with you and not acknowledged who you were. I just don't believe he would do that. It's late, and we are both emotionally wiped out. Could we just go to bed for now and sleep on this? I'm too tired to watch a movie, and too drained to pay attention to anything else."

"Sure, Mom. I'm gonna hang out here for a bit but will see you in the morning. I'm not mad any more, but it will be a while before I can accept all of this. Do you understand that?"

"Yes, I do." She kissed him on the cheek, hugged him and left the room. *Well, that's about as badly as things could have gone. Since I made a mess of my son learning about his father, I must make sure the rest of this goes well. I need to figure out a plan, but right now I'm too tired. Sleep first, plan later.* Rorie settled down for the night and fell asleep before her mind could take over and keep her awake all night with worry.

Donie shuffled into the kitchen to the refrigerator for another beer. His spirit was dragging, and his heart felt heavy. Sitting back down on the sofa in the same spot his mother had sat, he picked up the letter to read it again. For a moment, reading the letter felt en-tirely too intimate—his mother had written to his father declaring her love for him and the upcoming birth of their son. *Children shouldn't know this much about their parents.* Donie found that he felt uncomfortable as he finished reading. *I sure hope this guy has some explanation for why he met with me if he knew about my mother. I could never forgive him if he has done that to both of us. So Professor Clay Jacobs is my father—who would've thought that? I might like the guy once we get all of this sorted out. Who knows?* When he finished with the letter, he placed it carefully back into Clay's book, returning it to the shelf where it had lived for years.

Sipping his beer while he listened to music, Donie sat draped on the sofa, legs crossed, eyes downcast. A slight headache began in his temple. He decided to take Shama out for her nightly walk. Once this chore was done and Shama was settled for the night, Donie flopped on the sofa and soon fell into a dreamless sleep.

As a winter sun streaked through her bedroom window, Rorie woke clear-eyed and resolved. She knew what had to be done. She would ask Donie's permission first, but if he was okay with her idea, she would act—today! Dressing quickly in her jeans, a blue/green pullover fleecy and woolen socks, she rushed into the living room to set a fire in the fireplace. She startled when she saw Donie asleep on the sofa in his clothes. He had never made it to bed. Tiptoeing over to him, she brushed the hair away from his eyes just as he opened them. "Good morning, Kid. How about some coffee?"

Groaning, Donie pulled the thick handmade afghan over his head, and mumbled through the cover, "Sure, Mom."

Making coffee for the two of them was something she loved to do when he was home from college. She bought a special blend of beans from a local coffee shop and ground them herself. The sound brought another groan from the living room, and Rorie laughed out loud. "Up, Donie. It's going to be a great day! I have a plan."

With this Donie roused, tossed back the cover, and swung his socked feet to the floor. The fire crackled and popped, spewing embers at the wrought iron screen. He ambled over to warm his hands just as Rorie walked back into the room holding two identical, rust-colored pottery mugs with steam rising from them. "Here," she said as she handed him the coffee, "this will wake you up." She laughed at his look, with his thick hair askew and his clothes rumpled beyond repair. "You look like a waif. Do you want breakfast?"

"Nope! I want to hear the plan . . . right now!" Anticipation filled his face as the conflict between them the previous night vanished. Anger never lasted long between these two. With hope for reconnection between them, Rorie explained her idea to her son.

Nodding enthusiastically, he spoke over the rim of his cup, "Terrific, Mom. Let's do it. I'm ready."

Rorie picked up her cell phone and dialed the number Donie had given to her. On the second ring, she heard a familiar voice, though it sounded as if the connection was breaking up. "Hello?"

"Clay, this is Rorie. I understand you have met our son. I suspect the three of us should talk before Donie goes back to the university next weekend. When do you think you could come to Santa Fe? He wants to meet you again as his father, and I need the chance to explain this complicated situation to you. What do you think?"

"Sure, Rorie." There was a long pause. She waited. "I'm on my way to Kansas to tell Cassandra that she has a brother. I'll return to Taos on Wednesday evening. How about I come to Santa Fe on Thursday? Does this work for you and Donie?" Clay's breath was shallow as he formulated a plan with her.

"Excellent! I'll text you where to find us," her voice lilted with delight.

For Donie and his mother, the crawl of time until Clay's return became excruciating, though they sporadically continued their talks about Rorie's story. For Donie, excitement over meeting Clay again as his father kept him on edge.

Clay's trip back to Taos was uneventful, except that his mind would not shut down. *Rorie has a son. I have a son. We have a son. What must she have been feeling all those years thinking that I never responded to her letter? What a waste of precious time. Talk about love and loss! What in the world should I do now? And I've met him! He's a delightful young man. I can see Rorie in him . . . and myself.* His mind would not stop whirling as he made the long drive. Over and over again, he replayed the breakfast he had shared with Donie, his offspring, his child. The way the boy looked, his use of words, his gestures, those sparkling blue eyes lodged in a ski-tanned face with his hair falling down over his forehead. *I wish I had memorized everything about him when I had the chance. He's so bright and articulate. He seems comfortable with himself, unlike most college students his age. I hope the future includes the two of us having more discussions. I truly want to know him in a way that is not superficial. My, my. What surprises life holds!*

The final stretch of the drive seemed interminable; he was so weary from the inner struggle. Flame kept him company, though even the dog seemed uncannily aware of Clay's mood, keeping a low profile in her demands of him. Finally, Clay pulled into his driveway after midnight, abandoned the truck, and entered the house. The interior was cold since there was no fire to greet him. Without thinking about what needed to be done, he warmed up his bedroom with only a space heater, created a place on the floor for Flame, and crawled into bed. His head ached from the shift from the plains of Kansas to the altitude of the Taos mountains, as well as from all the stress he had conjured during his drive. Sleep came as a blessing.

Both Rorie and Clay slept deeply and soundly that night, one in Santa Fe, the other in Taos, both now aware of each other—only seventy miles apart.

About the Authors

Tom W. Boyd, Ph.D., is a retired professor emeritus of philosophy who spent most of his career teaching at the University of Oklahoma. He is the author of one book, *Lusting for Infinity*, as well as numerous academic articles and book chapters.

Barbara Skye Boyd, D. Min., is a retired professor of religious studies who spent her professional career in a variety of vocational positions, including serving as pastor of several churches. She is the author of one book, *The Wisdom Years, A Guide to Intentional Aging*, and numerous professional articles as well as poetry.

Tom and Barbara have four children, eight grandchildren and live in Santa Fe, where they continue to write. This is their first work of fiction.